The Final Trials of Alan Mewling

A.C. Bland

The Final Trials
of Alan Mewling

The Final Trials of Alan Mewling
ISBN 978 1 76041 223 4
Copyright © text Adam Clark Bland 2016
Cover image © karandaev

First published 2016 by
Ginninderra Press
PO Box 3461 Port Adelaide 5015
www.ginninderrapress.com.au

For SPG

(for fostering a love of words)

The Hierarchy of Officers in the Department of Various Affairs

Secretary
Deputy Secretary
First Assistant Secretary (Division Head)
Assistant Secretary (Branch Head)
Director (Section Head)
Assistant Director (Team Leader)
Subordinate staff

Principal Characters in the Department of Various Affairs

Alan Mewling	Acting Director Committees, temporarily replacing Robyn Rainbird
Antonia Ainsworth	Acting Secretary of the Department, temporarily replacing Denise Day
Barbara Best	a team leader in the Committees Section
Brian Gulliver	Deputy Secretary of the Department
Bruce Trevithick	a subordinate in the Committees Section
Carol Cunningham	an ex-Secretary of the Department, now a consultant
Daphne	replacement Executive Assistant to Quentin Quist
Edwina Troy	a subordinate in the Committees Section
Eris	briefly, a graduate in the Committees Section
Escher Burgoyne	Director, Workplace Health and Safety
Hector Rasch	Director, Security
Peaches Trefusis	briefly, Executive Assistant to Quentin Quist
Quentin Quist	Acting Head of the Consultation and Stakeholder Liaison Branch, temporarily replacing Valerie Venables
Stephen Morton	Team Leader in the Committees Section and long-time colleague of Alan Mewling

Principal Characters in the Bonny Brae Nursing Home

Clyde Adams	a resident sharing a ward with Hugo Faggoter.
Hugo Faggoter	a resident and Alan Mewling's father-in-law
Matron Frogmore	Director of Nursing

'Sterculinum publicum! – You public toilet!': insult in ancient Rome

1

Later, when the events of that time had passed into departmental folklore and the telling and retelling of the story had so blurred the facts that the core truth was, ironically, all that remained, he would recall earlier summers as though they had been part of some other life. And that's exactly what, in a sense, they were. Because everything that came before the precise moment when Peaches Trefusis unlocked the office door, sniffed the sourness in the air and spied 'it' sitting on the desktop – everything that preceded that moment – involved a different man.

That other man perceived himself to be of an exclusive caste – one tracing its origins, via the clerks of the British East India Company and the officials of His Majesty's Navy Board, back to the satraps of the Persian Shahs, to the Confucian bureaucrats of the Han dynasty and even to the scribes of the ancient cities of Sumer.

That different man knew of no greater service than the public kind and of no more important time for it than the four long weeks of January when, with the Parliament empty and the pre-eminent bureaucrats ensconced in their beachside retreats, the default cohort stepped up to ensure the seamless continuance of essential administrative processes.

For the less experienced middle-ranking and senior officers, this was their time: the moment of the aspirants, the season of the hopeful – a brief interlude when true mettle could be displayed, resolve could be revealed and a general suitability for higher office could be demonstrated. But for wiser heads, like Alan's, it was a time when nothing more needed to be done than the absolutely necessary, lest the absent be made to appear less competent than their understudies.

In Alan's view, January required a firm hand, a clear head and the ability to seem – by being entirely ordinary – unworthy of hostile attention. All three of these attributes he knew himself to possess in generous measure, without eugenic advantage. And hadn't he been one of the trusted ones, charged with the safekeeping of the nation, for the initial weeks of so many years?

Yet, for a few seconds after Peaches saw 'it' on Valerie Venables's desktop and, recognising it for what it was, screamed, Alan Mewling doubted himself. A sense of dread – of future catastrophe reversing at full speed to meet him – halted his search of the carpet under his workstation and caused him to look up at the underside of the operational surface, as if into the eternal unknown.

Then, as Peaches' cry disintegrated into slow breathy sobs, he reversed into the light on all fours with his recovered security pass in his hand, grimly relieved that the wait was over.

Grasping the edge of his chair and pulling himself up, he had no need to make any link between Peaches' distress and the sense of impending doom he'd experienced in the days since Christmas Eve. He simply knew that a profound moment of connectedness – an instant in which his future and his past had collided and coalesced – had finally come to pass. His life could never be the same.

For all that, though, he was surprised when, pushing past Peaches into Valerie Venables's office and seeing 'it' on the blotter, he beheld its ordinary proportions – proportions at such odds with its awful significance. In time, it would become a substantial fibrous pat, a mountain of dark, hard, shiny nuts and a viscous puddle in which there were vaguely familiar yet unidentifiable solids. It would be cracked and brown, smooth and green, dripped like a Pollock and dropped like an unbaked bun. It would be a number of chunky thumb-sized pieces arranged according to the requirements of some ancient native rite and it would trail endlessly, like the tail of a well fed python, across the creamy paper to droop over the desk edge. It would appear, too, in a spray of minuscule flecks over the entire surface, delivered with a force that spoke of terrible pressures, building and building until eruptive release was the only possible outcome short of explosive oblivion.

Later, he would have difficulty describing 'it' and in detailing other aspects of the scene: the position, for example, of the chair relative to the desk, and the juxtaposition of the telephone and of the In and Out trays. Some would say this was not surprising, given that the desk was without the photographs of Valerie's red setters – images which usually took up more than half of the available space.

But the truth of the matter was that Alan was mesmerised by 'it' and stood, transfixed, outside time, two steps inside the office, hardly noticing a young woman from one of the other sections shepherd the distraught Peaches away. Someone else entered the room briefly and, ignoring Alan, held a mobile phone at arm's length – much as one would a can of insect spray or a protective icon – in the direction of the desk.

More time passed, perhaps as much as a minute. Then, finally, the arrival of two men, within seconds of each other – Hector Rasch, the Department's Director of Security, and Escher Burgoyne, the Director of Workplace Health and Safety – broke the spell.

'Good God,' said Rasch standing next to Alan, staring at the blotter.

'I came as quickly as I could,' wheezed Burgoyne, shutting the door behind him. 'I've been in the plant room with the air conditioning technician.'

The newcomers looked at each other with undisguised loathing: Rasch, tall and cadaverous; Burgoyne, squat and florid. Alan would later think it peculiar and not altogether insignificant that neither of them seemed in the least surprised by 'it'.

'That item,' said the short man to the tall, pointing a plump finger at the material on the blotter, 'is a health and safety hazard which is about to be the subject of a provisional improvement notice. I have made arrangements for this office to be cordoned off, pending the issue of the appropriate documentation. Your assistance, Mr Rasch, is not required.'

'To the contrary,' said Rasch, looking at his rival with naked hatred, 'that object is the trigger of a Phase Two security incident, Mr Burgoyne. I have, accordingly, activated the relevant protocols. Your assistance may yet be required under my direction to deal with,' he looked at the table, '"it".'

Alan peered from one man to the other, wondering if they had lost their senses.

When the phone on the desk rang, all three of them looked at it with suspicion. Then the other two fell on the handpiece. They struggled before Rasch, the more agile, prevailed.

He listened for a moment, eyeing 'it' all the while, then said, 'Probably', 'No' and 'Yes', before finishing with, 'Of course. It's your decision.'

'Toni is on her way,' he announced.

They waited in tense silence. When Acting Secretary Antonia Ainsworth opened the door, all three men turned to face her.

Burgoyne seemed to shrink before Alan's eyes. He clearly believed that his defeat in the struggle for the telephone handpiece had already been his undoing.

'Good morning, gentlemen,' Toni said, moving quickly to the desk. She pushed her red-rimmed spectacles into her hair and bent low to examine 'it' from a distance of ten centimetres. 'Yes,' she said, 'it's definitely excreta.'

'I have a hazard containment team at the ready,' said Burgoyne, 'able to collect and remove the object.'

'And I have a group of forensic experts on close standby,' said Rasch. 'They will swiftly secure the item, pending scientific analysis and a formal enquiry…on your command.'

Antonia Ainsworth pulled a green ballpoint pen from her blouse pocket and poked at 'it'. 'There can be no doubt that it's excreta,' she repeated, staying low while looking up at Alan. 'And who are you?'

'Alan Mewling,' he announced, 'Acting Director, Committees.'

'Really?' she remarked, almost putting the ballpoint back into her pocket. Alan's face seemed familiar to her but it was, she knew, unlikely that so ordinary a satellite could previously have passed within her orbit. What to do with the pen? She dropped it into the waste-paper basket. 'Have you called a cleaner to take this away?' she asked Alan, gesturing towards 'it'.

'All departmental cleaning has been outsourced,' said Burgoyne.

'Then let's get someone in to do the job,' suggested Antonia, still looking at Alan.

'I'll consult the procurement manual,' he answered with purpose.

'And wait a month?' said Antonia Ainsworth, rolling up a peacock blue sleeve. 'I'll deal with it myself.'

'I wouldn't, with the greatest respect, advise that,' said Burgoyne.

'Nor, with even more respect, would I,' said Rasch.

But Toni, already bending over the blotter, would have the problem solved within seconds. 'It's excreta,' she said for the third time, neatly releasing the corners of the thick paper sheet from its green vinyl holder and pulling all four together.

'The security protocols,' spluttered Rasch.

'The hazardous material handling procedures,' echoed Burgoyne.

'Idiots,' said Antonia Ainsworth, carrying the paper sling (with bonus poo) from the room.

It was not yet seven-thirty a.m. on the very first working day after Christmas.

2

Burgoyne and Rasch followed Antonia, leaving Alan wondering – but for the missing blotter and the sulphurous whiff in the air – if he hadn't imagined things.

Outside, he rummaged in Peaches' top drawer for a Post-it note and commenced a message to Quentin Quist, who, as Valerie Venables's January replacement, was the prospective occupant of the desecrated office.

Alan's authorial efforts, hampered by the need to find the right tone – respectful, without seeming obsequious – had taken him no further than 'Quentin, rather urgent you see me,' 'Quentin, there has been an incident,' and finally, 'Dear Quentin', when Quentin Quist himself appeared, wearing an anxious expression and a Disney necktie.

Alan got to his feet.

'I've just seen Toni in the foyer,' the new arrival said, dumping an aggressive sansevieria cylindrica on Peaches' desktop, causing the soil to spill over the lip of the pot and into the keyboard. 'What's going on?'

Alan crumpled the last incomplete Post-it note and dropped it into the bin. 'Good morning,' he said.

'And why is it so bloody hot in here?' Quist asked, mopping his forehead and upper lip with his tie.

Alan, conscious that there were at least two witnesses in the nearby cubicles, ignored the accusatory tone of both questions. He couldn't help staring at the angry carbuncle on the tip of Quist's nose. 'We'd better talk in my office.'

'What's wrong with mine?' said Quist, eyeing the closed door.

Alan couldn't readily explain why he thought it inappropriate to discuss the morning's events in the place where they'd unfolded.

Quist dumped his briefcase and tennis racquet onto the desk, causing more soil to jump from the side of the pot plant into the keyboard.

'It won't take a moment,' said Alan, reassuringly.

'There have been changes to the January acting arrangements, haven't there?' asked Quist, 'and I've been passed over.'

'Not at all,' said Alan.

'No, no. I knew it,' Quist said, with bitter certainty. 'It's Dapin, again. And no one of any consequence' – he looked past his pustule at Alan – 'has seen fit to inform me.'

Debbie Dapin was the other embodiment of ambition in the Consultation and Stakeholder Liaison Branch and had been acting assistant secretary, instead of Quist, the previous summer.

'I suppose she's already in there,' he remarked, edging past Alan towards the glass wall, even though he'd see nothing with his carbuncle pressed against the surface (because of the closed blinds). 'My corpse is barely cold,' he uttered, melodramatically.

Alan, still aware of listeners in nearby cubicles, put a finger to his lips to communicate the need for discretion, hoping to save the younger man from any further lapses.

Quist allowed himself to be walked past two rows of workstations and between a pair of inflatable half-sized reindeer into the office Alan was to occupy for the next four weeks.

Alan pulled the door shut and transferred his unpacked box of personal items from the meeting table to the desk.

'Why the secrecy?' asked Quist. 'This isn't the first time I've been usurped and I don't care who knows it.' He refused Alan's offer of a chair.

'There's been an incident,' said Alan.

'An incident?'

'In your office.'

Quist folded his arms in front of his pigeon chest. 'What sort of an incident?'

'Someone…' Alan commenced, 'someone has…' His problem, again, was with the right words. He was initially tempted by 'someone has left a deposit on Valerie's blotter' but he knew this would sound prudish and ambiguous. Replacing the mercantile 'deposit' with 'faecal matter', resulting in 'someone has left faecal matter on Valerie's blotter', didn't greatly improve the specificity of the sentence, as Alan knew there were, logically, as many types of faeces as there were living species. 'An unknown person has placed a stool on our branch head's desktop,' though not so twee, was more likely to furnish confusion than clarification, while 'Someone has shat on Valerie's desk', though to the point and unlikely to give rise to multiple interpretations, worried Alan from a grammatical perspective – because of the confusion attending the past tense of 'shit'. This way of proceeding also seemed, because of its indisputable vulgarity, to be insufficiently respectful of the absent Valerie, while options making reference to 'ploppies', 'poos', 'poo poos', and 'number twos' all evidenced an undignified infantilism. 'Someone has crapped on our boss's desk,' while economical, was, in some indefinable way, again lacking in respect.

Perhaps, thought Alan, there was something to be said for an incremental process of communication.

'Someone,' he said, 'has used Valerie's desk as a lavatory.'

The colour drained from Quentin Quist's face. He removed his glasses and held them by a single temple. 'Number ones or number twos?' he asked, in a voice not much above a whisper.

As if the difference mattered, thought Alan. Perhaps he should have employed the baby talk option after all.

'Solids or liquids?' Quist prompted, presumably because he believed most of his inferiors to be innumerate.

'Only solids, so far as I know…'

'So we're talking about multiple…'

Alan could sense another reference to 'number twos' about to emerge.

'Only one,' he announced, realising his error immediately.

'One number two?' asked Quist.

'Yes.'

'Is nothing sacred?' He sat down and Alan took the other chair.

'Is it still there, in the office?'

'Toni removed it.'

'Toni?'

'Yes.'

'I see.'

'She thought it the easiest option,' said Alan.

Quist seemed to consider this last news for a moment and Alan knew better than to interrupt a member of the executive – even a temporary one – engaged in cerebral exercise.

Quist removed the fountain pen from his pocket and tapped it, nib end up, rapidly and repeatedly on the table top. 'Has anyone told Valerie?'

'No,' replied Alan. 'The, ah, "it" has only just been discovered.'

'What on earth could she have done to deserve this?' Quist asked Alan's rubbish bin. 'She'll be devastated, absolutely devastated.'

'I'm sure she will,' Alan agreed.

'Even if it turns out to be a random act of…whatever.'

'Yes,' said Alan, more to be supportive than because he followed his superior's train of thought.

'And that's what it must have been,' mused Quist, perhaps convincing himself. 'A break-in. Probably drug-crazed teenagers looking for…'

'Stationery?' asked Alan, recalling his own teenage longing for miniature notebooks and propelling pencils.

Quist ignored Alan's suggestion. 'That must have been why Rasch was here,' he continued. 'I saw him with Toni and Burgoyne in the foyer.'

At that moment there was a knock on the door and Rasch entered. Quist and Alan looked at each other, spooked by the security director's entrance on cue.

'You must be Quist,' said Rasch, looking at the replacement branch head's Disney tie, and pushing the door shut.

'I am,' said the younger man, without offering his hand.

Rasch pulled the remaining visitor's chair up to the table, so that his back wasn't to the door – his recreational reading was exclusively of spy stories – and forced Alan to shuffle jump his own seat twenty degrees around the perimeter.

Any diminution of purpose Rasch might have felt after his earlier interaction with Antonia Ainsworth had clearly become a matter of the subjective past. He had, Alan would later recall, a sense about him of great work in the offing. He was a man whose hour had finally come.

'Your office,' said Rasch to Quist, 'has been secured, pending the arrival of my forensic team.'

This announcement came as something of a surprise to Alan. As far as he knew, Rasch's Section comprised a pulchritudinous young woman who took wonky security pass photos on Tuesday mornings and two silent old men whose policy formulation responsibilities necessitated the careful plagiarising of other agencies' security documents and the still more time-consuming scrutiny of *Greyhound Breeders Weekly*. It did not include, to the best of Alan's knowledge, anyone who knew much about fingerprints, bloodstains or DNA.

'I anticipate,' Rasch continued, 'that their work will be concluded within a few hours. You should' – he nodded at Quist – 'be able to move in by lunchtime.'

'Anything we can assist with…' said Quist, staunchly. 'I regard this as a very serious…'

'Incident?' ventured Alan.

'Matter,' decided Quist.

'My view, too,' said Rasch, thinking that the acting Assistant Secretary might yet prove to be a useful ally, even if he was rumoured to be a first-class tosser.

'I suppose it is an outside job?' asked Quist.

'Job' wouldn't have been a word employed by Alan in the (then) prevailing circumstances but its use was consistent with Quist's clear preference for bubby talk when discussing human by-products.

'Why do you assume that?' Rasch asked, leaning forward.

Alan was about to say, 'Because there was no message left in the vicinity of "it" to give meaning to the act,' but the question hadn't been addressed to him.

'Well, it's inconceivable that someone from the branch or even the broader department would...' Quist's sentence again trailed off into oblivion.

'Defecate?' suggested Alan, when he was certain that there would be no resumption.

'Commit such a revolting act,' confirmed Quist.

'Ms Venables doesn't have enemies in the department?' asked Rasch.

'Those of us who engage in high-level policy development,' Quist averred in a superior tone, 'are well used to robust discussion and to exacting criticism, but our...'

Alan had no idea where the sentence was heading and refrained from speculation. Quist, however, looked at him expectantly and gave no indication of any intention to see the oratorical task through. Alan supposed that he had to suggest something. 'Professionalism?'

'Yes,' said Quist looking irrationally pleased with himself. 'Exactly. Our professionalism militates against...'

Alan and Rasch both waited for more words – at least enough to end the original sentence on this repeat occasion – but none came. As Alan didn't feel confident about completion a second time, Rasch filled the silence.

'I wasn't suggesting,' he remarked, 'that the perpetrator was a member of the Executive.'

'Of course not,' said Quist, hurriedly realising his earlier error. 'There are, however, other people in the department – aggrieved, embittered, unhappy individuals – whose intellect and aspirations are out of step or who, at some crucial moment, have been found...' His eyes fixed on Alan and swivelled quickly away.

'Wanting?' suggested Rasch, also avoiding eye contact with Alan.

'Yes, wanting,' agreed Quist.

Even Alan tried not to think about himself and about the ancient blunder that had albatrossed his career, forever excluding him from high office.

'But the dissatisfaction of such persons within our own branch,' said Quist, 'is inevitably with the department and, if I may say so, with the service's system of merit-based promotion, rather than with Valerie, who is, by any measure, a manager of quite outstanding…'

For all his faults, thought Alan, Quist had grasped the central tenet of the executive faith – that of Brahmin solidarity. He understood that one never criticised the other members of the priestly caste in front of the untouchables.

'A manager of quite exemplary…' reprised Quist, looking each of them in the eye, challenging them to complete for him.

'Ability and diligence,' said Alan, half truthfully on the first count.

'I see,' said Rasch, thoughtfully. 'That would mean that the act' – all three men knew which act he was referring to – 'was either one of wanton vandalism by someone who broke into the building and saw Ms Venables's desk as a suitable one on which to empty their bowels' – none of them believed this was likely – 'or one of non-specific defiance by a member of the department's staff'.

'An act,' added Quist, 'which was unlikely to be directed at this branch or its outstanding management.'

'Of course,' said Rasch.

The three of them quietly pondered this last option or perhaps nothing in particular.

'There is another possibility,' said Rasch.

'Which is?' asked Quist, conscious of the fact that, as an acting member of the executive, he should have been making his stamp on the discussion, even if no one he needed to impress was in attendance.

Rasch sat back in his chair and looked Quist in the eye. 'You were due to move into Ms Venables's office today.'

Alan's pulse quickened.

'That's true,' said Quist, looking puzzled.

'And that fact was presumably known to others, including subordinate staff, prior to the Christmas shutdown.'

'Yes,' said Quist.

Alan pulled a handkerchief from his pocket and wiped the sheen off his forehead.

'Perhaps it is you who has enemies,' suggested Rasch.

'Me?' said Quist, turning puce under his solarium tan. 'Impossible.'

'Do you have enemies?' asked Rasch.

'Too many to list,' Alan might reasonably have answered.

'A ridiculous suggestion,' said Quist, chortling with a touch too much effort. A droplet of sweat plummeted from the enraged tip of his nose onto the table where he smeared it to oblivion with his coat sleeve. 'Almost ludicrous,' he added, laughing heartily.

Alan wondered whether the mirth was hysterical – whether Quist had never before been prompted to calculate the numbers of those he'd humiliated, bullied and intimidated, and to thereby conclude that he was, in fact, the subject of unqualified, universal hatred.

'Now, I'm not foolish enough,' Quist said with a smile, 'to think of myself as someone who is the object of collective affection.'

That's a good start, thought Alan.

'However, I think I can confidently say that I am widely respected and, if you will, even admired.'

But not such a good finish, Alan concluded.

Rasch didn't look in the least convinced. Alan looked at the floor.

'That would be a reasonable précis of the situation, wouldn't it, Alan?'

Time stood still. Alan could hear the gentle chime of someone's computer starting, out in the open area, and he sensed a bead of sweat making its way between his shoulder blades down to the elastic band of his Y-fronts.

'Alan?'

'Well…I…yes…I suppose so,' Alan answered. 'Most certainly.'

Rasch looked from Alan to Quist and then back to Alan again. 'You're sure about that?' he asked.

Quist intervened before Alan could reply. 'You're right. It is worth confirming. Alan, do you believe that there is someone in our branch who dislikes me so much that they would do a poo on my desk-to-be?'

Alan's tongue was paralysed. His lips were soft, thick, lazy strips of plasticine.

'I'd be disappointed to learn, Alan, that a person or persons – even as many as two or three persons – have taken an irrational dislike to me… and that they have not been, well, person enough to come and discuss their feelings…discuss them with me. However, I can deal with it.'

Alan smiled gormlessly at Quist and then at Rasch.

'Now come on, Alan,' said Quist, drinking in his subordinate's humiliation. 'This is not a time for…for not coming forward.'

Alan was always panicked by the surprise employment of double negatives. He could say nothing.

'Well, that's that then,' said Quist.

'If, on further reflection, you can think of anyone disposed to acting against your interests, call me,' said Rasch, not at all convinced that 'that' had, in fact, been 'that'. He extended his hand to Quist. 'I'll be in touch as soon as my people have finished in your office.'

Without any acknowledgement of Alan, he left the room.

Quist pounced, as Alan knew he would, the second Rasch was gone. As was usual when the aspiring executive was angry, the words came fast and freely. 'Thanks for your loyalty,' he hissed. 'I'll be informing Valerie about this – all of it – when I next see her and I know she won't be impressed.'

'I'm sorry,' Alan replied, feeling that he had, indeed, done the wrong thing.

'And at a personal level, I won't be forgetting your failure to support me either.'

'I'm sorry about that, too,' said Alan, now feeling as though he'd committed an act of unspeakable treachery.

'All you had to do was agree with me,' said Quist.

'Yes,' said Alan.

'It was that easy.'

'Yes.'

'Yes, indeed,' said Quist heatedly, looking directly at Alan. 'Yes, indeed.'

Alan pondered his lap, knowing that Quist was staring at him, hungry for a glimpse of his quivering, cowardly soul. In primary school, nearly half a century before, he'd drawn a pair of breasts on the inside rear cover of his exercise book after mapping and naming the rivers of the Australian interior. He recalled the shame he'd felt when his Aunty Vi had been called to the principal's office to 'please explain'.

'You're not a team player,' said Quist after a pause that might have lasted as long as twenty seconds. 'And this has not, frankly, been a good start to a demanding January.' Quist rose and went to the door. 'Not a good start at all.'

Alan couldn't help but agree. They'd been biggish purple breasts with cheerful yellow aureoles and bright red nipples.

3

In ordinary circumstances, Alan would have visited the office each day during the holiday period to log into the daily media summaries and satisfy himself that there were no emails requiring his urgent attention.

That his scrutiny proved to be unnecessary each year, because the media reports were always about shark attacks and credit card debt, and because no one of any importance would have thought to contact Alan in the event of an administrative crisis, was irrelevant. He had never felt comfortable with the idea of a Christmas closure, not even in those years when, taking on the section head's role, the shutdown enabled him to move into his supervisor's office in private and thereby disinfect the surfaces without snide remarks on the more bizarre consequences of germ phobia.

In any normal year Alan would, by eight a.m. on the first day back, have been sitting at Robyn's desk with his diminutive spathyphyllum perched on the windowsill, the Section's work programme at the ready and his In tray contents prioritised, under tight control. He would already have logged onto the Internet to check the performance of his modest share portfolio and have fed his vital statistics – for the many-thousandth time – into the superannuation benefit calculator. He would also have eased Robyn's nameplate from its slots on the door and have gently tapped his own one – swathed in tissue paper since the previous January – into place. A mug of generic English Breakfast would have prepared him for the first wave of Christmas reminiscences, out on the floor. And he would most certainly have been around the cubicles, outside, to water the many pot plants left in his care by still holidaying colleagues.

But the particular circumstances of that morning had been far from normal, unexpected ordure aside. This was because Alan had woken at home on Christmas Day, more than a week before, dazed and nauseous, without any recollection of what had happened to him or to the security pass needed to access the building over the Christmas period.

The need to wait for the building doors to open on the first working day of the year had kept him from all of the things he'd normally have done, early in the day, to impose order on his temporary empire.

And then there'd been the events in Valerie's office and the subsequent discussions with Quist and Rasch. It was not inconceivable that it would take the rest of the morning for him to effect control…and Alan was not a man who felt at ease with the unknown.

He gazed out of the window at the building opposite, in which he imagined other acting directors sitting calmly at their desks, confident in the antibacterial regimes they'd instituted and otherwise prepared for whatever challenges the day might bring. Envy melded in Alan's mind with mouth-desiccating, bladder-weakening anxiety and with the sense of dread that had gorged on his equanimity over the preceding days.

He hadn't so much as looked at his emails; he had no idea what was lurking in his In tray and he couldn't recall which members of his staff would be present to aid his labours over the days ahead. For all he knew, too, the various plants he'd been asked to minister to over the break were long dead. The emptiness of his white board shouted his incompetence to the world.

The child in him wanted to cry, 'Not fair' and 'Why has this happened to me?' but he sensed that despair and defeat lay in wait down that path. And hadn't he faced greater crises? Was this one any different, except, perhaps, in degree? Was there still not time in which to make good the deficiencies of the day?

He breathed deeply and pictured himself working steadily to impose control, step by gradual step. And such were his powers of imagination in this one special respect that, when Bruce Trevithick knocked for the fourth time and opened the door, Alan looked little more than moderately surprised.

Trevithick, tall and thin with a dyed black goatee, was normally one of Alan's assistants in the Committees A Subsection. He had recently forsaken a fundamentalist brand of Christianity and a plain, devoted wife for sadomasochism and a live-in relationship with a transsexual plumber named Bettina. Alan beckoned him in.

Edwina Troy, a thirty-something brunette who held an equivalent position to Trevithick's in the Committee B Subsection, and Stephen Morton, the acerbic assistant director in charge of Committees C, followed.

Morton, who'd known Alan for nearly thirty years, spoke first. 'Someone over in Policy told us that you and Peaches discovered a brown offering on Valerie's desk.'

Alan wondered for a moment whether, as Acting Section Head, it was incumbent on him to restart things in the appropriate way by enquiring about his visitors' Christmas experiences. The prospect, though, of a detailed account of Bettina's ingenuity with the flaming brandy sauce or of her vicious dexterity with other Christmas accoutrements – perhaps the click-handle walnut crusher or the plastic-coated fairy light wire – filled Alan with apprehension. And he couldn't very well make enquiries of Morton and Edwina without quizzing Trevithick. He decided to bypass queries and answer the question put to him.

'Over the Christmas break,' he said, 'someone has, indeed, defecated on Valerie's desk.'

'So it's true,' said Trevithick, jubilantly. 'Someone left Quist a moving-in present.'

'Or a Chrissie tribute,' said Edwina.

'I can't think of any bastard more deserving,' said Morton.

'Me neither,' said Edwina.

'That makes it unanimous,' said Trevithick, assuming Alan to be of the same mind. 'What has he done about it?'

Morton snorted. 'Quentin couldn't manage an arsehole.'

'Now, now, that's enough of that,' said Alan. 'I suppose we're it for the day?'

Edwina put Alan's dead spathyphyllum on the table and sat,

prompting the others to take chairs. 'Barbara's supposed to be in later,' she said, referring to her supervisor, the fiercely reproductive Assistant Director, Committees B. No one, however, rated the likelihood of Barbara's attendance at better than 'unlikely'.

'And the rest of the Branch?' asked Alan.

'No one on the dark side, yet,' said Morton. The Stakeholder Liaison Section, normally headed by Quentin Quist, was led by two narcissists in his own image, Strasser and Mankiewicz, and otherwise staffed by a number of broken-spirited individuals widely reviled as 'the living dead'.

'And no one in International,' said Trevithick.

Members of the International Committee Support Section were rarely sighted before lunch; according to them, no one important in the bits of the world that mattered was contactable in the first half of the Australian day.

'But I did see some of the navel-gazers,' said Edwina.

The Policy Unit, headed by Debby Dapin, had the least interaction with committee members and stakeholders, and consequently boasted the lowest absenteeism.

'And there's someone in Corporate,' said Morton.

The key members of the Finance and Coordination Section, apart from the drunken director, Alistair McAllister, were an elderly Canadian dwarf known as 'the Elk' (who answered without demur to 'Elk') an obese Welsh belly dancing instructress named Brenda Jones ('Wednesday lunchtimes in the downstairs recreation area – ladies only, if you don't mind') and an unintelligible Sri Lankan (whose family name had been so long that it couldn't be accommodated by the department's email system and had been truncated to a mere 'Lingham' before becoming a less threatening 'Smith').

'Then we're not alone in the struggle,' said Alan.

'Tell us about the turd,' said Trevithick, eagerly.

'I don't know that there's much to reveal,' Alan answered.

'Start off with how you found it, then.'

Alan sighed. 'It was Peaches who saw it first,' he said. 'I was part way through moving in here when I heard someone scream from the direction of Valerie's office. I went straight there. Peaches was inside. She was deeply distressed. 'It' was sitting on the blotter.'

'There was just a single crap?' asked Morton.

'That's right,' said Alan, 'sitting on the blotter.'

'Was there a note with it?' inquired Edwina.

'It would be its own calling card,' said Trevithick.

'…a message,' Edwina persisted, 'saying who it was from?'

'Or who it was for?' added Morton.

'Nothing,' said Alan.

'Not a defiant "Up yours Quist",' asked Morton, 'pieced together from cut-up newspaper headlines and pasted sloppily onto ministerial letterhead?'

'No.'

'Or a chilling threat,' continued to Trevithick, 'smeared in brown on the windows: "Quentin, there's plenty more where this came from".'

'Disgusting,' said Edwina.

'No message,' said Alan. In fact, it occurred to him that there hadn't even been toilet tissue on or near the desk.

'Getting back to the crap itself,' said Trevithick. 'What did it look like?'

Alan tried to recall, in greater detail, the features of the object. 'I don't know. It seemed like…like…just another piece of faecal matter, really.'

Trevithick sighed. 'Would you say it was fat or thin?'

'Relative to…'

'Relative, to say, I don't know…to…to your own turds.'

Alan blushed. The thought of people learning anything from him about his own waste matter, even by deduction, was unthinkable. As a child, he had endured excruciating pain in order to avoid visiting school or public lavatories and as an adult he'd often gone to other floors to complete the task away from his colleagues. He would as soon have discussed sex with someone as engage in personal toilet talk.

'I guess it was about average,' he ventured, 'but I can't say that I know much about excreta at all.'

'…apart from that which we produce on the written page in the course of our duties,' said Morton jovially, with the intention of easing Alan's discomfort.

'Yes,' Alan continued, 'I'd probably say it was of an average size but it may be, of course, that what I perceive to be average is actually undersized or is…is…even, perhaps, well, large or huge by other people's standards.' He looked glum.

'We'll come back to the size of it, again, later,' said Trevithick, now confident in the interrogator's role. 'What about the colour? Tell us about that.'

Alan felt he was on significantly thinner ground. 'It was mostly green, as I recall…and white. I think it had fungus growing on it. Quite a lot of fungus, in fact: so much that it was furry, almost feathery.'

'Really?' asked Edwina.

'Mostly green and white but with some orange and red. Yes, some red.'

'A veritable palette of colours,' said Morton.

'And the shape: are we talking Montezuma's revenge – something a lot more liquid than solid, delivered with arse-ripping urgency – or something held hostage for days…something compacted and hard, that, when severed, dropped like a rock?'

'Trevithick, you're disgusting,' said Edwina.

'A late call but a good one,' said Morton.

Alan was still thinking about the answer – expelled in a liquid rush, or painfully and gradually squeezed – when there was a sharp knock at the door and Quentin Quist entered.

'I need to speak to you, Alan,' he said, 'in private.'

'Good morning, Quentin,' said Trevithick.

'Happy New Year, Quentin,' said Morton.

'I hope you had a good break, Quentin,' said Edwina, beaming.

Alan was silently astounded. Were these the three individuals who'd earlier concluded that the acting branch head deserved a dung decoration on his desk top?

'Thank you,' said Quist without any gratitude. 'Now, Alan, if we could…'

'We'll reconvene later in the day,' said Alan to the other three, getting to his feet.

They departed and Quist closed the door behind them.

'What did those dimwits want?'

'We were just having a chat,' said Alan, 'to establish where we were all up to.'

'Because Robyn wasn't sufficiently organised to give you a proper handover?' asked Quist, nastily.

This was typical Quist behaviour, thought Alan, the denigrating of his director and, at the same time, the casting of him in the Quisling's role. 'No, it was more a matter of ensuring that we have a common understanding of the work ahead, after the break.'

'I have to say, Alan, that I couldn't care less about your work programme at this exact moment. I have just had Rasch on the phone and he told me that he proposes to interview each and every member of the branch about this morning's…'

'Discovery,' suggested Alan, quickly.

'Yes, that's right. Each and every one, commencing this afternoon.' He looked at Alan expectantly.

'Well, I suppose he is obliged,' said Alan, 'to demonstrate that management takes incidents of this sort seriously.'

Quist snorted. 'You've missed the point, entirely,' he said. 'Each and every member: that includes me. He proposes to interview me and I am, in case you'd forgotten, your acting branch head.'

'Of course you are,' said Alan, wondering why Rasch's thoroughness was becoming his problem. 'He probably just wants to know when you were in, over the break, so that he can narrow down the time when the… the…"night soil" appeared.'

'No. No. I've already discussed that with him. He clearly regards me as a…' He made a swishing movement with his right hand to encourage the appearance of the required word.

'A suspect?' said Alan.

'Exactly,' said Quist.

'Surely not,' said Alan, hoping that he sounded sincere, after the earlier allegations of deficient loyalty.

'He thinks I may have done number twos on my own desk,' Quist sobbed.

Alan was deeply embarrassed. Did the man not have friends to whom he could unburden himself? 'He probably can't be seen to ignore you,' he said, almost sympathetically, 'if he's going to interview all of your staff and get their cooperation.'

'No, I tell you, I am a suspect.' Quist sniffed and searched his pockets for a handkerchief.

'He'll just be going through the motions,' said Alan, regretting his words as soon as they were out.

Quist gave up searching for a tissue, so Alan pulled a role of paper towel out of his box of things and tore off two sheets.

'We'll see how you like being interrogated,' snuffled Quist, dabbing at his runny nose.

How could it be any worse, Alan thought, than what I've endured this morning at the hands of Trevithick?

'And if I'm under suspicion,' said Quist, folding one snotty square into four, and in half again, before jabbing it like a cigarette butt into the parched soil of Alan's deceased spathyphyllum, 'no one here is in…'

'The clear,' said Alan with absolute certainty.

'That's right,' said Quist. 'Not even you.'

Recalling the lost hours of Christmas Eve, Alan sensed that this was true. He could not vouch for himself and he realised that the bolus on the blotter – an object to which felt no special or essential connection and which was not recognisably 'of' him – could yet prove to be his own dread creation. And if it was of his making, there could surely be little doubt about how it was delivered to its destiny.

'I need to think about my next step,' said Quist from the doorway.

'Yes, of course,' murmured Alan, barely aware of his own words.

4

Before Alan's feet could touch bottom in the ever-deepening slough of his personal despond, Morton knocked and entered. Alan blotted sweat from his forehead with an incorrectly monogrammed handkerchief he'd been given on a long forgotten Christmas.

'What did that nasty little prick want?' Morton asked, shutting the door.

Alan had known Morton for nearly three decades but had never come to terms with his unprofessional frankness. 'That nasty little prick' had shortcomings, of course – ones that would have prevented his elevation in the public service of Alan's youth – but that didn't mean it was anything other than grossly inappropriate for Morton to be voicing an honest assessment of him.

Morton, on the other hand, knew that while Alan found his contempt for Quist distasteful, there was little possibility of correction.

'Rasch is going to interview everyone in the branch,' said Alan.

'And let me guess,' said Morton, 'Quist is distraught because he hasn't been given a get-out-of-jail-free card.'

Alan said nothing.

Morton sighed. 'Well, it was never likely that he shat on his own desk, was it? The sad thing is that he's too stupid to realise that his interrogation would have been nothing more than a quick, cheerful chat designed to give the rest of us the impression that everyone, including management, was being questioned.'

Now it was Alan's turn to sigh.

'The man is an idiot,' continued Morton. 'But that doesn't mean he won't be able to provide Rasch with an extensive list of persons whose bowels loosen at the mere mention of his name and who'll consequently become first-tier suspects. We'll both be on that list: cast as players insanely envious of his success, resentful of his talent and jealous of his networks. You know that, don't you?'

Alan nodded glumly.

'On the plus side, it won't be a short list,' Morton murmured. 'The cretin. It's going to be a long four weeks.'

Alan sighed, again, in acknowledgement of an undeniable truth.

'At least I don't have to deal with him day to day,' said Morton.

His aversion to higher duties had seen him avoid time in the Section Head's chair for more than a decade. This made it inevitable that, owing to the sporadic attendance of the other assistant director, Barbara Best, Alan would be required to 'act' whenever Robyn Rainbird was absent.

'What is Rasch thinking, though, conducting any interviews at all? Surely the best approach would have been to sweep the whole thing under the carpet.'

An unpleasant domestic image lodged itself in Alan's mind and he struggled to prise it free.

'What does he think he'll uncover?' Morton continued.

That unsavoury image took shape again, now in reverse, with the carpet under which 'it' had metaphorically been swept being lifted.

'You're his compadre,' said Morton.

It was true that Rasch and Alan met for lunch on Thursdays, work commitments permitting. It was also true that they exchanged the insignificant, quidnunctive confidences that office warriors so often mistook for the stuff of friendship. Once, years before, they'd even met on a Sunday afternoon to sail model motor boats on a ceremonial pond next to a public building. But they hadn't subsequently encountered each other outside the safe confines of their employment and the working day lunch. Did the occasional sandwich together and a single miniature boating foray make them compadres? Alan wasn't at all sure.

'If Toni gets wind of what he's up to...' Morton mused.

Alan tried not to think about flatus, wondering whether toilet talk would plague him forever.

'…it will hit the fan.'

It seemed, at that moment, that nothing anyone would ever say to Alan, again, could fail to bring to mind the object he'd sighted earlier that morning on Valerie Venables's blotter.

He refocused resolutely on the present and on Morton's prediction that Toni would not be happy with Rasch's plans. Not for the first time, he wondered what sort of an executive Morton would have made, if he'd possessed a more pliant nature and a preparedness to work on his backhand.

'Yvonne would have stopped the whole thing dead' – Yvonne was the ex-secretary of the department – 'quick smart. But that won't be the end of it for us, not now. They'll take this opportunity to do a fast-track review of our functions.'

Alan shuddered, not thinking 'bodily'.

'And our responsibilities will be transferred or abandoned until there's nothing left.'

'Surely not,' said Alan.

'Then Valerie's office will be dismantled, the space will be used for some obscure corporate purpose and it will be as if we never existed. "Turd incident? What turd incident?"'

Alan thought about all the years he'd spent working in Committees A, putting useful processes in place, hiding the skeletons, subtly influencing the selection of more productive members and assisting the less competent committee chairs. He recalled all of the effort he'd expended, ensuring that meetings ran smoothly, that member entitlements were correctly administered and that meeting records were of the highest standard. That it could all be undone by a single piece of by-product was a terrible realisation. That he might have been the architect, engineer and quantity surveyor of his own precious monument's destruction was the very cruellest irony.

'Surely it won't come to that,' he reprised.

'Only if the anonymous shitter turns out to be a proven break-and-enter opportunist or someone on the inside they can quickly invalid out as a nutter. They're the only solutions that aren't embarrassing or subversive: the only ones that don't stain the management escutcheon and that permit things to continue as normal.'

Alan hoped that Morton wouldn't be repeating this assessment of matters outside, in the open plan, where the idea of feigning psychosis in order to earn early retirement and enjoy the notoriety attached to ownership of the faeces might prompt a rush of false confessions.

'Maybe that's what Rasch is aiming for,' muttered Morton, 'identification of a loopy fall guy. Or maybe he's playing it straight and saying nothing to you because you, too, are a suspect.'

Alan struggled with irrational panic. Surely no one could seriously regard him as a potential perpetrator. Not so soon.

'I haven't had an opportunity to speak to him,' Alan said, giving nothing away about his relationship with Rasch or his own anxieties.

'Are you having lunch with him today?' asked Morton. 'It is Thursday.'

Rasch, Alan thought, would have been mortified to learn that others knew of their luncheon meetings. 'Our gatherings,' Rasch was prone to saying, 'are in every respect subject to plausible deniability and the "need to know" principle…which means that others don't need to know about them and that, respectfully, you don't need to know why they don't.'

The phone rang; Alan picked it up and announced himself.

'It's your tailor,' said a muffled voice which Alan recognised instantly. This was the second eerily coincidental intrusion of Rasch into Alan's life that day. 'Your suit is not ready. I repeat, your suit is not ready – but I will ring you again next Thursday to tell you when it can be collected.'

'Thank you,' said Alan, 'I look forward to wearing the suit when it is ready.'

Alan had never had the heart to inform Rasch that everyone in the committees section joked about the sartorial messages the security chief left to indicate whether or not they could meet for lunch. That Alan had never been sighted wearing anything other than a plain white shirt, grey trousers and a blue sports coat, supplemented by a smart mustard cardigan in winter, had doomed Rasch's bespoke attempts at rendezvous spy craft from the moment of their inception. But Alan was a kind man who knew something of the sadness of exposed illusions and he would continue the tailor charade at cost to his own dignity before he ever revealed Rasch to himself as a fool.

'I gather,' said Morton, 'that we won't be getting any inside information today.'

'I suppose he's preparing for this afternoon's interviews,' admitted Alan.

The air conditioning sprang to life, almost as if to suck away the selfish, unworthy hopes Alan entertained: hopes that someone would yet be found by Rasch to take responsibility for the excrement that was poised to cast a blight over his bureaucratic future. But after the briefest tantalising gust of cool air, the system ceased.

Alan once again attempted to focus on the day-to-day and on what needed to be done to restore a sense of the normal. 'Is everything all right out there?' he asked, gesturing at the open plan workstations. 'Do I need to organise counselling for anyone?'

'Counselling! Because Peaches found a turd on a desk?'

'No. I suppose you're right.'

'If anything, they're revelling in it.'

'I see.'

'But once they find out that Rasch wants to interview them, all you Acting Managers will have to brace yourselves. The whingeing will be endless.'

'Best keep it quiet until it's official,' said Alan, mindful that staff complaints about Rasch's plans would further delay his unpacking.

'My lips are sealed,' said Morton.

'Do I need to do the Christmas thing before I look at my emails?' asked Alan, changing the subject.

Morton knew exactly what Alan was referring to. Some years before, complaints had been made in the period following the New Year about Alan's desk-side manner – complaints to the effect that that his enquiries about the festive season activities of subordinate staff displayed a lack of genuine interest in those persons as persons. Alan had been counselled and instructed to be more genuine, and a note (that no one would ever read) had been placed on his personal file.

The next year, Alan had conscientiously questioned all members of his team about their activities after all public holidays and had even begun to take a particular and earnest interest in the inadvertent poisonings, sozzled quarrels and deranged giftings which were the most memorable highlights of their Christmas reminiscences.

The enthusiastic and highly detailed response to his questions on this follow-up occasion led him to believe that he was making entirely appropriate enquiries and that he'd rectified the earlier personal and professional deficiency…until a number of staff had informed the acting branch head that Alan's questions were of an intrusive nature, in addition to being invasions of privacy. Alan had once again been counselled and another note (which no one would ever read) had been appended to his personal file.

Alan suspected mischief-making on the part of both sets of complainants and that the aggrieved persons were in each case the same. He didn't, though, rule out the possibility that he had failed to keep abreast of changing community perceptions of the private/public divide.

'The turd has eclipsed everything as the focus of interest,' said Morton, getting up. 'Christmas is now another country…and no one wants a visa.'

Alan was silently relieved.

5

Despite apprehensions about urgent messages that might be awaiting his attention, Alan resisted the temptation to turn on the computer. Putting his deceased spathyphyllum and the box of personal items on the floor, he sprayed all the work surfaces and drawer handles with disinfectant and wiped them clean with paper towel. Because the phone and keyboard were electric and might need to be used immediately, those objects were excused an antibacterial drenching and were, instead, swapped for pre-cleaned, plastic wrapped alternatives from the box.

Still wearing rubber gloves, Alan plucked Quentin's tissue substitute out of the pot plant and placed it in the bin. He then lifted Robyn Rainbird's stationery tray out of the top desk drawer and eased his own into place. With the various excess items stowed in the bottom shelf of the bookcase and the plant returned to the meeting table, he positioned his workbook and correction pen to the left of the keyboard. A number of the subordinate tools of his calling – a stapler, a single-aperture hole punch and a rather 'now' white-out roller – he placed on the keyboard's right.

Next to the computer itself he put a rectangular tartan shortbread tin, containing a number of non-self-inking stamps. This collection included Alan's favourite – 'Resubmit with emendations to Alan A.C. Mewling' – which was never used when 'Resubmit with amendments to Alan A.C. Mewling' was the more appropriate tool. Red, black and blue ink-pads held together by a thick brown rubber band nudged the right-hand edge of the tin.

Alan opened his workbook and, using the cheap black ballpoint from his shirt pocket, wrote the date above a tidy squiggle. Below, on five separate lines, he dot-pointed the morning's events.

Three things remained to be done before he could begin the day's work in earnest. Items cocooned in bubble wrap were removed from the box on the floor and carefully unwrapped. The first was a nameplate. It was slotted into place on the outer side of the office door. The second and third items were a numbered ticket dispenser and accompanying laminated sign. The sign read, 'Please take a ticket and wait quietly until your number is called.' The sign and the dispenser, together, supported Alan's unspoken yet emphatic claim to possession of a keen sense of humour. The dispenser was suspended from a drawing pin pushed hard into the door frame well above one of the drooping reindeer antlers; the sign was bonded to the adjacent glass wall with fresh Blu-tack.

Only when these last trappings of office were in place did Alan take his own place in front of the computer and reach forward to press the power button in the centre of the shiny black fascia.

As the steel spring behind the small plastic disc resisted his fingertip, he felt the whole building – for a moment he feared it was the greater universe – shudder. Then the monitor brightened to the accompaniment of cheers from the open plan. The air conditioning had, it was immediately apparent, begun operating at the moment Alan's computer was given life. Cool air ruffled his sparse cranial covering.

Alan looked at his screen, then slowly up and around, before shrugging off the coinciding of events as mere chance.

He typed his name and, working from memory, picked out the impossibly complex combination of numbers and letters that was his password. Others had to write their access codes on pieces of paper concealed in their drawers or attached to the underside of their desk utensils. This was because the formulation protocols required the use of alphanumeric sequences only able to be memorised by nuclear physicists, idiot savants and Alan (who took pride in the fact that he'd never had to complete the onerous 'Application to Reissue Password' form).

The email program opened in a blaze of red. There were more unopened messages than Alan had ever seen – frightening full screens of them. The cheerful ping that customarily announced the arrival of each new missive was immediately an irritating electronic stutter. Megabytes of new traffic rolled in. However, it seemed that all of the incoming items were mere carriers of a single attachment – an image which was, in every case, exactly the same size.

Many of the senders were from inside the department, with the bulk of the remainder from other government agencies. Nearly all of the messages had titles leaving no doubt as to their coprologous content: headings like 'Festive Faeces', 'Xmas Excrement' and (the not necessarily accurate but nonetheless intriguing) 'Christmas Encopresis'.

Alan opened the picture file attached to one of the earlier duplicate messages and saw that the image was an off-centre photograph of 'it' on Valerie Venables's desk, presumably shot by whoever had entered the room soon after his own arrival.

The pinging became less insistent and Alan ran his eye down the senders' list, wondering, again, about the lost part of Christmas Eve, trying not to think about the ways in which he and 'it' might (once) have been 'as one'. The only thing he could take solace from was the fact that there was no message in his In box from Personnel, addressed only to him, about unacceptable or indecent behaviour on the final working day of the elapsed year.

Deleting as he went, he quickly separated the emails of a non-faecal nature from the rest. Nestling below two not unrelated emails from the acting secretary headed 'Excessive Consumption of Office Stationery' and 'Outstanding Generosity – Staff Xmas Gifts for Needy Children' was an email from Quentin Quist entitled 'Cooperation with Departmental Security Unit'. Alan double clicked to open this last message. It was marked 'Triple Urgent', 'Super Confidential' and 'Copy Prohibited'… and that was as much as he could read before a red message box with oversized red text obscured the rest of the screen. The message informed Alan that his In box storage limit had been exceeded and that he needed to take immediate action (of an unspecified sort).

Alan knew that the storage quota had not been exceeded; he'd deleted dozens of messages only minutes before and he otherwise kept only the most important emails on his system for more than a day or two. Indeed, he suspected that, if he rebooted his computer, all would be well…but when he tried to close the screens before him, nothing happened. The oversized red text now flashed at him. Again, he clicked on the 'Close window' icon but nothing happened. He tapped gently on the space bar and then with more determination on the escape key. The flashing increased in speed and he felt he had no option but to depress the power button. He pushed on it. Yet again, nothing happened. Beeping noises now accompanied the flashing and he could feel his face burning and a crushing tightness in his chest. What to do? He sensed that time was of the essence. Decisiveness was in order. He leaned over and pulled the power plug from the socket.

The screen died as the air conditioning system wheezed to a halt. He flopped back into his seat to the accompaniment of groans and expostulations from the open plan.

This time he knew that the coincidence – the air conditioning changing at the instant his finger killed the power – was more than it seemed. He twisted the computer box around so that he could view the various wires and cables attached to its rear. There didn't seem to be anything new there and Alan was the sort of person – perhaps the only sort of person – who'd have noticed anything suspicious.

Next, he turned and carefully examined the bookshelves behind his desk. He saw nothing more suspicious than a mint condition, twenty-year set of portfolio budget statements – but did he really know, he asked himself, what the modern surveillance device looked like?

He was standing with his hands on hips scrutinising the ceiling when Trevithick knocked and entered. In his hand was a piece of paper which appeared to have been crumpled, used as a projectile and leaped up and down on.

Trevithick stood next to Alan, looking upwards. 'Something happening up there?' he asked.

Quentin Quist entered without knocking. He stood next to Alan and Trevithick, and also looked upwards. 'Is there a problem?' he asked.

'No, no problem,' Alan answered, wishing that the only air conditioning duct hadn't been a metre behind him.

Quist and Trevithick looked at each other and back at Alan.

'Everything is fine,' he confirmed, concluding that the other two believed him to be mid psychotic episode.

'Good, because I really don't have time to waste,' said Quist, implying thereby that Alan, by contrast, was unimportant enough to have countless hours at the ready for aimless frittering. 'May we have some privacy?'

'I'll come back later,' said Trevithick.

'I can move into my office,' said Quist, as soon as Trevithick was out of range.

'That's good,' said Alan, wondering what was so secret about the revelation and fearing that congratulations of a more personal and specific nature were yet required.

'Well,' replied Quist, expectantly.

'A wonderful achievement,' said Alan, opting for a compromise course by strengthening the superlative.

'Think it through, Alan.'

'You've worked a miracle,' Alan replied, left with no option but the attribution of unqualified merit to his superior.

Quist sighed. 'An Executive Assistant,' he said. 'I will need an Executive Assistant.'

'Of course you will,' Alan agreed.

'Because Peaches is…' Quist made a swift, clockwise, swishing motion with his right hand. 'She is…'

Alan wanted to say 'sitting at home, enjoying a glass of chilled Chablis' but didn't think that that was what Quist had in mind. 'Indisposed?' he ventured.

'That's right,' Quist replied. 'So, I'll need…'

'A replacement.'

'Yes.'

'Soon.'

'Most certainly.'

'Very soon.'

'Sooner.'

'As soon as this afternoon?'

'Even sooner.'

Alan could see, straight away, where this discussion was heading. If he wasn't vigilant, one of his (three) precious resources would be requisitioned to replace Peaches…and who knew how long she might be absent? Alan's team – such as it was – would expect him to vigorously resist any attempts at body-snatching. Quist, himself, would expect a show of resistance and so did 'the system'. After all, it was a truth universally acknowledged that there was no point in empire building if one's numbers (and the status they attracted) were to be eroded by opportunistic snaffling. And wasn't a 'just for the day' obsecration the thin end of the resource-stripping wedge?

Alan opened with dumb silence. It was a gambit that Quist hadn't expected and it evidently unsettled him. Alan peered at the floor.

As much as a minute passed before Quist broke. 'Look, I can't be expected,' he said, 'to talk on my phone and answer it at the same time.'

From a logical standpoint Alan knew that, in fact, Quist couldn't avoid talking on the phone if he was to answer it at any time. Alan stuck with silence but added some De Niro-like nodding.

'Perhaps,' said Quist, 'one of your people could…'

Alan did 'removing imaginary grit from eye with finger while holding glasses in other hand'.

'You must,' Quist said, 'have someone who you could…'

Pleading was never a good tactic, not even when followed by imprecations or threats.

'You know that I'm light on,' said Alan, still not making eye contact and rather wishing that Robyn Rainbird – or anyone, really – could have been present to see him at the top of his game. 'I'd love to help, of course, but I've got just three bodies to cover three subsections. Perhaps one of the other section heads could…' Alan did the swishing hand gesture that Quist often resorted to when the right word wouldn't come.

But the acting branch head wasn't done for yet. 'Whoever is available,' he said, cunningly, 'their phone could be diverted to Peaches' desk and they could do their normal work from there.'

'With respect, we both know that that's not realistic,' Alan replied. He sensed imminent victory and, though fearing the consequences, was not able to stay his sword. 'Someone supporting an officer as important and as busy as you could only be very hard-pressed.'

Quist gasped at the unexpected brilliance of this gambit.

'Even on a day like today,' Alan added, in case Quist wanted to argue that the first day back after Christmas was likely to be much less demanding than those to follow.

The fact that Peaches spent most of each day smoking at the rear of the building, tending to her décolletage in the ladies toilet and gossiping with the other grandmothers (wherever they were located on the floor) was a fact conveniently ignored by both men.

'Quite right,' said Quist, now thinking that Alan had resisted much more than was necessary and for much longer than the maintenance of self-respect and public dignity required.

In the silence that followed, Alan heard laughter from the open plan and mused on the oblivious continuance of life's small delights and dramas even as titans clashed.

'Seriously, Al,' Quist began, forgetting that Alan loathed being abbreviated, 'why can't the girl fill in for Peaches?'

The jocularity beyond the door peaked, in counterpoint to the seriousness of Quist's new assault.

'Surely she can be spared,' he continued, oozing a reptilian approximation of charm that took Alan all the way back to Sunday school and the tale of the original alfresco fruiterer. This unexpected change of tack halted Alan's momentum – as much because of its depersonalised reference to Edwina Troy as because of its chilling bonhomie. Alan knew, too, that failing to express disapproval of Quist's paternalistic lapse (in nominating the only female in Alan's section to perform the secretarial function) was to compound and be complicit in the sexist crime.

'The girl?' Alan asked, choosing feigned confusion over the just rage of the feminist sympathiser.

'You've only got one,' said Quist with a hint of impatience.

'Ah, yes. Ms Troy. Regrettably, she is the only person in her subsection.'

'Well,' said Quist, straining now to maintain a veneer of patient reasonableness, 'if the absence of any back-up staffing is the key determinant of unreleasability, I could always take the Elk.'

The Elk. Alan's jaw dropped. This was an appalling prospect. It was the Canadian dwarf who kept the Coordination and Finance Section Director, Alastair McAllister, away from the office in the afternoons, when he was at his drunken worst. To divert the Elk from this vital task would be a disaster of epic proportions for the branch and the department at large. Alan sensed that the tide had turned against him.

'He was at his desk,' Quist continued, 'when I went to the bathroom half an hour ago.'

'I suppose I could offer you Trevithick,' Alan countered, attempting to minimise his losses. 'I'd be prepared to cover for him, myself, in the event that any matters in relation to Committees A required attention.'

'No, I'm sure that he's got plenty to get on with,' Quist replied, certain that he'd at last chanced on a winning strategy.

'But he's the person I can most easily cover for,' replied Alan.

'And I'm sure you're no less busy than I,' said Quist.

The awful, grammatically inept reptile was going to have Edwina Troy or no one.

'I'll manage, somehow,' said Alan, trying not to sound unduly desperate, surprised that his own 'weight of responsibility' argument had been so cruelly turned against him.

'No, don't put yourself out,' Quist said. 'I'll happily take the Elk. I'm sure that Corporate can make do and it will be a wonderful development opportunity for him, working closely with an upwardly mobile senior officer.'

Alan wanted to be ill: not because of Quist's nauseating delusions as to his own importance and prospects, but because he didn't want to be held responsible for what might result if McAllister succeeded, after his customary liquid lunch, in returning to the building.

'The Elk,' said Quist, fanning himself with a file from Alan's tray, 'will do a perfectly satisfactory job, I'm sure.'

'I suppose you could have Edwina,' said Alan, now resigned to a complete route. 'I mean, it is just for one afternoon.'

'Only if you insist,' said Quist, enjoying himself.

The dreadful bloody brute, thought Alan. He most certainly would not insist. 'I'm sure that she'd be delighted to help you,' he said, avoiding complete humiliation and putting a brave face on the situation.

'Only if I can't dispersuade you, Al.'

Dispersuade. What sort of a word was that? Alan asked himself, mopping sweat off his brow with a piece of paper towel. 'Will you let her know? It will look better coming from someone as important as you.'

'No, I think it would be best coming from you, as…'

'Her acting section head,' said Alan.

'Exactly,' said Quist, sporting a victor's smile.

They were, again, in their proper roles. Alan had struggled and could claim as much. Quist had prevailed and would certainly claim as much. What needed to be done had been done and all was more or less well with the world…or would have been, had Alan not needed to inform Edwina Troy of her temporary redeployment, had Alan's email system not been flashing red warnings and had he not, earlier, discovered 'it' and seen that it was not good.

6

Alan's discussion with Edwina Troy about her temporary performance of the executive assistant's role did not go well.

'That sexist bloody pig,' she said at the halfway point, referring to Quentin Quist. 'Nothing he suggested would surprise me.'

Even with Alan's limited understanding of the sexual mores of the modern – or any – world, he rather thought there were some things that the acting branch head could suggest that would actually surprise. He wondered, too, what it was about pigs, relative to, say, goats, camels or other species, that made them the popular personification of gender prejudice (in addition to greed and policing). He supposed that pigs were the encapsulation of so many sins because of their preparedness to live in their by-products, instead of hunger striking for more salubrious surroundings.

'But you,' Edwina accused, 'it's not as though you're one of the hairy-chested ones…or even a fellow traveller.'

Alan knew that he should have felt dispirited about the metaphorical depilation and all that it implied about the way his female colleagues saw him, but he was, in truth, more troubled by Edwina's use of the sexist 'fellow traveller', notwithstanding the dangling unsuitability of 'hanger-on', its most tempting alternative. He saw, quite correctly, her use of the term as a measure of her distress.

'I'm so disappointed in you,' she said.

For as long as Alan could recall – all the way back to the mammary glands in his social studies exercise book – women had been disappointed in him. His face burned with shame – with the accrued shame of those manifold let-downs.

'I feel unwell,' said Edwina. 'I have to go home.'

'If there's anything I can do,' Alan mumbled.

'You've done enough,' came the reply.

Alan nodded sympathetically and, not feeling up to further pleading with Trevithick (as the default fill-in), diverted his phone. He steeled himself, as he left the room, to the disinfecting of his second workstation for the day.

'I'll be sitting at Peaches' desk,' he announced to Morton, who, staring up at the ceiling vents, complained about the heat before urging Alan not to enjoy himself in his new role as amanuensis to their leader.

Quentin Quist came out of the office and, fanning himself with a ministerial folder, watched Alan tip potting mix out of the keyboard and on to the carpet, and then shift a variety of Christmas trinkets from the work space into a bottom drawer.

'I thought I was getting the girl,' he remarked.

'I'm afraid she had to go home sick,' said Alan, hoping that his own self-abasement would make it unnecessary for any further discussion about developmental opportunities for the Elk.

'Pathetic,' said Quist.

Alan gave the keyboard a light spray with antibacterial mist and placed it, upside down, onto a strip of absorbent paper so that the fluid would drain away.

Quist leaned against the door frame, probably wondering if Alan was stupid enough to have engineered Edwina's absence. 'Some of these women ought to try real labour, out in the fields in the summer heat.'

So far as Alan knew, Quist had never done a day's labour without pen or keyboard in his life. It was also a fact that the conditions inside an office building filled with heat-generating machines and without functioning air conditioning could be more than unpleasant.

'I'll call you, if I need you,' the temporary Executive said.

'I'll be whatever help I can,' replied Alan, trying to sound agreeable.

He reached for the computer's On switch and cocked his head, ready to detect any resumption of air flow from the vent above. As his fingertip passed the point of no return, Alan heard the air conditioning system whoosh into action, then groan like an expiring mastodon and cease. Alan's eyes met Quist's.

'Well?' Quist enquired.

Alan hadn't imagined the brief recommencement and shut down. Surely Quist had sensed it, too.

'Did you notice…?'

'Notice what?'

'It's nothing,' said Alan. 'I just thought I heard…'

Quist shook his head and returned to his desk. 'And ring Burgoyne about this bloody air conditioning,' he called, 'before we have a revolution on our hands.'

Alan picked up the sterile telephone handpiece, called Burgoyne's number and was diverted to a recorded message telling him that technicians were at work on the cooling system. The problem was expected to be fixed within the hour but there was no indication of the time at which the message had been left.

When the email program opened, there were more messages (with the attachment that Alan didn't want to view) and, among them, ones jocularly enquiring about his role (if any) in the morning's events. He worked his way through the new arrivals, searching for text that didn't feed his doubt and fear.

The first of a number of official emails was a brief In Confidence message from Quentin Quist to all staff of the Consultation and Stakeholder Liaison Branch. 'Pressure of work,' it began, 'prevents me from meeting with you, but by now you will be aware that, at an unknown time over the Christmas period, a person or persons unknown left a piece of excreta on our branch head's desk.'

Alan noted Quist's attempt to prevent – by reference to 'our branch head's desk' – any speculation that 'it' might have been aimed at Quist himself. This did not surprise. Alan also noted Quist's reference to 'persons unknown'. This, by contrast, did surprise, as Alan was rather sure that defecation was not an activity which, like ballroom dancing, ping pong or (allegedly) sex, was improved by paired participation. Indeed, he recalled that the close proximity of another was usually inimical to achievement in the lavatory. On the positive side, though, Quist had used the word 'excreta' in the place of bubby talk poo synonyms.

'This matter,' the email continued, 'is being investigated by Departmental Security. Director Internal Security, Mr Rasch, has notified me of his intention to interview all staff of the branch as they return to work, commencing with those present on the date of this email. Although this is not yet a police matter and it is not mandatory that you attend any interview with Mr Rasch, your cooperation would be appreciated. Mr Rasch's office will contact you, individually, re interview times.'

Alan looked at his telephone, expecting it to ring at any moment. Calm yourself, he thought.

'I know that all of you,' Quist's message concluded, 'will feel for Valerie, Tango, Togo and Topsy in the aftermath of this shameful occurrence. I will keep you apprised of any developments.'

Inclusion of the names of Valerie Venables's red setters was a bizarre touch that would fool no one into thinking that Quist had a sensitive side. And Alan was almost certain, anyway, that the dog's names were in fact Pango, Pogo and Popsy. As for the promise to keep everyone apprised of any developments, Alan knew it to be without substance; Quist's management style was, if nothing else, highly secretive. Information was power…and power was never willingly diluted on Quentin's watch.

A message from Morton drew Alan's attention to the fact that 'Mango, Mogo and Mopsy would have been delighted by the presence of brown thunder on Valerie's desk as, like most mammals – with the exception of alpacas – dogs are habitual crap eaters and the obvious inspiration for the wonderful expression "shit eating grin".' Alan pressed Delete.

There followed a message from the Acting Assistant Secretary IT Security and Policy on the delays in email traffic as a result of large numbers of unauthorised images of human waste being sent within, to and from the department earlier in the day. Staff members were reminded of the requirements (unspecified) of the department's 'Appropriate Use of Email Policy' (not attached).

Another message from Morton was next on the display. It asked Alan whether he recalled a 'poo picture prohibition' in the 'Appropriate Use of Email Policy'. Alan deleted the message without responding.

Following was a message from Rasch; it contained a schedule of interviews with Consultation and Stakeholder Liaison Branch staff at twenty-minute intervals after an initial forty-minute stint with Alan at twelve p.m.

Alan's surprise at being first off the blocks over-rode the earlier advice he'd given Quist about the importance of everyone being interviewed… or to be more precise, the importance of everyone, including senior staff, being seen to be interviewed. Why, he wondered, had he been allocated double the time put aside for interviews with others, when he'd been exposed to 'it' for only a few seconds longer than Rasch himself? And why double the time when he, Rasch and Quist had already discussed motive and opportunity…and when Rasch surely knew Alan to be the sort of man who had no misapprehensions about the uses to which a toilet should be put (and to which, by contrast, a desk top should not be put).

What could Rasch have learned since their last meeting? Could he have already examined the building's electronic access records and the temporary pass register, and have deduced that Alan had left the building without his access card on Christmas Eve?

What if there were security guard reports about Alan drunkenly berating the mobile patrol, snoozing at his desk (unable to be woken) or trying to exit via the fire doors, having activated the alarms and summoned the fire brigade? Even worse, what if there was surveillance footage of him incoherently begging the foyer attendants to let him out of the building, of him clambering over the security gates or attempting, on all fours, to squeeze under them? What sort of link would any reasonable man have made between Alan's atypical egress (however achieved) and the despoliation of Valerie Venables's blotter?

Of course, Alan didn't know for certain that he had misbehaved in any of the above ways in the final hours of the working year but there was the possibility that he might have disgraced himself in some way (with or without excreta)…and that possibility was almost as troubling as the not knowing itself.

Alan forced himself to return to the screen. The very next message was marked 'In Confidence' and was from Quentin Quist. It urged any staff who felt the need for counselling following the 'incident' referred to in his earlier message to contact Personnel. This prompted Morton to speculate on the likelihood of a sudden sharp rise in coprophobia-related psychoses (necessitating compensation leave) in the department.

A follow-up message from Quist with the same security markings as the earlier one urged staff not to contact Personnel 'until advised to do so'.

A third email from Quist marked both 'Urgent and confidential' asked all members of the branch to delete all previous emails containing any reference to Personnel.

Alan looked through the one partially open blind into Quist's office and observed the occupant speaking animatedly on the telephone.

A dozen new emails beeped their arrival in Alan's In box and then all was silence. The first of the new batch was from Acting Assistant Secretary Personnel to all staff on the 'appropriate use of rest rooms'. Staff were instructed 'to restrict their toileting activities to areas designated as lavatories'. A message revoking this message was next and urged staff 'to restrict their toilet activities to the areas officially designated as lavatories'. A message revoking this message followed, instructing staff 'to restrict their toileting activities to toilets and lavatories within areas officially designated as lavatories, toilets or rest rooms'. Finally, a message revoked this last missive and required staff 'not to go to the toilet other than in toilets that had been officially designated as toilets (by means of departmental signage) or that were known to be toilets as a result of long-established custom and usage'. Staff members who didn't speak English were encouraged to contact the translation line to obtain a copy of this last email in a language of their choice. Non-English-speaking Aboriginal and Torres Strait Islander staff were invited to contact the Aboriginal and Torres Strait Islander Liaison Officer to obtain a translation in the tongue of their choice.

Why any individuals who didn't speak English would be using the email system (with its exclusively English content) in the first place was a mystery to Alan. He wondered, too, if anyone ever rang up with a request for translation into a truly obscure language – perhaps suggesting, 'My Puquna could do with an airing', 'Today I'm in the mood for Fingalia' or 'I'll have some Lule Toconote if you don't mind.'

A message from Rasch informed Branch staff that all proposed interviews had been cancelled and that Departmental Security had never intended to conduct an investigation into any incident that might or might not have occurred over the Christmas break. Any impression created by previous communications to the effect that such an investigation was proposed or underway was entirely unintentional and deeply regretted.

The Acting Assistant Secretary Personnel, in an email marked 'In Confidence', 'Urgent' and 'Priority Delivery', asked that all staff delete all of her emails regarding the appropriate use of toilets (however styled or designated) immediately. Quentin Quist, in an email marked the same, asked that all staff delete all of his previous emails too.

'Didn't I tell you that the shit would hit the fan?' asked Morton in an unclassified one-liner.

The last message in the batch was from Antonia Ainsworth's executive assistant and explained everything:

An act of vandalism took place in the office of Assistant Secretary Consultation and Stakeholder Liaison over the Christmas period. This has given rise to a number of official internal communications which have, in turn, been the subject of enquiries from the media. Staff are reminded that the unauthorised release of Departmental communications to individuals outside the Department is a breach of the Code of Conduct and may result in disciplinary action. Any contact with the media is to be through Communications Branch. In addition, the unauthorised release of classified communications may result in prosecutions under the Crimes Act. I lastly remind you of the requirements of the Department's 'Appropriate Use of Email Policy' (attached). All staff are to familiarise themselves with their responsibilities under the policy. In short, think before you press Send.
Antonia Ainsworth
Acting Secretary

Alan always thought before he pressed Send and he never communicated with the media, except to draw attention, through the mail in his private capacity, to the more egregious grammatical errors in the local newspaper.

Quentin Quist appeared at Alan's side. He looked pale and agitated. 'I'm going to a meeting over in the executive suite,' he said. 'I may be gone for some time.'

Alan looked at Quist's diary – to satisfy himself that there were no other meetings he needed to make arrangements for – and familiarised himself with the executive correspondence tracking system in the final minutes before the email system died and the air conditioning rumbled back into action. When Alan rang the IT help desk, a recorded message informed him that the system had been shut down for all but executive staff for the purpose of urgent maintenance. Alan smelled a rodent and busied himself reviewing the contents of his paper diary.

This activity would have been a useful distractions from his anxiety about 'it' had not been for the comments of people passing his desk on their way to the lifts and the conveniences. These remarks ranged from harmless yet amusing references to Peaches' sudden gender reassignment (the like of Morton's 'Peaches, sweetie, you've had the change and I'd sue the surgeon') through to the plainly insulting and too-familiar pronouncement of the Corporate Foliage Optimisation Executive: 'the Peter Principle, Alan, it shames us all, sooner or later.'

Alan focused, nonetheless, on the due dates for papers for the year's initial committee meetings, then reviewed the Section and Branch business plans to see if, part way through the cycle, there was anything in them that was still relevant. Satisfied that there was nothing hostile lying in wait for him – nothing the non-achievement of which could be finger-pointed home to him – he picked up a committee paper he'd written, in his capacity as Assistant Director Committees A, which he would now have to approve in his capacity as acting director.

Junior officers were often paralysed by questions of proper process when required to pass judgement in such situations – that is, on work which they had, in effect, submitted to themselves. But Alan was untroubled by procedural doubt. This didn't mean that he was beyond writing something amusing, in recognition of the circumstances, on the front page of a document – perhaps something along the lines of 'An insightful piece of work; well done' or even, more playfully, 'After a great deal of deliberation, I concur.' It did, however, mean that he could get on with the task of dispassionately considering what he'd originally written. And that's precisely what he did until eleven forty-five when, looking up, he realised that he hadn't eaten any morning tea and his thoughts went to his cheese sandwich lunch.

'He must be getting the mother of all bollockings,' said Morton, appearing from Alan's left. 'I may well open a bottle of Louis Roederer tonight, in an act of thanksgiving.'

'I don't know what you mean,' said Alan.

'He's over with Antonia, getting what for about mentioning the turd in emails, blabbing to the media and sanctioning Rasch's inquisition.'

'I wouldn't know about that,' said Alan.

'We both saw it coming.'

That they had was a fact of no moment to Alan. 'May I assist you with something?' he asked.

'Your loyalty is pathetic,' Morton replied. 'And quite unwarranted. Quist would have us both out the door without a second thought. Only the brain-dead and the unswervingly sycophantic suit his purpose and we're neither of those things.'

Alan pretended to see something in the document he'd just put down. 'Let me know if I can be of assistance,' he said.

'I've actually come to assist you,' said Morton. 'I thought I'd give you a break, give you a chance to stretch your legs.'

'How kind,' said Alan, 'but I probably shouldn't.'

Morton had been Quentin Quist's initial Public Service supervisor. Morton loathed Quist. Quist loathed Morton. Quist would not be pleased to see Morton in the Executive Assistant's chair, even for an hour or two.

'You've got to have a lunch break and I don't imagine it's been busy.'

'Rather quiet, actually.'

'Then it's settled.'

'Well, if you insist,' said Alan, rising.

'It'll be great seeing that bastard's face when he realises that I'm his Exec Assistant.'

'No, on second thoughts,' said Alan, sitting back down, 'I'd better stay.'

'Get going,' said Morton.

Alan dallied.

'Go on.'

Alan picked up his diary and pocketed his pen.

'Take as long as you like,' said Morton. 'I have no plans.'

7

Alan's father-in-law shared a room at the Bonny Brae Nursing Home with a taciturn Slav named Alf.

In Alan's green Morris Minor, with the front windows down in lieu of air conditioning, the journey took less than fifteen minutes. But for his driving gloves, Alan would have eaten his sandwich en route.

Someone new was snoozing in Alf's bed but Alan didn't ask himself the obvious question.

On the other side of the room, Hugo Faggoter lay on his back, wide-eyed, staring at the ceiling. His pyjamas were buttoned up to his dewlaps and his arms rested by his side on the blue oversheet. He was in precisely the position in which he'd been left by a personal care assistant four hours earlier. He would remain in that position until lunch was served and Alan raised the back of the bed to prevent him from drowning in the soup of the day – always lentil because of its stool-softening qualities. After lunch, Hugo would be rotated forty-five degrees and then, after dinner, a further forty-five degrees, so that after each meal his body and the bed would meet in a different way.

'How are we today?' Alan enquired, keeping his voice low, so as not to disturb Alf's replacement.

Hugo's gaze remained fixed on the ceiling. Nothing about him indicated that he'd heard Alan's greeting or that he was otherwise aware of his son-in-law's presence.

'You're looking chipper,' said Alan.

Hugo had said nothing to anyone for years and was evidently not about to break with custom.

What Alan had come to think of as companionable silence in the pre-admission decade they'd spent together had since been diagnosed by the geriatricians as a gradual retreat from the world, labelled 'dementia with underlying depression'.

This had come as a surprise to Alan. He thought they'd lived amiably enough, with Hugo spending his days on the veranda and his evenings with the radiogram. If they'd had little to say to each other, wasn't it because there was less that needed saying? If they'd gone out less, apart from Alan's absences for work, wasn't it because there was less worth looking for (and at)? And if Hugo preferred not to see the newspaper, was that really surprising, taking into account the increasing frequency of grammatical errors, pornographic underwear advertisements and accounts of the bedroom antics of people they'd never heard of – occupants of a world to which neither of them really belonged.

Alan had, in fact, been bitterly disappointed to learn that their silences were less about a reduced need to say anything than about Hugo's inability to think anything worth articulating.

'You're definitely on the up,' Alan said, as much to buoy his own spirits as to encourage any residual human presence within the shell of Hugo Faggoter.

He straightened the items on the top of the metal chest of drawers and hung the unread newspaper off the bed rail, just as he always did.

The geriatricians said that Hugo had lacked stimulation in his years with Alan and it was this conclusion that hurt Alan the most; experts, using scientifically established criteria, had judged him to be dull…and Alan had an abiding respect for experts.

It hadn't occurred to him that there might be anything wrong with Hugo until the event which he subsequently thought of as 'the cornflake incident'.

On the relevant spring Sunday morning, Alan had announced that breakfast was ready and Hugo had shuffled from his lounge chair to the dining room table. Normally at this point the old boy sat quietly while Alan tested the milk on the stove to make doubly sure that it had reached an appropriate temperature between tepid and warm. On this occasion, however, Hugo had shovelled at least a spoonful of the dry flakes into his mouth before Alan could add liquid to the bowl. A single spittle-drenched flake had dangled from the old man's chin like a badly glued stamp or the barely connected crust of a substantial sun-dried knee scab. Then, after the milk had been carefully poured over the remaining cereal, Hugo had peered into the depths, with his spoon at the ready, and asked the most profound of all the questions known to man: 'Why?'

Why breakfast? Why cornflakes? Why go on? Alan was never to be enlightened. The old man had placed his spoon carefully on the woven place mat and never spoken another word. The silence that had been broken less and less, even by the 'thank you(s)' 'please(s)' and 'would you be so kind as to(s)' of polite domestic intercourse was thereafter absolute.

'I see you've got a new roommate,' Alan said.

On cue, the occupant of the other bed announced in a croak, 'You won't be getting anything out of that one.'

There were numerous things that Alan might have noticed about the newcomer: his sunspot-mottled cranium, the white stubble on his wobbly jaw or, more disturbingly, the way his visible skin seemed so thin and dry that it appeared incapable of corralling his organs. However, it was the eyes Alan couldn't look past. They had an intensity which was difficult to reconcile with the fragility of the rest of the man.

'I like to think he hears me,' Alan replied. 'I'm his son-in-law, Alan Mewling.' Alan got to his feet and smiled, hoping he wouldn't be offered a fragile, arid hand.

'I need you to look at something,' said the newcomer, through cracked blue lips. His eyes raked Alan's soul. It was the second time that day that a malevolent entity had surveilled Alan's inner being and found it too slight to warrant serious predation.

'Certainly. How can I help?' Alan asked, filled with dread.

'Come closer,' said Alf's replacement.

Alan moved a step nearer, hoping that any assistance he might be required to render would not involve touching or by-products. The most innocent child would have been alert to the prospect of something unpleasant at this point but in Alan's case the trepidation he felt at impending human contact overwhelmed the urge to flee. 'May I ring a nurse for you?' Alan asked, trying to fix on the ancient's monstrous white eyebrows in order to avoid his gaze.

'It won't take a minute.'

Alan advanced another step. He was now just a metre away from the bed and consumed by apprehension. It wasn't that he was unwilling to assist. He wanted to help. But only, please God, in a remote and impersonal way.

'Closer,' said the ersatz Alf, beckoning Alan to position himself bedside.

Alan, now an automaton incapable of resistance, obliged. His thighs brushed against the mattress and it seemed to him that the manic energy burning in those eyes – those mesmerising eyes – was draining the life force from the debilitated host. He wondered, foolishly, whether he would be commanded to offer his neck in an act of regenerative obeisance – to make his own blood contribution to that all-consuming fire.

Instead, the old man pushed back the trolley table, lifted the bed cover and urged his disciple to look underneath. Alan was incapable of resistance. He tilted his head and beheld a huge, blue, vein-riven organ that was the true master of the being – its own blood-hungry parasite – and, at the same time, ghastly irrefutable proof of the triumph of the psyche over the eternal void, even in the shadow of the final reckoning.

Alan hoped desperately that he wasn't required to touch – to do anything more than stand in awe.

'What do you think of that?' croaked the priapic one, throwing a cautious glance at the doorway.

'Very…uh…impressive,' said Alan, dreading whatever was to come next.

'I'm keeping it.'

Alan gulped. Moments passed. He could hear the pulsating hum of a machine – probably a refrigerator – in a nearby room. 'Keeping it for…?' he finally enquired.

'Later,' said the high priest, with satisfied finality, carefully lowering the bed clothes. His eyes blazed all the brighter and, although the initiate knew he now had nothing to fear, he wasn't sure how to conclude the rites. 'Our secret,' said the old man, pulling the tray table up to its most protective position. 'Tell no one.'

'No one,' Alan murmured.

'I'm a true ginger,' the ancient said, nodding to himself.

'A true ginger,' Alan reprised, although he knew the claim to be no longer true, if, indeed, it ever had been.

Hugo Faggoter emitted a long, low groan that startled Alan and returned him to the present. He swivelled to see whether the old man had observed any of the concluded ceremony. Thus it was that he was standing exactly between the two beds – convinced that Hugo's focus had never deviated from the ceiling – when the Director of Nursing, Matron Frogmore, entered the room.

An oversized metal serving spoon dangled from her hip. She looked from Alan to Alf's replacement and, knowing of the latter's disposition for display, suspected the very worst. 'I hope that we've been behaving ourself, Mr Adams,' she said to the high priest.

Adams's hand held the tray table in place but the exultation in his eyes had been supplanted by the guilty humiliation of the beaten dog. Alan imagined harmless detumescence under the bed clothes.

'Because Matron has ways of dealing with bad boys, doesn't she?' said the nurse. She flourished the serving spoon and the ancient's grip on the table tightened. Perhaps there was still life below, after all.

'He's harmless,' she said to Alan, 'but I didn't want him frightening any of the female visitors, so it seemed best to put him in here, with Hugo, who only has you.' She tapped the enormous utensil twice on the closest edge of the true ginger's table, causing him to wince, then transferred her attention to the other resident. 'Aren't you lucky, Hugo, that Alan has come to see you? And on a Thursday, too.'

Thursday was the only day on which Alan didn't usually visit but, if Hugo felt himself lucky – and Alan couldn't see any particular reason why he should – he was keeping his gratitude very much to himself.

'My usual luncheon companion was detained at work,' said Alan, by way of explanation for his presence.

'Lunch won't be far away,' Matron Frogmore announced.

'Our secret,' said the true ginger, as soon as she was out of sight.

By the time Alan had elevated the back of Hugo's bed and tied a napkin around his neck, the luncheon trolley could be heard rattling along the corridor.

A cheerful African woman placed a single bowl, a spoon and a paper serviette on Hugo's tray. At the moment Alan removed the metal covering from the bowl, he could have sworn that Hugo was watching him but, in the time it took capture the first spoonful of aperient sludge, the watcher had gone.

A personal care worker raised the back of Clyde Adams's bed and left. The old man slurped greedily on his soup.

After the first half dozen spoonfuls, Hugo and Alan fell into their own steady rhythm and Alan's mind turned again to 'it', to the lost hours of his Christmas Eve and to the awful possibility that he had, in a moment of mindless stupidity, mounted Valerie Venables's desk and urged his own special tribute to Quentin Quist into the world.

8

Back at the office, Bruce Trevithick was sitting at Peaches' desk. The computer was on and the air conditioning had lowered the temperature to a comfortable point.

'Quentin did his nut when he saw Morton filling in for you,' Trevithick explained, not looking up from the monitor.

Alan winced.

'I told him,' Trevithick continued, 'that I'd help out until you got back.'

'That was most kind of you,' said Alan. 'I've been at Bonnie Brae.'

Trevithick knew all about Hugo and the nursing home. 'Any developments?' he asked, sympathetically.

'None,' said Alan. 'Here?'

On Trevithick's screen a naked fat man tied to a rotating wheel begged for more zucchini. He didn't, Alan thought, have the look about him of someone with a penchant for greens. Alan looked away.

'Quentin wasn't back ten minutes before he was recalled to the Executive Suite. And the media called.'

'About the…?' Alan asked.

'Uh, huh,' said Trevithick, still not looking up.

Alan's head swam and he placed a steadying hand on the edge of the filing cabinet. 'Which media?' he asked.

'TV,' answered Trevithick.

If Alan had asked the question 'which medium?', TV would have been a perfectly acceptable answer, for Alan had sighted a pair of broadcast vans parked on the footpath outside the main entrance on his way in, without making any connection between them and 'it'.

'The details are all here,' Trevithick said, gesturing in the direction of a notepad to the side of his keyboard.

'You didn't think to refer them to the Communications Branch?'

The man on the torture wheel sobbed. Alan tried not to look. Trevithick couldn't tear his gaze away.

'I thought that Quentin would want to do it. He was talking to all of the newspaper people before Toni called.'

'That can't be true,' said Alan.

'Begging them not to publish his earlier comments, actually.'

That could well be true, thought Alan. 'How do you know that?' he asked.

'I was listening in,' said Trevithick.

'Because?' said Alan.

'Because I had nothing better to do.'

'Well, best keep that to yourself,' said Alan, quietly. 'Is there anything else I need to know?'

'There's an emergency meeting of directors and assistant directors with Quentin in five minutes in the eighth floor conference room.'

There was barely enough time for Alan to visit the toilet and catch the lift up.

The man on the torture wheel – evidently denied the required zucchini – swore long and ingeniously.

'Are you OK to look after things here a while longer?' Alan asked.

Trevithick looked Alan in the eye for the first time. 'I was hoping for a lunch break, so I could go somewhere and change my bandage.' He pulled at his collar to expose the soggy gauze dressing which seemed to encircle his neck.

Alan didn't like to think about the activities which might have necessitated its application. 'I didn't really have lunch myself,' he said.

'But you did get out.'

'That's true.'

'Then, if I could leave early for the day…'

'The meeting shouldn't go for too long,' said Alan, committing to nothing. 'There won't be too many starters.'

'I don't know about that,' said Trevithick. 'He had me ringing around.'

'Ringing around?'

The naked man attempted to bargain, shocking Alan with the degradation he was prepared to endure for another green length.

'Section Heads and Assistants,' said Trevithick. 'Getting them in from leave.'

Alan wondered how many of the absent had answered the call. He knew that his section head, Robyn Rainbird, was uncontactable at a health farm, having coffee enemas, drinking spring water and endlessly chanting (to stop herself from fretting over the treatment of her Burmese at the cattery).

'He's cancelled their leave?'

'Just this afternoon's, for the meeting.'

'Is Debbie coming in?'

Debbie Dapin did everything she could to avoid interaction with Quist while he was in the branch head's chair.

'Not answering.'

That she wasn't contactable was no surprise.

'Piers will represent the Policy Unit,' Trevithick added.

Piers Faure was a data modeller. He would remember everything and contribute nothing.

'And what about Corporate?' Quist surely wouldn't be stupid enough to insist on the presence of Alastair McAlister, a dedicated liquid luncher, at an afternoon meeting.

'Smith will do the honours.'

Alan still couldn't relax. 'Barbara?'

'ETA about now, with the whole brood.'

'Ghost!' said Alan. (It was his strongest expletive.)

The last time Barbara's seven progeny had visited the Office, the results had been calamitous. Alan recalled the soggy nappy he'd found in his briefcase, the pizza triangle wedged into his disc drive and the drawings of defecating animals in permanent marker on his miniature whiteboard: strangely angry penguins, livid zebras and infuriated kangaroos delivering coffee-coloured scats of arse-tearing proportions. He didn't ask the obvious question: who, in Edwina's absence, would be prepared to look after the oldest half dozen of Barbara's children while she was in the meeting?

'More zucchini, I beg you,' cried the man on the torture wheel.

'I'd better be on my way,' said Alan, anxious to secure his office.

'I'll await your return,' said Trevithick.

After stowing his nameplate, ticket holder and related sign in his filing cabinet for safekeeping, Alan locked the door and caught the lift to the eighth floor. He went straight to the lavatories closest to the conference room, took the cubicle abutting the wall and draped the seat in clean toilet paper. Fear gripped him…from the inside: fear that one of the section heads or assistants recalled from leave had returned to the office late on Christmas Eve and seen something that would implicate him or point to 'behaviour unbecoming'. Perhaps one of their number was about to shed a dark light on events Alan had no recollection of – events which in some labyrinthine way connected him and 'it'.

Alan again racked his brain for the faintest, most insubstantial, additional recollection of that last working day – something that would hint at his innocence or, at the very least, give him cause for comfort. Nothing materialised. Everything after the moment, at about 3.30, when he had entered the Executive Suite with his bottle and trayed hors d'oeuvres was a blank.

From the occupied cubicle two down, there came the sound of a large, dense stool crashing through a meniscus unburdened by tissue paper or by fragments of any earlier contribution. A faltering, sibilant fart which became a single, unimpeded 'whew' celebrated the liberation of the prisoner. A brief intake of air then preceded a long, satisfied sigh.

Alan knew that only a peaceful, ordered life could result in such a satisfying sequence of events and he speculated on the particular element of contemporary public administration that might have nurtured such a mode of deliberate yet easeful evacuation. A memory of a long-abandoned file repository flashed into his mind and a feeling of unalloyed tranquillity embraced and enclosed him.

His musings were, however, brief. The outer door crashed open, the door of the only vacant cubicle was slammed shut and bolted. He heard a belt buckle clink against floor tiles, and buttocks slapping onto a seat. Then came a half-grunt, half-groan – the sort of noise he might have expected from the mouth of an overburdened water buffalo – and a prolonged watery eruption, followed by the rattle of the toilet roll holder, a curse and the crashing open of the same cubicle door, all in the shortest order, and at no point complemented by the sound of an emptying cistern.

Alan looked at his watch. One minute until the meeting commenced. He stood up, pulled a piece of tissue free of the roll, wrapped it around his finger and depressed the flush button (for appearance's sake). When he opened the door, using more tissue to prevent another contact, he was surprised to see Quentin Quist standing at the mirror, squeezing the carbuncle on his nose.

Alan shuddered. He hadn't heard the sounds of preliminary hand washing.

'I wasn't happy about you leaving Morton as my EA,' said Quist, without disengaging from the pustule.

'My apologies,' Alan replied, removing a miniature bar of soap from his pocket and unwrapping it.

'He's not a team player and it's not as though I'm not already under pressure.'

'No,' said Alan, creating a lather.

Quist abandoned his efforts to squeeze the yellow top of the pustule open and eyed Alan's labours with barely concealed contempt. Alan, by meshing and unmeshing his fingers, and rubbing the palms and backs of his hands, covered every conceivable germ-harbouring fold and surface.

'Don't spend all day at that,' said Quist, finally. 'We can't be expected to wait for you.' He left without passing his fingertips through the finest trickle of cold water.

Again, Alan shuddered. He rinsed, then wiped on a segment of paper towel. With a fresh piece of towel, he collected the miniature soap and deposited it in the bin. Finally, without so much as a glance at himself in the mirror, he wrapped a further piece of towel around his hand and opened the door.

In the conference room, all heads turned at Alan's entrance. The only vacant seat at the table was at the opposite end to the chairman, between Morton and Barbara Best, so Alan dropped into the closest chair against the wall.

'At the table, if you don't mind, Alan. We wouldn't want to be straining to hear your pearls.'

A couple of the more sycophantic attendees sniggered. Morton shifted his chair to allow Alan some squeeze-in space. Barbara, with a snotty-nosed toddler on her closest knee and a snoozing babe in a bundle on the other, had no room to move without rubbing elbows with the Sri Lankan, Smith.

'Before we begin,' said Quist, 'I want to respectfully acknowledge the past and present traditional owners of the land we are meeting on, the great, proud…aaah…traditional nations of the…um traditional land we are meeting on. It is a privilege to be standing on their…um…'

Martin Strasser, the acting head of the Stakeholder Liaison Section, sitting on Quist's right, was an ex-South African, widely suspected of white supremacism. He nonetheless scanned the faces of the dozen attendees for any hint of disdain or scepticism.

Alan's view was that reference to the 'great, proud…aah…traditional nations' was an over-egging of the pudding but he was well experienced in innocent dissembling, so adopted a facial expression that, after nights of practice in front of his bathroom mirror, he believed to be an appropriate mix of remorse, guilt and admiration. This was a task made difficult by the unmistakeable bouquet of stale urine emanating from one of the children at his right. Strasser meanwhile glared at Smith, who had form as a 'reluctant acknowledger'.

'I've convened this emergency meeting,' said their chairman, 'and most reluctantly recalled some of you from leave because of the difficult circumstances in which we find…' He made the water swishing motion.

'A turd?' asked Strasser.

'Ourselves,' concluded Quist, looking mildly irritated, 'the difficult circumstances in which we find ourselves. The secretary is on holidays in…' The swishing movement again.

'A well-deserved attempt at recreation?' ventured Strasser.

'New Zealand,' said Quist, looking properly irritated this time, 'but has been briefed and do I need to tell you? – especially, you, Alan, who were almost first on the scene – she is not…' More swishing.

'Skiing?' asked Strasser.

'Impressed,' said Quist, on the brink of apoplexy. 'She is not impressed at all.'

He looked Alan fixedly in the eye and for a brief moment Alan thought, there must now be evidence; it must have been me. But then Quist's focus moved to Barbara, where – but for the children – it would probably have rested for a while, before moving on to Smith.

'Not one little bit,' said Quist, swivelling back past Alan to fix on Morton. 'She may even have to cancel her leave.' This last piece of information was delivered as though it constituted a disaster of epic proportions.

Alan thought the possible postponement of the secretary's holiday to be an unfortunate thing but – as he'd never met Denise Day, attended a meeting chaired by her or spoken to her on the telephone – his sympathy was somewhat limited.

'And the Acting Minister,' Quist continued, 'is being…' Quist peered at the ceiling and most of the participants followed his gaze upwards.

'Tugged off by the principal adviser,' whispered Morton.

'Kept up to speed…' said Quist, looking even more intently at the ceiling, so that those who'd previously resisted the temptation to join him, now succumbed, '…with developments.' He looked downwards and everyone followed. 'I shouldn't need to tell you that we are not,' he continued, 'flavour of the month.'

The toddler next to Alan, as if belatedly inspired by Morton's earlier masturbatory jest, lunged at Alan's tie with sticky fingers and, securing a firm grip on the widest section, gave it a couple of sharp jerks. Alan, whose eyes had been on Quist, was ill prepared for such a vicious and unheralded assault. His upper body was pulled downward until he slid forward and off the chair.

Barbara murmured, 'Don't do that, darling,' without attempting to restrain the child, leaving Alan to struggle, from a disadvantageous limbo-like position, for dominion over his own neckwear. A tug of war ensued and the child squealed with delight.

'Alan, may we enquire why you suddenly thought this was the right time for games?' asked Quist.

Alan, with his attention momentarily diverted from the struggle, was pulled sideways by a second series of especially savage yanks and responded in the only sensible way, by throwing himself in the opposite direction and landing full-length on the carpet.

'Oh, someone help the fool up,' said Quist.

Morton went to Alan's aid, the two-year-old bawled and the infant on the other side, woken by the excitement, cried even more loudly. Barbara attended to her progeny in birth order, rather than 'loudest first', thrusting the baby into the arms of the horrified Smith and pulling the toddler onto her lap.

Alan, reassured by the distance between himself and his tormentor, resumed his seat and stuffed the dangling part of the coveted item into his shirt pocket.

Quist glared at him and the volume of the child's caterwauling doubled. Only one thing would restore calm and everyone knew what it had to be. 'Give the boy your tie, Alan.'

'But...'

'Alan.'

'But I...'

'Oh, if it's that much of a problem.' Quist came to the riotous end of the table and removed his Disney necktie – an item of apparel which no one had heretofore suspected to be of the ready-knotted, clip-on variety.

The child responded to Quist's approach by hiding his face in his mother's bosom. His sibling ceased crying at this point, too.

Anyone else would have regarded this as an unexpected early win but Quentin Quist, once committed to a course of action, would not be swayed by mere victory. He jiggled the tie about in an attempt to attract the older child's attention. 'Does the widdle man want to play with Mickey Mouse?' he enquired in a sickening falsetto. 'Does he want to play with Micky-wicky?'

The kid pushed the item away, sobbing and looking at Alan's plain, brown adornment.

'Look at the funny man's Mickey tie,' said Barbara, gesturing at Quist's already rejected offering.

'Won't,' the child answered, between sobs. 'Want the other one – that one.' He pointed at Alan's drab, half-hidden length.

Quist and Barbara both looked expectantly at Alan.

'But it's…'

'Want that one,' repeated the two-year-old.

The baby, in Smith's arms, started up again and Barbara gave Alan her most plaintive look.

He pulled off the desired item at the same time as Barbara in a resigned way pulled out a breast to calm the infant recovered from Smith. Everyone looked self-consciously away.

Alan proffered the tie but not with any enthusiasm and just out of the toddler's reach.

'Alan,' Quist warned.

The item was handed over and the recipient promptly stuffed the better part of it into his mouth. The chairman resumed his place at the end of the table, the baby suckled loudly and Alan peered – disarmed and shamed in some indefinable way – at a point a metre or so in front of Quist.

'Now, where had I got to?' Quist asked, patting Mickey – reinstated without the need for any display of dexterity – flat against his midriff.

'The Secretary was in New Zealand,' said Faure, Debby Dapin's fill-in.

'Yes, that's right,' said Quist, 'and she will make a decision about returning once she's seen…' He adopted a vacant look unaccompanied by either a swishing movement or scrutiny of the ceiling.

'The Whakarewarewa mud pools?' asked Strasser.

'Tomorrow's headlines,' said Quist, looking vaguely puzzled, 'which brings me to the point. The reason why the executive is not impressed with matters is that someone – someone in the know, someone from within – has been talking.'

The baby farted quietly and the toddler replaced the thin end of the tie in his mouth with the fat end, staring all the while at Alan.

'Talking to the media, Alan,' said Quist, heavily. 'And while I'm not necessarily convinced that it's someone in this room, there can be little doubt that it's someone in our branch.'

'Turds one minute, leaks the next,' whispered Morton.

'You've something to say about that, Stephen?' asked Quist.

'I was only wondering why you suspect someone in our own Branch,' Morton replied.

'Because they are in possession of all the facts,' snapped Quist. 'The fulsome facts. I have, of course, done my best to offset the worst of the damage to…'

'Valerie's desktop?' asked Strasser.

Quist sighed and his shoulders slumped.

'Our reputation?' asked Mankiewicz, the other assistant director in Stakeholder Relations, sitting on Quist's left.

'Yes, our reputation,' said Quist looking admiringly at his previously silent subordinate. 'Spot on, Mankiewicz. Exactly right. Well done. Yes, our reputation.'

Mankiewicz beamed.

'And I can't guarantee that our budget won't be compromised – severely compromised – when we get to June.'

'It's bloody ridiculous,' said Barbara, whipping a large pink nipple out of the infant's mouth and stuffing the attendant breast back into her blouse. 'Most of my life is about poo, in one way or another.'

As if to prove her point, the toddler reached down into the back of his pants and pulled out a handful of brown pebbles the identity of which – owing to their provenance and rich bouquet – could not have been disputed by anyone present. The child looked about, as if in search of a recipient, before reaching the just and inevitable conclusion that Alan deserved recompense for his surrendered necktie. Thankfully, Barbara intercepted the gifting. She pulled a tissue from her sleeve, scooped up the nuts and popped them into her handbag. A second tissue from the same place was applied to the sticky little fingers. The child was then dumped on the vacant maternal thigh and silenced by the swift transfer of a dummy from his sibling's mouth to his own.

'In the short term,' said Quist, 'a consultant will work with us to explore any issues that staff might have.'

'About poo?' asked Barbara,

'About our workplace culture.'

'Then it is about poo,' said Barbara under her breath.

'The senior executive will indicate later today who has been selected for this…' Swishing.

'Mission?' said Mankiewicz, emboldened by earlier success.

'Task?' ventured Strasser.

'Role,' said Quist, with certainty. 'Obviously, that person needs to be someone with an understanding of the important work we do – and of the special stresses that it places on us – while being completely…' He scrutinised the ceiling.

'Committed?' asked Strasser.

'Impartial?' asked Mankiewicz

'Simpatico,' said Quist, looking benignly at each of his lieutenants.

Simpatico with or to whom? Alan thought.

'Simpatico with the twin goals of staff welfare and maintaining the Department's integrity,' Quist answered.

'A departmental stooge,' murmured Morton.

'Someone who can manage the difficult task of balancing both sets of requirements,' said Quist.

'Carol,' whispered Barbara. 'It's a nice big fat consultancy for bloody Carol.'

Carol Cunningham was the previous secretary but one of the department.

If not Carol, Alan thought, then one of the other half dozen recently retired mandarins needing an entrée to the lucrative world of consultancies, enquiries and reviews.

'The acting secretary and I need to know that you are one hundred per cent behind us on…' Swishing.

'This,' said Mankiewicz and Strasser, simultaneously.

'This,' agreed Quist. 'That's why we are here at this time.'

The baby farted wetly, producing a noise that was mostly mallard. Morton and Smith giggled. Barbara popped the baby on the table and carefully pulled back the rear of the nappy to view the contents. Alan's sensitive nose detected something so stinky it prompted a gag response; he covered his mouth and concentrated on not dry retching.

'This not a laughing matter, Barbara,' said Quist.

'It most certainly isn't, Quentin,' Barbara replied.

Morton and Smith adopted straight faces.

'Management needs to know that we are not blabbing to the media,' – Quist glared at Alan – 'not undermining and sabotaging' – he glared at Morton – 'and not trivialising or underestimating the importance of supporting' – he glared at Barbara.

No one attempted a finisher, so Quist continued, 'supporting our hard-working executive when they are under siege.'

Alan's face burned with shame, even though he would as much have talked to the media as worn a Disney necktie.

'Are we together on this?' Quist asked. 'Are we as one?'

All heads nodded and the baby farted a third time. This time the sound was submerged mallard and only the toddler giggled.

'There'll be no formal announcements. Low visibility is the thing. But I can't stress enough that you need to carry your people with you on this and you have to emphasise to them the importance of keeping everything…' Unprecedented vertical swishing with the fingertips upmost.

'Top secret?' said Mankiewicz.

'Under wraps?' said Strasser.

'In house,' said Quist, looking at neither of them. 'And one more thing. Toni has generously released Daphne – who most of you will know is Carol's old executive assistant – to look after me until Peaches returns to us.'

To keep an eye on you, Alan thought. Morton winked at him, clearly on the same wavelength.

'I hope that you will all make Daphne welcome. She will be a real asset to us.'

Daphne was widely known to be a low-intellect, surly stickler for any and every departmental rule and the meanest custodian of a stationery cupboard in living memory. Working with her would be hell. Everyone nonetheless murmured assent to the proposition that she would be 'a real asset'.

'Even without this morning's brouhaha, we have a challenging time ahead, so let's do…'

'Our best,' said Mankiewicz.

'What needs to be done,' said Strasser.

'Both right,' said Quist. 'Now, before we go, I shouldn't need to ask but, hey, guys, are we the best public service in the world?'

'Yes we are,' came the half-hearted response.

'Oh, we can do better than that, can't we?' said Quist. 'I know we can. Are we the best public service in the world?'

'Yes we are,' came back a slightly more resolute reply.

'And again,' said Quist, 'with passion.'

'Yes we are,' came back a fake yet fervent response. Mankiewicz and Strasser high-fived over Quentin Quist's head. Smith looked around for someone to do the same with but found no partner. Morton looked to be about to vomit and Alan, who was probably the only person in the room who genuinely believed that he was part of the world's best bureaucracy, felt vaguely uneasy.

'That's much better,' Quist announced, standing and giving others permission to rise. 'I almost forgot. We'll be collecting money for a floral tribute for Valerie. Let your staff know.'

Another subtle attempt by the acting branch head, thought Alan, to fix in people's minds the idea that 'it' had not been intended for him.

Barbara, to her very great credit, was having none of it. 'Has there been a bereavement in her family?' she asked.

'No, Barbara. As you are doubtless aware, it was Valerie's desk on which the poo was…'

Strasser and Mankiewicz were both mute. The silence was absolute. No one moved. This was, for some reason Alan couldn't later define, a crucial moment. He sensed that to challenge Quentin Quist's take on the reasons for 'it' was to challenge that part of the Executive's larger plan which had been just been shared with them. To question was to place in jeopardy the future of the branch, the division and perhaps even the department itself. This was something mysteriously understood by everyone in the room.

'We will all contribute,' said Barbara.

'All donations to Alan – it's the least he can do – by lunchtime tomorrow.'

Again, Alan felt a mix of guilt and resentment but knew that resistance was futile.

'Then we are done,' said Quist.

Alan and Smith, left behind in the rush for the door, were the last to leave. Alan's lifelong habit of cleaning up after himself was defeated by the unrecognisable tangle of soggy and chewed cloth which – lying on the carpet, abandoned by Barbara's second youngest – had once been his necktie.

'Leave it, my friend,' said Smith, in one of the few immediately intelligible utterances Alan could recall him making. 'Leave it where it is.'

Alan turned out the lights and Smith pulled the door shut behind the two of them.

9

Alan returned to the Executive Assistant's desk outside Quentin Quist's office. A woman in her sixties with a wall eye, three chins and upper arms like a sumo wrestler's thighs, sat behind the desk earlier manned by Morton and Trevithick.

'Good afternoon,' said Alan. 'I'm…'

'I know who you are, Mr Mewling,' Daphne replied, through almost pursed lips. 'You'll find your items back at your workstation. I sent them back with Mr Thick.'

'Thank you,' said Alan.

'Thank you is not the point,' Daphne said.

Quentin Quist came to the door behind her. 'Daphne, is this man annoying you?' he enquired. 'Haven't you done enough, today, Alan, to hamper the cause?'

The EA rotated to the right and shifted her functional eye to the new arrival. 'I have the situation under control, Mr Quist. You can return to your executive duties.'

'Of course,' replied the nominal boss, retreating and closing the door.

The behemoth's gaze turned back to Alan. 'Now, how may I assist you, Mr Mewling?'

A sense of duty which Alan knew to be more often his undoing than not, forced him to mention the unanswered enquiries from the media. 'There were some phone messages,' he said.

'All referred to Communications Branch. I was, frankly, surprised that an officer of your seniority would be ignoring the acting secretary's instructions on the referral of all such enquiries to the appropriate area within the department.'

'I wasn't proposing to…' Alan began.

'And might I suggest, Mr Mewling, that you comply, during business hours, with the traditional rule with regard to your collar? Although you might not have contact with the public, you will find – even in the twilight of your career – the wearing of a tie to be a reassuring and respect-conducive practice.'

'I had one,' said Alan, 'but…'

'No buts, Mr Mewling. As the previous secretary used to say, "Dress the part to play the part."'

To Alan this seemed to be perfectly good advice only for apprentice thespians. He nonetheless made a mental note to think further about it.

'Dress, deportment and demeanour, Mr Mewling: the three essential preconditions of a professional approach to official duties.'

'I usually do wear…'

'Thank you, Mr Mewling.' Daphne returned to her screen.

Alan, defeated, returned to his office. Morton was waiting inside, gazing at the opposite building. Alan's In tray and his briefcase were sitting on the table next to the dead spathyphyllum. A large brown envelope, which doubtless contained the other items returned with Trevithick, sat on top of the tray. In Morton's hand was a necktie.

'That outrageous little prick,' he said. 'I've got a fair idea who's been blabbing to the media.'

Alan said nothing.

'I retrieved your default strangler.'

Alan always kept a spare tie at his desk, 'just in case.'

'It's all right,' said Alan. 'The damage is done and no one of any note will see me at this stage of the day.'

Morton clearly thought this assessment of things to be out of character. 'You'll feel better if you put it on.'

Alan rather doubted in the circumstances that this would be true, but accepted the tie and buttoned his collar.

Morton noticed for the first time the new briefcase Alan had brought in that morning. 'And is this an acquisition like Edward McTiernan's wig,' he asked, pointing at the briefcase on the table, 'indicative of an intention to work through your autumnal years?'

Alan had been given the item decades before but, until he'd left its ancient, much-loved predecessor in the office on Christmas Eve, had no cause to use it. 'I don't know about that,' said Alan. No one knew of his intention to retire within a matter of weeks while on higher duties, so as to have his leave credits cashed out at the optimal rate. He hadn't want to commit, publicly, to the plan until he was quite sure the conditions were right.

'The way this place is going, I wouldn't be hanging around if I were you,' said Morton. 'I'll certainly be departing sooner rather than later. How bloody dare Quist accuse me of being a wrecker.'

Alan nodded sympathetically. 'Was there much to clean up?' he asked, referring to the mess Barbara's older children usually left in the workplace.

'One of the computers is broken but I've taken care of the rest of it.'

'Thank you,' said Alan.

'I never told you,' said Morton, keeping an eye on the doorway, 'but last summer, one weekend, I found a copy of Quentin's executive psych test results on the photocopier.'

Alan created a perfect double Windsor as Morton watched.

'He registered high scores in all three areas.'

Morton smiled broadly and Alan couldn't stop himself from feeling quietly pleased. A high score in each of psychopathy and Machiavellian tendencies was rumoured to be permissible, even desirable, but to rank highly in narcissism as well – thereby achieving a high rating in all three elements of the dark triad – was widely known to be too much of a bad thing. While anyone with any sense was in charge of the department, Quentin Quist would not be permanently elevated to the executive and given his own branch to manage.

'But he still has hopes,' said Alan.

'Clearly,' said Morton. 'He's hanging out for a change in policy, for an exception to be made or for a reshuffle of secretaries.'

None of these seemed likely outcomes to Alan.

'And another thing.'

Alan wasn't sure that he wanted to be privy to any more revelations but he sensed that Morton would not be silenced.

'Someone in Personnel gave me a copy of his birth certificate.'

Morton motioned Alan closer. 'And his given name isn't Quentin.'

Alan got up and pulled the door shut.

'In fact, I can reveal to you that none of his given names is Quentin.'

'Are you sure?' Alan enquired.

Morton nodded but didn't elaborate. He was evidently determined to make Alan ask.

For his part, Alan would like to have been uninterested or disinterested. He'd never placed much importance in the theory that alliterative appellations enhanced aspirants' prospects of promotion to the executive. However, confirmation that Quentin Quist had renamed himself in order to improve his chances was important additional evidence of his intrinsic unworthiness for high office.

Alan sighed and looked fondly at the dead pot plant. 'What…what are his names, then?'

'You're going to love this,' said Morton. 'You're going to really love this.'

'Tell me.'

'His middle name is Atherden.'

'Atherden.'

'Yes.'

'And his first name?'

'Perhaps I should write it down, so that you can view it when you're fully prepared.'

'I believe I'm quite ready.'

'You think you are,' said Morton 'but it will come as a shock, I can assure you.'

Alan now thought that too much was being made of the matter. He speculated nonetheless on names that might stun or discombobulate him. Those of dead dictators, exotic animals and American Indian chiefs would all have surprised, but the names of African rivers, domestic appliances and sirens of the silver screen – designations the like of Limpopo, Kitchen Whizz and Tallulah – were the ones that could have been relied on to shock. The problem was that there so many watercourses, gadgets and actresses of the requisite types: too many.

'I give up,' he said, trying not to appear agitated.

'Come on. Guess,' said Morton.

'Where would I begin?'

'I'll give you a clue – it's something in this office.'

Alan scrutinised the walls, the desktop, the bookshelf, the filing cabinet and, finally, the floor. Nothing sensible came to mind.

'No, I can't think of anything,' he finally remarked.

'Nothing?' asked Morton, enjoying the game more than Alan could ever have thought possible.

'Nothing at all.'

'Think close to home – very close to home.'

Alan looked at Morton. Morton looked at Alan…and suddenly all was clear.

'No,' said Alan, 'Surely not.'

'If you're thinking what I'm thinking…'

'I think I am thinking what you're thinking,' said Alan, getting into the playful spirit of things.

'And you think his name is?'

'Morton,' exclaimed Alan.

'Yes?' said Morton.

'No, that's what I think his name is: Morton, Morton Atherden Quist.'

'Really?' said Morton, as though the possibility had never occurred to him.

'Yes,' said Alan.

'Well, no,' said Morton, 'it's not Morton, definitely not Morton…but you're close.'

'Stephen, then?' Stephen was Morton's pre-eminent given name.

'No, but I can tell you that you're hot, Alan. Very hot.'

Alan looked at the table they were sitting at, at the pen resting in Morton's shirt pocket and down at his own shoes. He thought of starting with the constituent parts of his brogues and then making his way up his trouser leg but he knew the endeavour to be a futile one. Something obvious was eluding him.

'I give in,' he finally remarked.

'Alan,' said Morton.

'Yes,' said Alan.

'No, that's his name.'

'What's his name?'

'Alan.'

'Alan?'

'Yes.'

'Alan Atherden Quist?'

'Precisely.'

'Oh dear.'

Quentin Quist had rejected as inadequate the Christian name which Alan had thought to be eminently consistent with upward mobility and even – until he'd indelibly blotted his copy book – with admission to the inner temple.

'I knew you'd be surprised,' said Morton.

'I think I'm beyond surprises today,' said Alan. In fact, this last revelation had left him deeply dispirited.

'You disappoint me,' said Morton.

Alan smiled wanly, looking at his watch. 'I suppose I should gather whoever's left and let them know about Daphne and the consultant.'

'Too late,' said Morton. 'Trevithick had to leave for a medical appointment. You and I are Committees Section at the moment.'

'Then I'll get everyone together, first thing in the morning. By then we might even know who the consultant is.'

'No surprises for anyone there. My money will be on Carol. Someone saw her and Toni eating together last month and she'd probably like a contract to pay for next winter's trip to Whistler or the new BMW.'

'We'll just have to wait and see,' said Alan.

'I'll be more interested in the true nature of the exercise than in who ends up doing it. Is it really about repairing the culture of this Branch or is there something else – something more devious – happening?'

For as long as Alan had known him, Morton had seen shadows in the shadows and meaning in the most accidental or coincidental of events.

'And another thing,' Morton said, gesturing Alan back within whispering range. 'One of my spies has given me intelligence – very hush hush – that might even explain the turd.'

Anything that could account for the provenance of 'it' – that could bring Alan a step closer knowing whether 'it' was of him – could not be ignored.

'According to my source,' said Morton, 'Quist told the zombies in May that he'd been thinking about all of the work time that was being wasted by staff in the Stakeholders Section. They all naturally thought this was a prelude to redundancies or a review of their work plan, but Quenty had something much more interesting in mind.'

'Go on,' said Alan.

'He wasn't thinking about banning morning and afternoon teas.'

More's the pity, thought Alan.

'…or about getting people to sign off before they go to the coffee shop.'

Still more commendable, thought Alan.

'He wasn't even thinking about a no gossip policy, a ban on footy talk or an end to the excruciating "how was your weekend?" Monday morning rubbish.'

All eminently worthy goals, thought Alan.

'No, he had an altogether more ingenious plan.'

Don't make me guess, thought Alan. I can't do it twice in one day.

'He was proposing a "log off before lavatory" regimen,' said Morton, triumphantly.

'I don't understand,' said Alan, thinking he must have misheard.

'No toilet trips in taxpayers' time.'

'Extraordinary,' said Alan, wondering whether he should be impressed or appalled.

'Either do it at home, before you get here, or sign off when you have to answer nature's call.'

'Truly extraordinary,' said Alan, now more inclined to admiration than dismay.

'He'd read somewhere about the amount of time a human being spends, in the course of a life, in the crapper, deduced that most visits take place in working hours and calculated – god knows how – that in the course of the average career' – Alan thought about his own terribly average career at this point – 'nearly two years of paid time could be spent in the restroom.'

'Truly extraordinary,' Alan repeated, now much more inclined to awe than outrage.

'He had all of the zombies signing off whenever they had to go and he was, according to my source, doing spot checks of the men's room to catch out the cheats – of which there were precisely…'

'None,' said Alan.

'Correct,' said Morton. 'Not a one. But then someone whinged to Personnel. Quist got all of the living dead together and read their horoscopes: having a toilet break at all was a privilege – lucky they didn't have to supply their own paper and hand towels – disgraceful that they had no interest in lifting productivity – pathetic that someone had felt the need to sneak off and complain – gut-wrenching that they would not, after all he'd done for them, come to him, if they really felt that they'd been…' Morton did the little water-swishing gesture that Quist favoured when the right word wouldn't come.

'Hard done by,' suggested Alan, rather pleased with himself.

'Unfairly treated,' said Morton, with a grin.

'So what was the outcome?'

'Don't rush me when I'm having a good time,' said Morton. 'It happens so rarely.'

'Apologies of the…' said Alan, swishing.

'Sincerest sort?' asked Morton.

'Unconditional kind,' said Alan, enjoying himself hugely.

'In short, the union rang the minister's office. The chief of staff spoke to the secretary. The secretary spoke to Toni. Toni spoke to Helen. Helen spoke to Valerie and Valerie stomped on the whole scheme.'

'When did all of this happen?' asked Alan.

'Back in May.'

'Yet none of us heard a thing about it?' said Alan, wondering whether the whole tale was too fantastic to be true.

'All of the zombies were silenced. Code of conduct. Upholding the reputation of the service et cetera, et cetera.'

This last piece of the tale seemed perfectly reasonable to Alan. The idea that anyone would knowingly breach the code of conduct after being warned about loose lips seemed incomprehensible to him.

'But why,' he asked, 'would anyone wait until now to have their revenge?'

'You're right, of course. It's not as though Quist has been without a desk in the intervening months…but, when you think about it, dropping a brown one in the big office over Christmas does make a louder statement.'

Alan tried to dismiss from his mind scenes in which booming flatus made the very walls of the building reverberate. He wasn't entirely convinced by Morton's delayed vengeance thesis. Apart from anything else, which one of the zombies still had spirit enough to turn a Yuletide movement into an act of reprisal?

'I know what you're thinking,' said Morton. 'That none of them would have the intestinal fortitude to defiantly shit where none have shat before…but imagine that you've been to a Christmas knees-up somewhere nearby on the last afternoon of the working year.'

This was something Alan had no difficulty doing.

'You've tied a savage one on – in order to dull the pain of a year in which Quentin Quist has foregone no opportunity to belittle and humiliate you.'

This was also something Alan had no difficulty visualising.

'And imagine that, when you return to the floor, half-pissed, perhaps to collect your keys and your bag, you see Valerie Venables's office – the very office Quentin Quist is to occupy in the weeks ahead – bare of her things, open and empty.'

This was, again, a scene Alan had no problem recreating.

'And you can't stop yourself from thinking that your bowels ought to be in the very same state: open and empty.'

This, too, was much too easy to envision.

'Then a voice spookily like your own, yet not your own, is saying to you – more insistently and persuasively than any voice you've heard before – "Get up on the desk, up on the desk" – and although a different voice – one you know to be the embodiment of all that is decent and civilised and right – is saying "Don't do it, you know it's wrong, so very wrong", you're helpless to resist.'

Morton mounted one of the visitors' chairs. 'You're suddenly on a chair and then – with the grace of a gazelle, the agility of an ibex and the poise of a – I don't know – a vicuña? – yes, a vicuña – you've attained the summit.' He stepped, unsteadily, on to the table.

'The tipsy, staggering fool you were only minutes before is no more and nothing can stop you now. The lone, so-convincing, so-credible voice you originally heard is now a chorus urging you on, "Drop your duds, drop your duds, drop your duds," and before you know it, your trousers and undies are on the deck and the voice of reason is drowned out by a still greater number of joined throats voicing a louder, more compelling yet terrifying refrain than your ears can surely bear. And they're commanding you, "Do the job, do the job, do it now, do it now" and louder, "Do the job, do the job, do it now, do it now" and, god help you, Alan, still louder, "Do the job, do the job, do it now, do it now."'

Morton crouched and Alan clenched his buttocks in grim resistance of the imitative urge.

'And suddenly,' said Morton, 'you can feel it coming, even before you know it can be true. The defecation reflex: it's unstoppable. As unstoppable as the Great War trains. You can sense the impulses from your spinal cord speeding through your parasympathetic nerves. They're racing to your descending colon and your sigmoid colon. Then your longitudinal rectal muscles are shortening. You can feel the pressure building. You can feel the internal sphincter around the anal canal relaxing. And, finally, yes, you sense its external pair relaxing. You open up and – with one final push, one gentle little push – it's delivered.'

Morton now appeared weary yet serene and Alan knew that the worst was over.

'You look down,' said Morton, 'and experience a sense of triumph: a feeling which can't be negated by creative exhaustion, separation anxiety or shitter's guilt.'

Alan unclenched and breathed a deep sigh.

'Maybe the voice of rectitude and responsibility re-emerges at this point and urges you to pick up your turd and walk – to make good your escape with it, before it's too late. But you aren't, in your exultant state, in the least interested. And anyway, the original voice will not be silenced. It says, "Go by all means but leave in the certain knowledge that that which is done cannot be undone. Yea verily, just as the mountains of Moab are immoveable, so is your tribute to he who goes by the name of Quentin but is really…"' Morton made the swishing motion and Alan obliged.

'Alan.'

'Yes, that's right, Alan: Alan.' Morton smiled and stepped from the table on to the chair, and from there to the floor. 'Have I convinced you that delayed vengeance is a real possibility and that there was motive, means and opportunity?'

'I don't know,' said Alan, feeling sorry that Morton had expended so much effort on an explanation which, on balance, was more theatre than logical exposition. 'Six months, as I said earlier, is quite a delay.'

'Not to avenge yourself on Quentin Quist it isn't. I've been waiting more than twenty years…and he's never – unfortunately for the retributive cause – been my direct supervisor.'

'As he is now, briefly, mine.'

'As, indeed, he is.'

Alan had much to think about, quite apart from the earlier matter of 'looking the part to play the part'.

'Keep everything I've told you to yourself,' said Morton.

'Of course,' Alan replied, reminded of some earlier experience.

'Twenty-three working days to go,' said Morton, referring to the remainder of Quist's incumbency. He pushed himself back from the table.

'Nearly one down,' said Alan, brightly.

'Quite so, and I'm not going to endure any more of it. I'm off. I'll see you in the morning.'

'Right,' said Alan. 'I'll see you then.'

Morton left and could be seen standing at his workstation, packing up for the day. Alan reinstated his nameplate, ticket machine and sign, and then positioned his In tray. The only item missing from the large yellow envelope next to his keyboard was his cheese sandwich…and he didn't feel, after everything which had already taken place, up to a confrontation with Daphne about its fate. Instead, he sat in front of his computer, took three deep breaths and depressed the On switch, expecting a repeat of the morning's air conditioning crashes. When the screen brightened without an obvious change in circumstances, he stood underneath the nearest vent in the office and then under one outside, to verify that cool air was still being expelled. When satisfied that all was well, he opened his In box and surveyed the afternoon's messages.

An email from Daphne informed him that the missing cheese sandwich had been binned because of its offensive smell. Affronted, Alan almost responded with a description of the various assaults the day had orchestrated on his own olfactory sensibilities, but he knew better, on second thoughts, than to expect understanding from a woman in Edna Everage spectacles. He reviewed the other new emails.

Ex-colleagues from outside the department continued to enquire about Alan's role in the arrival of 'it' – the most common theme being that every great bureaucratic scheme needed an experienced midwife. The few correspondents acquainted with Quentin Quist and who'd been tipped off to the fact that the landing pad was technically his at the time of the discovery, were delighted by events. The rest of the messages displayed varying degrees of sophistication in the deployment of toilet humour, invariably comparing the work of public servants to the labours of dung beetles, sanny men, gong farmers and subterranean shit-shifters. Alan found none of these communications in the least amusing. All were deleted without any response.

Ignoring stomach rumblings, he sent a meeting request to all Committees Section staff for the next morning so they would all be up to speed with events pursuant to the discovery of 'it' and so they wouldn't, more particularly, be surprised by the presence of Daphne or of the consultant (in the event that her work began immediately).

Hoping for therapeutic diversion in his real In tray, he resumed work exactly where a halt had been called for a luncheon never consumed, reading through a paper prepared by Morton for one of his committees. Alan prided himself on his diligence as a proofreader but Morton's work always received additional attention because of the time bombs in his drafts – text inserted in order to encourage supervisory engagement. For their previous section head, Desmond Napper, a lazy reader, the sleepers had consisted of hard to detect single words, usually sex organ referential colloquialisms. For Robyn Rainbird, a more vigilant scrutineer, Morton included readily detected, nonsensical excerpts from 1950s pop lyrics – sha la las, shang a langs, bebop a lu las and their like. For Alan, after some initial years in which composting and pruning references were inexplicably the norm, Morton ranged widely, presumably to entertain, rather than ensnare.

In the middle of an account of previous policy in the document under scrutiny, Alan found an excerpt from an engine repair manual (all torque and gaskets) and, part way through a paragraph on the budget implications of the relevant proposal, he discovered what may well have been a quotation from an Edwardian tract on the evils of masturbation (including grim predictions of fatal debilitation preceded by blindness). Finally, in a footnote that should have referred him to indigenous dog ownership statistics at the time of the Malayan Emergency he discovered some lyrical text comparing an unspecified task to the work of a potter shaping a topaz vase.

The content and expression were both otherwise satisfactory – Morton knew what he was doing and had been doing it for a long time – so Alan stamped the front page 'Resubmit with emendations to Alan M. Mewling', wrote 'Three sleepers located; especially nice work re topaz vase' immediately below, and then initialled and date-stamped the entire notation. Appropriate entries were made in his workbook and he placed the document with the three he'd approved that morning in a pile to his right. (He'd long since dispensed with an Out tray. What was the point, when no one came – as they had once done, twice a day – to remove the contents?)

There would be further papers requiring approval before the first round of Committee meetings in February but Alan's view was that the efforts made by the early birds had to be rewarded with prompt attention, enabling the leisurely making of corrections and improvements by the authors. He was not by nature a man who put things aside until the time they were due, thereby causing required changes to be made in a climate of panic and mistake-conducive haste.

He displayed the same care and common sense in his strictly impartial patronage of charity chocolate boxes in the open plan. Accordingly – and unable to resist the grumbling of his stomach any longer – he removed the change bag from his old briefcase and counted out enough coins for a chocolate from each of the boxes on display in his own Section's cubicles: one in aid of a vision-impaired ladies' basketball team intending to tour picturesque Lesotho; one to save a marsupial so small that it was effectively indistinguishable from a mouse (and so nutritious that it had not been sighted in decades); one to minister to unloved dogs and cats; one to provide obstetric services for underprivileged African mothers; and one to provide reading materials for illiterate Afghan schoolgirls.

Alan was undecided about the relative merits of these causes. He wasn't sure that a tour of anywhere picturesque would bring much joy to the blind lady basketballers – how would Lesotho be different from any other (unfamiliar) place they might have visited? – and it was probably the unloved cats and dogs which had ensured the extermination of the miniature marsupial. As for the obstetric services, Alan felt sure that it had only been a decade or two since he'd been urged to sausage sizzle, chocolate binge and lamington drive for the starving children of the same dark continent…and weren't obstetric services merely going to bring more hungry kiddies into the world?

Alan was by no means sure that the entire department, in more calorie-conscious times, could consume enough mystery meat, cocoa bean by-products and choc-coated sponge squares to have any impact at all on the steadily increasing number of ravenous African minors…who probably wouldn't think much of the most obvious solution to their problem: the cooking, canning and consumption of pre-loved First World pets unable to function as guide animals for the blind lady athletes.

If he had been free to choose a cause of his own, it would undoubtedly have been the Afghan schoolgirls' reading materials because, surprisingly, he felt he shared something indefinable with the oppressed, joy-deprived young women of that arid, war-addicted land…and because, he reasoned, reading was always going to be a more uplifting experience than goat or camel herding (burqa permitting) and being married off to your great-uncle.

He knew, however, that to sponsor one cause and not the others – or, more accurately, one cause and not all the others – would be to risk interrogation, incensed emails and frosty silences. The only safe path, even if there was hardly anyone around to observe an act of reckless favouritism, was for him to patronise every box in his own fiefdom – making a display of each transaction by laboriously counting out the necessary coins at each stop, shaking each change receptacle in a seeming attempt to settle the contents and then dallying over the act of selection, as though the wares weren't identical.

And having purchased once from a particular supplier, there could be no dispensation from the requirement to repurchase. Dietary necessity was no excuse, even though among the female staff dieting was the principal topic of conversation after hair, gymnasium ordeals and the achievements – from toileting to birthing – of the next generation. Even doctors' orders could not excuse; the reassuring and well-intentioned expressions 'One won't hurt you' and 'They're only small, after all' had presaged many a coronary and bypass.

With money in hand and a feeling of moderate anticipation, Alan stepped out of his door and toured the boxes, returning shortly after with five plain chocolate frogs: one for immediate consumption and the remainder for later dispatch.

In a calmer frame of mind than at any earlier stage of the day, he reviewed the January task list he'd agreed with Robyn Rainbird at their handover two days before Christmas, then – on the wall-mounted whiteboard – allocated tasks to both of his assistant directors.

He now felt himself to be in control for the first time since his arrival that morning. Peering at his In tray, he nonetheless reminded himself of a favourite aphorism – one that he liked to knowingly recall in the presence of *ab initio* administrators: 'For every constant, a thousand surprises'.

There would, though – he regretfully concluded – be no more surprises for his dead spathyphyllum. He reached over and jiggled the stalk from side to side and upwards, hoping it would come free of the soil. Finding, however, that the root system – balled and compact – was reluctant to part from the pot contents, he decided to nurse the whole, minus the pot, across to the bin. It crumbled, despite support, at the midpoint, leaving him holding the stalk and a few rootlet-attached lumps. He looked at the pile on the carpet, more quizzically than in desperation, then placed a sheet of paper – a printed email from Quentin Quist – next to it and swept most of the fragments aboard with his hand. He emptied one load into the bin and was nearly finished a second when Quist walked in.

No knock or greeting foretold his arrival. He stood almost on the paper's edge and looked at the last particles of dirt being encouraged by Alan onto the sheet.

'The vacuum cleaner, Alan. I can't tell you who invented it but I'm almost certain that the cleaners will have access to one.'

'My plant,' said Alan, clutching the table to his left to aid his ascent, 'I picked it up and…'

'Not interested,' said Quist. 'I came to say "Pens down" in the firm belief that crises like today shouldn't make us any less family-friendly.'

'I was hoping to spend another half hour or so,' said Alan.

'Just because you no longer have a family doesn't excuse you from setting an example.'

'For whose benefit?' Alan wondered, thinking about the deserted cubicles outside. His staff had long gone, just like his wife.

It was barely five o'clock but Alan did as he was told. He locked away his classified files, although no one else bothered with this formality, and organised the various items on his desk so that everything was in readiness for the next day. The empty pot he placed in a spare shopping bag which he then tied to the handle of one of his briefcases.

At the doorway, he paused to survey things: each item in its proper place, unclassified files in his tray and his jacket draped neatly over the back of his chair. If the day had not begun in orderly fashion, he could at least claim that it had concluded with a semblance of order.

Walking past Quentin Quist's office to get to the lift, Alan tried to appear invisible.

Quist was sitting at his desk. 'Try not to find another number two in the morning, Alan,' he called, without looking up.

If this plea had issued from the lips of almost anyone else, Alan would have thought it a joke – a dark one, but a joke, nonetheless. From Quentin Quist, though, it could be no jest; public administration and humour were, for Quist, mutually exclusive.

I never found it in the first place, Alan thought to himself, and you know I didn't.

'Most certainly,' he answered. 'Good night.'

<h1 style="text-align:center">10</h1>

In the lift the other travellers stared placidly at the doors and awaited the announcement of their arrival at ground level. Alan watched the floor indicator count down and speculated silently on what it was that Quentin Quist hoped to achieve by late support for a policy – the family-friendly one – he'd previously done his best to ignore. When the lift announced their arrival in the usual offended tone, Alan waited patiently for everyone else to alight. Only a young woman with matching red shoes and handbag, mindful of his courtesy, insisted on him leaving first.

Two steps into the foyer, Alan was halted by the sudden, buffeting force of a high-speed recollection. He gasped for air as his briefcases dropped to the floor and a small piece of Christmas Eve – his departure from the building – came back to him in one huge, walloping download. He staggered under the impact and looked slowly around the high ceiling in the bewildered way of someone suddenly present in both the present and the past.

The two men ahead of him turned their heads, their attention called by the noise of the briefcases hitting the marble tiles. Neither of them stopped. However, the young woman with matching accessories about-faced and processed all the relevant information: Alan's probable age, the look of shock on his face, his pallor, his hands now pressed against his chest and the grounded luggage. She put all of this intelligence together and feared that her plans for the evening – perhaps for a glass of wine, a bowl of pasta and a night in front of the TV – had been stymied by a myocardial infarction.

'Are you OK?' she asked.

'I'm not sure,' Alan replied, breathing heavily.

'Let's get you to a chair,' the young woman replied, gripping his elbow and looking around. 'This man isn't well,' she called to the occupants of the security desk.

The two guards, whose chairs faced the blazing daylight, swivelled to view Alan and his Samaritan. The more senior, a fifty-year-old with an orange tan, a buzz cut and the inverted A-frame figure of a weight lifter, unlatched the access gate and ambled over.

'He seems to be having a heart attack,' said the young woman. 'Can we get him to a chair?'

The guard looked from her to the pass dangling from Alan's neck.

'No, I think I'm…' Alan started to explain.

'Alan, are you having a heart attack?' the guard asked.

'He's probably had it already,' said the young woman.

The guard, who was well used to dealing with public servants, didn't miss a beat. 'Alan, are you having, have you recently had or are you about to have a heart attack or something resembling a heart attack?'

'No, it's just…' said Alan. An explanation failed him.

'Because if you are having a heart attack, you've picked the perfect time,' said the guard.

'A perfect time?' exclaimed the young woman.

'Yes, get his briefcases,' said the guard. He curled a ham-like arm around Alan's back and started walking him in the direction of the security desk. 'It's perfect timing because I've already got an ambulance crew on site.'

'It's very kind of you,' said Alan, 'but I'm sure I won't need to bother them.'

'No, look at yourself,' said the woman. 'You've suffered some sort of… shock.'

Not so much a shock, thought Alan, as a transportation. One minute he'd been gazing at the number display above the closed doors of the descending lift, trying not to read the words tattooed along the bust line of the middle-aged woman standing opposite him – and the next, on the opening of the doors, he was back in Christmas Eve with his peripheral vision shot, his balance compromised and his limbs acting independently of instructions and of each other.

He saw himself, wearing a paper party hat, lurch two steps out of the lift, then suffer a reversal (one step back) before looking to the left. Then he'd careered in the direction of the security exit, his head well in advance of the rest of him.

At the gates, he'd rested one hand on the pylon on each side of the middle chute and had leaned – his body at forty-five degrees to the floor – looking downwards, focusing his mind on what needed to be done next. He'd straightened up, keeping his right hand on a pylon, and patted his chest to locate the security pass needed to open the glass barrier preventing his escape. The pass wasn't, though, where it should have been. He'd therefore closed one eye to better assess the gate. He knew he couldn't slide under it. He knew he couldn't leap over it. So he leaned on the upper edge, with the bevelled glass biting into his diaphragm, and tried, by launching his legs and bottom into the air, to tip head-first to freedom. After three attempts, he almost did it, losing his glasses in the process but then losing the knack as well, at which point he became desperate. He tried a 'stagger up and over' strategy – something reminiscent of a Fosbury Flop – but his legs seemed to be made of lead at the launch moment. His torso was willing but nothing below was inclined to follow. He succeeded only in bruising his chest. Then he heard the lift chime and a familiar voice greeted him with slurred words which might have been 'Don't worry, Alan, I'll get us out of here.' The wide gate at the furthest end – the one used for deliveries sprang open – and they were through. Alan slurred a 'thank you', his glasses were recovered by the Good Samaritan and he was out into the early evening light.

Part of the Christmas Eve mystery was thus solved. Alan now knew how he'd exited the building without a pass; someone vaguely familiar had helped him leave.

In the present, people were anxious to help him too. He was seated behind the security desk. The woman and both security guards were watching him, waiting for further developments: pain down his left arm, some flailing about, perhaps collapse, even death.

'You'll find,' said the older guard, 'that your susceptibility to heart attacks will be greatly reduced by aerobic exercise.'

'It's too late for that,' said the young woman. 'He needs medical help, not lifestyle advice.'

Alan didn't think himself in need of either.

'He's already had the attack,' the young woman continued.

Alan knew he hadn't but the turn which events had taken was making him tense and he was aware of a tightness in his chest that couldn't have been indigestion – not after the consumption of just one charity chocolate.

'Or he's on the cusp of one,' the woman clarified.

This assertion didn't make Alan feel any better.

'It's never too late to implement change,' said the guard. 'Some aerobic work on the bike and the treadmill will be very beneficial. Then he can move on to weights. Within twelve months he could look like…like me.'

He turned side on and posed with his hands behind his head. Alan thought the stance ironically effeminate but still feared that huge muscles would break through the guard's shirt, like sausage meat through an over-filled casing.

'What do you think of that?' asked the guard.

Two young males, alighting from a lift, saw the end of the frieze and smiled knowingly to each other.

'Very impressive,' Alan conceded, 'but I don't think I've had a heart attack.'

'A seizure, then?' asked the woman.

'No,' said Alan.

'A mini-stroke?'

Alan shook his head.

'I've got a friend,' said the guard, 'who will fix you up with a program that gives you strength and display. If you just want a strong core or toned-to-the-max TVAs, you could do Pilates but why not have it all and look like a man should? Look what my friend did for Anselm.'

He gestured towards the younger guard, who seemed to Alan to have a very small head. Anselm turned lazily sideways and posed, then turned the other way to show the alternative view. He wasn't nearly as top heavy as his compatriot but Alan once again feared that flesh would defeat cloth as biceps (and other parts Alan couldn't readily name) swelled grotesquely.

'How far off are the paramedics?' asked the young woman.

'Anselm used to be a ninety-kilo weakling.'

And his head probably didn't look nearly as tiny, Alan thought, sympathetically.

'He has an introductory offer at the moment,' said the senior guard.

Anselm returned to his initial pose.

An elderly woman in bicycling gear and carrying a rucksack passed through the gates, not in the least interested in whatever was happening behind the desk.

'Not Anselm – sit down, Anselm. I'm talking about my friend who runs the gym. For a very competitive price, he can give you a program, three months membership and a free weekly boot camp. Have you ever done boot camp?'

Anselm got down on one knee and did the classic biceps display, mostly for the benefit of the young woman.

'Anselm, give it away, mate, before you make a fool of yourself.'

'Sorry, Boris,' said the chastened pinhead, who got to his feet, located his chair and slumped into it.

'I was asking whether you'd done boot camp,' said Boris.

Alan shook his head.

'Then you've experienced nothing, my friend: the combination of humiliation, contempt, ridicule and name calling – God, I love the name calling. It'll lift your performance by a thousand per cent. With group scorn, maybe half as much again. After six weeks, you'll wonder how you ever did without it.'

'But I already…'

Boris slipped a business card into Alan's top pocket. 'Tell Big George that Boris sent you and you'll get a discount on protein powder at the gym shop, as well as a good price for your program.'

'If this man has another heart attack, I'll be reporting you to the relevant authority,' said the young woman, as the lift doors opened and a paramedic guided a trolley into the open.

On it lay an elderly Indian, wearing the uniform of the department's cleaning contractor and an oxygen mask. A second paramedic hovered at his side, carrying a cylinder.

Boris pressed a button on the desk to open the wide gate through which Alan and his saviour had made good their escape on Christmas Eve.

'I've got another one for you,' said Boris to the paramedics.

'Two for the price of one,' said Anselm.

'Take him now and save yourselves a trip,' added Boris.

The occupant of the trolley, seeing Alan, became especially agitated and repeated a phrase which, from under the mask sounded like 'booraserp' and which, free of it, sounded even more like 'booraserp'. He tried to accompany this phrase with helpful gestures but was prevented by the restraint across his chest. The second paramedic encouraged him to put his mask back on and the patient, having failed to get his point across, complied.

'He's had a heart attack,' said the young woman pointing at Alan.

'I don't really think I have,' said Alan.

'Better let us be the judge of that,' said the lead paramedic.

'I really haven't had one,' said Alan in the knowledge that he could yet be spending the night in the emergency department.

'Then why did you say you had?' asked the young woman.

'I don't think I ever did,' said Alan, patiently. 'More a shock than a heart attack.'

Everyone waited expectantly for detail.

'Someone I hadn't expected to see,' he explained half truthfully.

'Let's look at you, anyway,' said the second paramedic. 'It won't take a minute.'

Alan could see that this was the least onerous of his options.

'Do you think you're all right to walk?'

'Certainly.'

'Then come to the back of the vehicle with us.'

Alan thanked the woman and the security guards for their concern but no one, himself included, was happy with the way things had concluded.

As he walked away, following the stretcher party, Alan heard the young woman complaining to the guards, 'He did say he was having a heart attack, didn't he?' and Boris commencing a sales job on her: 'You'll find that people are a lot less likely to lie to you when you're toned and rippling.'

On the back step of the ambulance, Alan submitted to minor tests and further questioning, after which he was warned about his blood pressure and released. The last thing said to him by any of the occupants of the vehicle was a barely discernible 'booraserp' from the detained patient, accompanied by frantic finger pointing towards the building they'd all left minutes before.

Alan scurried in the direction of the car park, anxious to put behind him the events of the day. He was not, however, to be free.

A toot on the horn of a nearby vehicle sounded as he approached his own. Rasch was parked four spaces away in a plain white sedan. He signalled Alan over and leaned across the seat to open the passenger door. The air conditioner was set to extreme cold and Alan wondered how long it would be before ice needed to be scraped off the inside of the windscreen. Rasch stared across the asphalt expanse at the campus.

Alan's interaction with the paramedics had been screened from view by the vehicles parked against the kerb; there were no enquiries to be answered on that score. He pulled the older of his two briefcases tight against his chest, more to protect himself from the blizzard-like conditions than because his restless right leg threatened to tip one of the bags onto the centre console or into the foot space.

Alan had nothing to say so joined in the gazing fixedly ahead.

'Sometimes,' said Rasch, after as many as five minutes, 'it's not easy for us to give of our best.'

'No,' said Alan.

'You don't agree?'

'No, I mean, yes, it isn't.'

Rasch nodded, still looking ahead. 'I was making progress, you know.'

In Alan's view, each day on which they attended their employment resulted in progress of sorts. How could it not be so when so much effort was expended to that end? He sensed, though, that it wasn't the Security Director's own contribution to the better order of the nation that was being referred to.

'Progress with?'

'The investigation.'

Alan noticed Rasch's lower lip quivering and hoped that he wasn't about to witness another discomforting disintegration.

'No one could claim that you weren't quickly on top of things.'

'Yes,' said Rasch.

'Securing the office and getting your forensics people in.'

'That's right,' said Rasch.

'Scheduling interviews.'

'True enough.'

'And generally seeming to have the situation under control.'

'All correct,' said Rasch, visibly rallying. 'I'd even tracked down an expert in defecatory bio-vandalism – the undisputed world authority on faecal crimes – and I had him poised to construct a profile of the perpetrator.'

'Extraordinary,' said Alan, always impressed by expertise, no matter how arcane and abstruse. 'How did you…?'

'Contacts in the intelligence community,' said Rasch, quietly, 'but my point is that, given some latitude, I could have had the whole thing wrapped up.'

Alan struggled with a vivid and unwanted image.

'With the culprit confronted,' Rasch continued, 'and escorted from the premises, all before the contagion had spread.'

Alan's very real fear of being fingered as the creator of 'it' was tempered by relief at the apparent rejection of the poo profiler's services. A more general sense of apprehension was, however, fuelled by the reference to contagion. Was Rasch suggesting that, once begun, the 'desk as toilet' phenomenon might take off or was he predicting an epidemic of disrespect or freedom of expression, things conceivably implicit in the anonymous shitter's art?

'It's all Burgoyne's fault,' said Rasch.

'How so?' asked Alan, shivering from the cold.

'Show me a health and safety officer who isn't a closet Trotskyite or, at the very least, an ex-union delegate.'

Alan's face must have indicated that he was not making the necessary or expected connections.

Rasch sighed. 'I rang the cleaning services contract manager and left instructions that all of the rubbish collected today was to be dumped on a tarpaulin in the basement. I wanted to recover the turd and its wrapping from wherever Toni had dumped them. I wanted to have them analysed.'

'By your excreta expert?'

'No, the professor's expertise is of an entirely different sort. I found a lab offering DNA analysis.'

'I see.'

'At the beginning of the staff interviews I'd scheduled, I was going to ask everyone to read and return to me a card summarising their rights and responsibilities. I wanted the lab to get their DNA off the cards and compare it to the DNA extracted from the turd.'

'Ingenious,' said Alan.

'Time-consuming and costly, too, but the combination of the professor's profiling and the threat of DNA analysis, carefully leaked to feed the rumour mill, plus the possibility of exposure through a special dob-in line, would almost certainly have prompted an early confession before too much expense was incurred. I'd stake my life on it. Why, if you were the faecant, would you hold out, knowing that the might of modern science – profiling and forensics – was marshalled against you… and knowing that there was a mechanism for anyone who'd seen anything suspicious to anonymously bring it to my attention?'

In fact, thought Alan, you might even surrender yourself to the authorities on grounds no more substantial than a suspicion that you'd scaled Mt Rainbird with a full rectum…giving yourself up even though your DNA had been obtained without consent.

'I had everything organised: the tarpaulin, the interview cards and the lab. And then I got a call from Burgoyne, running the same old hazardous waste argument – as if I was asking the cleaners to smear each other with the faecal matter or roll around in it, naked. He told me that he'd countermanded my orders and had, instead, left instructions that any cleaner sighting the turd, or the paper it was on, had to "down tools" immediately and phone the emergency OH&S number to summon a hazardous materials containment team.' Rasch shook his head.

'What did you say to that?'

'I told him to stay out of matters that didn't concern him – or words to that effect.'

'I see,' said Alan, suspecting that 'words to that effect' were ones which began by referencing the procreative act and urging Burgoyne to repair post-haste to Moscow, before noting his English ethnicity, and intimating that his parents were unmarried at the time of his birth.

'Within minutes, Toni called and I had to mission abort: no turd recovery, no interviews, no dob-in line and no DNA analysis. She was very, very cross.'

'Did she know about Burgoyne's plans?'

'Good question. He'd told her nothing about them. But I was able to put her in the picture.'

Alan winced. Exacting vengeance was, in his book, rarely a good strategy.

'If I wasn't going to get my hands on the prize – wherever it was located – Burgoyne certainly wasn't.'

There was only one thing Alan didn't understand. 'But you still have whatever evidence your people recovered from Quentin's office, other than the item and the blotter, don't you?'

Rasch shook his head. 'The desktop should have been a treasure trove but we got nothing.'

'Nothing,' Alan exclaimed, hoping not to appear too relieved.

'The turd was positioned dead centre on the blotter – you can see that from the photograph – but I still expected some splash marks out towards the perimeter. There were none. None at all.'

'I see,' said Alan, trying not to appear pleased.

'The faecant must have delivered the object from a low altitude, squatting on the desk, possibly with his feet on the blotting paper itself, while facing the door. I say this because we couldn't detect any shoe prints on the visitor's side of the horizontal surface.'

Alan tried to picture himself atop the desk on his haunches. All he'd ever known about the mechanics of excretion he'd learned from Morton's earlier performance but, this knowledge notwithstanding, he seriously doubted that he'd be able to achieve anything in the squat position. It seemed so unnatural.

'The professor informed me that three-quarters of the world goes to the toilet that way – almost crapping on their heels – but that doesn't help us much and, in any case, there's a remote possibility that the deed was done with the offender perched on the chair, possibly with the back against the edge of the desk to minimise instability, and with his hands on the closest edge of the horizontal surface to provide support.'

Alan tried to picture himself in a drunken state, balancing on the chair, with his bottom hovering over the blotter. This seemed to him to be an even more unlikely scenario, especially taking into account the careful maintenance of the countervailing forces needed to retain the positions of chair, desk and posterior, while relaxing enough to facilitate an outcome. He rated his prospects of achieving this in a sober condition as negligible and the same prospects, while drunk, as more remote than one or two in a million. This was most reassuring.

'Of course, if I had the blotter, I could probably tell which of the approaches was taken.'

'There were no fingerprints?' asked Alan.

'The blotter, again, is probably the key but the chair-top is fabric – nothing there.'

'And no note?'

'No note.'

'That's all very disappointing for you,' said Alan, feeling decidedly cheerful.

'I begged Toni to give me the key evidence but she said, "What's to be achieved by that?" I said, "Everything." She didn't agree.'

'Dear, oh dear,' Alan murmured sympathetically. His breath was foggy before him and the windscreen was beginning to ice over.

'I thought of coming back after hours and searching the executive suite but I knew it wouldn't be there. My bet is that Toni will have double-bagged it and dropped it off somewhere on the way home. Either that, or the turd has already been flushed and the blotter shredded. Either way, it's no go for me.'

'Very disappointing,' said Alan, feeling jubilant.

'But I do have a print-out of staff who accessed the building from Christmas Day to New Year's Day.' He handed a sheet of A4 paper across to Alan. 'Is there anyone on this list who strikes you as a potential perp?'

Alan looked down the page and then at the opposite side. No individuals from the Consultation and Stakeholder Liaison Branch were included – something that would, in other circumstances, have rather embarrassed him; someone from his team should have visited the office at least once during the break. Some of the names on the list were known to him but most were not.

'No one stands out,' he remarked. What made someone a likely desk dumper, anyway? What characteristics or attributes were the decisive ones? And why did Rasch think him in any way qualified to identify someone disposed to an act of that sort?

'Is there anyone on this list who might harbour a grudge against Quist or feel resentful about the department?'

Alan forced himself to review the names at the beginning of the list, on the not unreasonable assumption that the act had taken place early in the shutdown, soon after Christmas Eve. None of the individuals he knew seemed likely candidates, even though nearly all of them, quite properly, loathed Quist and should have thought ill of the department for employing and promoting him.

'Look at the rest,' Rasch encouraged.

Alan did as he was told but, again, there was no one who leapt out at him as an obvious desk defiler. 'I'm sorry,' he said, handing the list back.

'I don't suppose, having had a chance to think, today – about everything that's happened – you've got any ideas?'

'Regrettably, no,' said Alan. He would like to have recounted Morton's zombie theory, as it had the potential to divert attention from other suspects, including himself, but he couldn't risk being revealed at any time in the future as the source of information causing Quist to be blamed, indirectly, for the incident.

'No one has anything good to say about your Mr Quist,' said Rasch, eerily on cue, yet again. 'The consensus seems to be that he's a proper tosser and the more people I talk to about him, the longer my list of suspects grows.'

'You're convinced then, that "it" was aimed at him?'

'I'm keeping all options open.' Rasch yawned and reached over to scratch some ice off the windscreen. 'If you hear anything, will you let me know?'

'Of course,' said Alan.

'Then I'll be getting on.'

Alan got out of the car and only remembered, in the familiar surrounds of his own vehicle, that he'd failed to enquire about Rasch's Christmas.

At home, he ate a salad mostly comprised of vegetables from his own garden before settling into his favourite chair in front of the evaporative cooler with Goodman's *Le Matin, Le Midi and Le Soir* on the radiogram.

At five to ten he rose and consulted the Shorter Oxford. Instead of 'shit' being identical in the present and past tenses, and as a past participle, the relevant forms of 'shit' were, to his surprise, 'shitted', 'shit' and 'shat'. He was not pleased.

On retiring to bed and recalling the events of the previous twenty-four hours, he reminded himself that he hadn't had substantial cause to visit the lavatory in the second half of the day for many years and that – despite the possible ingestion on Christmas Eve of a handful of chips, a cocktail frankfurt and a sausage roll or two – he was unlikely to have consumed enough roughage to warrant an early evening 'visit' on Valerie Venables's desk top.

He was encouraged too by the recollection that, on Christmas morning – after waking fully clothed on the lounge room floor and vomiting in the kitchen sink – there were no signs on his person or his underwear of hasty defecation in the absence of abstergents.

Slightly (but not conclusively) reassured, he nodded off.

11

He slept fitfully. There were dreams in which – with a stunning musculature, tanned and oiled, draped in a tiny (yet more than adequate) loin covering – he engaged in an endless necktie tug of war with teams of straining, spiteful toddlers. The opposition was incongruously supported by a jeering crowd comprised of everyone he seemed ever to have known: people from school and work, a girl he'd fancied at ballroom dancing lessons, his ex-wife and even a wizened individual who'd prevailed on him, at a small Italian railway station in the 1970s, to fund a grandchild's emergency surgery. Alan had no one barracking for him in 'the tug' but knew, instinctively, that his Aunty Vi had packed him a thermos, and a cheese and beetroot sandwich. The entrepreneurial friend of the security guard – the one who ran the gymnasium – had despaired of him earlier in the contest.

'Your problem is that you don't want it enough. You don't hunger for it,' Big George had said as he was leaving. 'It' was presumably triumph or distinction or, possibly, the excitement of a life in which risk was not avoided at all cost, but welcomed as a difficult yet stimulating friend.

Alan wondered who was in charge of his clothes and how he'd get home in a semi-naked, oleaginous state if he was still friendless when the struggle was over. And over – in a version of the scenario that lasted long enough to reveal the inevitable outcome – it finally was. Alan was hauled ignominiously onto his face and dragged for a metre before he had the good sense to relinquish the tie (which, once in the possession of the victors, was cut into enough portions for each toddler to have a piece).

Filth of an indeterminate yet vaguely porcine sort – it was the stench that was telling – was pelted at him from all sides. He was then escorted from the sandpit and the departmental building in which it was incongruously located, by Rasch and his two elderly henchmen.

He was exhausted by the struggle, unable even to walk, and the two coursing enthusiasts had to drag him by the oily biceps through the booing, jubilant mob. Rasch carried a duffel bag into which the personal items from Alan's office had been dumped: his redundant single-hole punch and his dictionary, his ticket machine and his nameplate, his Roget's and his Fowler's, short course certificates of achievement, a resplendent spathyphyllum, his cardigan and his diary – all jumbled in together, as though swept off the desktop in a single powerful motion.

When Alan arrived at the office at seven a.m. it was with an illogical sense of relief that he observed the presence, in good condition, of all of the same items, spathyphyllum excepted.

The temperature was already tropical. No one else was yet in attendance. Humming to himself, he arranged his jacket on the hanger behind the door and positioned the sansevieria trifisciata he'd brought in from home at the centre of the visitor's table. At the entrance to his office the only remaining inflatable reindeer had slumped, overnight, onto its knees so that it seemed to be offering its upright rear to anyone who could be bothered.

After Alan returned with hot water for his tea, he tried kneading air from the antlers and the head down in to the front legs. Then, when that effort failed, he endeavoured, from the other end, to plump the front by squeezing air from the hindquarters forward.

Quentin Quist, pulling a full file trolley, appeared in the corridor en route to his executive office just as Alan felt he was getting somewhere and the reindeer regained its front legs.

'In the privacy of your own office, if you don't mind, Alan,' Quist said without the smallest hint of humour.

The interruption caused Alan to release his hold on the deflated buttocks. The antlers wilted and the head slumped downwards. He pulled the creature inside his office and stuffed it in the corner, between the filing cabinet and the wall, so that, after a good deal of artful prodding and poking, only its top half could be seen.

The air conditioning rustled the crêpe paper and tinsel streamers rimming the ceiling. That the draught was, on a day with scorching promise, as warm as breaking wind caused Alan, seated at his computer, to feel less apprehension about causing the flow to cease. Nonetheless, when his finger depressed the 'on' switch, he maintained the pressure, for he was reluctant to see the procedure through – loath to know whether the previous day's intermittent connection between computer and air movement was still in place. After ten purposefully counted seconds – in which he worried that the compressing of the spring might impair its later elasticity – he withdrew his finger and listened intently for a change above his head. When, despite the brightening screen, he could detect no cessation, he entered his password and turned in his chair to observe the quivering decorations over the window. They ceased dancing as he watched, and he heard a shout of exasperation from Quentin Quist's office.

The computer whirred and hummed behind him but he remained with his back to the machine, inspecting the walls for something untoward in the way of a miniature surveillance device, even though he knew – because the same failure had taken place when he'd logged on at Peaches' desk the day before – that the connection was not specific to a particular location or keyboard.

His scanning of the windows of the building opposite was no less irrational, yet he looked intently along the rows for a high-powered telescope or someone with binoculars. What he'd have done if he'd detected a watcher, he had no idea…and, in the event, no action proved necessary.

He turned and opened his mail In box. There were more jocular messages from old colleagues, seemingly prompted by the previous evening's news bulletins. Alan ignored them all in favour of a series of fund-raising notifications: one advertising an egg and bacon cook-off for coronary research, a second for a fun run against domestic violence and a third for a pavlova drive 'for diabetes' (presumably to support more research funding, rather than to increase the incidence). Alan could see immediate merit in the run – flight seemed the only sensible response to violence of any sort – but doubted the likelihood and appropriateness of fun (which could only be, in any event, of an inappropriately masochistic nature). As far as the suitability of the pavlova and bacon events was concerned, he couldn't, he reasoned, have been alone in his misgivings, as both seemed to be encouraging the very conditions they were designed to mitigate.

There was also a message from Quentin Quist, sent at 11.02 p.m., forwarding a daytime request from the minister's office to nominate media opportunities in the four weeks ahead and asking that the staff of the acting minister not be copied into any resulting correspondence. Another message, sent at 3.08 a.m., urged all Consultation and Stakeholder Liaison Branch staff to have money for Valerie's floral tribute to Alan by lunchtime. A further message, sent at 5.41 a.m., reminded staff about the need for record-keeping vigilance over the summer.

Alan sensed in these missives an increasingly desperate excuse for communication; he'd long suspected Quist of having devised a secret way of programming the delayed despatch of emails so as to create the impression of ceaseless diligence.

There was a message, too, from an unknown address headed 'Bruce Dermott Trevithick Jnr – Medical Illness'. Was there any sort of illness that was not medical? Even psychoses were medical, weren't they? Alan took the very grimmest view of tautology.

The message read simply, 'Alan, please see the attached certificate.' The attachment was in a familiar form and read, 'Bruce Trevithick is suffering from a medical condition and is unfit for work on 4 January.' It was dated the same day and signed Bettina Stern, Consultant Water and Waste Movement Operative.

Since when, thought Alan, had plumbers issued medical certificates? Had the world gone completely mad?

The second-last unread message on the list, from Edwina Troy, regretted to inform Alan that she would not be at work 'owing to illness of a family member viz. Pussils the cat'.

Alan made a mental note to contact Personnel to see whether, since he'd last enquired, pets had become family members for the purpose of carer's leave and whether plumbers' certificates were acceptable proof of medical incapacity.

The final unread communication was from Barbara. 'Sorry I won't be in, again. In confidence: terrible morning sickness. Will be in touch again when can attend. Edwina knows where everything is up to.'

Incoming mail dispensed with, Alan loosened his tie, ran his essential information through the superannuation calculator and then, no less or more satisfied with the outcome than he'd been on any previous occasion, composed an email to the most genial of the junior executives who were likely to have attended Brian Gulliver's Christmas Eve drinks. He wished the recipient a happy 2014 and opined that the most recent celebratory gathering had surely been their jolliest yet. (He thereby hoped for information on his state in the final unrecalled stages of the event – perhaps even reassuring intelligence to the effect that he'd not been drunk enough to consider toileting on a desk top.)

After sending the message on its way, he was inclined to enter the media portal and review reportage of the previous day's event. He knew, however, that he could no longer postpone with good cause a more pressing task – one which had required his attention from the moment Hector Rasch had revealed to him that 'it' had been extruded from a low altitude.

He pulled the blinds facing the corridor closed and shut the venetians against the external window. He then turned off the light, pushed his chair against the desk – with the back against the edge – and slid the keyboard to the side. With everything in place, he took a deep breath and attempted to mount the chair, much as he might have done on Christmas Eve, either on his way to the desk top or so that his bottom could levitate over it.

He tried the one-foot-on-seat method first, but found that he lacked sufficient push in his other leg to achieve the necessary lift off. Swapping legs didn't help, so he tried kneeling on the seat while gripping the back and gently rising. The first stage of this strategy – the kneeling bit – was difficult but doable. The second, requiring each of his legs to be drawn up underneath him, as a prelude to standing, proved impossible without the support of chair arms.

He next tried holding on to the sides of the padded seat – with the chair in the same position, back first against the desk – but the arrival of his second knee forced him to release his grip, causing his centre of gravity to shift and everything to crash backwards.

Dusting himself off, he tried kneeling on the seat while leaning on desk, then pulling his legs up, an approach which saw the chair career backwards (with Alan's hands still in situ) and caused him to briefly become a sagging bridge between the two objects before, again, crashing to the floor.

It was somewhat easier, he found, to get directly on to the desk, posterior first, making no use of the chair, to rotate and to then raise himself up from the all-fours position.

Once standing, he released his belt buckle, lowered his trousers and attempted to squat…but the conclusion he reached about the final part of this routine – the hover – was that it wouldn't be easy to expedite while drunk. As for the middle part – the ascent – it would have been nigh on impossible to achieve while balance-impaired in an office where the desk was well clear of the walls…although it might, he supposed, have been conceivable that the computer screen would provide some support for the rising.

On his haunches, he wondered about the biblical expression for defecation – 'covering one's feet' – because it seemed to him that the inevitable end result of evacuation while squatting could only be filth on his ankles and on his dangling shirt tail. For excretion to cover the feet properly, major modifications would need to be made to the human body – most notably the switching of the waste management and reproductive parts.

Focusing again on the purpose of his experiment, there seemed to Alan to be so many impediments to successful defecation while squatting that the popularity of the position in other parts of the world – vouched for by Rasch's professor – rather mystified him.

These ruminations were halted by a knocking at the door. Alan's rectum tightened to avoid the untidiest stage of the fear response. There followed a second more urgent series of knocks and furious rattlings of the doorknob. Alan clenched with greater determination; he genuinely feared that the lock would not hold or, worse still, that he'd hear a key inserted into the barrel and that he'd be discovered with his trousers down on the top of a desk not unlike the one on which the original act of abscission had taken place. This, he knew, would not be an easy thing to explain away.

He counted out ten seconds and then, with his trousers like shackles around his ankles, rose and penguin-stepped to the right side of the computer, where he took a deep breath, leaned close to the blinds and formed a small opening with his thumb and forefinger.

A surprised eye – even closer to the window than his own – peered at him from the other side. He gasped, withdrew and waited for the resumption of knocking and knob jiggling accompanied by demands for ingress. In the event, though, only the low hum of his computer accompanied the racing of his heart.

After what might well have been a minute, he waddled to the left-hand end of the desk and stealthily lowered himself in stages to the floor, where he pulled up his trousers and tucked in his shirt.

Any satisfaction he might have derived from the conclusion that he was incapable of mounting Valerie Venables's desk for any purpose while drunk, had been temporarily diminished by the disturbing sight of Quentin Quist's ghastly orb.

He opened the blinds at the exterior window and then tiptoed to the door, where he placed his ear to the surface. When the silence was sufficiently conclusive, he held his breath and carefully released the lock. No one barged in.

Then, assuming the appearance and demeanour of a man who'd done nothing wrong (or, at least, the look of one who thought it reasonable to simulate an act of cacation atop a desk that was only temporarily his), he opened the door and stepped outside.

Quentin Quist was nowhere to be seen.

Alan repositioned himself at the keyboard. A new message from Quist, sent within the previous minute and addressed to all directors, read, 'Your eyes only – crisis worsening – gone to Acting Secretary's office – will update on my return.'

By being aloft and inaccessible, Alan had probably avoided being apprised of Quist's feelings about this most recent summons.

In the media portal, the events of the day before had encouraged an alliterative apogee of the subediting art with headlines the like of 'Christmas Crap Crisis', 'Furtive Faeces Furore' and 'PS Poo Pandemonium'.

The most informed of the related accounts predicted the return of the secretary from recreation leave and referred to the Consultation and Stakeholder Liaison Branch as 'an arm of the Department long known to insiders as a plodding backwater, the sleepiest of hollows and a workplace untouched by time'. It described the consultative bodies as 'redundant assemblages of academic, bureaucratic and parliamentary has-beens' and described the committees' work as 'the very flimsiest excuse for timeservers, place men and assorted ministerial mates to consort for the purpose of wining and dining at taxpayers' expense'.

The associated editorial described the same committees as 'the last bastion of jobbery, self-congratulation and meetings-for-meetings-sake' and then as 'institutionalised boondoggling of the very worst sort'. It advanced the existence of the committees as reason enough for a thorough review of the branch's functions – functions which it noted, grumpily, had been mysteriously immune from the cost-cutting to which other areas of government had been subjected for decades.

The disdainful references to Alan's workplace as one 'untouched by time' were echoed in an adjacent cartoon. It featured a Dickensian counting house scene in which rows of stooped, prune-faced elders wearing winged collars and bookkeeping visors worked at high desks by candlelight with quill pens. At the front of the room in which they laboured was a raised platform on which a larger desk supported a cocoon-shaped turd the size of small motor car. An array of squiggly lines radiated from this object to denote an unpleasant smell. A wizened ancient at the closest desk to the over-sized bolus remarked balefully to the others, 'Something malodorous in the wind, gentlemen.' On the turd itself was written the word 'CHANGE'.

Alan imagined that members of his principal committees would not take at all kindly to being labelled as 'academic, bureaucratic and parliamentary has-beens' and might even be angered at the description of their deliberations as 'meetings-for-meetings-sake'. Yet it was the description of his own organisational unit as 'a plodding backwater' that most troubled him. It troubled him because the unpaid work he'd done at nights and weekends over many years, the pressure he'd so often been under in responding to urgent requests of various sorts, and the intellectual acuity that had been required of him – not the least in orchestrating committee outcomes of some utility – all spoke of a different reality: one in which the Consultation and Stakeholder Liaison Branch was a demanding, dynamic and vital place to work.

Alan had never expected public approbation; not even in the days before error had blighted his future. But by the same token he'd never understood, having worked so hard for so many years, why the society whose interests he served was so quick to judge him or, more truthfully, to take such a set against him. Even if, for the sake of argument, his efforts made no useful contribution to the maintenance of democracy, social stability and societal advancement, it could not be said that they did significant harm. And didn't he and his like play their part in the national economy: paying taxes, consuming goods and doing their bit to avert zero population growth?

Yet, if Alan had been frank with himself, he'd have conceded that the rank ingratitude of the populace was the very thing that invested public service with nobility and with the feeling that it was less about the wage contract than about self-sacrifice and altruism. What he did intuit, though, was that no amount of railing against public contempt would change the essential dynamic or deal with the problem at hand. And it was the matter of public criticism of the committees which his resurgent professionalism now returned him to.

The charges levelled were ones with which Alan was well familiar.

They were not infrequently made in letters to the minister or in the press by individuals who had been overlooked for appointment or had, after a turn at the trough, not been reappointed. However, the committees had never before been the subject of an editorial or a cartoon. This was an attack on a new scale: one requiring rebuttals of unprecedented ingenuity and unassailable rigour.

Alan walked out into the open plan, to the cubicle which was normally his own, and unlocked the drawers underneath the desk. From the bottom drawer he removed a manila folder marked 'Criticism of Committees – Responses To'.

Back in his temporary office, he printed the offending newspaper articles, editorial and cartoon for the inevitable file. If his future – his post-retirement future – was to bear any resemblance to the one he'd planned, the days ahead would not be easy ones. In many ways, though, he was, he reassured himself, at the top of his game – his intellect sharpened by innumerable years of analytical effort, his strategic skills refined by decades of struggle and his attention as capable as ever of the narrowest focus. Indeed, if there was a man still able to snatch respect and redemption from the jaws of public ridicule it was surely one not unlike Alan A.C. Mewling.

And yet, when he picked the cartoon up from the printer and noticed that the face of the speaking clerk in the front row rather resembled the one he saw each morning in his shaving mirror, he struggled to maintain his resolve. His heart quailed even though he knew that the similarity between the cartoon character and himself could only have been a coincidence.

He opened the retrieved folder on the desk, brought the ministerial briefing template up on his screen and, in the certain knowledge that busyness was, for him, the only proven antidote to self-doubt, typed the heading 'Urgent Briefing For Acting Minister – Criticism of Expert Committees'.

12

The briefing note (which made no direct reference at any point to excreta of any sort) took Alan longer than anticipated. This was not because he needed to invest the key points with a freshness and vitality demonstrative of renewed effort, but because he took the additional, risky step of including statistical information on outputs – numbers which, on every previous defensive outing, he'd claimed were too difficult to collate and too easy to disaggregate. It took him an almost unprecedented three cups of tea to complete the task and, once it was done (and the document had been despatched to Quentin Quist's In box, in anticipation of a formal request), Alan scurried down the hallway.

Only one cubicle was free. The atmosphere was heavy, as it always was, with the frustration of repressed emotions and fettered initiative, and the bitterness of gradually eroded ambition. Yet the silence cloaked, on this occasion, an anxiety well beyond that which was normal and certainly beyond that reasonably associated with the possibility of disappointed excretory expectations. Alan almost walked away but, in the knowledge that delay might cause a disruption to his daily routine, seated himself. He cleared his mind, leant forward and waited for the usual prompt expulsion. This time, however, there was not to be the smallest hint of an internal response.

This was most unusual, for, notwithstanding the unpredictable demands of the working day – the emergency meetings, crisis confabs and urgent requests for briefings and input – and notwithstanding the interruptive potential they held for toileting regimens, Alan had never been constipated. In the periods when long days and nights at the keyboard had made others sallow and bloated, and had retarded their normal functions, Alan had never been stopped. In fact, he had secretly prided himself on his regularity; he saw it as, perhaps, the most significant private sign of his suitability for office and as the most fundamental proof – no pun intended – of his oneness with his work.

Remembering in a vague, half-recalled way that performance anxiety was its own outcome, he tried thinking of nothing in particular and found that, instead of achieving a state of ataraxia, his head filled with images of colleagues hoisting up their skirts and whipping down their trousers to contribute to a steadily increasing pile of *merde* on Valerie Venables's desk top. He rubbed his eyes and squeezed them tightly shut, imagining big, slow mudslides in a more substantial variant of the waterfall antidote for bashful bladder.

Nothing resulted. He resigned himself to a gentle push. Still nothing resulted. He pushed more insistently. Again, nothing resulted. He took in a deep breath and pushed for as hard and as long as he could, until he thought it very likely that his head would explode. The only result was a short, gaseous splutter, a preliminary to…nothing at all. Conceding defeat at last, he reached for the paper.

It was as he folded the desired sheets into an impenetrable quire – modern departmental toilet tissue was always of the flimsiest quality – that he realised something new and significant about the circumstances in which he and Peaches had found 'it' the day before, viz. that there had been no lavatory paper (either used or still fit for purpose) in sight. Valerie's office, he realised, had been in every conceivable sense 'paperless'.

Bearing this in mind, he again cast his mind back to the state of his person on Christmas morning and looked for any indication, no matter how minor, that his always rigorous standards of personal hygiene had been allowed to slip in the period since he'd previously showered. Relieved, he could recall no stains or marks on his underclothing indicative of a want of abstergential effort.

So it was that there were, he mused, numerous pieces of circumstantial evidence that pointed to his innocence of the aboral outrage in Valerie's office.

There was the fact that it had long been his custom to attend the lavatory in the mornings and the fact that he'd been compelled to 'make a visit' on Christmas morning (making an 'in-between' voiding unlikely). There was also the fact that he'd not needed to go in the afternoon for decades. Add to that his demonstrated inability to squat with ease on either a desk or a chair while sober, let alone drunk, and the undeniable truth that, on Christmas Day, when he'd removed the clothes he'd slept in, there were no signs that he'd engaged in a spontaneous or opportunistic act of evacuation (without a thorough 'tidy').

Yet he knew that he would be incapable of rest until he'd learned something more about events between the last sober moment he could recall on Christmas Eve – travelling in the lift up to the executive suite with his angels on horseback – and the point at which his recovered memory of attempts to leave the building began.

He shut his eyes and attempted to recreate the instant when, perhaps half an hour after catching the ascending lift, he had probably opened the oven door and breathed in the gorgeous, rich aroma of plump, baked prunes and sizzling bacon. He hoped that, by immersing himself in that sensuous moment, he could trigger the return of fragments of memory able to act as a foundation for more substantial recollections – recollections which would bring back all of the lost hours and enable him to say with certainty, 'It was not of me.'

At this point he sniffed the (washroom) air as part of the process of remembrance and his mind worked hard to ignore the olfactory contrast between his actual and revisited circumstances. But when a quacking duck (or something very much resembling one) called from the cubicle to his right and a response sounded in the cubicle to his left, he reluctantly knew himself to be no longer in the kitchenette and no longer in that under-appreciated time before his life had been assailed by uncertainty.

When a louder call came from the right and a commensurate reply came from the left his senses placed him in yet another reality – one characterised by reed beds, an insect chorus and life on the wing.

And then a different kind of report – was it the explosion of a hunter's rifle or the outer washroom door thrown open with excessive force? –

dismissed for good any residual feeling of comfort…and Alan was back in an undesirably white-tiled present.

He rose in a hypnopompic state – much as one would from a deep summer afternoon sleep – arranged his clothing and opened the door.

Quentin Quist was bent over the basin. Alan couldn't explain how, with just a view of the man's posterior, he could recognise him with such certainty…but he was absolutely confident of the identification and, in consequence, strongly inclined to retreat. Quist straightened, yanked savagely on the paper towel dispenser and, on sighting Alan, sighed, before proceeding to dry his forehead and the back of his neck. Alan's legs had already carried him towards the basin and he reached, in resigned way, into his pocket for the miniature cake of soap he always kept there.

Quist's eyes were puffy and his face – or the portion of it that wasn't concealed by the plaster square covering his nose – was red. Alan struggled to find words which expressed a modicum of sympathy for the ever deepening mire in which circumstances had placed the acting branch head.

'These things are never easy, are they?' said Alan, in a kindly way.

'What things would they be?' Quist responded.

'Catastrophes,' said Alan, quietly.

'I didn't realise you had so much experience of them,' said Quist in unexpectedly conciliatory tone. 'You should have told me earlier.'

'I didn't mean to…' said Alan, with the dry soap in his hand.

'If I'd known, I would have handed the reins over to you straight away.'

'No, I wasn't criticising, I was…'

'No, no, you're right,' said Quist, even more reasonably. 'Despite my intelligence, drive and proven problem-solving skills, I'm poorly equipped to handle disasters of this…'

'Magnitude?' suggested Alan.

'Type,' countered Quist. 'And you know, Al, thinking back, I should have deferred at the very earliest hint of crisis to your superior intellect, experience and diligence.'

Alan was fearful of the direction things were taking. He'd seen Quist play the 'too reasonable' part before and he knew it could precede a rage of terrifying ferocity and duration. 'I apologise, if I…um…I certainly didn't mean to…'

'No! You never do, do you?' shouted Quist, suddenly trembling with anger. 'You never do.'

Alan could hear frightened silence from the cubicles. 'No,' he said, looking at the floor and thinking it best to be amenable.

'No?' exclaimed Quist, empurpling with each second. 'No? Did you just say no?'

Alan noticed a vein fiercely pulsing at Quist's temple. 'Yes, but I meant yes,' he replied.

'Oh, you don't know what you meant, do you? You've got no idea. You've got no idea at all.'

'No,' said Alan, very quietly, in case he'd once again got things wrong.

'God help us,' said Quist. 'God help us.'

Alan transferred the soap, still in its packet, from his right hand to his left. Sweat trickled down his brow.

'Just send me a draft minister's brief,' said Quist, turning towards the door. 'See if you can get that much right.'

'I've already…'

'Don't argue with me,' said Quist, turning back. 'Just do it, you fool. Just this once, try to be of some…'

'Assistance?' asked Alan.

'Help,' said Quist, heading towards the door. 'Just try to be of help.'

It occurred to Alan that neither of them had at any point mentioned the incident at the window. He completed his ablutions with a heavy heart, reminding himself that there were but a few weeks until he turned fifty-five and until the date – two days before his birthday – on which his superannuation entitlements were at their peak, making it foolhardy for him to postpone retirement. He reminded himself, too, that the early relinquishment of higher duties would cause him no great harm. He could step aside for one Quist's cronies – Strasser or Mankiewicz, assuming that

Morton, as usual, refused the opportunity – and see out the last few weeks of his career in a subordinate role. He might even take some certificated leave if his doctor was amenable; he'd hadn't a day off because of illness in many years and his sick leave credit was huge.

While he hadn't envisaged that his final days in harness would be spent in his normal job, if the alternative was a ceaseless stream of humiliations and demeaning encounters, then some distance on the organisation chart between himself and Quist was probably for the best.

Back in his office, Alan loosened his tie even further – the temperature seemed to have risen significantly in the previous half hour – and took solace in some well-practised revisions to his 'notice of intended retirement' letter.

Morton knocked and entered as Alan pressed 'Save'. He was wearing a red striped shirt without a tie. There were moisture circles at his underarms and his face was shiny with sweat.

Alan had never subscribed to 'casual Friday' but tried not to let his disapproval vis-à-vis the coloured shirt show.

'How are your genitals?' enquired the newcomer without any preliminaries.

Alan was horrified. Questions about his excreta one day and his reproductive organs the next! What was the world coming to?

'I beg your pardon?' he asked.

'Your crotch.'

'Yes, I think I recall where my genitals are located.'

'Well, how are they?'

'You're enquiring because…?'

'Mine are in a shocking state.'

'I'm sorry to hear that.'

'I've got the nastiest rash.'

Alan considered this admission, wondering why it was that Morton felt it necessary to reveal to him, in the accusatory tones of an aggrieved sexual partner, the condition of his privates.

'And it's suppurating up my crack.'

'I see,' said Alan, breaking eye contact; he was not used to such frankness, even from Morton.

'I've been driven to distraction.'

'I'm sorry to hear that too.'

'And I've barely slept.'

'Most unfortunate.' Alan still had no idea where Morton was headed.

'I'm left with no option but to lodge a form.'

Alan considered his options. 'For?' he enquired.

'To notify an employment-related infirmity.'

Alan felt, at this point, that the two of them had, at last, made some progress. 'Right,' he said. 'And that's the appropriate way to proceed because?'

'Because my naughty bits and adjacent parts are red raw,' Morton spat.

'Yes, I think we'd pretty much established that,' Alan said. 'I'm trying to determine something about causality. Your nether regions, they're in an undesirable state because?'

'Of fungus…or, more probably, fungi.'

Alan tried again. 'Which is (or are) work-related insofar as?'

Morton shook his head in disbelief. 'Insofar as no one in this organisation seems able to ensure the sustained operation of a simple air conditioning system and thereby prevent the building from turning into a fucking steam bath.'

'Now, now. There's no need for that sort of language. You've made your feelings abundantly clear.'

Indeed, everything was, finally, clear…and Alan felt guilty about having his computer on. He thought about turning it off, before concluding that he couldn't deal with the attention that would result if Morton twigged to the bizarre relationship between his (Alan's) computing and the building's cooling system.

'Apologies,' said Morton, 'but the scratching, it's driving me mad.'

'For what it's worth, you have my sympathy,' Alan said, 'but, that notwithstanding, you'll need someone with medical qualifications to attest to your condition.'

'You needn't worry,' said Morton, seeming almost cheerful now that his manager had given in-principle recognition of his impairment, 'I'll get a doctor's certificate. I wouldn't be asking you to scrutinise my precious.' His eyes chanced on the reindeer – the horns and head of which had mysteriously deflated to the benefit of the hindquarters. 'And while on the subject of extremities,' he added, 'it seems that those appendages could do with some stiffening.'

'I suppose you've seen the media,' said Alan, changing the subject before Morton mentioned Viagra or 'a sharp old rub'. 'I've sent Quentin a brief for the minister.'

'Criticism of committees?'

'Criticism of committees, with some of the material we've previously kept in reserve.'

'I'm not sure even that will do the trick this time.'

Alan recalled Morton's abolition predictions of the previous day and shuddered. 'I've added statistics.'

'Ah, new and improved ministerial briefing, now with added stats: more persuasive than ever.'

'Desperate times.'

'Of course.'

They both thought about the struggle ahead.

Morton's hand strayed towards his crotch.

'Was there anything else you wanted to report?' asked Alan, hoping to avert the removal of another layer of skin, deep within the furthest reaches of Morton's underpants.'

'Not really,' said Morton, looking distractedly at the errant hand, 'but I was thinking in the shower this morning about everything that's happened and it occurred to me that someone wasted a great opportunity by not crapping on the keyboard.'

Alan winced. 'Things are quite bad enough, as they are, don't you think?'

'We do live in interesting times.'

'Quite. Quentin has already been called to a meeting this morning with the acting secretary.'

'I drank a bottle of the Cristal last night,' said Morton, 'and I didn't share.'

Alan wiped perspiration from his forehead.

'And I see Quenty's up to his tired old tricks,' Morton continued, 'with the early-morning emails and the file trolley. Those things aren't going to get him off Rasch's suspect list.'

'I didn't know there was one,' said Alan.

Morton smiled. 'I don't expect you to tell,' he said, 'but my sources indicate that Rasch is more intent than ever on solving the crime. Operation Brown Christmas is to be his career highlight: the coup to boost his profile and propel him into senior management. When you next lunch, he'll almost certainly reveal to you that he's found himself a shitologist – an expert – to track down the faecant, and is setting up a stoolies line' – Alan winced – 'so that anyone with inside info' – he winced again – 'can inform.'

Alan was rather satisfied that he was, this once, more up-to-date with Rasch's goings on than Morton (whom he suspected of inappropriate relations with the pulchritudinous young woman in charge of security pass photos).

'But he won't be shortening his list any time soon,' Morton continued. 'Everyone in the department without a colostomy is a suspect and even members of the bag brigade may be required to furnish alibis before this episode is through.'

'He'll doubtless do whatever he thinks best.'

'For himself, most certainly,' said Morton. 'It's the ministerial correspondence that I'm more worried about…because the unwashed are going to write in their thousands. Nothing surer. Every smart arse and amateur comedian will have a point to make.'

'There'll have to be a special unit to deal with it,' Alan said.

'No, I reckon Quenty will try to dump the task on us. You'll need to have all your arguments at the ready.'

'He couldn't ask us to handle the corro,' said Alan, genuinely surprised. 'The briefing I've sent him is just the beginning of our efforts to defend the committees. The workload is going to be enormous.'

'He'll try it on. You know he will. He hates us: both of us.'

On cue, Quentin Quist appeared in the doorway. The Band-Aid had disappeared to reveal a large red crater with a sticky yellow centre, almost doubling the size of the host proboscis.

'Good morning, Quentin,' said Morton, not missing a beat. 'I was just discussing ministerial media opportunities with Alan.'

'Yes, thank you. A word, if you don't mind, Alan.'

Morton smiled cheerfully, got up and left. Alan meanwhile wondered if he was to receive a rare apology from Quist, further to the altercation in the washroom.

'He seems to be spending a lot of time with you,' said Quist.

'He was actually distressed by the overnight media,' said Alan.

Quist looked at Alan, as though his subordinate had surreptitiously broken wind. 'Really? He didn't look too upset to me.'

'And he has medical issues.'

Quist sat and motioned Alan to shut the door. 'What's wrong with him?'

'I'm not sure it's appropriate for me to divulge the precise nature of his condition. Privacy and all that.'

'Is it cancer?' Quist asked, a little too eagerly.

'Nothing that serious,' said Alan.

'He'd better not be angling for time off.'

A drop of perspiration – at least Alan hoped it was perspiration – dropped off Quist's crater and onto the open diary on the table. Alan couldn't bring himself to wipe it up and he was aware of an itching sensation in the vicinity of his groin.

'I'm sure he'll struggle on.'

'Mind you, we'd probably see productivity increase if he took some leave.'

There was no point in disputing this unfair judgement while ever Quist was in one of his moods, so Alan focused on the droplet making its way through the morning interview spaces and into lunchtime. He tried not to think about his private parts.

'Further to my email,' said Quist, 'Do you have many media opportunities?'

'I think I'll be sending you a nil response.'

'I can't go back to the minister's office with nothing.'

'We don't have any big issues on the agenda for upcomings and I can't think of any retirements or reappointments.'

'You don't have a single committee member on their last legs?'

'They're all very sprightly.'

'No one with a terminal illness?'

'Not that I'm aware of.'

'Or snowballing dementia.'

'It wouldn't be easy to tell.'

'We can't have them tested?'

'It would create a very dangerous precedent.'

'For?'

'Public life, generally.'

'I suppose you're right. Maybe could encourage one of your older members to resign, instead?'

'To create a media opportunity?' Since when, Alan thought, had the manufacturing of fodder for the nightly news broadcasts been the responsibility of the bureaucracy?

'There's got to be someone you can hurry out the door.'

'I'm not sure that's appropriate conduct for...'

'Just find me an opportunity.'

Alan made a note in his workbook.

'Have you met with your staff to let them know about the consultancy?'

'Morton may be it, today. Trevithick and Edwina are both unwell.'

'What about the other woman: the one with all the children?'

'Barbara Best?'

'That's her.'

'Between ear infections, three-day fever, whooping cough, chicken pox, scarlet fever, tonsillitis and hand and foot and mouth...'

'But she didn't look unwell when she attended the emergency meeting I called.'

'No, I was referring to the illnesses which her children…'

Quist sighed and shook his head. 'Why we employ them I don't know.'

Alan thought it best not to mention Barbara's morning sickness and, instead wondered whether there was anything to be gained by a gentle reminder that zero population growth wasn't government policy and that someone had to have children to pay taxes to fund public service pensions. In the end, though, he opted for the least inflammatory response.

'I don't suppose anyone was to know, at the time she commenced with us, that she'd eventually have eight children.'

'Eight children! Good God! Doesn't she own a TV?'

'I've never enquired.'

'Well, we're one day back and three-quarters of your already scarce resources are absent. That hardly reflects well on your management style, does it?'

Alan wondered why it was that the high rate of absenteeism in the section was his fault alone, and not as much the responsibility of his psychotic senior manager, inadequate contraception and midlife sadomasochism. He would like to have said, 'If there's someone better equipped for the task, I'd be happy to do a handover,' but he had plans. And hadn't he earlier resolved that he wasn't, in the final summer of his career, going to be defeated by circumstances…at least, not without a fight?

The droplet in the diary halted at five o'clock, as if working to rule, and made a sharp left-hand turn to the gutter of the page.

'How much have you received for Valerie's flowers?'

'I've been too busy to chase anyone up. But I think we'll be light on.'

'Don't base your estimates of attendance in other sections on the clear lack of commitment in your own. And don't be expecting me to make up the shortfall for the bouquet.'

'Of course not,' said Alan.

Quist was not known for digging deep when it came to contributions.

'Did you get my briefing for the acting minister?' said Alan, hoping to change the subject.

'Yes, it's all right, I suppose, as far as it goes. I'll get back to you with amendments.'

'Certainly,' Alan replied, almost sure that Quist hadn't even opened the emailed draft.

'But that will have to be after you've collected our consultant, Ms Cunningham, from the executive suite and brought her over to my office.'

So Barbara and Morton's suspicions had been on the mark; the ex-secretary had picked up the consultancy. Alan wondered if Morton's associated suspicions – that an investigation of the branch's culture was a mask for some more sinister mission – would also be proved true. From a more mundane perspective, he wondered why it was that someone who'd spent nearly a decade in charge of the department needed to be escorted, like a small child or a demented great-grandfather.

'And then, while I'm getting her up to speed on some of the finer points, you'll need to pack up here and move back into the open area.'

Alan's heart stopped. Without any discussion or prior warning, Quist was ceasing his higher duties: finding him, after fourteen summers – summers in which he'd performed the managerial role to the quiet satisfaction of all concerned – to be incompetent or no longer up to the task.

Alan racked his brain to think of the one incident that had decided Quist on this humiliating course of action. It could well have been the confrontation in the toilets but it could also have been – knowing how unpredictable and precipitate the acting branch head could be – something as trivial as the reindeer incident or as bizarre as the business of the eye through the blinds. Then there was the already failed collection for the floral tribute and the previous day's contest for possession of the necktie. In fact, the more Alan thought about it, the more possible triggers for this indignity there were, going all the way back to his arrival, soon after Peaches, in the executive office the morning before – an occurrence which, in Quentin Quist's mind, had made Alan, as much as Peaches (or more), the discoverer of the turd and the undisputed cause of all the consequent tribulations.

Alan concluded that he should have taken pre-emptive action immediately after the most recent scene with Quist in the lavatory. He should have told Quist that he would no longer perform higher duties and would revert to his normal assistant director's position. He should have walked – as Morton would have put it – before they made him run. But might have beens were pointless. It was all now much too late.

13

'Are you still with me, Al?'

'This is a very disappointing outcome for me,' said Alan.

'Harden up, my friend. I need an office for Carol,' said Quist. 'You're still in charge of your team – if you can call it that – still a part of the branch management cohort, still a part of my inner sanctum and inner circle, still doing your bit to decide the plays, to keep the ship on course and…'

'So, I'm still acting director?'

Quist laughed. 'Oh, Alan, you don't mean…you don't mean to tell me that you seriously thought I'd…' He laughed even harder. 'You do, don't you?' Tears began their journey down his cheeks.

Alan's face burned with embarrassment.

'You thought I'd…'

Quist gasped for breath, he was laughing so hard. Alan smiled weakly and when Quist motioned towards the roll of paper towel on the desk, tore him off a couple of sheets.

'Such a delicate flower. You thought I'd terminated your higher duties,' Quist said when his face was dry. 'Didn't you? Admit it.'

Alan nodded reluctantly.

'When I've never, as far as I can recall, expressed any doubts about your performance, when I've only ever supported and nurtured you… and sung your praises at every opportunity to my senior management peer group.' Quist shook his head. 'Sometimes I wonder why I bother.'

Alan blinked. He wondered if he was hallucinating.

'People are a funny lot, aren't they?'" asked Quist.

Alan smiled weakly.

Quist dabbed at the crater with the soggy paper towel and once he'd soaked up enough goo, crumpled the sheets and threw them at the bin. They landed short but he made no attempt to retrieve them.

'Well, you'd better be off,' he said in a disappointed tone. 'It doesn't do to keep an ex-secretary waiting, does it?'

'No.'

'And on your way out, remind Morton that it's Twelfth Night over the weekend.'

'Certainly,' said Alan, mystified but not foolish enough to delay escape by requiring clarification.

'We don't want Carol thinking we've been unduly festive, do we?'

'No,' Alan answered, even more comprehensively lost.

'And give Burgoyne another call about the air conditioning.'

'Certainly,' Alan answered.

As soon as Quist had gone, Alan clawed at his crotch, turned off each of the programs running on his computer and shut down. The air conditioning sprang to life the very second that his screen faded to grey.

On the way to the executive suite, Alan spoke to Morton, who was sitting by himself out in the open plan.

Morton understood the significance of the Twelfth Night reference immediately. 'He wants the Christmas decorations down,' he said. 'Debbie told him a few years ago that it was bad karma to leave them hanging.'

At Alan's home, the miniature tree, artificial mistletoe and single string of fairy lights (non-flashing) were always packed away on Boxing Day, consistent with cherished domestic notions of tidiness and timeliness.

'But we could be forgiven some tardiness in getting everything down,' Morton continued, 'as some of attributes of Twelfth Night seem to be the norm around here for most of January.'

Alan knew exactly what attributes Morton was referring to.

'If you could nonetheless make a start on the decorations, your medical condition permitting, that would be much appreciated.'

'You know,' Morton replied, 'I've been accused over the years of not being a "can do" kind of guy, but I think I can accommodate you. However, it would probably whet my appetite for the task if I knew that you were likely to affirm, once my compo form has been lodged, that my condition is a result of the temperature problems in this building.'

Alan had no time for negotiation and was inclined to caution anyway, even though the days of invalidity retirement for less-than-debilitating reasons were long gone and there was no prospect of Morton getting cash compensation for his affliction. 'Were you ill-disposed over the shutdown period?'

'Ill-disposed vis-à-vis?'

'Downstairs,' Alan gestured.

'Not so much as a cinder of prickly heat or an inch of athletes foot.'

'Were you otherwise itchy before your return to work?'

'Otherwise?'

Alan blushed. 'You know, around the corner?'

'You mean "up the back passage", "in the vicinity of the starfish" or "anywhere near the quince"?'

Alan blushed again. 'I suppose so.'

'I can assure you I most certainly wasn't.'

'Then,' said Alan, 'you can consider me very much inclined to support your claim.'

'I'll have all of this stuff down within half an hour,' said Morton rising and looking at the closest decorations.

'Quentin's office first and then mine, if you wouldn't mind.'

'You can't deal with a detumescent reindeer, a few baubles and a couple of strings of tinsel?' Morton asked, grinning.

'I've been asked to collect the consultant from mahogany row and move her into my office.'

'Jesus,' said Morton. 'You haven't been…?'

'Not yet, but I am vacating my office.'

'They're throwing you out of your office to make way for a consultant!'

'Well, not just any consultant,' said Alan, 'but, look, I've really got to go.'

'You can't leave me hanging like that,' said Morton, walking with Alan.

'I'll be back, soon enough.'

'No you don't. Name, please.'

Alan had hoped to avoid being with Morton when the news broke. 'It's Carol,' he admitted.

'I told you it would be her snout in the trough, didn't I?'

'I have to go.'

'Didn't I?'

'You did,' Alan admitted.

'It's a disgrace,' said Morton, mightily pleased.

Alan caught the lift to the ground floor and passed a different set of security guards to those who'd attempted to convince him of the benefits of bodybuilding the day before. Into the daylight, he walked across the courtyard and entered the foyer of the department's other tower.

Years before, a proposal to link the towers with an above-ground walkway had been thwarted by a coalition of protesting departmental officers and environmentalists, concerned about the fate of the two nearby, near-dead, gargantuan gums. Both trees had since expired but had not been cut down owing to a second wave of protest, demanding dignity in death for the twin giants and asserting that they should fall in their own good time (inevitably on one of the towers, at which time the department would be accused of placing the lives of its officers at risk).

In the foyer of the second tower, Alan came face to face with old friends.

'Hi, Al,' said the older of the two beefcake bodyguards from the day before. 'Have you had a chance to think about the great offer I told you about?'

'I'm giving it very serious consideration,' said Alan, not stopping.

The lift doors opened and Alan froze at the site of a slim platinum blonde dressed incongruously in ski gear.

'Don't stand there,' said the secretary.

'I'm sorry,' said Alan, struggling, for the third or fourth time that day, not to let fear empty his stomach.

He positioned himself at the rear of the lift next to a brace of tennis racquets, some luggage, a set of skis in a travel case, and an upright object which was poking through its brown paper covering – evidently a carved totem pole.

The secretary did not speak to Alan; she did not normally have dealings with officers at his level. Alan did not speak to the secretary; he'd only ever sighted her in the distance – from the back of the auditorium in which she delivered intermittent briefings and encouragements to lower middle management staff.

Her proximity to him bothered her not in the least. His proximity to her made him decidedly anxious; the urge to throw up passed but he was conscious of his itchy crotch, of the need to attend a lavatory and of an urge to blurt that he was not the creator or the discoverer of it, on the off-chance that she was about to hear otherwise.

He fretted, too, about the skis, the racquets, the statue and the luggage, and whether it would seem paternalistic or in some other way offensive to offer to help with them when they reached the thirteenth floor.

In the event, the secretary made the haulage call for him. 'Stand back,' she said, gathering up her handbag, an overnight bag, two suitcases, the skis, the racquets and the graven image, before making her exit.

Alan followed her empty-handed, like an incompetent royal attendant, through the electric doors into the executive suite: four offices guarded by four executive assistants who could all have been sororal relations of the termagant who'd taken over Peaches' desk the day before.

All four of the women looked from the secretary's baggage to Alan's unburdened person with disbelief. All four rushed forward to relieve their leader of her load, then three of them hustled her into her office, to the accompaniment of clucking, cooing and sympathetic remarks. More solicitous murmuring could be heard from inside, before the door was shut.

The larger pieces of luggage were propped, by the most junior of the assistants, against the walls between the two desks closest to the biggest office – nestled in the luxurious leaves of the ceiling-high semi-tropical pot plants which hid much of the imitation wooden panelling from view.

The last of the brown paper fell away from the wooden statue revealing a giant displeased Tiki which – with an exposed tongue – was considered too unsavoury for public display. It was turned to face the greenery.

All order restored, the remaining assistant turned to Alan. 'You're here for…?' she enquired.

'Carol,' said Alan. Decades had passed since senior managers were referred to as 'Mr' or 'Mrs' or 'Ms' but Alan still felt uncomfortable referring to someone who'd once been so important by her given name. 'I'm to take her down to the Consultation and Stakeholder Liaison Branch,' he said, smiling.

The assistant's upper lip curled a little. 'And your name would be?'

'Mewling, Alan Mewling,' he answered, waiting for the rest of the curl.

When the distaste didn't transition to fully fledged contempt, the relief he felt was boundless.

'Take a seat,' she said. 'I'll let her know you're here.'

He sat in one of the three visitors' chairs opposite the entrance and gazed at the vegetation – a growth so lush that he half expected to hear songbirds warbling, trilling and whooping, and to see pangolins snuffling about in dense leaf matter obscuring the carpet from view.

He wasn't tempted by any of the tennis magazines in a neat pile on the nearby coffee table. In truth, he'd braced himself for another rush of Christmas Eve recollections, for it was in the same reception area in the next chair that he'd waited with his bottle and his carefully covered trays of angels on horseback on the last afternoon of the working year.

The three absent assistants returned and looked through him, having decided from his appearance that he was a minor departmental functionary (the modern equivalent of Furphy's deputy assistant sub-inspector) warranting no respect in and of himself, and no vicarious deference as the acolyte of a personage of note.

Apart from phone calls made and received, the only sound was that of expertly harried keyboards: more than a hum, less than a rattle and too much like something light and many-legged moving fast across a hillock of tiny brittle bones.

Mid-reverie, the door to Alan's left opened and the experience he'd expected (but then thought unlikely) engulfed him. It was Christmas Eve once again and Brian Gulliver was motioning him over, telling his executive assistant to 'up stumps', and offering Alan his hand. Alan was once again juggling his bottle and his angels, proffering the wine when there was no other solution to the shortage of hands, and reciprocating Christmas greetings. Gulliver was ushering Alan through his office and asking, as he always did, about Alan's year. Alan was enquiring as he always did about the well-being of the Gulliver spouse and progeny, and about Christmas holiday plans.

Formalities concluded – without, disappointingly, any mention of Alan's impending retirement or any thanks for the wine (the most expensive Alan had ever purchased) – they moved through the internal door into the meeting room and from there into the kitchen. There, as usual, Alan pulled on an apron and began preparing the food.

It was a role he'd first performed nearly twenty years before when Gulliver had been a mere acting assistant secretary, and when a feminist executive assistant had drawn the line at party preparations for a group mostly comprised of men.

Alan separated cocktail frankfurts in preparation for boiling and turned on the oven in readiness for party pies, his angels and frozen curry puffs. Then he opened packets of chips and nuts, removed dolmades and artichoke hearts from their tins, liberated various cheeses and sliced up a range of tropical fruits.

He'd attended the first of Gulliver's Christmas drinks as a guest – he was certain that had been so – and, for the immediately following years, had been invited by a handwritten card 'to have a glass of Christmas cheer and help out an old mate'. With passing time, any pretence of mateship and of voluntary attendance had disappeared and, after Gulliver had been gazetted a deputy secretary, there'd been only emailed meeting reminders alerting him to the time, the location and the need to arrive early.

Alan had wondered whether the orders to attend and cater weren't petty vengeance for those occasions when, as Gulliver's original public service supervisor, he'd had to remonstrate with the boy over clumsy expression, deficient filing, poor timekeeping, slovenly dress and security breaches.

Alan put the first trays of savouries in the oven and, removing his gloves (but not his apron), made three quick trips into the boardroom, placing platters and bowls of nibblies around the meeting table against the only unbroken length of wall.

Some of the older hands acknowledged him but to most of the guests he was invisible or, at best, an object of moderate amusement – as any late middle-aged man in an apron emblazoned with 'World's Greatest Mum' should have been. Alan wore the apron beyond the kitchen to prevent a repeat of the embarrassment, years before, when a new member of the executive had introduced herself in the mistaken view that he was someone important.

He still held vague hopes of a valedictory tribute during the speaking part of the proceedings but busied himself in the interim, replenishing the crisps and nuts, replating the hot titbits and moving from little group to little group with top-up bottles.

Numbers were, he noted, down on previous years – there were probably forty-five to fifty people at the peak – but that did not prevent the usual rituals from taking place at the usual times: the usual ribbing and ribaldry when he entered the room at the one-hour mark with plates of cocktail frankfurts, and the customary cheering and whistling when he served the prune and bacon sizzlers soon afterwards – all of this before Brian Gulliver's vaguely subversive recounting of the blunders of the almost finished year in a speech always preceded by the assurance that 'Alan, our old friend and caterer, hears nothing at all at this stage of proceedings'.

Finally, at the point before the non-stayers started to drift away, there was the traditional toast to Alan himself, in recognition of his culinary efforts. No mention was made that it was, or might have been, his final Christmas appearance. There were, as a consequence, no sneering remarks to the effect that he knew how to man a hole punch, that he'd once been the idol of the typing pool, or that he could teach youngsters a thing or two about folioing. There was, however, chortling in response to Gulliver's rhetorical preliminary, 'To our lovely and attentive caterer, Alan: where would we be each year without him? Where would the department be without him? To Alan,' Gulliver had continued.

'To Alan' came the lukewarm response.

Glasses were raised and Alan attempted to look pleased, without fixing on anyone in particular, before returning to the kitchenette.

He'd kept himself a modest selection of delicacies on a paper napkin but someone passing through – probably in a drunken search for the toilets or more wine – had knocked them off the bench onto the floor, from where they could only be despatched to the bin. So, Alan sat out of sight of the swinging door and sniffed at the bouquet of a much-deserved glass of Shiraz. Before, however he could put lips to rim, his name was called and he was – disappointed and slightly dazed – back in the present and staring up at the Habsburg jaw of Carol Cunningham.

14

Carol had been an outsider when appointed secretary in the early 1990s – someone whose career had been spent in the central agencies and for whom the opportunity to head a middle-ranking department, well away from the engine room and bridge of government, was pleasing enough but, at another level, a little disappointing.

In those days, there were cutting edge agencies – administering where none had gone before; powerful agencies – reviewing the activities and spending of the rest; and sexy agencies – doing intentionally secret things or boasting an international presence. There were quirky agencies too – engaged in quasi-academic pursuits or focused on strange places; and then there were the unremarkable workaday rest. The department which Carol Cunningham was required to head was very much of the last category.

Under a name so long at one point that it spanned ministerial letterhead twice, it was, even in those years, a peculiar collection of programs comprised of the bits and pieces, bibs and bobs and odds and sods left over from previous reorganisations of ministries and agencies: a bizarre grab bag of functions, the diversity of which constituted a cerebral challenge to the second-ranking ministers to whom it was usually allocated and an even greater challenge to the still more reluctant mandarins entrusted with its day-to-day administration.

Carol Cunningham wrestled and grappled and tussled and struggled with the disparate components of the portfolio until she knew about every last project and interaction. She had then masterminded an internal restructure of such breathtaking scope and frightening expense that it left barely an officer at the same desk or in the same work unit and and – because it marked the end of corporate-funded pot plants for staff below executive ranks – was thereafter referred to as the Great Deforestation (by those not already disposed to calling it the Great Confusion).

Despite the fanfare and self-congratulation which followed hard on the heels (or, more accurately, the wheels) of the last unloaded truck, it was quickly apparent that the synergies, efficiencies and new ways of working which had been advanced with such certainty as rationales for the reorganisation had been thwarted by something indefinable beyond the silos, knowledge protection and process retention which had stymied earlier, less ambitious exercises.

The lazy, lumbering, resentful old beast would not be transformed into the sleeker, keener, fleeter-footed creature of Carol Cunningham's fondest imaginings and, though awards were bestowed and CVs were puffed, nothing was gained. And much, including certain boxes of files recording the department's least glorious moments, was lost.

Having engaged, restructured and trumpeted, Carol expected to be returned to the high-profile heart of government before any cracks appeared in the freshly plastered edifice of her creation. But even though she networked assiduously, played tennis year-round with persons of influence and hinted ceaselessly at her availability for a more 'strategic' appointment, her moment had come…and gone. She had retired at sixty-five to a think tank and then, post-seventy, after a long holiday and a facelift, had offered her services one last time in the cause of the public good.

There had been no obvious takers or tasks until someone had spent a penny (or a decimal sum of a larger, inflation-adjusted denomination) on Robin Rainbird's desk. That single act had fertilised Carol's hopes to a degree she would not have thought possible only weeks before. Endless panoscopic vistas of opportunity suddenly opened up for her, and long-buried aspirations – even to return to a full-time role at the centre – were disinterred and galvanised. Such had been the impact on Carol Cunningham of a single bowel motion well away from the point and moment of its secret birth.

Alan looked up into the ex-secretary's hungry eyes and saw ambition more naked than any he'd previously sighted – ambition already so bare that stadium lights and professional depilation could not have revealed any more of it to view. He rocked forward to regain his feet.

'You're not the Alan Mewling who…?' Carol Cunningham asked.

Forgiven, perhaps, but never forgotten, Alan's great mistake would haunt him, it seemed, forever.

'I'm afraid so,' he answered, bravely.

Cunningham pulled at the sleeves of her blue pinstripe jacket and adjusted her lapels in the reflexive, unthinking way in which Christians from peasant societies had once crossed themselves at the mention of the Evil One. 'Never mind,' she said, less in absolution than to signal her impatience to achieve, to be acknowledged and to then be given her just reward (in quick order).

'May I carry anything for you?' asked Alan, anxious not to repeat the mistake he'd made by failing to carry the secretary's baggage.

'Certainly,' Carol Cunningham answered.

One of the EAs came forward with a gym bag and a satchel. Alan took charge of them and led the way to the lifts, where he was obliged to put down the satchel to press the button.

When the doors opened, the Corporate Foliage Optimisation executive who'd insulted Alan the day before was waiting to alight with his trolley and the various accoutrements of his calling.

'Columbus discovered the New World, Alan,' he said as he passed, 'and you discovered…'

'Thank you,' said Alan, anxious not to have his role in the previous day's events revealed to his charge.

'What was that man saying?' Carol asked as they descended.

'I'm not quite sure,' said Alan.

In the foyer, Boris was also eager to engage. 'Remember what I told you about name calling and group humiliation,' he said, as Anselm strained the stitching on his uniform shirt with a rotating pose.

'Good-oh,' said Alan.

'What was that about?' Carol asked, twice bewildered.

'I have no idea,' he lied.

Coming out of the foyer of the other building, the woman who'd assisted Alan with his briefcases the previous afternoon glared at him and hissed, 'You ought to be ashamed.'

'And that young woman?' enquired Carol, a third time baffled.

'Disturbed,' he said.

At Quentin Quist's office, Carol and Daphne air-kissed.

'I'll take your things to your office,' Alan said when the virtual osculations were complete.

'You can leave them here,' Daphne replied, 'with me.'

The door opened behind the EA and Quentin Quist appeared with a fresh plaster strip on his nose.

'Ah, Ms Cunningham, Quentin Quist, acting assistant secretary. Delighted to meet you. I have long been the hugest fan.'

Carol Cunningham ignored the offered hand and sailed past Quist into his office.

'Don't stand there like a fool,' said the embarrassed acting manager to Alan. 'Take those things to Ms Cunningham's office, immediately.'

Quist shut the door. Alan looked at Daphne for guidance.

'You can leave them here, Mr Mewling,' she said.

Alan deposited the bags, as instructed, and made towards his office to pack up his own things. Morton seemed to have made poor progress with the removal of the Christmas decorations in the open area. Alan's office, though, had been attended to, with the exception of the reindeer, which, instead of being deflated and packed away for future festive seasons, had been topped up, then positioned on Alan's table in front of a Santa of like scale, crotch to hindquarters, joined with blue tack so that interruptus could only be achieved by the application of force. Alan gave his groin a quick scratch then exerted the necessary force. The two parted, as new lovers invariably do, with the greatest reluctance. With a tissue over his fingers, Alan opened the animal's valve and then Santa's, before squeezing the left-over stale air out of both, well away from his body, and then folding them up.

With two bulging supermarket bags, Morton appeared in the doorway just as Alan, having returned all of his possessions to his cubicle, was giving the office desk a final wipe.

'Quentin sent me off to get morning tea for Carol,' said Morton without even glancing at the table.

Alan said nothing about the inter-species tryst.

The shopping bags seemed rather full for a gathering of two or, if Daphne was invited to join the executive, of three…especially as the ex-secretary looked more starved than well fed, but the decision wasn't Alan's to question.

'You'd better deliver, then,' said Alan. 'She's in with Quentin.'

Morton rested the bags on the floor and raked a thumb up and down his crotch. Alan looked away.

'It's not a private cake and arse party,' Morton said. 'Quenty emailed everyone. It's the full branch red carpet in the tea room at eleven.'

'I wouldn't have thought that was a good idea,' said Alan, recalling that the consultancy was supposed to be a low-visibility thing.

'Crazy,' said Morton.

Crazy indeed. No matter what task Carol was really among them to do, she would not be welcome. And their reduced numbers would hardly impress upon her their dedication and commitment.

'I'm to get the rest of the decorations down while you do your magic in the kitchen.'

Alan wondered if, between recalled and real-time kitchen duties, he was going to spend the better part of his morning in apron and disposable gloves. 'So there's no one in this branch except you and me to do whatever is needed in the way of menial tasks?'

'It appears not,' said Morton.

'We'd better get on, then.'

In the event, it took Alan less than ten minutes to prepare everything. The fare, mostly generic products and discounted items, would disappoint, for too little cash was, as always, expended for there to be a satisfactory result. Yet, what decades of service in the public cause had taught Morton about buying cheap, they'd taught Alan about the crucial nature of appearances:

about the importance of making things seem a good deal better than they actually were. Thus it was that once he'd worked his magic, the tea room tables seemed to contain a veritable feast; at least the moment between first sight and first bite would be moderately pleasurable.

Alan returned to his vacated office for one last check before it became Carol Cunningham's…and found Quentin Quist tapping his nameplate into the slot on the door.

'Don't say anything,' said Quist, under his breath.

Carol had evidently decided to move into Quist's temporary office, obliging him to move into the one he had earmarked for her.

'Some morning tea will raise your spirits,' Alan said, following Quist inside. 'A bit of bun and a cup of tea always perks me up.'

'Bugger the morning tea,' said Quist, bitterly. 'She doesn't want to attend and neither do I.'

Alan wondered what was to happen to the food he'd just put out. 'What would you like me to do with the food?'

'Didn't you hear me?' Quist interrupted.

'Of course,' said Alan. 'I was just wondering what to do about the…?'

'Cancel it but get Morton to collect the money, so I'm not out of pocket.'

Alan's face indicated what he thought about Morton's prospects of extracting funds on an off pay week, after all of the additional expenses associated with Christmas, for a non-event that no one had requested, to welcome a woman no one wanted around. It was hard enough squeezing money out of some individuals for scheduled events immediately after pay day but, if word leaked out that Quist had advanced money to purchase food this time around, almost no one would contribute.

'They'll graze on it during the day,' said Quist. 'Why shouldn't they pay?'

'You know they'll claim they didn't.'

'Oh, all right, they can get together but do it quickly and quietly, and make sure they cough up for Valerie's flowers while they're about it.'

'Would you like to kick off the contributions?'

'To myself? For food I've already paid for? Are you a halfwit?'

'For Valerie's flowers.'

'Take a single gold coin out of the food money.' Quist sat and faced the computer.

'And is there anything you'd like me to say at the morning tea?'

'About?' Quist reached towards the On button.

'You and Carol?"

'With respect to?'

'Why you're not in attendance.'

'You'll think of something.'

Quist depressed the switch and Alan wondered whether the IT hoodoo he'd experienced would now pass to the new occupant of his office. The screen brightened and the air conditioning didn't so much as stutter.

'An urgent task of some sort?'

'Say whatever you like. I honestly couldn't care less.'

'I'll tell them something urgent has come up and that Carol will talk to us all when she's settled in.'

And that's what, with some embellishment, Alan would have announced to the little group of no more than twenty gathered around the home-brand cakes and biscuits, the generic dips and the partly warmed saveloys…had Morton not collared him at the entrance to the tea room and given him still more bad news.

'Don't look now,' he said in a whisper, 'but the young woman in the dark suit in the corner, giving Smith and one of the zombies a lecture on risk management, is our new graduate.'

'What do you mean?' asked Alan, looking warily over Morton's shoulder at a buxom young redhead poking Smith in the chest with a revivified celery stick.

'Your newest staff member is here to commence her working life as a public servant.'

'I know nothing about any graduate,' said Alan.

'Well, she had you down as her supervisor.'

'There must be some mistake.'

'Be that as it may…'

'And the graduate program doesn't start until the beginning of February, anyway.'

'She got her offer of a place by mail yesterday and booked the first available economy seat.'

'Possibly so, but not until February.'

'She told me she couldn't wait.'

'But she can't just start when she feels like it,' said Alan. 'New staff don't tell the department what to do. We are in charge, aren't we?'

Morton shrugged.

'Well, aren't we?'

'You and I were never in charge.'

'You know what I'm saying. Have you rung Personnel?'

'I didn't need to. She was on the phone to them when I went down to the foyer to collect her.'

'And?'

'It seems that we can put her on a temporary contract until the other graduates commence.'

'But we don't have to, surely?'

'Probably not, but she won't be turned away.'

'What do you mean?

'She doesn't seem to understand the meaning of "no".'

'She won't come back in a month?'

'She most certainly won't.'

'Doesn't she realise that we are in the midst of a crisis?'

'How could she not know? We're all over the media.'

'And you're certain she's ours?'

'More than ours. She's actually yours.'

'But she couldn't have come at a worse time.' Alan peered at the young woman haranguing the hapless Sri Lankan. 'If this campaign against us, and against the committees, gains any momentum at all, we'll be stretched like never before. And that's without having to handle the correspondence.'

'Don't tell me Quist has allocated that to us already.'

'Not yet, no, but my point is that we don't need, in our darkest hour, the additional work that's necessary to get a graduate started in a meaningful way.'

'Certainly not,' said Morton, tweaking his crotch.

'And, as you know, it takes time to bring someone new and impressionable on board, to teach them the rudiments of public administration and inculcate in them a respect for objective decision-making and process.'

'It most certainly does,' said Morton. 'But I don't think this young woman will be all that interested in the rudiments. She wanted to know when she'd be meeting the minister, where her office was and who her personal assistant would be.'

'Did I just hear you say that she wanted to meet the minister?'

'That's right.'

Alan looked over Morton's shoulder, again. The graduate was lecturing a fresh zombie.

'Has she no idea?' he asked in a low voice.

'None at all. It's a generational thing.'

'I hadn't realised that things had deteriorated so much, so quickly.'

'We'll have to keep her busy if she's not to create havoc.'

'And we thought things couldn't get any worse,' Alan remarked.

'Let's have some morning tea,' said Morton, patting Alan on the back. 'We can regroup and strategise later.'

'And the name of a new staff member is?'

'Eris,' said Morton. 'Like Erin, except ending with an "s".'

'Eris as in E-R-I-S?'

'That's right.'

'Then the portents are terrible,' said Alan, ashen.

'Why?' Morton asked.

'The wedding of Peleus and Thetis? The judgement of Paris? The fall of Troy.'

'I know about the Trojan horse,' said Morton.

'It was Eris, the uninvited wedding guest, who provided the Apple of Discord.'

Morton had no idea what Alan was talking about. 'The Apple of Discord, eh?'

'This is a sign of the very worst sort,' Alan said.

'Then I take it you'd prefer not to be introduced?'

'It will have to happen,' said Alan 'but let's get morning tea out of the way first. No man should struggle against bitter destiny on an empty stomach.'

They turned and, locating the Jatz, fell as one upon a plastic container of hommus that contained more preservatives and artificial colourings than the year-old rainbow cake to its left and proved to be even less flavoursome than the tasteless tasty cheese to its right.

15

Later, when things then unknown were seemingly known and the mysteries attendant upon that time were of little further moment, it seemed incongruous to those in the tea room on that morning that they could have been assembled without some fleeting official reference to the ghastly discovery in Valerie Venables's office and to Carol's unsettling arrival.

Yet Alan's brief speech, without any specific mention of 'it', of the absent consultant or of any recent untoward events – other than the early commencement of the new graduate – seemed to reassure attendees that they could, in fact, rise above the challenges then confronting them.

It was, some later said, Alan's finest moment: a masterful demonstration of the public servant's craft – of persuasive obliquity – but others were to say it was the clearest pointer to how disingenuous, deceitful and dissembling he had become.

The graduate broke with all precedent by delivering an address-in-reply outlining her qualifications, her expectations of her workmates in the months ahead and her excitement at the prospect of a key role in root and branch public sector reform. Her new colleagues listened in mute disbelief until the ten-minute mark, at which point Morton filled a break for breath with furious concluding applause and Alan delivered inescapable thanks for 'a most illuminating address'.

Strasser and Mankiewicz, presumably under instructions from Quentin Quist, collected contributions for both food and flowers at the door as attendees departed, relieving Alan of the need. A couple of the zombies tidied up the tables.

Back in the open-plan area, Alan and Morton discovered that in their absence all of the recent committee files, including those belonging to

Barbara Best, had been removed from their cabinets. In each sling was an A4 piece of paper bearing the date and the words 'Removed with the authority of Quentin Quist, Acting Assistant Secretary, Stakeholder Liaison and Committees.'

A substantial pile of phone message slips – some completed by Daphne, some by Quentin Quist and some by persons unknown – sat next to Alan's phone, weighed down by his stapler; Alan's review of the pile confirmed that they all related to calls from committee members. A Post-it note stuck to the top message read 'See my email and ring them personally. QQ.'

Morton, peering over Alan's shoulder, observed that calling them impersonally might have been a better way of proceeding, bearing in mind the morning media. Alan, mindful of the graduate sitting expectantly at the adjacent meeting table, decided it best not to respond.

'We'll organise a spot for you this afternoon,' he said to her. 'Your early arrival happened to catch us by surprise.'

'Any vacant office,' the graduate responded, 'will be suitable while things are being organised.'

Morton shot Alan a look that said, 'I told you so.'

'I don't think you'll be getting an office just yet,' Alan said, gently.

Morton struggled to suppress a smile.

'I don't understand,' said the graduate.

'Directors and above get the offices.'

'Although they're hardly ever in them,' said Morton, 'owing to meeting dependence.'

'And those of us in subordinate, yet still important, roles sit out here in the open plan.'

'But I've got three degrees,' said the graduate.

'I'm afraid you aren't out of the ordinary in that respect,' said Alan. 'Morton, here, has five and not one relying on advanced standing or credit for previous study.'

It was true. Morton had acquired, with the assistance of study leave, post-nominals comprehending most of the letters of the alphabet and would have enrolled to capture some of the more elusive consonants had it not been for the recent tightening of the studies assistance criteria.

'I have an honours degree in change facilitation,' the graduate reminded them, 'a masters in risk management and a Doctor of Commerce in Leadership.'

Whatever happened to the days, Alan thought, wistfully, when graduates knew about the Peloponnesian Wars? 'Yes, I recall you telling us about your qualifications in the tea room,' he said, 'and I'm sure they'll all prove to be very useful. But for at least a while you'll need to sit with us, out here, in the open area.'

'We sit in cubicles,' said Morton, 'and if you've been following events in the media, the irony won't be lost on you.'

Alan shot Morton a warning look. 'Perhaps you could duck down to corporate, old chap, and get the approval for a reshuffle, so that Eris can be co-located with us.'

'Always pleased to trigger accommodation hysteria,' Morton replied, getting up.

Alan and the graduate waited until they were alone.

'Five degrees and he does your errands!' the graduate said. 'How many do *you* have?'

'The modern public service,' said Alan, sidestepping the question, 'is all about teamwork – about working together to get the right result – and we don't stand on credentials. The most valuable attributes you'll bring to your work in the decades ahead will be flexibility and a willingness to pitch in, in pursuit of collective goals.'

There'd been a time when Alan would have scorned these qualities in favour of professional objectivity, attention to detail and an understanding of processes or, perhaps, a grasp of English grammar. Those days had, however, long since passed.

'Of course,' said the graduate. 'When do I get to meet the minister?'

Alan took a deep breath. 'Morton didn't explain ministerial access to you?'

'No.'

'It's unlikely you'll get to meet the minister for some time. Those interactions are at the higher levels of the department. I, myself, have not met the current minister.' Or any of his five predecessors, Alan might truthfully have said. 'But within short order you'll probably be writing submissions to him and – ' Alan recalled his discussion with Morton the previous day about the expected flood of letters from the public re 'it' – 'even the occasional piece of correspondence.'

'I see,' said the graduate. 'What about the secretary?'

'You wouldn't normally be having much to do with her, either, but that doesn't mean we won't be keeping busy on her behalf.'

The graduate looked decidedly glum.

'In the meantime, I'll give you some background reading and Morton can get you on to the IT system.' He handed her a copy of the department's annual report and a folder with information on the operation and membership of the various committees. Together, these materials could be relied on to keep a graduate busy for at least a day.

'And who will be my orientation buddy?"'asked the graduate.

'Buddy' was a term Alan abhorred but he engaged, nonetheless. 'I would normally have been your buddy, as you put it, but I'm currently acting as the section's director – regrettably, without an office – so Morton will do what is necessary to get you on your feet and I'll supervise your day-to-day activities.'

'So I won't have a buddy?'

'Think of Morton as your quasi-buddy.'

'All right.'

'Morton,' Alan felt compelled to add, 'is a very competent and experienced officer but a little unconventional, so you should take anything he says to you *cum grano salis*.' Perhaps the metaphor was wasted on the graduate. 'With a grain of salt,' Alan added.

The graduate looked no less puzzled.

'Don't take everything he says to be the truth.'

'But how will I know what's true and what's not?' the graduate asked.

The question was a good one.

'Trust your instinct,' said Alan, not because he thought this an especially useful instruction but because he couldn't, at that moment, think of anything else that would assist.

The graduate's attention turned to her reading materials and Alan switched on his computer, conscious of the fact that he'd been offline for more than an hour. Even before his fingertip made contact with the power switch, the air conditioning ceased and some of the ripest language Alan had ever heard indoors emanated from the bay behind him, while from his front there was a less blush-making chorus of curses and moans.

'We've been having difficulty with the cooling,' Alan explained to the graduate.

Back on the screen the most insistent of the emails in his In box was marked 'Urgent' and headed 'Read this immediately.' It had been sent by Quentin Quist only three minutes earlier and was comprised entirely of upper text which read, 'WHO IS THE WOMN YOU ARE MEET WITH? WHY ARENT YOU TALK TO COMMITTEE MEMBERS LIKE I ASKED YOU TWO? SEE ME IMMEDIATELY.'

Alan glanced in the direction of Quist's office. The blinds were drawn and the door was shut.

An earlier message from Quist in more temperate terms required Alan to 'ring committee members immediately, discourage engagement with the media and tell all that Acting Minister best placed to defend'.

A still earlier message read, 'No need to respond to last night's request for media opportunities.'

A belated faecal JPEG arrived as Alan was reviewing the remaining messages. He wanted to respond to the sender with 'Are you an imbecile? Do you think I could have avoided seeing this at least 100 times in the last 24+ hours?' but stayed his fingers.

At Quentin Quist's door, he was instructed to enter. Inside, he could see none of the files which had been retrieved from the cabinets while he and Morton were at morning tea. The only deduction he could reasonably make was that they had been taken for the use of Carol.

'You wished to see me?' Alan said when Quist didn't look up from the file he was reading.

Quist didn't respond. On the window ledge, a huge magpie savagely attacked a smaller colleague.

'Quentin?'

Quist put the file down but didn't turn round. 'Why haven't you followed my instructions?' Quist asked in a low voice, almost a whisper.

'I've been settling the new graduate in,' Alan answered.

'That woman you've been talking to is the new graduate?'

'That's right.'

'So, you're telling me,' Quist continued, 'that you've been wasting time on an *ab initio* when I not only had work for you to do that necessitated your immediate attention, but had left you a message which made my requirement clear?'

'Not exactly,' said Alan, determined not to be cowed this time.

'Not exactly?' asked Quist

'Yes, because at the time I was talking to her, I wasn't aware of your requirement.'

'I see,' said Quist.

'Yes,' said Alan, emboldened by his lie. 'Not in the least aware.'

'True though that might be, when I mean immediately, Alan, I actually do mean immediately, not when convenient, not at your leisure and not if it's not too much jolly trouble.'

On the ledge, the feathered giant delivered the coup de grace.

'I'd better make a start then,' said Alan.

'That would be so appreciated,' said Quist, trembling and barely able to contain his rage.

On the ledge, the dominant bird gorged on the bloody entrails of the vanquished.

'But not before we've had a discussion about my secretarial support.'

If Quist and the world at large expected another display of resistance from Alan, they were to be disappointed. He'd already done as much as his spirit would allow.

'What can I do for you?' he asked.

'You can start by answering my phone. I'll divert it to you.'

'Certainly,' said Alan. 'But –'

'– but what?'

'I was wondering how I put anyone through to you if your calls are already diverted to me.'

'Don't bother, then,' Quist snapped.

'I was only trying to –'

'No, no. If it's too much trouble for you.'

'Well, it's not a matter of trouble. More a matter of –'

'Oh, get out,' Quist shouted. 'Get out now.'

'Would you like me to shut the door?' Alan asked.

A groan, followed by a stapler whizzing at high speed past Alan's right ear was all the answer he received. He shut the door anyway.

In the open-plan area, Alan noticed, with some satisfaction, that the temperature was appreciably lower than in Quentin Quist's office. Morton had moved the graduate temporarily into the cubicle opposite his own, normally occupied by April Wong, and was digging at his crotch with one hand, while sorting the message slips left next to Alan's phone with the other.

'How many degrees does that man have?' the graduate enquired, looking admiringly in the direction of Quentin Quist's closed door.

'Why do you ask?' Alan responded.

'He has an office and gets to shout at people,' she said.

'Quentin is acting as our assistant secretary while the permanent branch head is on leave and I'm not quite sure what qualifications he's got.'

'He has, as Alan knows all too well, a degree in hospitality,' said Morton. 'After three years of intensive study, he was able to open a beer bottle, boil an egg and make a bed.'

'Morton,' Alan warned.

'And even now, he can hail you a taxi, iron your blouse and procure you a gigolo in no time flat.'

'Morton, that's quite enough.'

'Alan is of the old school,' Morton explained, for the benefit of the graduate, 'blindly loyal to the swinish senior management of this organisation and horrified at the prospect of any dirty linen.'

'Really,' said Alan, exasperated.

'You need, therefore, to take whatever he says with a grain of salt.'

'It seems that everything here needs to be taken with salts,' said the graduate, returning to her reading.

Alan thought about making clear the singular and non-laxative qualities of the substance in question but concluded that such clarifications were unlikely to be of much benefit and that it was probably wiser to attend to his In box. It contained three additional 'please call' messages. He printed them out and added them to Morton's pile.

'It's not just these I have to call,' said Alan. 'Quentin wants me to do the lot.'

'Ridiculous. We'll divvy the task up or you'll be here all weekend. You can do the conveners, we'll each do the members of our own committees, and we can split Barbara's lot fifty-fifty, with me doing A to M inclusive, and you doing the remainder.'

'That seems sensible,' said Alan.

'The way ahead this time: are we encouraging public engagement by the members or discouraging it?'

'Discouraging, this time, definitely discouraging. The acting minister is to be left to do the defensive work.'

'Any other instructions, before I begin?'

'No delegating,' said Alan, nodding in the graduate's direction.

'Understood and I'll make my calls from one of the meeting rooms, so Quentin doesn't overhear me helping out.'

'I'd better stay close,' said Alan, again nodding in the direction of the graduate and thinking about her stated desire to make contact with the minister and/or the secretary.

'We'll touch base at…'

They both looked at their watches.

'Twelve-thirty?' suggested Morton.

'Twelve-thirty,' Alan agreed.

Both men believed the task before them to be an important one to which they were uniquely suited, and both proceeded, in very different ways, to the same end.

At twelve thirty-five, as Alan was part-way through his last call, Morton returned with an A4 sheet. He sat and waited for Alan to finish.

'Twenty-two willing to play it our way,' he announced when Alan was free. 'One whereabouts unknown in south-east Asia, one in police custody, likely to be bailed later today, and three messages left. One problem child, Professor Kllppin, determined to go his own way.'

'Well done,' said Alan. 'I've spoken to nineteen, left messages for three, couldn't make contact of any kind with another two and encountered three rebels who've promised me to hold off on independent action until the acting minister has had a go.'

'And I received a surprising amount of unsolicited advice on cleaning up crap,' said Morton, 'instruction of the real and metaphorical sorts – plus offers of air freshener, stain remover, a big breed doggie poo scoop, some man nappies and basic tips on how to tell the difference between a desk and a dunny.'

'I also had cleaning advice,' Alan said, 'in addition to grumbling and lamentation.'

'It takes all types,' said Morton, mopping his forehead with a tissue.

"I'll let Quentin know about the uncooperative ones.'

'And I'll have a shower,' Morton pointed silently in the direction of his undercarriage, 'before repairing to an air-conditioned lunch venue.'

'Your phone?' asked Alan, nodding, again, in the direction of the graduate.

'Diverted to voicemail.'

'Excellent.'

Alan sent an email to Quentin Quist indicating that the task was largely done and naming the four recusants. He then turned his mind to the graduate: could she be safely left alone over the lunch period? He thought not. Yet there was, perhaps, a way he could yet be free to visit Bonnie Brae.

'I have a lunchtime commitment,' said Alan to the young woman, 'and, in consequence, I need to raise a somewhat delicate matter with you.'

'Is it about change facilitation or risk?' asked the graduate, eagerly.

'Yes, in a sense, I suppose it is.'

'Then I should be able to help you,' she said, leaning forward.

'I rather hope you can,' said Alan. 'You see, I need a promise from you.'

'A promise?'

'Yes. I need your promise that you won't, while I'm away, attempt to call the acting minister or the secretary…'

The graduate thought about the undertaking she was being asked to give, calculating the opportunities she was being asked to forgo and wondering how their forfeiture would impede her ascent to the very top.

'…or any of the deputy secretaries…'

'Yes.'

'…or first assistant secretaries…'

The graduate saw her prospects of making an early splash diminished with each additional proscription.

'…or any assistant secretaries.'

And finally saw them incontrovertibly dashed. 'But I could speak to them if they rang me, couldn't I?' she asked.

Alan was conscious of his shirt clinging to his back, of sweat pooling at his belt line and of an intensifying desire to claw at his nether regions. He switched his computer off as he spoke. 'I think they're unlikely to do that at this early stage of your career, especially as they don't yet know you're here to assist them.' Alan knew, immediately, that he'd said too much. 'And it would not be wise to proclaim you arrival by broadcast email. There is a rule against unauthorised "whole of department", "whole of division" and "whole of branch" emails.'

'But I haven't signed up to any rules,' said the graduate, 'and no one has brought any email protocols to my attention.'

Warm air caressed Alan's bald spot.

'They're a condition of your employment, nonetheless, and I have now told you about them, so you can't claim – not that it would assist you – that you didn't know.'

'Are there other rules I don't know about that I need to know about?'

'Rather a lot, in fact, and I'll tell you about them in a moment. In the meantime, I need to know if I can rely on you not to send any department-wide or division-wide messages saying, "I'm here for you."'

'I won't, if it really isn't permitted.'

'I can assure you that it isn't.'

'Then, no, I won't be bulk messaging.'

'And can I safely assume that you'll not be emailing the acting minister or members of the executive…to alert them to your expertise and to encourage contact?'

'What about the other dos and don'ts?' said the graduate, sidestepping the question.

'There are, as I've already indicated, quite a lot of them,' said Alan. 'I'd start with the ones that are about your rights and obligations as an officer and employee: the twenty statutes and related regulations, the directions, rules and instruments, the industrial agreements and then the various policies, guidelines and procedures referred to in it.' He began transferring the relevant folders from his cubicle shelf onto the graduate's desktop.

'But getting back to my question,' he continued, 'can I safely assume that you won't be emailing the acting minister or members of the executive? Because, if you can't give me an undertaking, I will have to give you a formal direction…and I haven't had cause to issue one of those in more than thirty years.'

The pile of folders containing the employment-related information started to teeter.

'Not if it's going to cause trouble,' said the graduate, steadying the pile. 'Am I really expected to be familiar with all of these?'

'I'm not finished yet,' said Alan, starting a second stack.

'So many of them,' said the graduate, looking despondent. 'How does anyone…'

'Every file begins with a single folio,' said Alan, adding more folders to the rising store.

The graduate did not appear to be comforted by the aphorism, so Alan tried again. 'Every journey begins with a single step.'

'Maybe I should have selected a different journey,' said the graduate, now looking distraught.

'I don't know that things will be very much different in any other department,' Alan said, adding still more folders.

'I meant the private sector.'

'Ah, yes, the private sector. I understand things can be very different there – and sometimes not.'

The graduate reached for a tissue. She looked to be defeated. Alan thought that, perhaps, he'd revealed too much, too soon.

'But regulation,' he said, balancing one last folder on top of the second teetering pile, 'is as much our friend as our enemy.'

The graduate wiped a tear away.

Alan was not a man lacking in empathy. 'You'll feel better after you've had something to eat,' he said in a kindly tone.

'I don't know that I will.'

'Did you have something on the plane?'

'Not very much,' she answered in a tiny voice.

'Page 47 of the Committee Members' Guide is what you want: local restaurants reviewed by Morton and then, over the page, the more modest eateries – coffee bars and such – reviewed by me.'

The yellow cover of the guide poked out from under the mountain of folders. Alan wondered if he shouldn't try the French waiter's table cloth trick.

'No, I think I'll go out and find a gym,' said the graduate, pulling herself together.

Alan was quite sure there were no gymnasia in the guide. The committee members were all beyond any pretence of physical fitness.

'Well, enjoy,' he said, without any confidence that pleasure was the desired goal.

16

Antonia Ainsworth gave no indication that she recognised Alan from the morning before. Although most of the other occupants of the lift were well known to him, no one spoke to Alan in the presence of the woman who, until a few hours before, had been their acting secretary. It was always thus: silence in the presence of the gods (who must have thought their underlings strangely incapable of the smallest talk).

As they arrived at the ground floor, Alan was surprised to feel a hand on his shoulder, to detect the aldehyde top notes of Chanel Number Five and hear Toni whisper in his ear, 'It will never be found, Alan. Not until hell freezes over.'

He nodded understanding. His peers, thinking that they'd witnessed an exchange of some importance, looked at him with heightened respect.

At the security barriers, he brushed his access pass over the sensor. The gate refused to open. He would have tried a second time but for the flashing light and beeping that emanated from within the closest pylons. The noise and display both ceased at the approach of a hefty female guard – short-haired with a silver nose ring – who asked Alan to step to one side. His first thought was that Rasch had found evidence of an incriminating sort and that he – Alan – was, at last, undone.

He was steered to the security desk.

'It's the T10 for Security 1,' said the female guard.

Her male companion grunted and stabbed numbers into the telephone base.

Alan's pulse raced, his mouth was dry and he wanted to both vomit and scratch. What would now happen to him? Would he be taken somewhere, to await the arrival of the police? And what would his workmates say when they saw him on TV, arriving at court with his cardigan pulled over his head? He could only be thankful that Aunty Vi had long since passed on and that Hugo was oblivious to world events. Neither of them would have to share the burden of his terrible shame.

Just as importantly, what would happen to his pension? The urge to vomit now superseded the desire to scratch. He tried breathing deeply and then burped a number of times. The two guards looked at him with unbridled suspicion. A T10, he thought, must have been a rather bad thing to have become.

'Security 1, Roger to your T10,' said the male guard. 'We have Alan Mewling, a Caucasian male, early sixties, eighty kilos, one hundred and sixty centimetres, currently detained without restraints or force at location 6, repeat location 6, awaiting your further orders, over.'

Alan might have bridled in other circumstances at being described as early sixties when he was still days short of fifty-five, but he'd always been thought to be older than he was and consistency in this respect brought, strangely, a sense of normalcy to an otherwise abnormal situation. Looking at the uncluttered desk top, he suspected that by being less dangerous or notorious than a T11 or 12, yet more interesting than a T9 or his normal quotidian self, he'd briefly added spice to an otherwise dull day for the two guards.

'Say again, over.'

Colleagues passed backwards and forwards, all avoiding eye contact, not wanting to know.

'Roger that,' said the guard on the phone.

Alan wondered if anyone would visit him in prison. Who, he worried, would keep an eye on Hugo if he was incarcerated for a long spell? Who would make sure the old chap ate his lentils? Who would read to him from the newspaper?

The female guard looked questioningly at her companion.

'After a quick word, he's free to go,' said the male guard, beckoning Alan close. 'Security 1,' he added, in a low voice, for Alan's benefit, 'will meet you at your car.'

Alan gaped at him in bewildered surprise. The female guard meanwhile looked Alan up and down; yes, he might be released but he would never again be innocent.

'At your car,' the male guard repeated.

'Thank you,' said Alan without due cause.

At his vehicle, he paused before getting in. There was no white sedan nearby but, as he slipped behind the wheel, Rasch emerged through the sliding side door of a green Mercedes van parked in the next bay. He was wearing polaroids, a hat and a long, grey beard.

'I expected you more than an hour ago,' said the security head, getting into the back of Alan's vehicle. 'What have you been doing?'

'Unavoidably detained,' said Alan, without irony.

'This vehicle doesn't have a radio?' asked Rasch, looking at the expanse of uncluttered dash.

Alan was aware, thanks to TV, that secondary noise sources were often used to confuse listening devices at clandestine meetings. 'We could talk in yours,' he said, nodding in the direction of the van

'No. Drive away,' said Rasch, looking out the back window at the cars in the row behind.

'You know I'm going to Bonny Brae?'

'We can't talk here.'

Again, Alan suspected that a game he had no recollection of playing was well and truly up. He deduced that Rasch was either going to bargain with him for a confession or give him a chance to escape, for old time's sake. He was, however, disinclined to flight. Where would he go? Asia? South America? How would he survive? And how could a man who'd spent his entire working life in the bureaucracy – a man thoroughly (or mostly) convinced of the merits of a career civil service – how could such a man fail to stand out in countries desperate for efficient, impartial public administration? If forced to choose between flight and confession, he'd own up, even though he still had no recollection of committing the crime.

'Drive off,' said Rasch, crouching down in the seat, so as not to be sighted by any onlookers.

The speed with which Alan pulled on his driving gloves probably persuaded Rasch that he was possessed of the necessary urgency. The usual bumpy ride probably convinced him that they were doing more than seventy kilometres per hour, at which point the Morris Minor was capable of more but its driver was not.

When they were clear of the campus, Rasch sat up and peered out of the back window, again. Alan was given no instructions to 'Step on it' or to take any sudden turns, so concluded that they had made good their escape.

'I didn't see anyone watching or following us,' he said.

'The best policy is always to suppose you're being watched.' Rasch sat up but kept the hat, the sunglasses and false beard on. 'There have been developments,' he said.

'I see,' said Alan, preparing himself for the worst.

'At first I concluded that it must have been one of the cleaners.'

This possibility wasn't one that had previously occurred to Alan. Why would the cleaners foul their own domain? If, however, it was true, he would be greatly relieved – and thankful that there was no longer a need to bone up on the geography of Paraguay or the declension of Laotian adverbs.

'They have access and they're around after hours.'

'That's true,' said Alan.

'But you're wondering why?'

'I am,' Alan admitted.

'Put up to it by Burgoyne, I'd assumed, as part of a plan to heighten his own importance and to prevail over me – to put me to the test.'

'But, if that's true,' said Alan, 'it could have happened at any desk… in any branch.'

'I thought that too, until I went to the Contracts Section this morning and looked at the cleaning complaints file.' Rasch nodded to himself. 'One hundred and seventy-three complaints across the department in the last twelve months.'

'How extraordinary,' said Alan.

'And ninety-seven of them lodged by Quentin Quist.'

'Astounding,' said Alan.

'More than half of the departmental total from just one man.'

'Complaints about?'

Rasch pulled a list from his pocket. 'Inadequate vacuuming, dust on bookshelves, mop marks on kitchen floors, paper towels packed too tightly in the restroom dispensers, rubbish residue in bins, scum in the washbasins, grime on restroom doors, slime on the urinal outlet, accreted glug on door handles, excreta residue in toilet bowls, smells of many and various sorts –'

'Enough,' said Alan. 'I follow.' Waves of nausea flooded over his sterile promontories.

'So the cleaners certainly had a motive or motives,' Rasch continued. 'But then I heard from the contract manager – and you need to keep this under your hat, absolutely hush-hush – that a second turd was discovered last night.'

They veered dangerously to the left. Alan jerked the car back on course and Rasch lurched onto his left shoulder.

'Discovered early in the shift, by one of the senior cleaners, in the eighth-floor conference rooms.'

This was potentially excellent news because, although Alan still feared that he might, on Christmas Eve, have left faecal matter on the desk that was about to become Quentin Quist's, he thought it most unlikely that he'd delivered different faeces in different places on the one drunken occasion.

'Was it' – fresh didn't seem to be an appropriate descriptor for a substance which, by its nature, was always residual – 'did it look to be recently…?'

'Whether it was delivered recently or some time ago hasn't been established because we haven't been able to locate it.'

'Two faeces missing in two days,' thought Alan. 'How can that be?'

'And there are problems communicating with the fellow who found it.'

Alan had a fair idea what these difficulties were about, for when there was an Indian test match on TV, cleaners were as scarce as taxi drivers.

'He had a heart attack on sighting the thing.'

A light went on for Alan and he recalled the man on the stretcher who'd preceded him to the ambulance on the previous afternoon.

'He had a heart attack because he found faecal matter?' Alan asked.

'I assume it was the shock, after Burgoyne's irresponsible talk vis-à-vis the hazards associated with the original turd. I told you, didn't I, that he had the cleaners on alert last night, ready to cry Henny Penny at the faintest whiff of poo?'

'Booraserp,' said Alan recalling the words the agitated cleaner had repeated from under his oxygen mask.

'That's right,' said Rasch. 'Those were the exact words he was said to have used. How did you know?'

'I saw it all.'

'You saw the second turd?' asked Rasch.

'No, I saw the cleaner carried from the building.'

'Oh.'

'What does booraserp mean, anyway?' asked Alan.

'Brown snake, according to one of his colleagues: exactly how people around the world, regardless of their culture, describe a turd.'

'There is no doubt about brown?'

'I'm informed that he is quite definite about the colour.'

Brown was better than good for Alan, for brown spoke of recent provenance and Alan was certain that he had not vacated his bowels in recent days on departmental premises. Brown thus contributed to the increasing weight of evidence in favour of his innocence of the original atrocity and was, in consequence, the very best colour a subsequent turd could be…unless a copycat perpetrator had commenced work less than twenty-four hours after the discovery of the original faeces, and 'it' had been his (Alan's), after all.

'While I was reading the contract file,' Rasch said, 'a relative of the cleaner rang from the hospital accusing the department of harbouring reptiles on Commonwealth premises: "brown" and "snake", however, mean something very different to me.'

'Quite so,' said Alan.

'Before meeting you, I searched every chair and desktop on the eighth floor in vain but couldn't find it. I'm going to speak to the patient, as soon as I've got the medical and legal clearances.'

They turned into the car park at Bonnie Brae and Alan wondered why Rasch had, once again, revealed developments to him. He wondered, too, which turd Toni had been referring to in the lift.

'I'll try not to be too long,' he said.

'No, I'll come in,' said Rasch. 'No point in sitting here…without air conditioning or a radio.'

'These places,' warned Alan, 'are not for the faint-hearted.'

'In what way?' asked Rasch.

'This is our future,' said Alan, 'barring nasty cancers, coronaries and fatal accidents.'

'All the more reason for me to come in.'

Alan's conscience told him that further discouragement was the proper thing but he knew also that Rasch's presence might prevent recurrence of certain rituals in the other bed. He could, at a pinch, concede that Clyde Adams had once been a true ginger – there was little psychological cost in that – but any additional rites or observances were beyond him, after the trials of the morning.

They signed in at the front desk and were admitted through the one-way doors.

'Just like work,' said Rasch cheerfully.

An elderly male wearing a red wig – perhaps he, too, had once been a true ginger – and a tartan gown, fixed on Rasch within metres of the door. 'Have you found the file?' the old man asked.

'We're looking for it, now,' said Alan, accustomed to dealing with the demented.

'Even more like work,' said Rasch when they were out of hearing distance.

'It's best not to make eye contact,' said Alan.

Within a few metres of the second door, an elderly woman in a cocktail frock and floral apron had equally specific enquiries to make. 'I don't suppose either of you nice young men would like to play with my bunny's nose?' she asked.

'Not today, Dora,' said Alan, 'but put me down for next week.'

'And your friend?'

'Schedule him in, too.'

Entries were made in a notebook recovered from the apron pocket and they were free to continue their journey.

'How did she know my name?' asked Rasch, 'to slot me in.'

'She doesn't need to know it,' said Alan. 'She only needs to feel necessary.'

'The similarities keep coming,' said Rasch.

'Really?' Alan enquired.

'Actually, that last experience was more like a marriage than work.'

'I don't follow,' said Alan.

'The scheduling,' said Rasch.

Alan was relieved of the need to make clarifying enquiries about this last remark by their arrival at the room shared by Clyde Adams and Hugo Faggoter. Both residents were *in situ*: in almost the same positions they'd occupied at the time of Alan's departure, the day before. Hugo was staring upward as usual and Clyde was facing the wall. To the trained eye there would only have been two things obviously different about the tableau: the front page of the paper hanging off Hugo's bed rail and the text on the clipboard attached to his bed end. On the latter, instead of the usual charts and tables, with their indecipherable scrawl and notations, was a message in large black letters intelligible to both visitors from the doorway. It read, 'Alan M to see Matron.'

Alan directed Rasch into the chair furthest away from Clyde Adams and whispered, 'I have to see the woman in charge. You can talk to Hugo or read him the "To Let" advertisements from the paper. They're the ones he seems to most appreciate. But don't engage with the chap in the other bed.'

'Got it,' said Rasch, peering at Clyde Adams.

'Not even if he pleads,' said Alan.

'Roger that,' said Rasch, peering even more intently at Adams.

17

Alan found the matron in the alcove which, separated from the hallway by a screen, doubled as her office.

'Hugo has been talking,' she said.

Alan thought, straight away, of gangster films in which an announcement to the effect that someone had been communicative could trigger plans for a rubbing out, a hit or a ride, in contrast to a statement to the opposite effect, prompting the encouragement of squealing, singing or general loquaciousness.

'Was he saying anything in particular?' Alan enquired.

'He seems to be saying the same thing over and over again.'

Alan reflected on Hugo's life and attributes. 'He can be a bit persistent on matters to do with French food and lawn maintenance,' he offered.

'Of course.'

'However, I wouldn't say he was ever one for pointless repetition.'

The director of nursing took a file from the draw to her right and reviewed the top folio. 'It was originally thought he was saying "hooray".'

'Repeatedly?'

'Yes.'

'That is odd,' said Alan.

Reiterated expressions of joy didn't seem consistent with Hugo's circumstances – nothing about his nursing home life called for celebration – and irrational elation hadn't been part of his persona at any earlier time. Indeed, he'd personified the lugubriousness thought to be appropriate in senior public servants of his era…and which Alan still regarded as preferable to the unrelenting, inane glass half full optimism of bureaucrats of more recent times.

'But then a number of us positioned ourselves close to him and turned off the TV,' said Matron.

'And you heard?'

The director of nursing sighed. '"The wave", "the wake", "the hate", even "the ace", before we finally settled on "the haste".'

The popular choice reminded Alan of the names of vulgar music ensembles of his youth.

'"The haste?" Are you sure?'

'Yes, I definitely heard "the haste" and so did two of the other staff.'

'"The haste", "the haste",' Alan murmured. Hugo couldn't claim that there was anything approaching urgency in the rhythm of turnings and meal deliveries that were – bed changes and ablutions aside – the high points of his daily routine. Alan also mused that haste was not considered a desirable concomitant to sound decision making in the public service of Hugo's time and that, in his autumnal years, too, the old boy had been determined to do things in his own good time, abhorring any unnecessary rush.

'Any condemnation of haste would make sense on a number of levels,' Alan concluded, 'but is it usual for someone to attempt speech after years of silence?'

'I'd have to say it is most unusual.'

'I see.'

'Most unusual, indeed.'

Alan pondered this judgement. What was to be done next? Hugo had always chosen his words with the utmost care. Should he now be encouraged to say more, if his utterances were mere incoherent remnants of past communications: words or phrases randomly detaching themselves from a dwindling store of daydreams, imaginings and memories, no longer corralled by inhibitions or etiquette or any sense of propriety? Alan thought not but, as usual, he would set his store by the judgement of experts.

'I've consulted a psycho-geriatrician,' said the director of nursing, 'and he is of the view that while Hugo is unlikely to interact, again, in any meaningful way, oral self-expression may reduce the anger that he presented with when he first came to us…and which we've been dealing with pharmacologically ever since.'

Alan recalled that there had been an incident a couple of weeks after Hugo's arrival at Bonnie Brae, involving lunchtime lentils in flight – but would he have described this as demonstrative of anger? Again, he thought not: who wouldn't, after a time, have rejected the same food served the same way, every day? Still, he supposed the staff couldn't be expected to go about their duties under threat of airborne vegetarian sludge. Stupefaction had probably been for the best.

'So we're going to reduce his antipsychotics, give him some antidepressants and think about some stimuli…which is where you come in.'

'Yes,' Alan said, sitting up to indicate that he was both engaged and ready to assist, even if experts had previously held him responsible for the diminution in Hugo's interest in the wider world.

'It would be helpful for us to know something about his interests, because there don't seem to be any entries against "hobbies" in his admission papers, except… Well, I can't quite decipher…'

She turned a file on the table around, so that Alan could read the opening page. Her finger guided attention to a field headed 'Hobbies and pastimes' against which there was a smudged entry in an unrecognisable hand.

Alan studied the text from a number of angles before revealing its secret. 'I believe it says "euphonist".'

'"Euphonist", of course. How clever of you,' said Matron, looking at the text more closely than before.

'Yes, almost definitely,' said Alan.

'And what would a euphonist be or do?'

'Think musical instruments,' said Alan.

'Instead of "euphemisms: proponent of"?'

Alan smiled in case the enquiry was intended to be jocular. 'Appropriate as that may be, no, it's definitely musical.'

Matron silently mouthed the word "euphonist" a number of times, then thought for a while, before shaking her head. 'A hint?' she asked.

'Think horn.'

They both recalled the unsavoury habits of the true ginger.

'Brass, instead of wood,' said Alan in a helpful tone oblivious to any double entendre.

'Brass as in oompah pah?'

'Brass as in oompah pah.'

'Oompah pah brass as in this?' She played an invisible trombone, vigorously working the slide.

'Shorter,' said Alan, getting into the spirit of things.

'As in this, then?' She played an invisible trumpet.

'Fatter,' said Alan.

'Fatter,' she mused, before gripping an imaginary saxophone. 'Fatter as in this?' She improvised expertly.

'Wider,' Alan clarified.

'Fatter and wider. Wider. Are you sure?'

'Quite sure.'

She thought for a few moments. 'No, I have to admit, I'm stumped.'

Alan tucked an imaginary euphonium under his right arm and, although he'd not produced a note on any instrument at any time in his life, tootled cheerfully away. 'Four valves, like the trumpet,' he said, 'with tubing gradually increasing in diameter to an upright bell.'

'I can't see it,' admitted the director of nursing.

Alan shrugged. 'Well, I wouldn't say it was a popular instrument relative to say, the cornet or the flugelhorn, but it was Mr Faggotter's instrument of choice.'

'Would you say that he was passionate about playing it?'

'I don't know that he was passionate about it but he could certainly get agitated if people called a euphonium a baritone.'

'What's the difference?' Matron asked, more out of courtesy than interest.

'The number of valves: four in a euphonium, three in a baritone.'

She had expected a more interesting answer. 'But he wasn't, you say, passionate about the playing of it?'

Alan recalled what he could about Hugo's state of mind when playing the euphonium. 'I think he found it engrossing and satisfying but was he passionate? No, definitely not.'

The look on Matron's face said 'Probably just as well', presumably because she didn't imagine that the playing of the wider, fatter underarm instrument, even in an understated way, would have a calming effect on her other charges.

'So what was he excited about?'

'I don't that think that excitement was encouraged in his day.'

'Then was there something…anything that he enjoyed doing?'

'He liked talking about great French restaurants he'd visited…'

Matron raised a disapproving eyebrow.

'…and he liked French cuisine, accompanied by fine wines.'

'I don't think he'll be getting haute cuisine or fine wine here, do you?'

'I think he also enjoyed waging war on a lawn pest called the scarab bug.'

'We had our lawn cemented over last year,' said Matron, 'as an economy measure.'

'Lawns can be expensive,' said Alan.

'What about his employment?' Matron enquired.

'He certainly spent a lot of time at it, before he retired,' said Alan.

'And then?'

'He never talked about it again.'

'Oh dear. Perhaps we'd better return to the euphonium.'

'Yes,' said Alan. 'I have his instrument – a Besson Prestige – in its case, safe in the garage. I could give it a polish and bring it in, in the morning.'

'That's good,' said Matron, not at all keen, 'but I think we should begin with some recorded music, don't you? And see if that prompts any response. Then, if that goes well, we could consider giving him the instrument itself.'

'Of course,' said Alan, irrationally disappointed.

'Do you have any CDs of relevant virtuosi? We could play them to him on a portable device, through earphones.'

There weren't, so far as Alan was aware, many works for the solo euphonium or for duos, trios and quartets. The instrument was one the virtues of which were best displayed without accompaniment or in the company of its own kind.

'I think there are some brass band records in the Faggoter collection.'

'Vinyl?' asked Matron, perhaps expecting to be told 'shellac'.

'Regrettably, yes,' said Alan, expecting to be disappointed.

'No, we can do 33⅓. It's the 78s we have trouble with. We have a turntable in the recreation room. I'll have the handyman move it into Hugo's room in the morning and you could come at, perhaps, lunchtime.'

'Lunchtime would be fine,' said Alan, feeling relieved that there would be no need for martial music before midday.

Matron closed the file, signalling that the discussion was over. 'We have a plan,' she said.

'We do,' said Alan even though experience told him that planning was a mostly futile activity.

'Are you going to look in on Hugo before you leave?'

'A colleague who came with me is with him,' Alan answered.

A worried look crossed Matron's face. 'Then let's walk together,' she said.

Past silent wards – rooms where shells of human beings were fed and turned and toileted because that was all that remained to be done for them – Matron and Alan made their way back to the room shared by Hugo Faggoter and Clyde Adams.

Matron's shoes squeaked on the shiny linoleum, and the huge metal spoon swung back and forth from her belt. A waft of disinfectant reassured Alan that when his time came he'd have little to fear but commercial broadcasting and the bodily indignities and duration of the final phases.

As the pair neared their destination, Alan thought he heard the words 'our secret' above the noise of the nearby televisions. Matron heard them, too, and a look of reluctant understanding passed between them.

In the room, Hector Rasch sat in the chair next to Clyde Adams's bed, staring vacantly at a point on the opposite wall where there was not so much as a Namatjira or a Bristol stool chart to warrant attention. He seemed not to notice the new arrivals.

Alan waved his arms about to attract Rasch's attention but the replacement supplicant saw nothing. A second look passed between the director of nursing and Alan but they both knew there was nothing to be done after the event.

Matron approached the clipboard at the end of Hugo Faggoter's bed and removed the note left earlier for Alan. At the same time, Clyde Adams looked Alan in the eye and mouthed the words 'our secret, too' while pulling the tray table up to protect the blanketed area immediately over his groin.

'No more warnings for Clyde,' said Matron, straightening the sheet under Hugo Faggoter's chin. 'His days in the sun are over.'

The miscreant gripped the edge of the tray table, anticipating the deployment of the giant spoon but no punishment was forthcoming. Instead, Matron knelt in front of Rasch and looked into his eyes.

'Is he going to be all right?' Alan asked.

'A strong cup of tea, with lots of sugar, and he'll be fine.'

'Then we'll be on our way,' said Alan, conscious of the time.

Matron walked with the men to the reception area beyond the last of the security doors and waited quietly with Rasch while Alan brought the car around.

'Until tomorrow,' she said, 'when we will acquaint ourselves with the euphonist's art.'

Alan surprised himself with a flamboyant tootling motion. 'Until then,' he said.

18

The official mobile phone Alan was required to carry while on higher duties started ringing as they pulled out of Bonnie Brae. He wouldn't have expected Rasch to answer the device while incognito and had no expectation that he would deal with it while still dazed by events in the nursing home. Alan certainly had no intention of breaking the law by answering it himself while at the wheel. It rang out four times before an unsettling and unexpected chime announced that someone – presumably the caller – had sent a text message.

At that point, Alan pulled over to the side of the road, removed his gloves, replaced his driving glasses with his reading ones, and recovered both the unit and its instruction booklet from his top pocket. He read aloud the most pertinent directions, cursing his lack of dexterity as he followed them, to finally view the message. It was from Quentin Quist and the initial sentence was all capitals: WHY WONT YO ANSWER YUR PHONE?

Alan thought about responding to this question but knew the process to be one procedurally beyond him. He read on. 'Send flowrs give simpathy before you return offic so I have a announcible.'

'I think Quentin Quist wants a floral tribute and sympathy,' he informed Rasch, 'so he can tell the senior executive that the branch empathises with him in a time of crisis.'

'Saving it for later,' Rasch murmured, looking straight ahead.

'Or maybe he wants me to send the bouquet to Valerie,' Alan mused. He reread the message. 'Yes, that must be it.' He looked at Rasch. 'Will we find a flower shop?' he asked.

'Our secret,' said Rasch.

'Good. We'll do that, then.'

Alan put on his gloves and glasses, and drove to a nearby shopping centre which he knew to host a florist. When they arrived, he slotted the vehicle into the first available space. 'Will you be all right here, while I duck inside?'

'The vigour,' Rasch murmured. 'The terrible vigour.'

'Yes, quite,' said Alan, making no sense of this pronouncement at all. 'I won't be long.'

Inside the shop, the florescent display was made unremarkable by flashing hats and canes, and brightly coloured inflatable objects on sticks. A threadbare, man-sized gorilla clutching a sign that read 'I'll deliver for you' sat on a stool next to the cash register. Alan wondered why anyone would open the door to someone dressed as a silverback.

He nevertheless managed to negotiate the dispatch of a large bunch of the brightest, most cheerful blooms to Valerie, Pango, Pogo and Popsy at the holiday address earlier noted in his pocketbook. He wrote a message on a tiny card that failed to mention ectopic excretion but, instead, expressed the hope that the branch head would enjoy her holiday. The cost, including delivery, was probably well in excess of the sum collected earlier in the day but Alan thought this small act of defiance to have been worth the investment.

Buoyed by his disobedience, Alan repaired to the café next door with a view to acquiring a celebratory pair of curried egg sandwiches and two cups of tea. All of the ready-made offerings seemed to contain pesto or grilled bell peppers, and nothing resembling sliced white bread was an advertised possibility. Similarly, there seemed to be nothing on the list of fillings that vaguely resembled egg or curry. Worse still, Alan had to choose between twelve different varieties of tea before the transaction was complete. Yet, he eventually returned to the car with ham and cheese toasted focaccias – pesto and charred strips of slimy capsicum politely but firmly declined – and tea in paper cups.

'Take this,' he said to Rasch, offering him Twining's English Breakfast: black with four sugars and enough added tap water to make the liquid immediately drinkable. 'It will do you good.'

Rasch said and did nothing.

Alan took off the lid – he never trusted them to remain in place – then held the cup up to Rasch's unresponsive lips. 'Come on, old thing, do give it a try.'

The liquid mostly dribbled down the other man's chin onto his shirt, but enough went into his mouth for him to taste the sweetness so that, when Alan offered the cup a second time, he assisted with swallowing and, finally, held the vessel unaided.

Alan placed the focaccias on the rear seat, then drove off. 'Soon we'll be back at work,' he said, 'and you can't let others see you like this. You have to pull yourself together.'

Rasch stared vacantly ahead.

'Life goes on,' Alan said, thinking about the ways in which the inexorable rhythms of things could be best illustrated to the benefit of the passenger. 'Policies continue to be formulated, implemented and monitored, meetings continue to be convened, minutes are written, and plans continue to be devised and never implemented.'

Rasch appeared no more engaged.

Alan almost added, for shock effect, 'Desks continue to be despoiled and serpentine turds continue to be discovered by cleaners in meeting rooms,' but decided to stay his tongue. Yet, in those unspoken words, he realised, might yet lie the key to Rasch's revitalisation. The problem was, though, that use of the key could yet lead to his own undoing.

At the penultimate traffic lights before reaching the department, he pondered this conundrum. Remotivating Rasch, if it resulted in the security director's return to a normal state, was an undoubtedly desirable thing, but what if it led to his (Alan's) own apprehension as the faecant? For how long could he, in good conscience, refrain from use of the restorative tool – having exposed, as it were, Rasch to Clive Adams – even if it ultimately placed his own reputation at risk?

With the department tower blocks in sight and without any improvement in Rasch's condition, the need to make a decision became urgent. Alan once again pulled over to the side of the road, prompting honking horns and rude gestures from drivers in more modern vehicles.

He unlocked his seat belt, reviewed his options and turned to his passenger. 'Hector' – Alan had never before used Rasch's given name and hoped that it might prove to be a breakthrough tactic – 'can you hear me?'

No response.

'Have you any appointments this afternoon, Hector?'

He hoped to reset the security director's psyche by focusing on the demands of the immediate future, but, once again, there was no response. Rasch sat as mute and as unreachable as ever and Alan knew that he had, at last, no option but to speak about the matter he'd hoped to avoid any mention of.

'The person,' Alan began, quietly, 'who left excreta on Valerie Venables's desktop, and who would seem to have left faecal matter elsewhere in our building on a subsequent occasion, is still at large.'

Rasch stirred almost imperceptibly.

'That perpetrator,' Alan continued, affecting the language that Rasch would most relate to, 'could strike again at any moment.'

Rasch's brow furrowed.

'They could be at their dastardly work as we speak and if you are not on the case – employing all of your wit and energy, your skill and experience, your guile and cunning – to apprehend them, we remain at their mercy…'

Rasch turned his head towards Alan. In his eyes was the faintest glimmer of recognition.

'…never knowing whether and when we will arrive at our workstations, at our desks or at our meeting tables to find more…faeces.'

Rasch's upper lip curled.

'And that person will go on doing what he – or she, because it might well be a she – has been doing, encouraged by the notoriety he or she has earned, by the scorn they have caused to be heaped upon us…'

Rasch's jaw clenched.

'…and by the shame which has accrued to every last one of us, tainting our souls, infecting our spirits, feeding on our insecurities and permeating every aspect of our being like the ineradicable stench of…'

Alan tried to think of the worst things he'd ever smelt – perhaps a

Third World turd stone; dog faeces in a locked, hot car; a flyblown sheep; unaerated compost; vomit; freshly ground mozzarella; or rotting nappies.

'…like the ineradicable stench of burning flesh,' he finally announced.

Rasch gulped. 'Christ!' he said, huskily. 'Burning flesh.'

'Yes,' said Alan, recalling the sack of Rome, a departmental barbecue and the incineration of Dresden.

Eye contact was made and swiftly broken.

'The department needs you, Hector,' said Alan softly.

'Yes,' said Rasch.

'The service needs you.'

'Of course,' Rasch answered.

'The nation needs you.'

'Absolutely.'

And it was at this point that Alan played his ace card. 'And without you, the Burgoynes of this world and all they stand for' – Alan had, in fact, no idea what Burgoyne stood for post-Gorbachev, other than a substantial increase in the daily allowance paid to workplace health and safety representatives – 'all that they stand for, will prevail and we will be plunged into eternal darkness.'

'Never,' said Rasch, fixing Alan with a look of the steeliest determination. 'Not while there Is one last breath in me.'

Alan drove the last 800 metres into the departmental car park. Before the car had come to a halt, Rasch was out the door, without any pretence of secrecy, and gone.

Alan bit into one of the focaccias as he walked across the car park and could taste basil and garlic. He rather supposed he was tasting pesto and it wasn't all that bad.

The automatic doors to the building were wedged open and the two guards who had earlier apprehended Alan barely gave him a second glance as he walked past them and through the security gates.

If he was not mistaken, it was hotter inside than out and warmer even than it had been before he left.

As he walked past Carol's office, Daphne announced, without looking up from the papers she was sorting, 'Mr Quist has been looking for you, Mr Mewling, and it's nearly ten to three.'

If heads hadn't turned in the nearest bay, Alan wouldn't have bothered with an explanation, even though it had been many years since he'd last returned late from a lunch break.

'I didn't get out until late and then Quentin asked me to organise Valerie's flowers.'

Daphne continued sorting.

Quentin Quist wasn't in his office, so Alan continued to his desk. Morton was wearing a pair of dark blue satin shorts and was so engrossed in the department's media page, that he didn't notice his supervisor's arrival. However, on hearing Alan's wallet and keys returned to their customary place in his top drawer, he also announced, without looking up, that Quentin Quist had been in pursuit.

Alan wondered whether he should deal with the matter of the shorts immediately or wait until Morton offered an explanation.

'I borrowed them from Mankiewicz,' said Morton, as though reading Alan's mind. 'Easier access to the itchy fundamentals.'

Alan decided that for the moment, bearing in mind the medical dimension to the situation, no response was the best response. Besides, he'd noticed that the graduate was not at her desk.

'No idea,' said Morton, still not looking up.

'But she came back from lunch?' Alan asked.

'Definitely, but Quentin gave her a copy of the department's risk management plan, and soon after – while I was on the phone – she shot off towards the lifts, whereabouts unknown.'

'Perhaps she went to Personnel,' said Alan, 'to sign a contract.'

'With the pessimist's primer in hand?'

Alan's anxiety levels began a steady climb to familiar heights. The undertakings he'd sought from Eris before lunch might not, he mused, have been comprehensive enough to protect the department's risk gurus from interrogation and judgement. Alan turned to his machine for reassurance.

'I see that someone has called a halt to media opportunities,' Morton said, 'seeing as we are now front-page regulars.'

Alan's brightening screen was accompanied by an increase in the velocity of warm air being pushed down from the vents in the false ceiling. He turned the machine off, straight away, and heard the air conditioning cease. Cheers rose from all sides.

He counted silently to five and, when certain that Morton wasn't watching, depressed the button again. To the accompaniment of groans and cursing, the flow recommenced but at a much reduced rate. Morton, head still down, absent-mindedly scratched his crotch from the outside, seeming to have noticed nothing.

Alan opened his In box, hoping for a cheery 'I've just ducked down to Personnel' from the absent staff member but found, instead, an urgent message from Quentin Quist. 'That awful woman – the one who knows everything – I don't want her in my office again. YOU MUST KEP CONTROL OF YOR STAFF. You are a manager. Mange.'

On the bright side, Alan mused, the torrent of messages about the previous day's events had subsided to a trickle and a couple of his missing committee members had communicated their willingness to leave the defence of their reputations to the acting minister.

Positive though these events were, his sixth sense told him that it would be unwise to let the situation with respect to the graduate go entirely unattended. He whipped off an email to the risk assessment business unit, copied to Morton, asking if anyone had seen a tall, athletic, redhead named Eris, who was his section's new graduate.

Morton read the email as soon as it arrived, then twisted to face Alan. 'Which way did they go? How many were there? How fast were they going? I must find them, I am their leader.'

Alan was not amused. 'As if things weren't already bad enough for us,' he said, 'our weakest link is out there, unsupervised. Perhaps we should go looking.'

'She could be anywhere,' said Morton, draping a sodden face towel, from the bowl of iced water next to his keyboard, over the top of his head, sideways so that it covered his ears. 'And we should both avoid unnecessary exertion in this relentless heat.'

An email from someone in the risk assessment unit, copied to Morton, read, 'Young and restless not sighted here. Will let you know if she turns up.'

Alan wondered if he should return to the executive suite in case Eris had decided, after all, to go straight to the top.

'It's a big department,' Morton said. 'And even if we cover every floor between now and home time, we won't get into all of the offices.'

'I suppose you're right,' said Alan.

'How about a brief distraction,' Morton asked, picking up a document, 'further to more momentous events and with a view to cheering you up?'

'What did you have in mind?' said Alan, doubtfully.

'Twenty-five interesting things about excrement,' replied Morton.

'About excrement?'

'Yes.'

'Couldn't there be only ten?' Alan asked, in a kindly tone, aware that Morton derived no small pleasure from his temporary enthusiasms.

'I actually have many more than twenty-five,' said Morton

'What about fifteen? That would, surely, make a not insubstantial inroad into the...'

'Some of them are brief, able to be appreciated in an instant.'

'I'm not sure,' said Alan.

'You will be amazed and enlightened,' Morton promised.

'Let's start and see how we go then.'

Morton brightened up. 'The average weight of a human turd is hotly disputed, with estimates ranging from two hundred and fifty to four hundred and fifty grams.'

He waited for a response.

'If you say so,' said Alan.

'The normal water content is eighty to ninety per cent and a single, modest poo contains as many living cells as the human body.'

'I see.'

'There are between one hundred and fifty and five hundred different bacteria in it, at a per gram concentration of ten to the power of twelve… and only about ten per cent of them have been identified.'

Alan nodded.

'The customary brown colour is because of a compound called stercobilin which results when bile is digested by colon bacteria.'

'Yes.'

'And after a night on the grog you get the runs because ethanol is like rocket fuel to your intestines, preventing your colon from absorbing the normal amount of water.'

'Remarkable.'

'Human faeces contain as little as eight per cent of the calorific value of the originally ingested food.'

'Understood.'

'The principal minerals are calcium and phosphorus, with the also rans including sodium, potassium, magnesium, chloride and sulphur.'

'Noted.'

'And it usually takes humans sixty hours to process food.'

'Uh-huh.'

'Squatting is a more effective form of delivery because it offers a more direct route out of the body by causing the levator ani muscles to straighten out the normally twisty rectum.'

'I see,' Alan said, keeping his doubts to himself.

'Number nine, I think it is, yes…'

Alan knew Morton was cheating but didn't demur.

'The number of infections able to be transmitted by faeces is around fifty, including hepatitis, typhoid, scabies, salmonella, giardia, meningitis, cholera, various types of parasites –'

'Thank you,' said Alan. 'Let's move on.'

'Of course. The South American pigs called peccaries live in groups and all members of the group crap in the one place at the centre of their territory.'

Alan had no recollection of the attributes of the peccary but he rather admired their disposition to tidiness.

'Llamas,' said Morton, 'also crap in defined places, as do wildebeest.'

'Those last two should be separate facts counting towards your twenty-five,' said Alan.

'Forget that I mentioned the wildebeest, then,' said Morton.

'And the llamas?' said Alan.

Morton pretended not to care. 'I'll withdraw them as well.'

'That's all very well, but it's not as though you never said anything about them.'

'Llamas? What llamas? Number eleven: bears don't crap while hibernating; they self-plug.'

Alan shook his head in disbelief.

'Sharks produce spiral faeces.'

'Acknowledged.'

'While a horse will drop as little as five kilos a day, an elephant will produce up to a hundred and thirty kilos of partly digested roughage over the same time period.'

'That's a double-up, again,' said Alan.

'And?'

'It ought to count as two.'

'The point, if I may say so, is one pertaining to contrast.'

'It still ought to be two.'

'You're only denying yourself.'

'Be that as it may, they were, by any measure, two different facts.'

'Then I'll off load the elephant shit…all hundred and thirty kilos of it. Happy?'

'Moderately.'

'Good. There are more than seven thousand species of dung beetles.'

'And?' said Alan.

'And what?'

'Well, that's hardly about excrement per se.'

'You're not making this easy for me.'

'You can't just ignore the rules.'

'All right then, I'll do number fifteen again.' Morton scrutinised his lists. 'What about this? The Bantu can defecate on request.'

'I suppose I'll accept that,' said Alan.

'Aardvarks hide their poo in hollows about ten centimetres deep, thereby providing the enclosed seeds of the cucurbit fruit – which only aardvarks seem to eat – with the perfect circumstances for germination.' Morton looked at Alan, expecting him to be impressed and, when failing to elicit intimations of wonderment, moved on. 'Geese crap approximately every twelve minutes.' Morton looked at Alan, again. 'Come on,' he said. 'You have to admit that that's impressive.'

'In its own way, I suppose it is,' said Alan.

'Number seventeen, then: most camel shit is so desiccated at the time it's delivered that it can be burnt straight away.'

'Fair enough,' said Alan.

'From the front end to the back end, it can take a cow nearly 100 hours, which is among the longest internal journeys.'

Alan could have objected – on grounds of relevance again – but what would have been the point?

'Bird droppings are white because of uric acid.'

'Yes.'

'The ancient Egyptians used gazelle dung in hair tonic and, generally, against infections.'

Alan shuddered.

'While certain breeds of penguins, when brooding, have been known to propel their poo up to sixteen inches away from the nest.'

'Lovely.'

'Meanwhile, imported dung has been used to trick undersexed male giraffes into thinking that other males were in the vicinity and to get them competing for local females' attention.'

'Very cunning. Are we near the end yet?'

'Two to go,' said Morton. 'Fossilised excrescences are known as coprolites and the largest was excavated in Alberta. It was twenty-five and a half inches in length.'

'Remarkable,' said Alan.

'Lucky last: civets, which caused the SARS outbreak in China in 2002, well, their poo can also be the bearer of coffee beans which, once roasted, are used to make the world's most expensive coffee.'

Alan had been anticipating the mention of civets at some point but was pleased, nonetheless, that his beverage of choice was tea.

Whether it was all the talk of faeces or the peristaltic consequences of the focaccia he'd eaten on the way from the car, Alan had hopes of a movement, so retired to the lavatories.

The air was cool but heavy with recent achievement. The furthest of the four cubicles had an 'out of order' sign on its door and the middle of the remaining three was occupied, forcing Alan – if he was to continue – to take an immediately adjacent spot. He sensed that delay would be inimical to an outcome, so proceeded, even though he knew he'd need to make a special effort to clear his mind of proximate humanity in order to make good his ambitions.

In the event, though, it was the hint of a noise, the faintest intimation of a rustle, that dashed all hope and ruined the enterprise, even before it was properly begun. Alan could have sworn he'd heard a page turn. He listened and, yes, there it was again, the aural footprint of a folio being lifted and let drop. Someone in the lavatory, just a few feet away from him, was reading a file.

The thought filled him with revulsion. How anyone engaged in the basest of human functions could sully the record of their endeavours – posterity's evidence of their labours – was beyond him.

There followed the sound of a throat being cleared, of bodily movement, of a flush and of a cubicle door being opened. Alan waited quietly for the sound of the outer door to signal the departure of the reader. Trying not to think of all the files he'd read in the course of his career – of the thousands, perhaps millions, of folios his fingers had caressed – he surveyed the back of his own door. Someone had written at eye height, 'Denise, give us the 35 hour week.' Underneath that someone else had written, 'Bugger Denise, who wants to work an extra 30 hours.' Below and to the right of this exchange, someone else had written text which, after careless alteration, read 'Quentin Quist is a prize aunt.'

Alan dressed himself and, when all had been quiet outside for more than a minute, concluded that the coast was clear. He stepped out.

Quentin Quist was standing at the basins dabbing at his nasal Vesuvius with a piece of paper towel. The scene would have been a disturbing rerun of the one earlier in the day but for the fact that, over the basin to Quist's left, was a departmental file on which rested a blood-encrusted Band-Aid.

'Do you spend all your day here, Alan? It's no wonder you get nothing done. And why aren't you answering your phone? I expect you to be available 24/7. I require it. The department requires it and, furthermore, the service requires it.'

Alan waited for the nation to require it, but the states and territories either couldn't agree or their peoples – young and free – had other things in mind.

'I was driving when you called, en route to arrange the flowers.'

'The flowers, yes, well, that's something you've achieved today, if not without being reminded. I'll see you in my office in five minutes and you can bring that' – he pointed to the Band-Aid-bearing file – 'with you.'

Before Alan could object, Quist was gone.

Alan carefully washed his hands and then, with a strip of paper towel to prevent contact between flesh and cardboard, jiggle-tilted the Band-Aid into the rubbish bin. Slipping the file under his left armpit, he washed his hands a second time and did the customary paper towel routine with the door handle, evacuative aspirations unmet yet again.

19

Morton removed the towel from the top of his head and plunged it into the bowl of iced water. 'Quentin is back.'

'I was just with him in the toilets,' said Alan.

'Passion will flourish in adversity.'

'There's been no sight of the graduate?' said Alan.

'Still MIA.'

Alan turned his computer off and the air conditioning ceased. Hardly anyone cheered.

'Do you have any updates on your committee members?' he asked.

'Three of the lost are now found and the number of recalcitrants remains steady at two.'

'Thank you,' said Alan. 'I'll be in with Quentin.'

'You can't bear to tear yourself away from him.'

'You're not funny.'

'Reconcile yourself to it now. He'll never leave his wife for the likes of you.'

'Use your networks to see if you can locate the graduate.'

'Don't come crying to me when he's used you and flung you aside like an old rag.'

Quentin Quist, wearing a fresh Band-Aid, was playing solitaire on Alan's previous computer. A quarter of the screen was visible in the portable mirror sitting on the meeting table – presumably for pustule-monitoring purposes.

'One moment while I finish reviewing this secret document,' Quist said, unaware of the reflection. 'We wouldn't want you to be seeing anything you shouldn't, would we?'

Alan nodded.

'Now you can enter.'

Alan stepped inside.

'Sit,' said Quist. 'You received my message about that woman?'

'I did,' said Alan, allowing the file from the washroom to slide from his underarm, down his side, onto the table, before he settled into a chair.

'I hope I made myself clear.'

'I believe you did.'

'I don't want her in my office again.'

'No.'

'Not ever.'

'Yes.'

'She was rattling on about the risks involved in making beds, ironing women's clothing and engaging sex workers.'

'I see.'

'Bizarre. Quite bizarre. Where we recruit them from, I don't know.'

'The universities.'

'I suppose that explains it all,' said Quist, almost sadly. 'They let anyone in nowadays – pay and stay – and everybody graduates with honours. It wasn't like that in our day.'

Alan didn't believe that he and Quist had ever shared a halcyon day of the academic sort but nodded gravely.

'It's time we considered alternative sources,' Quist continued.

'Of graduates?'

'Yes.'

'Alternatives to tertiary institutions?'

'Why not?'

'Why not, indeed?' said Alan, mystified.

'Now, what can I do for you?' Quist enquired.

'I think you said you wanted to see me.'

'Did I?'

'Yes.'

'Did I, indeed?'

'It may have been about the briefing for the acting minister or, perhaps, you wanted an update on contact with committee members.'

'Yes, the briefing,' said Quist, getting up and collecting a document in a plastic sleeve from the tray on his desk. 'I think the substance is fine but' – he sat down again – 'frankly, the expression was appalling and the punctuation was almost hilariously bad. I've made the necessary corrections.'

Alan knew what to expect: commas and apostrophes in strange places, whiches turned into thats, thats into whiches, tenses randomly varied, genders neutered and sentences plundered of rhythm and reason.

'Not your best effort, I'm afraid, but I suppose I have to make allowances for the recent…' Quist's right hand stirred the air.

'Faecal matter?' asked Alan, surprising himself.

'Unfortunate events,' answered Quist.

'I'll take care of your changes,' said Alan, anxious to be gone.

'You're never too old to learn a thing or two from your superiors, are you? I'll sign the final page and you can make my amendments. Get Morton to do the twenty-three copies and shoot them up to the Liaison Office this afternoon before the four o'clock run.'

'Certainly,' said Alan.

Quist got up and retrieved a sinister black fountain pen, the size of a premium cigar, from his top drawer. It was the sort of thing that persons unaware of Stalin's attachment to the red pencil might have imagined the dictator using to select colleagues and loved ones for the gulags and death.

Quist signed the final page and added his customary paraph before inserting the date. 'I see you're coveting my hardware,' he said, pushing the capsule into its nib-protective top. 'This is a piston-filled Mont Blanc 149M Meisterstuck and, before you ask, I can reveal that you won't be getting any change from a thousand for even a second-hand model in good condition.'

'Ghost,' Alan exclaimed.

'At home I have a Caran d'Ache Year of the Dragon fountain for official business. It's a truly exquisite instrument worth nearly three times the Mont Blanc. The beauty of the implement invests the signing act with a sense of…' He looked expectantly at Alan.

'Gravitas?'

'More a sense of…' Quist's facial expression said, 'Come on, you can do it.'

'Purpose?' asked Alan.

'…of occasion,' said Quist. 'I can't let you actually use the Meisterstuck, because the nib is handcrafted eighteen-carat gold, but you could hold it, if you wished' – he proffered the dark monster to Alan – 'to experience the sense of destiny and unfettered power which it imparts.'

For one misguided moment, Alan was tempted to reach out and touch…but good sense prevailed before he shamed himself. 'I'd better not,' he said.

'Ah, you're probably right,' said Quist. 'If you don't appreciate precious objects and have no aspirations to greatness, what's the point?' He returned the implement to its drawer.

Alan thought he could hear Morton shouting, out on the floor.

'What are you packing nowadays?' Quist asked.

A plastic click-action ballpoint, with its retention clip and top visible for all to see, nestled in Alan's shirt pocket but neither he nor Quist acknowledged its existence.

'Something rather ordinary, I'm afraid,' said Alan.

'Horses for courses,' said Quist.

Alan didn't know whether there was insult implicit in the aphorism but his response would probably have been the same, either way. He contrived a look that was part dumb incomprehension and part benign assent.

'Now,' said the acting branch head, presumably as an introduction to further business, 'I need to…'

The phone rang.

Quist picked up the handpiece and said in a voice two octaves above his normal pitch, 'Quentin Quist's office.'

Alan looked away to hide his surprise.

'I can certainly see if he is available,' Quist announced in the same high voice. 'One moment, please.'

He put his hand over the mouthpiece and whispered, 'I'm pretending to be my executive assistant,' as if impersonating a subordinate of the opposite sex was a perfectly ordinary thing to be doing in the performance of one's official duties.

'Putting you through,' he announced in his secretarial capacity.

'Quentin Quist,' he confirmed in his normal voice.

He listened intently. 'Really?' he said. 'On whose orders?'

He listened again. 'There's no chance you've got this wrong?'

Alan peered at the maggot-ridden avian corpse on the windowsill.

'The optics are terrible,' said Quist. 'And I have work that has to be done, today – well, yes, they may all say that, but mine really has to be done today – yes – the toilie incident, for the minister's office – perhaps three or four, five at most – that would be excellent – you'll have it unlocked? Good – thank you – no, I'll be working, ah, elsewhere but I certainly hope that you do.'

He replaced the handset. 'Everybody is being sent home,' he said, 'because of the heat. Everybody except you and your people.'

By 'people' he presumably meant Morton and, possibly, the graduate.

'I'm afraid I need you to put together a first draft of the standard words for the ministerial correspondence re our crisis, by close of business today.'

Alan knew that argument was futile but he knew, too, that things would go better with Morton if he could truthfully say he'd put up a struggle. A half- hearted protest was therefore in order.

'The burden seems to be constantly falling on my team,' he said.

'Yes, well, I don't expect you to understand the complex weighing up of resources and priorities, capabilities and timelines which results in executive tasking decisions, Alan. However, I do expect you to do as instructed.'

'Morton and I will always do our best,' said Alan, 'and we'll certainly devise the standard words you want, but I should let you know that our capacity to deal with the correspondence itself, when the time comes, is very limited.' Alan was prepared to sustain early losses in order to win the war.

'The corro,' said Quist, 'will have to go somewhere at the appropriate time. It's not going to self-answer, is it?'

'That's true but the other work to be done, to deal with our current crisis – on top of our normal committee business – will be more than my team can manage.'

'You have your graduate.'

'But the work of other sections is largely unaffected by the crisis.'

'We are all affected by the crisis,' said Quist, 'in one way or another. But you can be assured that I will be making decisions about work allocations, taking into account all relevant factors, at the appropriate…' He looked expectantly at Alan.

'Time?'

'No.'

'Juncture?'

'No.'

'Moment?'

'Yes, at the appropriate moment. But I will need your team to answer the first couple of hundred emails today to demonstrate to the acting minister that we are dealing promptly with this crisis.'

The crisis had, at one level, become a mere matter of responsiveness – using the term in its most limited sense – to public opinion.

'But my team today is Morton and me.'

'Morton and I,' corrected Quist, 'and I fail to understand why that's my fault.'

'It isn't,' said Alan, ignoring the solecism, 'but wouldn't a more sensible way of proceeding be to get approval of the words we propose to use before commencing work on actual replies.'

'Back yourself,' said Quist. 'You're an experienced officer and Morton isn't entirely incompetent – not all of the time. You've got to get at least half of the responses right, haven't you?'

'On past experience?' Alan said.

Quist's lip curled. 'You know, Alan, when I last looked, the words "Assistant Secretary" were on my door, not yours.'

Alan didn't have a door, because Quentin Quist had requisitioned the office it was attached to, and there were no designations – nameplated or painted – on any departmental office doors anyway (not since the days when doors in their hundreds had been removed so that offices weren't, technically, offices, but rooms into which subordinate staff could be moved in pairs and trios). Nameplates were situated on adjacent walls. But since when had the facts been of any relevance to a contention advanced by Quentin Quist?

Alan could honestly tell Morton that reasonable resistance had been mounted. No further effort was thus called for.

'Would it be okay for the two of us to work outside the building?' he asked, anticipating later representations from Morton vis-à-vis the worsening condition of his privates.

'Unfortunately, I need to be able to contact you, to monitor progress.'

Alan took that to be a preliminary refusal. 'I do have my mobile.'

Quist chortled. 'Your mobile. In your case, it's more of a fashion accessory than a means of communication, isn't it?'

Alan didn't follow. No one had ever before accused him of being au fait with matters of fashion.

'What else could it be?' Quist continued. 'You don't appear to ever answer the thing.'

Alan might have objected to this statement but, instead, decided on a different tack. 'It would be remiss of me not to tell you that the heat will have a deleterious effect on Morton's medical condition.'

'Ah, yes. I was wondering when Morton's malady – the one I'm not allowed to know about – would be advanced as a reason for non-compliance with my wishes… And as it so happens, I have agreed to arrangements for your team to work in more temperate conditions. You can up stakes to the departmental library. It has windows that open. I hope that this will meet with Morton's approval, even if it falls somewhat short of a miracle cure.'

The library was a separate building to the towers and had been the very first of the departmental premises on the campus, back in a time when air conditioning was considered a luxury.

'Thank you,' said Alan, defeated.

'Or should I be dealing directly with Morton as regards the compatibility of proposed work arrangements and his increasingly delicate constitution?'

'There won't be any need for that,' said Alan, thinking that he didn't need Morton to be pushed by managerial ghastliness into playing the sick leave card.

'Good,' said Quist. 'Write the standard words. The first two hundred emails are being sent to your section In box. I'll be in touch.'

'Yes,' said Alan.

'And tell Morton that those shorts are unacceptable in the workplace – entirely unacceptable. Casual Friday is all very well but football shorts take the whole thing too, too far.'

'I'll get onto it straight away.' said Alan, intending nothing of the sort.

20

Morton, without surmounting face towel, was on his feet, dropping things into his carry-all when Alan approached.

'Is that your brief back with changes?' he asked. 'Has the great obnubilater completely buggered it?'

'Not entirely,' Alan replied, under his breath. 'Is everything all right out here?'

'Couldn't be better,' said Morton.

'I heard shouting.'

Morton shrugged. 'We've been given an early mark because of the heat. Everyone is being sent home.'

'That's not exactly the case,' Alan said. 'We…' – he hesitated – 'You and I are required to…'

'If it's just the twenty-three copies of the brief up to Liaison, I'll do them straight away and we can still be out of here in a flash.'

'It's not quite that simple,' said Alan, bracing himself for protests. 'We do need to send the brief on its way, but we've also got to do standard words for the excreta emails.'

'Standard words? Now?'

'Yes.'

'That bastard,' said Morton, glaring in the direction of Quentin Quist's office.

'And we've got to answer some of the emails as well.'

'Some, as in?'

'Two hundred, give or take a few.'

'Before the standard words have been approved?'

'Yes.'

'But that doesn't make any sense.'

'Yes, I've been through all of that with him.'

'And?'

'He doesn't care.'

Morton shook his head and sat down. 'This is madness.'

'It is,' said Alan.

'And why are we always the ones who have to go the extra yards? Why do we always get the shit sandwich?'

'I warned him that we couldn't be relied on to handle the rest of the correspondence, when it arrives, within existing resources.'

'Yes, but in the meantime we've still got the briefing, the standard words and the first two hundred emails. We've got all of that to deal with this afternoon.'

'We'll do what we've done before to handle the correspondence and we'll get through it.'

'We won't be out of here this side of midnight,' said Morton. 'And what about my crotch?'

'We'll work in the library, where it will be cooler.'

'I still don't understand why it always ends up being us.'

'I rather think you explained that earlier today.'

'Because he hates us?'

Alan put a finger up to his lips.

'I don't care if he hears me,' said Morton, loudly. 'I've had a gut full.'

'Think fifty-four eleven,' said Alan, referring to the age (in years and months) at which his and Morton's superannuation entitlements peaked. 'Think about fifty-four eleven,' he urged.

'The bastard,' said Morton, in a softer voice.

'I'll go and make the twenty-three copies of the brief,' said Alan. 'Why don't you get things organised in the library?'

'No, I'll do the brief,' said Morton, 'while you pack your things. And then we'll go together.'

'All right then,' said Alan.

'And here's the graduate's mobile number, if you want to track her down.' Morton handed Alan a slip of paper.

'How did you get this?' Alan enquired.

'Personnel,' Morton and said, avoiding eye contact.

'They wouldn't normally give out a private phone number.'

Morton shrugged

'Morton,' Alan warned.

'I told them I was someone important.'

'Yes?'

'And I demanded it.'

'You didn't say you were…?' Alan gestured in the direction of Quist's office.

'Maybe I did. Maybe I didn't.'

'Good God,' said Alan. At the very moment Quentin Quist had been impersonating an executive assistant, Morton had been impersonating Quist, raising his voice at someone from Personnel. 'Tell me nothing further. It's best I don't know.'

'Whatever's best,' said Morton, 'Give me the briefing paper.'

Alan handed the sheets over.

Morton scrutinised the proposed amendments. 'We're not making any of these, are we?'

Alan shook his head.

'Then print out a fresh version and I'll make copies.'

Alan did as he was told – turning on his computer made no difference to the temperature or air flow – and Morton headed off with a box of bulldog clips in the direction of the printer.

Alan scratched his crotch and thought about Eris's mobile telephone number. If he rang it, he would probably be complicit in Morton's deception. But if he failed to establish the girl's whereabouts and she was haranguing some hapless member of the executive, things would be even worse for him, as her nominal supervisor.

He could, he supposed, always deny knowing how the phone number had been obtained, but what could he say if he was accused of supervisory negligence, having failed to take all reasonable steps to locate the girl once the number was actually in his possession?

The path ahead was clear. He picked up the number and dialled. For a moment he believed he heard the phone ringing nearby, but after a few rings there was nothing more.

He made a note in his workbook of the time at which he'd called and then, as the last of the people in adjacent bays packed up and left, collected the various pieces of stationery he and Morton would need to complete their work in the library. He packed his bag and turned off his computer – again without any discernible change in the climate.

When Morton returned a few minutes later with a copy of the brief for the file, he found Alan returning all of the employment framework materials supplied to the graduate to the shelf they were kept on.

'I'm back.'

'All done?' Alan asked.

Morton nodded. 'Let's get on with the rest of it.'

'That's the spirit,' said Alan.

At the EA's desk, Daphne was applying lipstick with the aid of a compact.

'Have a pleasant weekend,' said Alan.

'I will,' she replied

'And then go and fuck yourself,' said Morton, underneath his breath.

A clutch of the zombies got in the lift one level down, having taken the fire stairs to avoid walking past Quentin Quist's office. They looked at Morton's shorts but refrained from banter or criticism. Alan also wished them a pleasant weekend.

'We'll be making up the lost time,' one of them reassured him.

In the foyer, the guard desk was unattended. Through a door to the right of the security gates and along an enclosed walkway, Alan and Morton made their way via a second door into the library. To their left was the self-help loans desk and to the right a vacant office. In front of them were, side by side, two large tables for group work, each seating six. Beyond the tables stretched rows of shelves, no more than a third of which were filled with books and out-of-date journals. Around the edge, abutting the windows were carrels in pairs – back-to-back snugs – which had once had their own computers. There had once been magazines and newspapers, too, in the grab racks between the big tables and the shelves, as well as a librarian in the office, and an assistant to execute the loans, put away returned volumes and shoosh the talkers. But the library had long since been de-staffed and the subscriptions let lapse.

Rumour had it that the head of Corporate Services was surreptitiously de-accessioning the stock, monograph by monograph, and would find herself in receipt of a large cash bonus when the last volume was finally gone. Alan thought it more likely that in one of the next few economy drives, the shelves, carrels and remaining books would disappear – probably over a long weekend – and be replaced by workstations, after which point, with the addition of air conditioning, the library would be a footnote matter in the departmental history, if and when it was ever written.

Alan opened windows on either side of the big tables while Morton unpacked the section laptop computer and plugged it in. Alan ducked behind the loans desk to turn on the printer sitting there, so that they could obtain a paper copy of each of the emails they were required to answer. They would read each and every one of them in order to devise the standard words they were expected to use in answering the first two hundred and which would, in theory, be used to answer the flood of snail mail that would soon follow.

Each message was numbered by Alan as it was printed and was placed in a pile on the table. The pile was then divided in two and each of the men worked his way through his half, stapling the multi-page documents, taking the occasional note and ordering the pages into smaller sets.

Not a word passed between them, even though there was much that, between others, would have required negotiation. Morton sighed from time to time and even guffawed at one point but failed to divert Alan from the task at hand. It was only when, a few pages from the end, a breeze swept up some of the sorted papers that Alan was finally distracted.

He and Morton both lunged forward at this point to pin down the threatened piles with their forearms and, having prevented further take-offs, turned to each other and laughed – partly at the circumstantial synchronicity of their action, partly in recognition of their ungainly positions, bent over the table, and partly at the joy of the cooling breeze.

Alan almost, in that instant, forgot about the events of the preceding day.

'I'm nearly finished,' said Morton, not moving.

'Me too,' said Alan.

They gathered and secured their bundles, Alan recovered the escapees, and Morton reviewed his notes.

Then Alan read and distributed his final four sheets into their proper bundles. 'Would you like me to begin?'

'I'm just as happy to,' said Morton

'Then away you go,' said Alan.

'I've got seven bundles,' Morton said. 'My biggest is the "disgraceful goings on, abolish the department and abolish the public service" one, to which I'd respond with' – he read from his notes – 'thank you for emailing the minister, department is answering on his behalf, government taking active steps to downsize the public service, already achieved a significant reduction in staffing and budgets – that sort of thing.'

Alan nodded and added 'further savings/reductions are anticipated, the minister will take your views into account in the context of future resourcing decisions – something like that.'

'Got it,' said Morton writing down the additional text. 'My next biggest bundle is of the sarcastic and humorous material – stuff like "appreciate how hard it can be distinguishing a toilet from a desk", "at last something productive and useful from the bureaucracy" and "what was wrong with the In tray?" and even, "there is clearly not enough constipating red tape in the average public servant's diet".'

'How disappointing,' said Alan.

'To which I'd respond with an unadorned "thank you for taking the time to inform the minister of your views", without giving in to the comedic impulse and without any censorious "the government takes matters of this sort very seriously".'

'I agree,' said Alan, 'simple thanks, no jokes, no judgement.'

'A bundle about the same size is the one of party political correspondence and in it I have everything from "it didn't happen under the previous government" and "it wouldn't have been permitted under the previous government" to "working for this government would have a laxative effective on me too" and "I also haven't needed the smallest dose of Gregory's Powder since the night the current government was elected".'

Alan winced. Once upon a time communications of the most vulgar sort wouldn't have been dignified with a response.

'For those,' Morton continued, 'I'm proposing the usual thank you and text along the lines of "the government doesn't take this incident lightly, is taking appropriate steps to get to the bottom – on second thoughts, maybe not get to the bottom, perhaps to establish the reasons behind – not the behind, either – the reasons for the incident, but is not able to comment on the attitudes of previous administrations, whether permissive or prohibitive, to previous occurrences of this sort.'

'If any.'

'Yes, if any,' Morton agreed.

'And for the public servant angle, something about confidence in the professionalism, objectivity and commitment of the public service would be good.'

'Of course.' Morton typed. 'And what about "confident that the employment framework, including the code of conduct, provides appropriate deterrents for people who might be tempted to engage in behaviour of this type"?'

The mention of 'behaviour of this type' prompted Alan to think more seriously about 'it' than he had done since they'd commenced the task. This led, inevitably, to a rejuvenation of speculation, self-doubt and suspicion about his own role in events. There was to be, he realised, no release for him, until the truth, however terrible, was known.

'Where were we, again?' he asked.

'The prophylactic role of the employment framework.'

'Probably not,' Alan said.

'Because of the "still missing" follow-up turd?' asked Morton.

'I didn't know you knew about it,' said Alan.

'I didn't know that you knew about it,' said Morton.

'Knowledge regardless, let's not go with that last segment, in case there are confirmed further incidents.'

'Okay,' said Morton, amending his notes. 'Next, I've got committee-related messages – criticisms of the work, criticisms of the members, criticisms of how they were selected, suggestions re better appointments, that sort of thing. And I'd propose we respond with our existing material – "vital advisory functions acknowledged by current and previous governments", "members selected so as to tap into substantial pools of experience in government and public administration", "selection based strictly on merit, taking into account the experience of existing committee members" and maybe "delighted to add nominations by informed members of the public to the list of possible candidates in the event of vacancy".'

'I'd replace the mention of the pools with something less liquid.'

'You're worried about sewage?'

Alan nodded. 'And finish up on merit.'

'So, no community consultation about future membership?'

'Best not.'

'Fair enough,' said Morton. 'Now I'm into the small bundles. I've got aggrieved and retired public servants complaining about an unhealthy work environment and an exploitative culture, talking about flight responses to bullying, pointing out the emetic consequences of work in the bureaucracy, and expressing surprise that – and I quote – "there isn't more shitting all around the place".'

Alan shook his head in disgust.

'So,' Morton continued, 'I think we'd respond with the usual stuff about "government having clear expectations of public servant's behaviour", "demanding the highest standards of conduct", with some additional rattling on about "respect, dignity, courtesy and consultative decision-making and not tolerating bullying or harassment" – that sort of thing.'

'All good.'

'Now to my favourites: the "citizens who've identified business opportunities – that is, who are trying to interest the minister in commercial poo stain removal systems, workplace toilet training, Teflon desktops and antibacterial laminates, binding agents that last exactly seven and a half hours (plus an hour for the lunch break), odour-absorbent office products, chairs that convert into toilets, toilet cubicles that double as workstations, toilets that analyse any by-products (liquid and solid) for purposes not revealed, and toilets that are fun to use.'

'Fun to use?'

'Presumably on the assumption that, if the toilet is an attractive place to do the deed, there will be less incentive to use a non-toilet as a toilet.'

'How extraordinary,' said Alan, who, though uncomfortable with the term 'non-toilet', was always bemused by the private sector's disposition to bizarre innovation.

'I can't see Quentin agreeing to the fun toilet,' Morton remarked.

On cue, Alan's mobile phone rang. Quentin Quist was on the line, calling from a location where fragments of a hundred conversations, champagne explosions and merriment combined to make communication more a matter of intuition than even guesswork. Alan cobbled together bits and pieces of speech to deduce that a progress report was required.

'We've mostly written the standard words,' he said, 'based on analysis of all of the correspondence, and we'll shortly start work on the replies.'

Alan heard fragments of words and then nothing. He put the phone down. 'That was Quentin,' he said to Morton, 'and although it was difficult to hear him' – Alan didn't reveal that their leader was calling from a celebration – 'I think he said he was behind us all the way on this.'

'Gosh! What a boost that is,' said Morton. 'Knowing that Quentin is supportive of my efforts, I can honestly say that my world is a different place. I don't mind spending my Friday night on a futile task. In fact, I would now willingly spend the whole weekend at it, knowing that QQ was backing me up.'

'Where were we?' Alan asked.

'I think we'd agreed that certain persons were unlikely to be fans of the fun toilet.'

Alan would like to have known something about the ways in which the lavatory experience could be made 'fun' but modesty and the need to progress precluded further enquiries. 'Yes, I think you're right,' he said. 'Was there anything else?'

'My final category,' said Morton. 'The hippies, greenies and alternative energy enthusiasts.'

'What are they up to?' Alan asked, as if enquiring about the activities of a group of old friends.

'They're criticising government policy on human waste treatment, pushing for more government support for composting, silage and recycling, endorsing the enviro friendly toilet (in all its forms) and, most importantly, wanting to know why the poo power of public servants isn't being harnessed to heat and light public buildings.'

Alan's lips pursed in revulsion at the thought of a national capital lit by flatus. 'How would you like to respond to them?'

'I'm thinking that we'll refer the ones about public buildings to the minister for finance,' said Morton, 'in her capacity as the minister who determines minimum standards for the fit-out of government offices, then send the remainder to the minister for the environment.'

'Agreed.'

'And that's it, unless you've got anything different.'

'I'll need to adjust my bundles slightly,' said Alan, 'but the only real difference between mine and yours is that I've got some statisticians.'

'Isn't that funny,' said Morton. 'I had an eye out for them, as always, but didn't end up with a solitary one.'

'I've got three and they're asking, "How many other incidents of this type have there been under the current government and how many under the previous government? How many in departments versus statutory authorities? How many in the offices of different-level executives? How far, on average, from the drop point to the nearest gender relevant facility?" Et cetera, et cetera.'

'*Très* weird,' said Morton.

'I initially thought we'd refer these to the minister responsible for

the public service but concluded that we should answer them with' –
he read from his notes – '"It has not been possible to verify whether or
not comparable incidents have taken place with any frequency under
the current or previous governments. Any such incidents have, however,
not been sufficiently widespread or frequent to warrant systematic cross-
Portfolio data collection, enabling more detailed analysis."'

'Nice,' said Morton, typing furiously. 'I'll press Print.'

Alan collected from the printer a sheet on which the agreed responses
were numbered. He made minor amendments to the responses (which
Morton fixed immediately) then combined Morton's piles with his own
and began writing the numbers of the appropriate responses on each
message, before passing each completed one across for answering. Morton,
meanwhile, had set things up so that he only had to type in a number for
the relevant text to be inserted into the response template.

They knew that the messages taking multiple approaches and requiring
combined responses were the most exacting to deal with, so completed
them before any of the others. They started on the first of the simpler,
single-approach bundles, the work of the public service abolitionists,
at approximately 8.15, Morton having declined a tea break. At 8.50,
partway through the replies to the aggrieved public servants, Alan had to
shut the windows to keep the insect world at bay. They finished with the
hippies, recyclers and alternative energy advocates at 9.25 and Morton
sent the final version of the standard words to Quentin Quist's In box
shortly thereafter.

Along the way, Alan had learned about proposals to make toilet
attendance entertaining (including toilet paper bingo, tickling fingers
from below, and canned laughter triggered by downward pressure on the
seat) and had learned a good deal about environment-friendly lavatories:
urine diverting and pit composting, direct drop and vacuum flush, and
those with fan-forced, convection and tumbler-assisted aeration. However,
by the time he and Morton bade each other goodnight, any pleasure
he might have derived from this knowledge was entirely discounted by
exhaustion.

He half expected to be assailed by Rasch in the deserted car park but drove away without incident, to eat cheese on toast for dinner, accompanied by a single glass of Shiraz. Before bed, he applied anti-fungal cream to his crotch and between his toes.

In the night, he dreamed of an epidemic of desk defiling and fleets of ambulances carrying away whole villages of cleaners to the accompaniment of a discordant euphonium symphony played by Rasch and the flower shop gorilla, Burgoyne and Aunty Vi, Matron Frogmore and the Corporate Foliage Optimisation Executive, Hugo Faggoter and Daphne the EA, Quentin Quist and the graduate, the secretary and the True Ginger, various combinations of security guards and assorted others, all under the baton of none other than Maestro Mewling.

Shortly before dawn, he was awoken by the ringing of the work mobile phone on his bedside table. When he answered it, he heard the sounds of energetic lovemaking and then a child say 'hello' five or six times, before twin adult expletives signalled a premature end to the nearby intimacy.

'Give the phone to mummy, darling,' said a voice Alan couldn't quite place. 'Give it to mummy.'

'Won't,' came the reply, followed by a slap and howling before the call ended.

21

The following day should have been like any other Saturday: devoted to domestic endeavours that, while supportive of the salary-earning component of the week, inevitably resulted in a sense of guilt at important administrative matters not attended to. That guilt was usually alleviated in part by the fact that social and political phenomena unmonitored and not responded to were rarely made any worse by bureaucratic inattention. It was usually attenuated, too, by the knowledge that Alan could, on being alerted to any development requiring his consideration, be at his keyboard in a state of heightened readiness in less than fifteen minutes.

On this Saturday, however, a comprehensive sense of defeat, rather than of guilt, predominated. It had its origins in his:

FAILURE to achieve a morning bowel motion, despite the addition of a large quantity of prunes to his muesli;

FAILURE to fend off a feeling that he was personally responsible for events unfolding in the media, including the rumoured recall of the minister from leave;

FAILURE to locate any recordings of the solo euphonium, despite a thorough search of discs in both the house and the garage;

FAILURE to elicit any response from Hugo to any of the rousing replacement pieces played to him in the activities room at Bonnie Brae – the activities room because it was easier to wheel his bed there than to dismantle and reassemble the stereo;

FAILURE to establish whether or not Rasch had made a full recovery from his interaction with Clyde Adams – he was not answering his phone; and

FAILURE to satisfy himself that he was not and could not have been the person who delivered in Valerie's office, notwithstanding Rasch's firming list of other suspects and his own deductions of the previous day.

The last of these failures and the possibility that one foolish unhinged action on his part had been the cause of the chaos of recent days obviated the small satisfaction he normally derived from viewing a wardrobe full of carefully ironed white shirts and a freezer replenished with little plastic containers of beef casserole.

The feeling of impending doom which had first colonised his psyche on Christmas Day and had staked its claim to every last reach and purlieu of his consciousness in the following days, intensified mid-afternoon, as Alan was driving home from Bonnie Brae…such that he felt compelled to retire to bed straight away and remain there, though wide-eyed and desperate for rest, until the following morning. He might, finally, have dozed for a few minutes before dawn but true rest eluded him entirely.

As he sat, exhausted, on the lavatory a few minutes after six a.m., the words from Scripture occurred to him: 'Come unto me, all ye that labour and are heavy laden and I will give you rest.' He thought briefly about attending morning prayer or holy communion but it had been so many years since his last observances that he couldn't recall the times of any local services. He knew, too, that there was something intrinsically cowardly about running back to God when the going got tough.

He rose from the WC without result and staggered to the lounge, where he broke with custom by turning on the television. An expert – who probably knew nothing of the perils of constipation – spoke about the prospect of a cabinet reshuffle in the event that the minister was required to step down. The PM professed every confidence in the minister and the department; the minister professed every confidence in himself and the secretary; and the opposition spokesman for various affairs professed confidence in no one and called for blood.

By the time Alan was out of the shower, breaking news was that the PM and the minister were in discussions, and that an announcement was expected at any moment. 'The Poo Affair' was, according to a different commentator, about to claim its first scalp. Alan thought, not for the first time, about the disconnect between reality and big political events, about pebbles dropped into ponds and butterfly wings in the Amazon jungle, but mostly about himself and the terrible sequence of events which his lapse – he'd now reverted to thinking himself entirely responsible for the faeces – had set in motion.

If the minister was forced to step down or, worse still, was sacked, the search for the person ultimately responsible for 'it' would surely intensify and the scientific and law enforcement resources of the nation, dwarfing the efforts of Rasch's shitologist and the commercial lab, could yet be applied to the problem of identifying the person who'd been relieved of his/her daily burden on Quentin's work surface.

Alan's only hope was that some misguided idiot, possessed of a credible motive and opportunity, and hungry for notoriety, would own up before any real progress was made with the investigation and that the authorities would leap at the opportunity to announce the mystery solved.

Flight, which had previously seemed a pointless option, crossed his mind again but, as before, he concluded that he was unlikely to long evade the authorities. He'd doubtless appear promptly on an Interpol watch list and, even if he chanced upon a place from which he couldn't be readily extradited, would inevitably be a prime candidate for rendition. He recalled what the Mossad had done to Adolf Eichmann.

The best course would probably be to carry on as usual and maintain a veneer of calm until he was confronted…and to then claim that he had been framed. Accordingly, he dressed, packed his briefcase and drove to work.

It being a Sunday, the security desk was unmanned and the lift went straight to the seventh level. Walking past Carol's office, Alan glanced to his left and noticed a large portable whiteboard on which appeared the names of all of the committee members in alphabetical order, crossed or ticked according to some scheme of not immediately discernible intent. He halted to take in the full list but before he could survey any useful portion of the detail, Carol, dressed for tennis, appeared at his side.

'All in due course,' she announced, pulling the office door closed behind her.

Alan blushed but there was no one to explain himself to or to see the flush of embarrassment rising from his neck up into his cheeks.

He continued along the floor to his bay, where to his surprise, he found Morton, also dressed in shorts and a T-shirt. 'Good morning,' Alan said.

Morton hurriedly shut the document he was working on. 'I just ducked in to collect some things I left here on Friday,' he replied, rising from his chair.

'How is your…?' Alan gestured in the direction of Morton's crotch.

'On the mend, thank you, but I don't intend to hang around. I've tried the local switch but there's no air con at all.'

'These things are sent to try us,' said Alan. He placed his briefcase – his old one – onto his chair.

'Carol is in,' said Morton, 'plus some of the zombies, and I think I spotted Full Bottle.'

Full Bottle was Morton's nickname for the bibulous Scot in charge of Coordination and Finance.

Alan unpacked his briefcase.

'You look terrible,' said Morton.

'I'm not sleeping.'

'You won't be the only one. Have you seen the media? Our minister will be getting it in the neck. Nothing surer.'

'It's all very unfortunate,' said Alan.

'I suppose someone has to cop it. That's how ministerial responsibility works.'

Alan thought about all of the times ministers had escaped well deserved punishment.

'So,' said Morton, 'my money would be on a prompt sacking if he won't do the honourable thing, followed by a faction negotiated reallocation of the spoils.'

'What a pity.'

'I've been thinking about the likely replacements,' said Morton.

Alan had never liked the speculation about ministerial comings and goings. There was something unseemly about it when the worst of ministerial sins – haste, bad policy and the appointment of inept staff – were hardly ones unique to the ministry.

And what was the point, really, of replacing the minister? Until the government itself changed, there was unlikely to be a change in policy, and even then things mostly stayed the same.

'Well, if I can't tempt you with ministerial possibilities before I head off,' said Morton, 'what about twenty-five further fascinating facts about faeces?'

Alan wondered why Morton's interesting particulars to do with poo always seemed to come in groups of twenty-five. 'Are there really that many more?' he asked, sitting down.

'Would I be offering if there weren't?'

Alan reasoned there was probably no point in delay – Morton's enthusiasms could rarely be sidestepped – and if he got through another twenty-five early in the week, he probably wouldn't have to endure a further tranche – assuming that there were even more in reserve – later, when he would probably be under pressure and his resilience would be on the wane.

'Look, if you can't do the whole twenty-five,' Morton continued, 'I could give you a taste – five or six of the more interesting ones.'

'No, I think I'm up to the full twenty-five.'

'Good for you,' Morton answered, unfolding a sheet from his top pocket and launching in. 'Number one: Japan's biggest toilet maker, Toto, has produced a motorcycle that can travel three hundred kilometres on a single tank of crap gas.'

'Is that really about excretion?'

'Well, someone had to create the crap that gives off the gas.'

'Yes, but the excreting itself is a distinct, discrete process.'

'I'm not following you.'

'Go on, then.'

'Number two: when eels return to the sea to spawn, and change from freshwater fish to saltwater fish, they swim three thousand or more kilometres without feeding and, after their anal orifices close, their eyes expand to four times their normal size.'

'I don't see that that's about excretion, either.'

'I suppose you're right, especially with respect to their eyes, and it's really about non-excretion, but let me continue – they get better.'

'All right.'

'Number three: the deadly respiratory disease histoplasmosis is just one of a number of nasties contracted from bat shit and, when contracted near the Egyptian pyramids, was thought for some time to be the result of an ancient curse on tomb defilers.'

Alan thought this fact to be relatively interesting, so made no objection.

'Number four: Sir John Harrington designed the first flushing toilet in the 1590s, two and a half centuries before Thomas Crapper took advantage of household plumbing to introduce his own flushing throne.'

'But…'

'And Napoleon described Talleyrand as "a pile of shit in a silk stocking".'

'These facts are all fair enough but none of them – not one – has been about excretion per se.'

'Number six: one thousand cattle produce eight hundred and fifteen grams of methane daily but a thousand giraffes produce just a hundred grams.'

'Interesting enough but –'

'French kings regularly held meetings on the crapper and Haile Selassie, for fifty-eight years the ruler of Ethiopia, was so feared, even in death, that he was secretly interred under the private shitter of the military leader who deposed him, General Mengistu.'

'Those last three were only peripherally about excretion.'

Morton continued reading from the sheet. 'Number nine: poo transplanting, more accurately known as faecal microbiota transplantation or MTS, has been used since the 1950s to fight deadly colitis as well as inflammatory bowel disease, irritable bowel syndrome and constipation. Poo from a compatible donor is inserted via an oral tube –'

'Stop,' said Alan.

'Stop?'

Alan had a hand over his mouth.

'Are you going to throw up?' Morton enquired.

'Let's move on,' said Alan.

'Hmm. Something less troubling then. What about this one? "An enterprising Indian in Jaipur has been making paper out of elephant dung, using 1,500 kilograms of droppings every week."'

Alan nodded assent, with his hand still over his mouth.

'A few years ago, the director of the Prague zoo – a man called Bobek, whose name literally means dung – commenced selling one-kilo containers of elephant poo to the public and the product has been all the rage with Czech gardeners.'

'How nice for them,' said Alan.

'The percentage of surveyed Australians who admitted, a couple of years ago, to using a mobile phone while on the toilet: forty-eight. The percentage of Chinese: sixty-six.'

Alan could have objected, but decided there was little point; nothing was going to stop Morton this far in to his list and there couldn't, surely, be too many more facts to go.

'In Hong Kong there is a twenty-four-carat solid gold lavatory, weighing exactly one ton.'

Short was nearly always good.

'Experts have recently agreed that in ancient Rome –'

Alan's ears pricked up. Anything to do with the classical world was of intense interest to him.

'– visitors to the public toilets – the *latrina* – would wipe using a sponge on a stick handed to them by a toilet slave: an *atriensis detergeo* or "wiping steward". The ancient Romans also engaged in fart concerts or symphony infatonis where they let rip with *incantus infalatio* or "flatulent operas".'

'Though interesting, that really ought to count as two,' said Alan.

'More Rome, then, seeing as you liked that one.' Morton ran his finger down the page. 'Hmm. Number fifteen: the Ancient Romans invented the toilet tax. To fund the construction, in the middle of an economic crisis, of some of Rome's most notable buildings, the Emperor Vespasian introduced a range of new tributes, including a toll on the public toilets he'd built around the city. The toll or tax, known as the Vespasian, was widely criticised but the emperor responded by stating "*Pecunia no olet.*"'

'The money doesn't smell,' said Alan.

'That's right,' said Morton. 'And while I'm on the subject of Vespasian, I have discovered that only two of the famous Parisian open-air urinals called *vespasiennes* remain: one of them outside the La Sante prison in southern Paris.'

'I'll let that entire collection count as one towards your twenty-five, even though the last bit was really about urination,' said Alan.

'Thank you,' said Morton. 'Perhaps this next one will be more to your liking. In ancient Rome, they had a goddess of the sewer system called Cloacina, who they'd borrowed from the Etruscans and then merged with Venus. But the true toilet god was Crepitus, to whom you prayed if things weren't good in the arse department. Neither of these gods is to be confused with Stercutius, who was the god of dung generally, and in the agricultural sense.'

'Do you expect me to count that as one?'

'I thought you were keen on classical stuff.'

'I am, of course, interested in the classical world. Who isn't? But I don't see why that should put me at a disadvantage.'

'Hardly a disadvantage. How can it be to your detriment to know more facts?'

'About excretion?'

'Yes.'

Alan shook his head.

'May I continue?' Morton asked.

Alan nodded.

'The part of Hobart's Museum of Old and New Art where visitors spend the most time is the mirrored room in which a number of shitting machines – works of art entitled "cloaca" – are on display. The staff of the museum put food into each machine and then, like magic – or science, really – you know what comes out the other end.'

'How can that be about excreting,' asked Alan, 'when the act is performed by a machine?'

'It's still shitting,' said Morton. 'Comestibles in, crap out.'

'I'm not convinced.'

'If that's the way you feel about it, I won't count it towards my twenty-five.'

'Count it by all means.'

'I most certainly won't – not if you feel as strongly about it as you evidently do.'

Alan felt, justifiably, that sometimes he was, as Aunty Vi had often reminded him, his own worst enemy.

'Number seventeen, attempt two: the Maori have thirty-five words for dung. I'm not going to give you any of them…and you know why.'

'I'd promise not to count them…just to hear your Maori pronunciation.'

'Continuing with a Maori focus: if Maori warriors are unwell, cowardly or have done something forbidden – something regarded as *tapu* – they could make things good by biting the shithouse, as the gods were said to congregate there for the food of the dead.'

'The food of the dead?'

'Yes.'

'Which must have been the…'

'I guess so.'

'Let's move on.'

'Ginsberg, Updike, Hemingway, Auden and Bukowski all wrote poems about crap.'

'That last one – maybe even the last two are definitely not about excreting,' said Alan.

'Just sit back and enjoy the experience,' said Morton. 'Go, as they say, with the flow.'

Alan shook his head in disbelief.

'In the high Andes,' said Morton, 'they burn cow and llama dung but not horse.'

'Where on earth…?'

'As I told you, the high Andes.'

'No, I meant where did you find out about this?'

Morton shrugged. 'You read stuff,' he said, 'and the nuggets lodge.'

'Nuggets of this sort shouldn't,' said Alan. 'There are more important things to commit to memory, surely.'

'Moving along,' said Morton. 'Number twenty-one: in 2010 the German town of Lunen, north of Dortmund, became the first town in the world to use animal manure in a dedicated biogas network. They are generating 6.8 megawatts of power, enough for twenty-six thousand houses.'

'But the Chinese have been using biogas for many years,' said Alan. He'd seen a TV program on the subject.

'I'm coming to them,' said Morton. 'In *Gulliver's Travels* one of the futile and bizarre pursuits at the Academy of Lagado was the returning of poo to its original condition as food. Elsewhere in the academy a doctor was combating flatulence by inserting bellows up –'

'Yes, yes, moving along,' said Alan.

'King Wenceslas III of Bohemia was speared to death while enjoying a crap in 1306, King Henri III was assassinated in the water closet in 1589 and some say that Edmund II of England was stabbed while dropping one in 1016. George II died of natural causes on the toilet in 1760.'

'Surely that's four and you're well and truly done.'

'They're all about royal deaths while delivering.'

'Oh, go on, then.'

'In ancient Mexico the term for "gold" meant "shit of the gods".'

'Delightful.'

'Lucky last: the toilet seat is likely to be the least contaminated surface encountered by the average office worker. It's likely to host only forty-nine bacteria per square inch, whereas the keyboard can have nearly three thousand, the mouse nearly two thousand, the phone receiver more than twenty-five thousand and the desktop twenty-one thousand. This means that the toilet seat is nearly fifty times cleaner than the desk top.'

Alan eyed his desk top with revulsion. 'I have to get on,' he said.

'I would have thought that unwise, in front of a witness.'

'No, I mean that I have to make progress.'

'You weren't entertained?'

'Thank you,' said Alan. 'I'll see you tomorrow.'

As soon as he was alone, Alan transferred his In tray from his desk to the table, disconnected the phone and keyboard (so as to reduce the risk of electrocution) and reached for the antibacterial spray. With twenty-five thousand plus bacteria per square inch, the phone handset was his first priority.

<h1 style="text-align:center">22</h1>

As he made the surfaces safe, Alan wondered whether Morton had intentionally saved the bacterial details until the end of his account with the aim of unsettling him. There had been a time, the previous January, when, after finding a photocopy of Morton's kitchen renovation plans on the photocopier, he'd had to speak to him about the use of departmental resources for private purposes. Although relations seem to have returned to normal within a few months, experience told him that career-long vendettas had been fuelled by less substantial disagreements. He racked his brain for other indicators of ill will in the intervening period and was still thinking about signs of disaffection which he might have overlooked or misinterpreted when the voice of Quentin Quist called him back to the present.

'He's gone,' called the temporary executive from the end of the bay. 'It's official.'

Alan wondered what aspect of Morton's departure had triggered formal notice.

'I just heard it on the car radio,' Quist added. 'I imagine it's all over the media.'

'The media!' Alan exclaimed. What interest could the media conceivably have in Morton? he wondered.

'We'll need incoming minister's briefs for the replacement.'

Alan processed this last piece of information, deducing with some relief that Morton wasn't the focus of journalists' interest, after all. But then the true state of affairs dawned on him: that a personage of note – no less than a lawfully commissioned minister of the Crown – had been brought low by faecal matter that could well have originated in the Mewling colon. There had, of course, been greater tragedies in the political life of the nation but there had probably been none more bizarre or unsettling.

'You look dreadful,' said Quist, now close. 'I didn't realise you were taking all of this so personally.'

Are you so obtuse, Alan wondered, that you can't see what this means for us?

'You're not going to throw up, are you?' Quist enquired.

'I'm not sure,' said Alan, thinking it very likely, indeed, that he might hurl over his supervisor and/or his freshly sanitised desk top.

'Then go,' said Quist, stepping backwards and extending his open hands as if to fend off a vomit torrent. 'Go.'

Alan stumbled towards the lavatories, where he lent over a basin until the worst of his nausea had passed. Then, not feeling ready to return to his workstation and hoping that residual fear might yet be used to evacuative effect, he occupied the closest cubicle.

His hopes were, however, promptly dashed…because, on being seated, he observed, at eye level, a piece of chilling graffiti. The text, though unadorned by exclamation marks, supplementary images or underlining, embodied all of the vitality of active language without the too obvious assistance of an adverb. Written in black pen in solid upper case letters approximately a centimetre high were two words which could not have more profoundly misrepresented the actual situation vis-à-vis Alan's bowels. The words read, 'ALAN SHITS.'

Alan gasped and clutched at stabbing pain deep inside his belly.

'ALAN SHITS.'

He used a piece of toilet paper to clean his glasses, then leaned forward to more closely scrutinise the writing. The words weren't, disappointingly, the foundation of a metaphorical statement (for example, 'Alan shits us' or 'Alan shits anarchists, everywhere') but were seemingly about cacation. That being so, they were, on any ordinary day, likely to be a true enough statement about any or all of the Alans working in the department. Bowel movements, Alan reminded himself, were a normal part of human functioning, as unremarkable as eating, sleeping or the pursuit of domestic or vocational order. But in the prevailing circumstances, any suggestion that anyone in particular might defecate was more than a bald statement of functional fact. Such an assertion was either a revelation by someone in the know – someone who might, with the passing of the minister, feel more disposed to speaking out – or a false claim made by someone with the worst of intentions.

Alan licked his right forefinger and, trying not to think about the sticky contact it made with the toilet door, scrubbed at the offending text. The 'L' in Alan faded but the rest of the letters were unchanged. Not to be defeated, he pulled the ballpoint from his top pocket, studied the text for a few seconds, then turned the ghostly 'L' into a 'D'. He added a down stroke to the 'N' so that it looked more 'M'-like and then scrawled 'ME' at the end. ADAM SHITS ME the altered text read.

He hoped that the various Adams with whom he'd laboured over the years wouldn't be plunged by these amendments into depressive episodes or be prompted by them to embark on workplace killing sprees. He couldn't, however, have left things as they were.

For the same reason, he couldn't pull up his trousers, go to the basins and from there back to work. He needed to continue the search for calumnies, he told himself, because his accuser, having taken one opportunity to point the finger at him, was unlikely to have passed up other opportunities.

He examined the rest of the door, the side walls and the surfaces on either side of the pedestal. Apart from a brief moment of panic when his brain confused 'ANAL' and 'ALAN' and he consequently believed someone to have claimed 'ALAN HURTS MY ARSE', he discerned nothing alarming, apart from the fact that more space was taken up by unflattering conjecture about Quentin Quist's sexual predilections and genital dimensions than by speculation about the preferences and proportions of everybody else.

Alan wondered how Quist could ignore the rich and extensive store of scorn when using the facilities and why he hadn't also taken action to de-identify the inscriptions in which he featured. The old maxim about 'any publicity' surely didn't hold true of toilet wall ruminations to the effect that one was possessed a tiny organ (used exclusively for self-gratification, same-sex excesses and congress with canines). It certainly wouldn't have held true of an aspersion suggesting a connection between Alan and the events which brought down the minister – not that he'd seen such a thing. Accordingly and nonetheless, he abandoned all hope of a movement, pulled up his trousers and then, when he was certain the coast was clear, went to the next cubicle to inspect the graffiti there.

He discovered nothing more troubling than two segments of text in a hand reminiscent of Morton's. The first, an instruction read, 'After delivering a Quist, wipe, lower the lid and flush', and the second, a vulgar limerick about a young woman from Aberystwyth, demonstrated linguistic ingenuity of an extraordinary order.

In the third cubicle, next to a graphic representation of mating rhinoceroses, he discovered a statement which read, 'McAllister did it' (which may or may not have been about recent events). Next to the toilet itself, was text in an unfamiliar hand which read, 'Quentun Qwissed shit on his oun desk'. Alan left both allegations as they were.

In the fourth cubicle, the name of someone thought to share the penile shortcomings and sexual peccadillos elsewhere attributed to Quist had been repeatedly redacted using a marker. The thick black strips covered the walls, the door, the lid and even the ceiling, evidencing a prolonged struggle between defacer and censor. Try as he might, Alan couldn't locate a single reference to Quentin Quist in the remaining notations other than one below the coat hook in inch-high letters reading 'QQ is a hung like horse', and a larger one along the left-hand edge of the door reading 'Quist is a genius'. There was little doubt in Alan's mind about which cubicle in the row was most frequented by his temporary supervisor.

It was in the fifth and final cubicle, near the very bottom of the door, almost lost in an impossibly cluttered plethora of rhymes, aphorisms, advertisements, obscenities, and diagrammatic depictions of bizarre sex acts that Alan at last discovered the words he had dreaded all along.

He got down on his haunches to read them and had to get so close to the door that his deflected breath repeatedly fogged his glasses. Their meaning was as clear and unambiguous as an eye gouge.

They read, 'Alan M did the shit'.

There were, Alan knew, no other Alans whose family name commenced with M then working in the department. The reference had to be to him…and by stating that he was responsible for 'the shit', rather than 'a shit' or 'multiple or various shits' or even 'the shit that was a specific piece of work thought to be of poor quality', it was clear that he stood accused of the delivery of the faecal matter which had sent Peaches home, busied the media, triggered an avalanche of correspondence from the citizenry and brought down a Commonwealth minister.

Alan wet his finger – a different finger – and rubbed at his name, without success. Deducing that stronger measures were necessary, he pulled the departmental ballpoint from his pocket and holding it at forty-five degrees to the offending script, tried to block out 'Alan M'. But even with the pen thus tilted, the ink would not flow. Horizontally, the result was predictably no better, and holding the pen point downwards before applying it to the door was also an effort in vain; Alan's previous ministrations had apparently exhausted the supply or clogged the ball.

He was left with no option, if he was to leave the cubicle with his name obscured, but to use the implement in a way which ensured its ruin – a usage which, being tantamount to the wilful destruction of government property, would make him the perpetrator of a criminal act and rank him in his own estimation with killers, rapists, thieves and drug dealers. He took a deep breath and stabbed at the word 'Alan' half a dozen times, trying to create pits and cracks in the text with the metal tip. A number of his attempts hit the mark but most were wide of the targeted letters.

He paused to ensure that all was quiet outside and, when satisfied that he was in fact alone, placed his thumb and index finger on either side of 'Alan' to focus his attack. He stabbed a further five times, at which point the barrel of the pen came apart and he used the opposite end, with the stop removed, to lift the broken paintwork.

His thighs ached and, from deep inside him – somewhere unable to be specified – there was unfamiliar throbbing pain. He stayed in the squat position and picked away at the splinters until only the words 'id the shit' remained. Satisfied, he rose and left the scene of the crime.

In the cubicle next door – the one covered with black and blue redaction strips – he sat on the dropped lid. Both ends of the pen barrel were jagged and broken; he clutched at it, anyway, and forced himself to review the options open to him now that his colleagues – or at least one of them – saw him as the culprit.

He could resign before any further accusations or evidence resulted in him being arraigned – perhaps citing the stress of recent times and the inevitable reorganisation of the department as the triggers. However, with just days to go until he turned fifty-five, such a move would be bound to attract suspicion.

An alternative was to approach someone in authority – maybe Rasch – and reveal his doubts. Perhaps his DNA could be taken for analysis and he could submit to polygraph or truth serum testing…but what if he'd talked himself into responsibility for the turd? He'd always had a tendency to self-guilt. Whenever there was collective blaming at school or work, he always felt particularly responsible…and a brief glimpse of a police car could have him nonsensically speculating on whether he'd committed, or was capable of, atrocities.

Responding to this consideration, a small voice inside his head – hesitant and low – said something that, only a day or two before, he wouldn't have tolerated but which he now knew to be true: that the executive might not require very much at all in the way of evidence in order to be persuaded of his certain guilt. And what if he wasn't guilty at all? He reasoned that an altruistic confession – to end the uncertainty – was untenable now that the opprobrium would be so much greater. He had to continue.

He heard the outer door open and was horrified when a knock at his cubicle door followed.

'Al, is it you in there?' Quentin Quist asked.

Alan hadn't, in all his fifty-four years and three hundred and fourteen days, engaged in converse with another human being while in the lavatory. Now this taboo, too, was apparently to be disdained.

He cleared his throat and attempted to answer. 'Yes.' A single word was all he could produce.

'Do you think you'll be long?' Quist enquired.

'Can whatever you require of me wait a minute or so?' Alan asked.

'No, I don't want you…in any sense,' Quist answered. 'I need to go.'

Something about tag toileting seemed to Alan to be indefinably disgusting, even if the first occupant was, like himself, fully clothed, sitting on top of the lid…and there wouldn't, consequently, be one bottom after another on the warm seat.

'But there are other cubicles, Quentin,' said Alan.

Silence.

'But I always use yours,' said Quist '– the one you're in.'

'I see,' said Alan. He well understood the importance of habit, but…

'How much longer do you think you'll be?' Quist enquired.

It seemed that it wasn't possible, even in the lavatory, to escape management depredations.

Alan flushed for appearance's sake and opened the door. Quist moved forward and the two men stepped to the left and the right in a dance before Alan flattened himself against the door and Quist brushed past, unfastening his belt as he went.

Alan went to the basins, certain that in such circumstances he had no option but to maintain his innocence until he was proven – to himself and the wider world – to be incontrovertibly guilty.

He washed his hands more hurriedly than he'd done in years and let the tap run at high velocity to mask the sounds of whatever might have been happening in the cubicle.

23

Alan draped his cardigan over the back of his chair and turned on his computer, without bringing the air conditioning system to life. Disconcerted, he shut down the machine, then started up a second time but, again, there were no signs of change above or around him.

From the direction of Carol's office he heard a woman's laughter. Poking his head over the partition, he saw the graduate and the ex-secretary, both with tennis racquets in hand, walking towards the lifts.

'That foolish young woman is in for a surprise,' said a soft voice behind him.

He turned to face the Corporate Foliage Optimisation executive.

'And you might want to get out of here, as well, Alan. Quist is in the building.'

'We've already engaged today,' said Alan.

'Each to their own,' said the man in green, picking up his tool kit and bucket, and heading purposefully towards the fire stairs.

Alan wondered what had been meant about Eris being 'in for a surprise' and, what it was that the acting branch head had done to earn the plant man's ire; he supposed that the former could have something to do with the accuracy of Carol's serve and the latter with complaints likely to have been made about the state of departmental vegetation. Still further re the latter, that one man could have alienated so many of those with whom he had so little contact was surely a remarkable thing.

On cue, Quist appeared at Alan's side. 'Who was that I saw you talking to?' he asked.

'The plant man,' said Alan, 'but we weren't really talking.'

'He reminds me of someone,' said Quist, 'someone I can't quite place…but that's not what I'm here about.'

Alan half-anticipated an apology for his untimely eviction from the lavatory but was, of course, to be disappointed.

'We'll need to recover that ministerial briefing we did last week on the committees and rejuvenate it for a new minister, who won't have the background.'

Alan felt anxious about the changes he'd failed to make to the draft after Quist's last scrutiny of it.

'I'm thinking that it needs a fresh approach,' Quist continued. 'No more fudging the question and faffing around at the edges, no more obscuring the brutal realities and avoiding the fundamental truths.'

Alan thought this a certain recipe for disaster. 'A re-evaluation can sometimes be illuminating,' he said.

'And I'm just the man to cut through and add value,' said Quist.

'You are,' said Alan. 'Do you want me to send you the most recent version again?'

The paper copy Quist had made his changes on was still in Alan's bottom drawer.

'I think not. All those tired ideas and that lumpy prose. I don't want it infecting my thinking. I'll start from scratch.'

'How wise,' said Alan.

'I'll do the hard task while you start changing the correspondence from Friday night, to take account of the change in minister.'

'I didn't realise that the PM had already selected a replacement,' Alan said.

'Ah, he probably hasn't but I've narrowed the likely contenders down to three.'

That didn't make Alan unduly optimistic but he was obliged to plug on. 'So, which one do you wish me to make reference to in the correspondence?'

'I was thinking that you might do all three.'

'All three,' Alan exclaimed. 'That will be very time-consuming.'

'But you evidently came for the day,' said Quist, motioning towards Alan's casserole container.

'So, all three names inserted in the signature box and then the two losers deleted, once it's clear who the PM has decided upon?'

'No, I was actually thinking that you could do the three separate versions.'

Making three sets of amendments to the existing replies would certainly take Alan all day.

'But what if the replacement isn't one of the three you've chosen?'

'How likely is that,' said Quist, 'taking into account my contacts, my IQ and the finite number of possibilities?'

'But on the off chance?'

'Then nothing lost, really, and you'll be an expert at making changes by that point.'

Alan wasn't convinced.

'And if it turns out that the new minister is one of my three, think about how good I'll look – how good we'll look – when, within minutes of the appointment, all of the responses, with the right details in them, land in the new chief-of-staff's In box for approval.'

Alan could, at this juncture, have pointed out that it would take some time for the new appointee to set up his or her office, that they would have bigger things in mind than correspondence about faeces and that the problems of the predecessor would inevitably be accorded little priority by the staff of his replacement. He could also have pointed out the waste of resources involved in making three versions of the correspondence and that Sunday was his day off, even if he often decided to spend some of it in the office. He could, moreover, have observed that he'd been allocated more than his fair share of futile tasks over the previous thirty-three-plus years of service to the taxpayer. However, resistance at this late stage of his career seemed a matter of too little and certainly too late.

'I suppose I could make a start,' he said.

'Awesome,' said Quist.

'But I can't promise that they'll be finished today.'

'I'll send you the three names.'

That should have been the end of the exchange but Quist showed no sign of moving.

'We live in tumultuous times, don't we, Al?'

Alan nodded agreement.

'I don't suppose you've had any further thought about who might have been behind the thingummy…?'

'The thingummy?'

'The, ah, number two.'

Alan shrugged.

'You see, it occurred to me,' said Quist, 'that I may have assumed the worst about the y'know.'

'The y'know?'

'The poo.'

'Ah, yes,' said Alan. 'Now I'm with you.'

'Because I was thinking that, well, there may have been nothing in it.'

Alan recalled, from Morton's briefings, that human excretion was substantially water, but it could hardly be said that there was nothing in it, especially bearing in mind the minerals and trace elements, the fibre and the one hundred and fifty to five hundred bacteria per gram at a concentration of ten to the power of twelve.

'I was thinking that it might just have been a case of someone passing by and feeling the need to go.'

Alan wondered whether Quist was having fun at his expense.

'Before they could, like, make it to a toilet,' Quist added. 'A lot of people at that time of year can't even do a fluff without fear…because of the alcohol and all the rich food.'

'But whoever it was got up on the desk, didn't they?' Alan asked.

'In the absence of a toilie, they did.'

'When the facilities were just a few metres down the hall.'

'Yes, but that would have been because they had to go, urgently.'

'In which case, it would have been easier and tidier to use the drawers.'

'Their own drawers?' said Quist, aghast.

'The desk drawers.'

They both looked at Alan's under-desk cabinet, wondering what might be lurking within.

'Unless he or she didn't have time to open them.'

Alan wondered how someone so stupid could have been entrusted with the temporary charge of a whole branch of the nation's public service. 'In which case they would probably have done it on the floor,' he said.

'Except for their concern that others might have stepped in it, slipped over, hurt themselves, and so forth.'

Alan now wondered how someone so stupid could have been promoted over all of the personable and modestly gifted yet sedulous people he had worked with over the years. 'Perhaps you're right,' he said.

'Anyway,' Quist said, 'between the need to go and the Everest imperative, there might have been nothing malevolent in it.'

'The Everest imperative?' Alan asked

'They climbed it because it was there.'

'So you're suggesting that someone anxious to expedite a bowel motion mounted the desk because it was there?'

'Uh-huh.'

Quist looked inordinately proud of himself and Alan wondered how someone so profoundly stupid could have been preferred for promotion over even him, notwithstanding his great mistake.

'It's an interesting possibility,' he said.

'But we can't sit here all day engaging in idle speculation, can we?'

'I suppose not,' said Alan.

'And for both of us, duty calls.'

'Yes, indeed,' said Alan.

'Al, look me in the eye,' said Quist, 'and tell me we aren't the best public service in the world.'

'I can't,' said Alan.

'Then I probably don't need to ask you whether we are in fact the best public service in the world.'

'You probably don't,' said Alan.

'But I might anyway.'

'I thought you would.'

'Then I'm not going to disappoint: Al, are we the best public service in the world?'

'We are,' replied 'Al' with what he hoped was sufficient enthusiasm, even though he thought it self-evident that he and Quist, together, could not constitute a public service for even a small African nation or a European micro-principality.

'Are we the best public service in the world?' Quist asked again, a good deal louder.

'We are,' Alan enthused, also louder.

'One last time,' said Quist. 'Are we the best public service in the world?'

The question echoed around the floor.

'We certainly are,' replied Alan, hoping that increased conviction made up for his inability to shout and that Quist would not find his effort wanting.

'Give me five,' said Quist.

Alan's efforts had apparently been sufficient.

Their upraised hands met, Quist left and Alan made prompt use of the antibacterial gel from his top drawer.

Quist soon afterwards sent him the names of the three ministerial finalists. As predicted, it took Alan the remainder of the morning and most of the afternoon to create three versions of the two hundred-plus emails that he and Morton had previously answered for the acting minister for various affairs on behalf of the (probably departing) minister. There was doubtless an IT fix that would have done the task in a fraction of the time but Alan had nothing especially urgent to do – he wasn't at work because he had to be – and the time passed quickly.

He ate his lunch at his desk, and the cool conditions outside meant that, even without air conditioning, the temperature was pleasant enough. At one point he noticed that he'd been humming to himself, having momentarily forgotten about the gravity of the situation he was in.

At 5.07 Quentin Quist emerged from his office, pulling the loaded file trolley behind him. 'I'm off,' he announced.'

'Have a good evening,' Alan replied, in an effort to demonstrate that he wasn't one to hold grudges.

'I'm only changing venues,' said Quist, nodding in the direction of the trolley.

'The burdens of higher office,' said Alan, amiably.

'Yes,' said Quist, making no effort to depart.

He looked at Alan. Alan looked at him.

'Was there something else you needed me to do?' Alan finally asked.

'Ah, no. Not exactly…but…ah…I don't suppose that by any chance, you kept the original two hundred responses – the ones from Friday afternoon?'

'No,' Alan answered. 'Why?'

Quist looked at the ceiling and then at the floor. 'It probably won't matter.'

'Is there a problem?' Alan enquired.

'Only that, well, it seems that the media might have misunderstood the state of play earlier in the day.'

Alan's antenna thrummed. 'In relation to?'

'The minister.'

'Are you suggesting that he hasn't resigned?'

'I, well, yes, as a matter of fact, I am. It seems, instead, that he's refusing to go.'

'I see,' said Alan, deducing immediately that his day's work had been in vain and that Quist had probably spent the afternoon watching events unfold on TV on his computer. Perhaps Alan should have felt relieved that matters weren't as bad as they'd seemed to be when he'd thought himself to be the likely creator of faeces that had triggered a ministerial dismissal. But he could see little reason for satisfaction in having been the likely cause of a ministerial crisis.

'But he could yet be dismissed,' said Quist, 'or he could see reason and walk.'

'I suppose he could,' said Alan.

'We'll just have to see what tomorrow brings, won't we?'

'Yes,' said Alan.

'No need to recreate the original two hundred responses tonight,' said Quist

'I won't,' said Alan.

'But I'd have Morton make a start on them, first thing in the morning.'

A nod was all the acknowledgement Alan could muster.

'I'll be going, then.'

'Yes,' said Alan.

'You're not squiffy with me are you, Al?' Quist asked, with a smug smile.

'Not at all,' said Alan, masking misery and rage about the wasted day.

'Then I'll see you tomorrow.'

'Yes,' said Alan, through clenched teeth.

Quist, at last, pulled his trolley away.

Alan listened intently for the lift chime and, on hearing it sound, dropped his head into his hands. Between his futile day's labour, his unresponsive bowels, his possible role in the delivery of 'it', the ministerial crisis and the likely reconstituting of his committees, he would have sobbed had he not sensed someone approaching from the far end of the floor.

Alastair McAllister, head of the branch's Business Management Unit, placed a whisky bottle and shot glasses on Alan's visitor's table, hitched up his kilt and dropped into a chair. He seemed, to Alan's surprise, to be sober. Experience, however, told Alan that this was unlikely to make the man any more intelligible; his Scottish accent was thicker than sun-hardened porridge.

'I'm just on my way out,' said Alan, anxious to avoid a repetition of his Christmas experience.

'It won't take a minute,' the Scotsman may well have replied, 'and I think you can spare a minute for me.'

'I can,' said Alan, recalling that his interlocutor was not a man to be crossed.

McAllister removed the stopper from the bottle and poured himself a double.

'Not for me,' said Alan.

'Dinnae try me wi' your refusals,' said the Scotsman. 'I'm already more than cranky.'

A second double nip was poured and from the accompanying words Alan thought he caught 'That odious turd, Quist, gets my dander up.'

'If I understand you correctly,' said Alan, 'agreed, absolutely.'

'To his airly, grisly death,' said the Scot, raising his glass.

It seemed impolite not to respond positively. 'Without delay,' Alan answered, raising his own glass.

They drank and Alan felt every last molecule of the spirit hit his stomach. He coughed twice. McAllister motioned him close. From the words that followed, Alan discerned more than he expected to, including 'Quist and that auld bitch', 'secret costings' and 'just one sorry, last committee'. From the follow-up utterances he divined 'makes me sick to the stomach'. He thought about the notations on Carol's whiteboard and had no misconceptions as to what was being plotted beneath his very nose.

'Can I tempt ye with another,' McAllister asked, 'seeing as it's Sunday.'

'I'd better not,' said Alan.

'Then I'll make it a wee one.'

They repeated the previous toast and downed their drinks. Alan felt distinctly light-headed.

'I should hae retired years ago,' McAllister said, peering at the carpet. 'This place has gone from bad to worse, and then some.'

Alan wondered whether the sudden intelligibility of the man's speech had anything to do with the whisky.

'I would hae left, you know, when that cretin Quist was promoted but for that Elk.'

'Ah, yes, the Elk!' said Alan, knowingly.

'He's a right terror on the grog,' McAllister confided. 'and who'd hae kept an eye on him, if nae me?'

'Quite so,' said Alan, wondering how it was that he could ever have subscribed to the popular view that it was McAllister who was the dangerous drunk and that it was the Elk who did the department a service by keeping the Scotsman away from the office in the afternoons. Life played, he mused, the strangest tricks.

'Between the two of us,' said McAllister, again motioning Alan close, 'I can tell ye, that I have that wee Elk picked as the one who did the bonny jobby on the desk ae that fool.'

'Do you?' said Alan.

'However, I cannae say for sure that it was nae me or, for that matter, that it was nae…you.' The Scotsman fixed Alan with a bloodshot, unwavering gaze and nodded, knowingly.

Alan felt the colour drain from his face.

Then McAllister chortled and slapped him on the back. 'Just joking,' he said. 'But if Quist dinnae do the noisome brown thing on his own desk, I tell ye, that wee Elk is the man. No one hates Quist more than the Elk.'

After McAllister left, Alan ruminated on the man's candour and was not inclined to drop either the Canadian or the Scotsman from his own list of possible suspects. But, as always, at the back of his mind was the very real and persistent likelihood that he, himself, was responsible for 'the bonny jobby on the desk ae that fool'…and this was not a possibility that would fill him with any less anxiety as the night wore on.

He went home via the supermarket, where he purchased a large quantity of mandarins – having recalled a colleague's claims as to their outstanding purgative properties – and a thick bunch of rhubarb stalks for stewing – Aunty Vi's second-line constipation remedy when castor oil had failed.

On the answering machine was a message from Rasch. In a voice choked with emotion he announced, 'Life is but a fleeting thing. A man must leave his mark or accept hollow obscurity.'

Alan was concerned for the director of security's mental state and called the only number listed under 'Rasch H' in the right suburb in the phonebook. No one answered.

He lay awake most of the night, again, certain in the knowledge that the restructuring of the committees would erase the only mark he believed himself to have made. That he, too, would have to accept 'hollow obscurity' now seemed inevitable.

24

Alan woke, exhausted after the briefest rest, and staggered straight to the shaving mirror. His face would have appeared grey and shapeless but for his eyes: startling red slits atop empurpled sacks. He sat for a while on the side of the bath before showering and on the edge of the bed before struggling with his underpants and socks. Breakfast was beyond him but he filled the kettle, having once been told by an Asian acquaintance that hot water in the mornings was an invaluable adjunct to well-being – code for 'an aid to regularity'.

Opening the kitchen blinds to better view the day, he noticed, with a start, an unfamiliar van in the driveway. His mind ran to scenarios in which his house was surrounded by men in camouflage and a megaphoned voice urged to give himself up before there was bloodshed.

The van was parked so as to prevent him from driving his Morris Minor away. Its driver nowhere in sight.

A chime sounded and Alan concluded that the front door was better answered than broken down. To his surprise, Rasch, with much of his face obscured by a Mexican moustache, was waiting on the step with a large buff envelope in hand and a newspaper tucked under his arm. Alan let him in. There was no trace in the visitor's bearing or demeanour of the previous day's despair.

'Do you have coffee?'

'I think there's instant somewhere.'

'You've heard the news?' Rasch asked, looking around.

'Not the latest.'

'According to this morning's media, the minister is still refusing to budge, his supporters are counting the numbers and he's getting cross-factional support.'

He held up the newspaper. The headline read, 'POO AFFAIR: MINISTER UNMOVED'.

'A terrible situation,' said Alan.

Rash dropped the newspaper onto the kitchen bench.

'I went to the hospital yesterday and spoke to the Indian cleaner. He definitely saw a long brown snake-like object on Thursday evening. So, I went back to the eighth floor by myself last night and found this.'

He dipped into the envelope he was carrying and withdrew a bedraggled length of brown cloth which Alan recognised immediately.

'As I found it on the carpet and as it's long, brown and snake-like,' Rasch said, 'I'm assuming there was no follow-up turd and that we're back to the original faeces and faecant.'

The confidence in his own innocence which Alan had intermittently derived from the knowledge that he couldn't have been responsible for any follow-up bolus was no more. His hands trembled as he pushed a teaspoon and then a knife into the coffee rock, no longer powder, which had formed in the bottom of the tin over the previous decade.

'Is that all you've got?' Rasch asked, observing Alan's efforts and concluding the worst.

'I'm afraid so,' said Alan.

'Then I think I'll do without.'

'That might be best,' Alan admitted.

'So I've been up most of the night, rethinking things, and every point takes me back to Quist…but as the perpetrator, instead of the target.'

'I thought you suspected one of the cleaners,' said Alan, leading Rasch into the lounge room.

'I did until I recalled that I didn't see a lot of fibre in the faeces. They eat a lot of veg on the subcontinent, you know.'

'But I'm surprised you're back to Quist.'

'I had a bad feeling about him – from the moment I first sighted him on the day of the discovery.'

They sat.

'He's not a very nice person,' said Alan, 'but why would he defecate on his own desk?'

'Territory marking?'

'Isn't that usually done with…um…liquids?'

'Hmm, you're probably right.'

'They're a lot less messy,' said Alan.

'I don't think you're concerned about that when you're telling the rest of the animal kingdom to steer clear of your turf.'

'I suppose so,' said Alan. 'But I'm still not convinced Quist would have…'

'Or it could have been an attention-seeking or sympathy ploy.'

Alan shook his head.

'What about a dominance ritual?'

Alan shook his head again. Dominance would surely have involved defecating on the desks of subordinates and, at the very least, on the desks of each of the section heads.

'Or a votive offering to the god of all matters shit-related?'

'Do you think there is one?'

'There's a god for everything, isn't there?'

'Maybe.'

'Or it could have been divination-related.'

'In the privacy of his home, I guess so.'

'Or how about this? – a set-up, so that he could showcase his crisis-management skills.'

'That's a possibility, I suppose.' Alan thought back to the moment when he'd revealed the existence of the excreta to the acting branch head…and he knew in his soul that Quist's shock had not been feigned. 'But unlikely. I can vouch for the fact that he was genuinely disturbed when I told him what was in his office that Thursday morning.'

'You're sure?'

'And it's not as if he's been covered in glory since.'

'That is disappointing,' said Rasch, 'because I'd been doing some digging into his past with interesting consequences. Did you know that his name isn't actually Quentin.'

'Yes, I'm aware of that,' said Alan.

'And as a youth, he was a promising gymnast.'

'Meaning?'

'He was lithe.'

Now Alan understood. 'But getting onto the desk wasn't going to require the agility of a gymnast, was it?'

'Have you actually tried it?'

Alan wasn't about to admit to a re-enactment. 'Quentin might be the key to the puzzle,' said Alan, 'but I doubt that he's the culprit.'

Rasch sighed. 'There's no chance that Valerie left it for him? "Here, all of this metaphorical crap, plus this actual crap, is yours."'

'She loves her job.'

'Then I suppose I'm back to people who might have been unhappy about having to work for Quist: someone not willing to look him in the eyes and say "up yours", someone spineless, someone for whom silent protest was the only option.'

Alan thought that the odds of the act being silent, bearing in mind the mode of protest in question, were poor, but kept his own counsel. He was more worried about investigative attention shifting to the timid and cowardly, about someone reporting on his presence in the building late on the last working day of the year, about video footage confirming his drunken state and about Rasch putting two and two together with the usual even number result.

Alan knew that it was time to put scruples to one side and place his own best interests foremost but it was hard for him to ignore the moral compass he'd employed to avoid the ethical reefs, shoals and shallows which had made shark food of less principled voyagers on life's perilous seas. In the final analysis, though, he told himself that the action he was contemplating was less a deception than the galvanising of a plausible alternative reality and was unlikely, in any event, to unduly delay the revealing of the real truth (whatever that might yet prove itself to be). By such specious reasoning is the full range of shameful acts, from petty domestic treacheries to murderous outrages, justified…and Alan understood this, even as his heart denied the fact.

'I happened to hear something interesting over the weekend which might be of interest to you,' he finally announced.

'Go on,' said Rasch.

'But I'd rather no one knew you heard it from me.'

'You're able to tell me in the very strictest confidence.'

'It's about Quist and his staff.'

'Ultra, absolute, completest discretion.'

'It seems, before the executive intervened at the behest of the minister's office, he had his subordinates flexing off before they attended the lavatory.'

'And?'

'You don't see?'

'Nope.'

'You didn't think it is more than coincidence that the object left on his desk was…faecal?'

'Well, it was never likely that some wandering shitter was going to drop a penguin on the desktop, was it?'

'But that's my point: "it" was the very thing you'd have expected some one still angry about the toilet initiative to leave.'

'Of course.'

'It could have been any one of his staff.'

'You're right,' said Rasch.

'And they're all tragic, broken-spirited wretches at the lower levels.'

'The very people I had in mind.'

'Precisely,' said Alan, happy to have Rasch think the idea his own.

'If the minister is sacked today, I'll apprehend and interrogate every last one of the cowardly swine.'

Alan loathed himself.

'They won't know what hit them,' said Rasch.

There was a manic glint in his eyes and a frightening image materialised in Alan's mind of the director of security in the role of Torquemada, Grand Inquisitor, applying the hole punch, the stapler and the bodkin to the extremities of various innocent zombies strung up in the tea room. Alan supplemented self-loathing with disgust.

'My cruellest and most unusual punishments,' said Rasch.

Alan added shame to the mix.

'When did the toilet thing happen?' Rasch asked.

Alan almost answered, 'If it was me, some time on Christmas Eve.' Sleep deprivation was now, he reasoned, affecting his thinking. 'You're asking about Quist's ban?'

'Yes.'

'In March.'

'You really should have brought this to my attention earlier.'

'I only just heard about it.'

'There's no time to be lost,' said Rasch, standing. 'I'll see myself out.'

Alan watched him reverse out of the driveway and drive off in the direction of the department. There had still been no mention of the security camera tapes and what they revealed about Alan's condition on Christmas Eve.

Filled with remorse and not optimistic about his evacuative prospects, Alan repaired to the lavatory, where a wave of passing weariness picked him up and rolled him gently through soporific shallows onto snoozy sands.

He dozed for nearly two hours, slumped against the side wall, and would perhaps have slept longer had it not been for irritating entreaties to wakefulness from a far-off place. The work mobile phone rang and rang on the kitchen bench until Alan's eyes blinked open and he realised that he'd slept in for the first time in more than three decades of public service.

Horrified, he rose and started towards the door, only to be brought crashing down by his own trousers, fettering his movements as effectively as any set of manacles. Later, he would think that the gash on his forehead, the following unconsciousness and the blood which pooled around him on the floor were karmic consequences of the evil step he had taken to divert Rasch's attention away from himself onto those especially timorous and oppressed persons who'd been inconvenienced (in every sense) by Quentin Quist's time-keeping reforms.

When Alan recovered consciousness, he pushed himself up into a sitting position, looked in astonishment at the blood on and around him, and located the cut above his right eyebrow.

This time, he took care to remove his shoes and then his trousers before carefully rising to take his bearings. He wiped his hands clean on toilet paper and, rolling his shirt into a ball, used the cleanest parts of it to spread the blood on the floor around with his feet. Logic soon told him that his efforts to mop up the mess were in vain and he tiptoed, with his fingers brushing the walls on either side, to the shower. Following propitiatory sacrifice, there must always be cleansing.

25

It was ten forty-five by the time Alan was out of the shower. He rang the office before driving in and his phone was answered by April-May Wong, one of Morton's assistants in the Committees C subsection, back from Christmas leave. She informed him that Quentin Quist had been looking for him, that Morton had attended the ten o'clock directors meeting in his absence and that the air conditioning system was (still) not working.

Once in the building, Alan caught the lift to the floor below his own and took the fire stairs to avoid any nastiness from Daphne. Halfway up he encountered Escher Burgoyne, glowing from the exertion and dressed in dark blue overalls. The occupational health and safety director was carrying a wrench, some gaff tape and a spray can of WD40.

'Don't even think of complaining to me about the air conditioning,' the fat man announced. 'I'm taking the stairs specifically to avoid whingeing.'

'You have my sympathy,' said Alan.

'Just because I'm English doesn't mean that I'm immune to it, you know,'

'I'm sure it doesn't,' said Alan.

'Between temperamental air conditioning compressors, rogue turds, and so-called colleagues trying to undermine me at every turn...'

'It can't be easy,' Alan said.

'What about you?' Burgoyne asked, thinking himself in friendly territory and pointing to the plaster over Alan's right eye.

'I slipped in the shower,' Alan announced. The true story was one which would have prompted undesirable speculation about him toileting in some peculiar, lofty, desk-like way.

'Come the revolution, every worker will have a safe and attractive domestic ablutions facility.'

'I'm sure they will,' said Alan.

Burgoyne looked up and down the stairwell, then motioned Alan closer. 'Everyone seems to have their own theory about who dropped that arse goblin on Quist's desk. What's your take on it?'

The theory which had deprived Alan of peace and sleep since the discovery of 'it' was one he was not yet prepared to reveal, and the alternative he'd put to Rasch was one which he believed had already brought him misfortune.

'I haven't yet formed a view,' he said.

Burgoyne motioned him even closer and, as he spoke, Alan could feel the fat man's breath on his ear.

'My advice would be to look no further than the apparatus of the fascist state – to the traditional instruments of the workers' oppression.'

'I'm not sure I…'

'The secret police.'

'I'm still not sure I…'

'Who,' said Burgoyne, dropping his voice to a whisper, 'heads our own Gestapo?'

'Who?' said Alan.

'Who is our own Heinrich Himmler?'

'I have no idea,' said Alan.

'Rasch,' said Burgoyne.

'You think Rasch was responsible for the…?'

Alan was astounded. This was one possibility which had not previously occurred to him.

'It stands to reason,' said Burgoyne.

'It does?'

'You know the fascist state will brook no opposition.'

Did Alan know? He wasn't sure he did.

'That turd has given him the perfect excuse to investigate us all, as a preliminary to death squads, show trials and concentration camps.'

'But rumour has it that he's been told not to investigate anything.'

'They want you to believe that. He wants you to believe it, too. But what does the history of terror teach us?'

'I don't know,' said Alan.

Burgoyne looked up the stairs and then down. 'It teaches us that no one is safe.'

'Of course,' said Alan.

Burgoyne resumed a normal distance. 'I'd better be on my way, comrade.'

'I wish you success with the air conditioner,' said Alan.

'Death to the imperialist aggressors,' said Burgoyne, recommencing his journey downwards.

'And to the running dog fellow travellers,' said Alan for politeness's sake.

He scaled the remaining stairs in his own journey and went, once on his own floor, directly to his bay.

Quentin Quist wasn't in his office, but April-May Wong was speaking animatedly on the phone in Chinese. Trevithick meanwhile was listening to someone on his own phone, and Morton and the graduate were nowhere to be seen. Edwina Troy was transferring numbers from a propped-up file on to a spreadsheet.

Everyone turned in their seats to face Alan and he gave them all a wave which by any objective measure was more a tremor than a true gesture. They turned away, as he noticed, sitting on his keyboard, a large brown turd, coiled like an Indian snake charmer's basket reptile.

Alan thought it odd that no one else in the bay appeared to have noticed it. He looked to the left and to the right, and when he was sure no one was watching, bent over and sniffed from a distance of ten centimetres. His nose detected…nothing.

He picked a document up off his desk and waved it from the object toward himself a number of times. Still his nose detected nothing. Finally, when he was sure, again, that no one was watching him, he removed a ballpoint from his pocket and, like Toni before him, poked the object with it. At the instant he perceived the surface to be impenetrable, he could hear Trevithick's laughter.

'It's painted plaster of Paris,' said his subordinate. 'The children made lots of them on the weekend and came in with me last night to distribute them.'

'Very funny, I'm sure,' said Alan. He picked up the coprome and dropped it into the bin.

He was still standing, removing his diary from his briefcase, when Carol's door opened and Quentin Quist and Morton appeared in the doorway, laughing and looking admiringly at each other. Alan ducked, to avoid being seen. If he'd been asked to account for this action, he'd have found it hard to furnish an explanation, for Carol was able to meet with whomsoever she wished, and Morton and Quist, though sworn enemies, were not prevented by law or convention from sharing a moment of levity. The truth of the matter, however, was that Alan felt – like someone sighting adulterous acquaintances at a restaurant in a far-off town – that he'd seen something he shouldn't have.

He turned on his computer (without any impact on the atmosphere) and pretended to be busy with his diary, so that, when Morton and Quist appeared next to him, he had an excuse to look surprised.

'Ah, Alan, you've finally made it in,' said Quist.

'I'm very sorry I'm late, Quentin.'

Quist eyed the Band-Aid on Alan's forehead with suspicion. It occurred to Alan that he was suspected of imitative mockery even though accurate piss-taking would have required a plaster across his nose.

'I slipped in the shower.'

'Morton filled in for you at section heads,' said Quist, 'so all is not lost.'

'Thank you,' said Alan to the lauded one. 'That was most kind of you.'

'Not at all.'

'I'll let him bring you up to speed with matters,' said Quist, turning and leaving.

The instant he was gone, everyone else turned in their chairs to look at Morton.

'Actually, there's not much to tell,' said the centre of attention, going to his workstation. 'Except that the graduate will be working with Carol on her project until further notice, sharing her office, the air conditioning is still not fixed, and the secretary has encouraged everyone to not be distracted by the ministerial crisis at a time when we are in the spotlight. Oh, and Valerie loved her flowers, Alan. She emailed Quentin and told him she was especially touched by the card that went with them.'

Alan's intuition told him that this was not a full account of events.

'I'll make a start redoing the Friday afternoon emails,' Morton said to Alan. 'Quentin told me about yesterday's mixed disaster.'

Alan tried to mask his surprise. That Morton would be so agreeable about redoing a task he'd thought pointless first time around was more than mystifying.

'We'd better let you make progress,' said Alan, 'and I'll catch up with the rest of you once I've looked at my emails.'

Everyone turned back to their screens, so Alan logged on, deleted more jocular messages from his In box and was partway through the morning's media clippings when his phone rang.

On the line was Brian Gulliver's EA. 'Brian was wondering,' she said, 'if you had a spare moment to pop up and see him.'

The deputy secretary had never before required Alan's presence in the non-festive part of the year; this unexpected summons filled Alan with apprehension. 'Calm yourself,' an inner voice said. 'Even if your guilt has been conclusively established, by means not yet apparent, it's unlikely that someone as important as a deputy secretary would be enlisted to dismiss you.'

'Don't bet on it,' a different voice urged him. 'If senior members of the executive are needed to approve minor purchases, higher duties and staff transfers, why shouldn't one of the Gods be required to action your dismissal?'

'Are you there?' asked the EA.

'I'm sorry,' said Alan. 'When would he like to see me?'

'Would now be convenient?'

'Certainly,' said Alan. 'Do I need to bring anything with me?'

'As in?'

'Documents and so forth.'

'He mentioned nothing to me.'

'I'll be there shortly.'

Quentin Quist, when informed that Brian Gulliver had requested Alan's presence, reached for his coat. 'Does the first assistant secretary know?'

'I came straight to you,' Alan answered.

'Did you ask what the proposed discussion would be about?' asked Quist.

'I was told I didn't need to bring anything.'

'So I can't even tell the first assistant secretary what the meeting will be about? How will she know whether she should join us?'

'I got the impression that Brian wanted to meet only with only me.'

Quist laughed. 'And how likely would that be, Alan? Honestly?'

'I was once his supervisor,' said Alan.

'Yes, and we all know how much he treasured that experience.'

'I suppose so,' said Alan.

Quist rang Brian Gulliver's EA and placed his phone on speaker mode.

'It's a personal matter,' the EA said.

'A personal matter,' Quist mused. 'Of what sort?'

'Of the private and confidential sort,' the EA said. 'Thank you for calling.'

The speaker light went out.

'That uppity little bitch,' said Quist. 'Did you just hear what she said to me, an acting branch head?'

Alan nodded glumly.

'I am speechless,' said Quist. 'And…' His left hand encouraged passing breast-high waters.

'Appalled?' suggested Alan.

'Disgusted,' said Quist. 'And I don't care how personal, private and confidential the discussion is. I don't care if you're talking about…' His right hand did the horizontal water whisking thing.

'Feelings?' suggested Alan, nominating the most embarrassing subject that in his estimation could ever be discussed by two men.

'Whatever. But if you discuss anything to do with work, anything even remotely to do with public administration, I will want to know about it, the minute you return. Do you understand me?'

'Perfectly,' said Alan.

'And no telling Gulliver that I require you to report back to me.'

'No.'

'And as soon as you're back, I want you to speak to Trevithick about his practical jokes. They're not funny. In the current circumstances, they're the very opposite.'

'Yes.'

'Robyn might tolerate this sort of thing in her section but I can tell you that artificial ploppies are not tolerated in mine and I will not countenance them while I am acting branch head. Trevithick has come perilously close to a charge under the code of conduct. He's only escaped punishment because I've been so busy with other things. That said, if the fakes get any media attention, he'll know the true meaning of discipline.'

Did Quist really think that taking disciplinary action against Trevithick over a few false faeces would have been a prudent move? Who, at the end of the day, Alan wondered, would have been the officer bringing the service most into disrepute: the joker or his judge?

'I'll speak to him,' said Alan.

'Go.'

Alan left before Quist changed his mind.

26

'Strength and power,' said the security guard named Boris at the first gate. 'Other men will fear and admire you.'

'Rippling muscles,' said Anselm at the second gate. 'Women – many of them with shapely bottoms and large breasts – will worship you.'

As usual, in the executive suite, Alan was asked to take a seat. He placed himself in the only available space between two furiously texting, beautifully suited women whose cabin-compatible roller bags and leather satchels announced them to be top-dollar consultants.

As a trio of public servants left Brian Gulliver's office, Alan glimpsed through the open door a slice of the view across the suburbs to the mountains and was transported, for the third time in as many working days, back to Christmas Eve. He was pushed back into his chair by the impact of the download and gasped at the vividness of the recollection. Neither of the consultants looked up from their iPads.

Alan saw himself at the connecting door between the meeting room and Brian Gulliver's office. He had cleaned the long tables, vacuumed the floor and packed the dishwasher one last time. He'd also placed the leftovers on a covered tray in the fridge for persons unknown, because that's what he always did. With his own baking trays washed and dried and placed in a carry bag, he'd then knocked on the door to announce that he was done and say his customary farewells.

He'd earlier thought that this might be the appropriate time to mention that his fifty-fifth was less than a month away and that, in consequence he wouldn't be available to assist with future Christmas parties. However, he'd realised that this announcement would have been less about alerting Gulliver to the need to line up a replacement caterer than about eliciting from the deputy secretary some acknowledgement of his contribution to the work of the department and, perhaps, an indication that he would be welcome back to work, should he ever decide to return.

Not wanting to appear needy, he resolved to be silent about his intentions. It gave him some satisfaction to think that Gulliver's EA would report to Brian the next November that Alan had left the department – perhaps even that he'd been snapped up by another agency – and that inconvenient and costly alternative catering arrangements would need to be made.

Still back in Christmas Eve, Alan knocked again at Gulliver's door and the deputy secretary called to him to enter. Gulliver was sitting with his back to the desk, in a visitor's chair in front of the floor-to-ceiling windows. The suburbs stretched out before him and a glass of red wine sat on a low table at his side.

'I came to say farewell,' said Alan.

'You're finished, then,' said Gulliver, dabbing at his eyes with a tissue.

'All done,' said Alan.

Gulliver cleared his throat and Alan suspected that he'd been crying.

'Get yourself a glass.'

'I shouldn't,' said Alan. 'I haven't had anything to eat and I'm driving.'

'It may be our last opportunity,' said Gulliver, shaping the tissue in readiness to blow his nose.

Alan couldn't imagine tears being shed at the tardy realisation that he was soon to retire or for the careless, even cruel, way his help with the catering had been acknowledged earlier. He deduced the worst: that Gulliver was about to tell him of a tumour left for too long and of follow-up excisions, poisonings and burnings in the cause of securing 'more' – more of everything, except cancer.

Alan steadied himself, because with every one of his colleagues who fell, it seemed that his own survival prospects were diminished, as though, like wildebeest, there was danger in reduced numbers. He secured a glass and positioned the chair at the opposite end of the low table.

Gulliver, who seemed to have composed himself, poured the wine. 'I've had bad news,' he said.

'I'm sorry to hear that,' said Alan.

'In the new year, after Denise returns from holidays, the PM will announce her move to one of the central agencies. I had been led to believe I would be succeeding her as secretary but…' His eyes misted over and he reached into his pocket for another tissue.

Alan looked out at the houses, streets and trees filling the valley before him: the environs of ordinary folk who could only aspire to life's lesser prizes.

'But one of my colleagues – my female colleagues – has been given the nod.' He sniffed, gulped and mopped at the tears which again coursed down his cheeks.

Alan wondered why it was that people so often felt compelled to burden him with their confidences.

'I've been given the consolation prize: three years in bloody Geneva.'

Alan, who hadn't travelled anywhere at public expense for more than a decade – and even then, had only ever made the 'up before dawn, home by ten p.m.' day trips to capitals on the eastern seaboard – found it hard to regard a three-year posting to Europe's most perfect lakeside city as a cause for lamentation. But he knew more than a little about ambitions thwarted and cherished hopes denied, so endeavoured to place himself in Gulliver's hand-crafted brogues. 'Very disappointing,' he murmured.

'It was all I dreamed of – all I ever wanted to be – and the time for it was now. If it was ever going to happen it was now, but, instead, the whole thing has been a waste.'

Alan sensed that remarks of a sympathetic nature were in order. 'But how many of us make it as far as you have?' he said, gently. 'And how many of us have the opportunities you've had to put your stamp on things, to influence policy and shape the future?'

Gulliver laughed.

'And to have played a role – a key role – in public administration at the national level.'

'To have got so close to the summit,' said Gulliver. 'So near and yet so far.'

'But isn't the work what matters?' said Alan. 'In Geneva there will be important things that need doing. And there'll be no rest for you when you return. There will be tasks – important tasks – which only you will be able to get done.'

'Oh, Alan, do you really believe that anyone of us makes a difference? Anybody of reasonable intelligence with a masochistic disposition could do the work. That's the point of bureaucracy. Besides, the system operates in spite of itself.'

Gulliver topped up their glasses. 'You must know that,' he said in a kindly voice.

Alan shrugged.

'No one in the know,' said Gulliver, 'thinks it's an effective or even second-best way of doing things.'

The deputy-secretary studied Alan's face. 'No, Alan, tell me it's not true. Tell me you're not still a believer. Not after all these years.'

Alan's face burned and he looked away.

'Oh, you poor bloody fool.'

They both gazed out at the mountains.

'You must have had your doubts?' Gulliver suggested. 'At some stage.'

'No, not really.'

'You've never looked around and thought, this is madness made systemic?'

'No.'

'Not when you've rewritten something a dozen times or slaved for months over something that was never actually required or when you've worked overnight to comply with an urgent deadline? Not when a document you've written, which did the job, was completely stuffed up by someone above you in the food chain who didn't understand the problem or the circumstances or didn't make the time to? Not when something that was crucial, which you've given your soul to and worked on night and day, is overtaken by events? And don't pretend that you've not put in the hours. I see your car outside at all sorts of strange times.'

Alan was emboldened by the wine to speak up, but in a quiet, certain way. 'The system isn't perfect. I know that. The department is like any big organisation. But the point is that we usually get to the right outcome, don't we? We usually arrive at the right destination and thereby give people out there' – he gestured towards the suburbs – 'confidence in public administration and good government.'

'But at what cost?' said Gulliver, 'because, for every little cluster of bludgers, clock-watchers and idlers, there's someone who, for whatever reason, is prepared – without additional pay – to get in early, work through lunch, stay until midnight and work on the weekend to keep things going, at cost to themselves and their families. The system only operates because there are individuals like them at all levels who are prepared for their own peculiar reasons to pitch in – some for only a while, some in bursts and some for the duration. The system will take what they have to offer because without them it would fail.'

Alan thought about the previous three decades of his own life and knew this to be true.

'Let me be very clear about this, Alan: the system doesn't just accept and desire your sacrifices, it demands them, for without your above-and-beyond efforts it must die.'

'And you,' Alan asked, 'you pitched in only because you thought you could make it to the top?'

'What other motive can there be, once you understand, as any thinking person must, that the system will consume whatever human energy it is offered, that it doesn't need to reward most of those who go the extra yards and that it logically can't reward all of those who offer more. No, the great challenge in these circumstances is to be noticed and rewarded, to not be so remarkable at a job that you can't be allowed to leave but to be remarkable enough to warrant promotion…and, finally, to ascend the summit. To make it to secretary is everything – the only thing.'

'The work,' said Alan, 'the good work we do: it can't be irrelevant.'

Gulliver scratched his head. 'The work: well, it mostly won't do any harm and I suppose that it's a good thing to keep people busy. If nothing else, their incomes buy goods, keep businesses afloat, pay taxes and keep the economy ticking over, et cetera.'

Alan felt deeply dispirited. Had his sacrifices meant so little? He drained his glass. Gulliver refilled it and acquired another bottle from a cupboard near his desk. He placed the new bottle on the table.

'Until today I never really understood what motivated you and how you carried on after your…your mis-step.'

Alan didn't want to relive that tragic period. What was the point? Besides, he'd now drunk more than he was accustomed to and could conceivably become emotional if he recalled too much about long-past events.

'I kept going because it was the right thing to do.'

'But there must have been times when you thought about what might have been…'

'Of course,' said Alan. 'But there was no changing what had happened.'

'So we both ended up making sacrifices in vain.'

Alan might reasonably have pointed out that there had been no hope of glory to sustain him through the saddest years, no promotions to keep him motivated, no expressions of respect and admiration to bolster his sense of personal worth, and no other indicators of executive favour to assure him that his efforts had been noted. He might also have pointed out that Gulliver hadn't had to live with mockery prompted by the mere mention of his name, as Alan had been required to do in the years immediately after his blunder, and that there was no all-expenses paid overseas posting to reconcile him to dashed ambitions as the finish line came into view. There had only been his belief that there was something inherently worthwhile about their calling and that the most mundane tasks performed by the lowliest clerk were, as contributions to the collective good, invested with just as much nobility as the complex, big-picture decisions made by the secretary and the senior executive cohort.

Yet, according to Gulliver this thinking was laughably misguided, even deserving of pity. The possibility that the deputy secretary's reading of the circumstances could have been correct and that he, Alan, could, by implication, have misread matters so comprehensively and for so long, was unthinkable. He might at this point have declaimed on the essential role played by conscientious, impartial and uncorrupted public services in modern democracies…but he knew that this truth was not to the point.

He drained his glass and, when Gulliver refilled it, downed the contents, again. When the deputy secretary attempted a follow-up refill, he slopped wine over the table. Alan didn't care.

'To older, simpler times,' said Gulliver.

'To old, simpler times,' Alan replied.

They clicked glasses and drank, and the toast led Gulliver neatly on to a survey of old colleagues – people with whom he and Alan had once worked – and where their labours had taken them. It was an exercise the deputy secretary had done before; the names were remembered without hesitation in alphabetical order, and their current or pre-retirement classifications were able to be specified with absolute certainty. None of the recalled individuals had enjoyed a rise as brilliant as Gulliver's and therein, of course, lay the impetus for the exercise.

Alan sat drinking quietly as trajectories more remarkable than his own, were scorned and mocked as fitting for drudges, dullards and drones. The list was long, the shortcomings of those on it were not readily glossed over and the worst journeys to mediocrity were much too satisfying to be abbreviated by summary or abridgement.

More than half an hour passed with nothing more than the occasional murmured intimation of attention from Alan. Gulliver was reliving the soul-deadening, snail's-paced failure of someone called Simmons or Simons or Simpkin – someone Alan couldn't recall at all – when Alan, who'd been brooding about the system's exploitation of the naturally diligent and the preternaturally selfless, decided he had endured enough.

'To Geneva,' he announced rising unsteadily and sloshing wine down his shirt front.

'Bugger Geneva,' said the deputy secretary.

'No, to Geneva,' said Alan,

'All right, to bloody Geneva,' replied Gulliver rising and spilling wine down his front.

They drank.

'And cuckoo clocks.'

'Cuckoo clocks?' asked the deputy secretary, swaying dangerously.

'They make them in Switzerland,' said Alan, offering a steadying hand.

'So they do.'

They drank again.

'And to alpine horns and pristine lakes.'

'To horns and lakes.'

They drank again. Their glasses were both emptied.

'And to taxpayer-funded international travel,' Alan continued.

'Now you're talking.' Gulliver topped them both up, getting as much onto the carpet as into their glasses. 'To first-class junkets.'

They clinked and guzzled.

'And to a tax-free salary,' said Alan.

'To untaxed Euros.'

They clicked and guzzled again.

'With reimbursed living expenses.'

'Hold on, we need another bottle.'

Another bottle was duly obtained, opened and part-emptied.

'Where were we up to, again?'

'To expenses, living and otherwise,' said Alan.

They clinked and drank, yet again.

'And to the rental income from your Australian residence, regrettably taxed.'

'To the rental income,' said Gulliver.

This time they raised their glasses and drank, without clinking.

'To the annual trip home, courtesy of the taxpayer.'

'To the annual trip home.'

This time they didn't even bother raising their glasses, before drinking.

'And to all of the other hardships and privations you'll have to endure,' slurred Alan.

Gulliver placed his glass on the table. 'And what the hell did you mean by that?'

'Nothing,' said Alan.

'Nothing?'

'Nothing,' Alan repeated, matching Gulliver's gaze, despite swaying gently backwards and forwards. 'If you must know, I feel genuinely sorry for you, banished to Geneva.'

The deputy secretary studied Alan's face for signs of malice. 'Do you?'

'Yes, I do.'

'You're drunk,' slurred Gulliver.

'I am,' said Alan, starting to cry…but for himself and his wasted decades, rather than for the hardships and privations to be endured by the Swiss-bound Gullivers.

'Now, now. Don't get yourself worked up,' said the deputy secretary. 'It's only three or four years. I'll survive. You'll see. It'll pass in a flash.'

Alan placed his glass on the table edge, from where it dropped onto the carpet. Looking at the wasted wine, Alan's tears intensified.

'Ah, don't worry about that. Plenty more in the bottle. Plenty more bottles.'

Alan wiped tears from his eyes.

Gulliver, uncertain about what he should do to comfort his old supervisor – feeling that he should, however, do something – opted for a 'drunken mate' hug.

Alan broke down, entirely.

'It's not as though I'll be gone forever,' said the deputy secretary, crying, too. 'And who knows? Maybe you could even come and visit – get a cuckoo horn and an alpine clock.'

Alan's sobs now convulsed his body.

'And by the time I get back, you'll probably be in charge of the place. Wouldn't that be a turn-up for the books? You in charge of me again… and we could retire together… I mean at the same time.'

This was too much for Alan, even in his distraught state. He pushed himself free of Gulliver's arms, knocking the deputy secretary off his feet. Their third or fourth bottle – the very fine wine that Alan had brought as a farewell gift – was tipped at the same time off the table, so that its contents gurgled ingloriously onto the carpet.

Alan lurched towards the door and the last thing he heard as the lift carried him away was Brian Gulliver plaintively calling his name.

27

'Alan. Alan. Come on. Look at me.' Brian Gulliver was on his haunches between the roller cases of the top-dollar consultants. 'Are you okay?' He passed a hand from left to right across Alan's line of sight.

Alan blinked, looked at Gulliver, then at the two consultants and finally at the watching EAs. He was, he realised, no longer drunk, distressed and descending on Christmas Eve, but back in the present.

'He's all right,' Gulliver announced.

'Do you want me to get the first aid officer,' one of the EAs asked.

'Do we need to get you a first aid officer, Alan?' said Gulliver.

'What about a glass of water?' asked one of the other EAs.

'Some water?' said Gulliver.

'I'll be fine,' said Alan. 'I'm just a bit dazed.'

'Dazed?' asked Gulliver.

Alan wondered what additional information he could offer that would support his claim. 'I had a knock on the head this morning,' he announced, patting his forehead to locate the plaster he'd applied to the gash. 'But I'm fine now, really.'

'I think you should have a glass of water,' said Gulliver.

Alan rose.

'Take it easy,' said one of the consultants.

Alan accompanied Gulliver into the deputy secretary's office and they sat in visitors' chairs – possibly the ones they'd occupied on Christmas Eve – facing the huge, empty desk. Alan glanced at the carpet in front of the windows and thought he could detect a faint crimson stain.

An EA placed a glass of water in his hands.

'Feeling any better?' asked Gulliver.

'Much better, thank you.'

'Good. How was your Christmas?'

'Very quiet,' said Alan. 'Did you and Bernice have a pleasant break?'

'Very pleasant, thank you.'

'That's good,' said Alan, not knowing where to look to avoid the deputy secretary's piecing gaze.

'I didn't expect to return to work so soon but the little problem in your branch head's office has given rise to bigger problems. So here I am.'

'All very unfortunate,' mused Alan.

Gulliver looked at his watch. 'I thought we should talk about Christmas Eve.'

'Yes,' said Alan, hoping that he wasn't about to be reminded of the hugging episode or, worse still, to be told that he shouldn't get the wrong idea about the embrace and that the deputy secretary was confident in his – his own – heterosexuality. Remarks of this sort would be wearisome in the extreme.

'We'd both had quite a bit to drink.'

'We had,' said Alan.

'And although my recollection is patchy, I have a feeling that I may have disclosed to you, some things that I, perhaps, should have kept to myself.'

'I don't recall a great deal about Christmas Eve,' said Alan intent on saving the deputy secretary and himself embarrassment.

'You don't?' said Gulliver, looking relieved. 'Nothing about cuckoo clocks?'

'No,' said Alan, trying to appear convincingly puzzled. 'I remember finishing the tidying up next door and I have a vague idea that we may have had a celebration of our own but I'm ashamed to say that I don't recall anything about it except that I spilt some wine on your carpet at some point.' Alan's dissembling had all the hallmarks of shame and was therefore, entirely convincing.

'No use crying over spilled wine,' said Gulliver heartily, 'but, if you do recall anything about our discussion, I would rely on your discretion: the discretion you are well known for.'

'Yes,' said Alan, 'certainly.'

Gulliver pinched the knees of his pinstriped blue trousers and rose. Alan followed.

'I knew I could rely on you. And you can, in turn, rely on me to ensure that you're not a casualty in any of the fallout from the goings on in your branch.'

'Thank you,' said Alan, thinking about Morton's prophecies and the lists of names on Carol's whiteboard.

'No, thank you for making the time to drop by,' said Gulliver, extending his hand.

'Have a good year,' said Alan.

'You too,' said Gulliver, without mentioning any of the things he might have: the assistance he'd provided Alan in leaving the building on Christmas Eve, the beautiful wine Alan had given him on the same day or Alan's impending attainment of the minimum retirement age.

The audience over, Alan caught the lift to the foyer without any flashbacks. He now had, he thought to himself, all of the lost recollections, except the final, crucial one.

'Women will offer you their bodies with the previously mentioned breasts and bottoms,' said Anselm to the horror of his pair, the heavily built woman with the silver piercings.

'Men will look up to you as their alpha male,' said Boris to the amusement of his pair, the security guard who'd waylaid Alan on behalf of Security One the previous Friday.

On his own floor, Alan passed Eris on her way to the washroom.

'I've got an office and a mentor,' she announced, 'and I'm working on my backhand.'

Alan mustered a polite smile and thought about the Corporate Foliage Optimisation executive's prediction that things would not go well for the young woman.

Quentin Quist affected surprise when Alan appeared in his doorway

'What! Finished talking confidential, personal and private matters?'

'Yes,' said Alan.

'Was there anything work-related you should reveal to me as your superior?'

Alan was not invited to sit.

'He wanted to talk to me about who would cater at his Christmas drinks in future years.'

'Because?'

'Because we didn't have an opportunity to discuss the matter on Christmas Eve.'

'No, I meant why wouldn't you be available in future years?'

Once embarked on the liar's path, inspiration came quickly to Alan. 'He thinks I may be tempted to retire and wanted me to nominate a replacement caterer – someone with appropriate experience and qualifications, and someone more important than me, whose own status would say something to attendees about the deputy secretary's position and power.'

Quist paled, doubtless recalling that his hospitality training had not been limited to ironing, bedmaking, decanting and procuring.

'And who did you suggest?'

'I wasn't able to nominate anyone at this point.'

'But did you have anyone in mind – you know, on a...' The rotating hand.

'A shortlist?'

'Yes.'

'I said I'd have to think about it.'

Quist looked Alan in the eye and Alan, to his own surprise, returned his supervisor's gaze, without flinching.

Quist was the first to break. 'And that was it?'

'That was it.'

'Then I'll let you go, but should you need someone to test a shortlist with – not that I'd know the first thing about catering and such – I can barely bake a bean, ha ha – make sure that you get in touch...'

'I'll certainly bear you in mind,' said Alan.

'For testing the shortlist.'

'For testing the shortlist.'

'I'd be delighted to assist.'

'But bearing in mind how busy you are, I suppose it's unlikely that you'll have the time.'

'No, no. I'll make the time,' said Quist, 'soon, if necessary.'

'All right,' said Alan.

'For you…and Brian.'

'I'll go, then,' said Alan.

'Yes, but don't overdo things. You've gone the extra mile in recent times – in all times, really – and, well, a knock on the bonce' – he chuckled – 'can be a nasty thing, really.'

'I'll take care.'

'And if you feel unwell, don't think twice about working a half day and heading home to rest.'

'Thank you, Quentin. I think I'll be fine.'

When Alan returned to his cubicle, the time displayed on his computer was eleven thirty-five. On his keyboard was a small trihedric cardboard sign featuring a stick figure in a squatting position excreting brown pebbles. Over the image was superimposed the red bisected circle internationally known to denote a prohibition.

'Is that what I think it is?' said Alan.

'I'm afraid so,' said Morton. 'We've all got one, from Personnel, because of the secretary's workplace health and safety responsibilities. I signed for yours, so don't lose it, will you?'

'How ghastly,' said Alan.

He was conscious that he hadn't accomplished any of the things he was accustomed to achieving at work in the mornings. More importantly, he'd not enquired about April-May's Christmas, had failed to tell Trevithick that a plumbing consultant's sick certificate did not meet the relevant guidelines and had not followed up his earlier enquiry to Personnel about the permissibility of a family leave application arising from the alleged illness of a Burmese blue named Pussils. In his experience, it was always advisable to deal with the most difficult matters at the very beginning of the day.

'How did you go with Gulliver?' asked Morton, typing furiously.

'Nothing problematic,' said Alan.

'Excellent,' said Morton.

'Once I've looked at my emails,' Alan announced in a louder voice, for the benefit of all of the adjacent section members, 'I'll find a vacant office and catch up with each of you.'

He enlivened his screen. Apart from a message from the director personnel explaining that the poo-proscribing desk signs were to be prominently displayed until further notice, nothing seemed to require Alan's attention, so he sent a message to the Personnel helpline enquiring about the status of Pussils – was he/she/it able to be regarded as a family member for the purpose of carer's leave or not?

He then logged on to the meeting room booking system and noticed that a room large enough for four was vacant at the other end of the floor. He accordingly secured it for the hour ahead and sent Morton an invitation to join him. He turned his computer off and heard the air conditioning system spring to life.

'I don't suppose you'd be interested in any further interesting facts on poo?' Morton said, even before he was through the door.

'No. Not at present.'

'They're all new. Not a one recycled.'

'No.'

Morton consulted his notebook. 'What about lavatories and international toilet habits.'

'Most certainly not.'

'Or, I know, defecation and related activities in the ancient world.'

'How ancient?'

'Would BC do?'

Alan couldn't help himself. 'Are there many aspects you haven't already apprised me of?'

'A few, yes. We haven't, for example, been anywhere near ancient Greece.'

'Later in the week, then.'

'In the meantime, did you know that seven hundred million Indians crap in the fields every day?'

Alan made a point of never purchasing foodstuffs from the sub-continent.

'And that 19 November is world toilet day?'

Alan was heartily sick of all 'days'; it seemed to him that barely a one passed without an impost on his wallet and without him being reminded of some vile medical condition or revolting human deficiency. 'We've got things to do,' he said, 'and the day is escaping us.'

'You'll want to find out what else happened at the directors' meeting.' Morton flipped to a different section of his notebook. 'I didn't want to say in front of the others that Quentin's sources in the parliament and the party have told him – in the strictest confidence – that the PM will advise the GG to sack the minister later today.'

'Extraordinary.' said Alan.

'The secretary has cancelled deputy secretaries' and first assistant secretaries' leave for the duration of the crisis. All sections are to meet this afternoon – on the secretary's instructions – and are, together, to read the media guidelines, the code of conduct and the workplace health and safety guidelines, all of which will be forwarded to section heads by business management units before two o'clock.'

'Right.'

'Oh, and Quentin wants us all to read the Official Secrets Act.'

'Because?'

'I wasn't game to ask.'

"The whole statute?

'He didn't specify any particular sections.'

'Well, I suppose it isn't the Tax Act.'

'Yes, it won't take all day.'

'Anything else?' Alan waited for Morton to make known the other (secret) matters he believed had been discussed in his meeting with Quentin Quist and Carol.

'That's it,' said Morton. 'Apart from the fact that I'm making progress with the Friday afternoon emails and should have them finished soon after lunch.'

'Well done. Send Trevithick in.'

While he waited, Alan loosened his tie. The temperature seemed to have increased markedly in a matter of minutes.

Trevithick came in and seated himself. Alan noticed a number of burns on his forearms the size of one-cent pieces.

'Sorry about the imitation turd this morning,' Trevithick said. 'Quentin nearly had a meltdown when he saw the one on his desk.'

'I'm at a loss to understand why you even contemplated leaving one on his desk.'

'At the time, I thought that the office was still yours. I didn't know you'd moved back onto the floor.'

'Quentin is not happy. He told me to warn you that you're perilously close to disciplinary action.'

'For the fake bum eels? He'd be a laughing stock.'

'I'm not sure that would dissuade him, so it would be prudent to discourage the children from further creative efforts of this sort.'

'I think the girls are bored with it. It's just my son who'll be disappointed.'

'Perhaps you could hide the makings.'

'Little boys and poo. You know what they're like.'

Alan nodded, more in sympathy than in agreement.

'Morton told me about everything that happened on Friday and I've seen the media over the weekend.'

'It's all most unfortunate,' said Alan. 'Who'd have thought that matters could get so quickly out of hand?'

'And there are rumours doing the rounds,' said Trevithick, 'that a lot more turds – real turds – were discovered on Friday morning but have been hushed up by the executive…and that we are in the midst of an epidemic of executive desk shitting…which is why the dep secs and FASs have all been recalled from leave.'

'To protect their desks?'

Trevithick shrugged.

'Rumour is never a reliable source of intelligence,' said Alan.

Trevithick was not to be stopped. 'And a friend of mine who works up on the tenth floor says that your buddy, Rasch, has been hanging around the toilets in disguise.'

'For what conceivable purpose?' said Alan.

'Apart from wanting to go?'

'Yes.'

Trevithick leaned close over the table. 'Some say he's DNA-testing the toilet seats after each use. Others reckon he's recording the times at which people are using the cubicles.'

Alan sighed. 'Look, even if he knew the precise time at which the original faeces were left or…or…had obtained DNA from them in order to carry out a matching exercise, the scale of the undertaking would be enormous.'

'At least he hasn't been seen cross-dressing and hanging around the female facilities.'

'It's all too stupid for words,' said Alan.

'I'm just telling you what others are saying.'

'Well,' said Alan, 'I hope you're not contributing to the scuttlebutt, telling others about these…' Words failed him but he refrained from water whisking.

They discussed Trevithick's sick leave and agreed that it was best if he reapplied for uncertificated personal leave. They then discussed pending work. Alan made no mention of a likely reorganisation of the committees. Until he was officially told about a restructure, he was determined that his credo would be 'business as usual', exercising the same diligence and professionalism he'd always brought to his employment, notwithstanding Brian Gulliver's views on the bureaucracy's ingratitude.

Alan's interactions with April-May Wong were over with quickly. He enquired about her family's festive season, having learned in a previous decade that enquiries about the Christmases of persons unlikely to have Christian antecedents were considered to be insensitive. He made no reference to Christmas, notwithstanding the fact that Christmas holidays customarily occurred at Christmas, and that agnostics and atheists of Alan's acquaintance comfortably referred to the period in the traditional way, without investing it with any spiritual significance.

April-May's family, Alan learnt, had worked hard over the festive season, with doctors doctoring, cleaners cleaning and restaurateurs restaurateuring (and various combinations thereof).

April-May listened impassively to Alan's reassurances as to the secretary's concern for her welfare and safety, and affected interest in his recommendation that she talk to Morton, her direct supervisor, if she felt at any time apprehensive as a result of recent events.

'No need worry about April-May, Alan. She not frightened by poo. In cleaning business, you learn fen bian your friend.'

'Your friend?'

'Round-eye customer, they wipe bench, vacuum carpet, mop floor and squeegee window before cleaner come but no one want to clean up fen bian.'

'I see,' said Alan.

'If we lose our job because of poo,' April May continued, 'April-May look after you, Alan. You hard-working man. Be good cleaner. I give you round-eye pay, not Chinese rate, and you clean toilet in place where no da bian or fen bian…or not so much.'

April-May had long been suspected of operating a cleaning business from work but because most of the related communications were in Chinese or via a hand-held device – and because any task allocated to her at work was completed to an excellent standard overnight, presumably outsourced to one of the doctors, restaurateurs or cleaners – no disciplinary action had ensued.

'I will bear that in mind,' said Alan. 'Most kind of you.'

Edwina Troy next entered the room.

'Trevithick told me everything I needed to know about Friday's goings on,' she said.

'We need to have a chat about Pussils,' Alan said.

'Yes. He's feeling very much better, thank you.'

'I'm very pleased to hear that,' said Alan. 'But it's your leave, really, that we have to discuss.'

'Why is that?'

'I have asked Personnel whether Pussils can be reasonably regarded as a family member for the purpose of carer's leave.'

'Are you suggesting that he's not a member of my family? My friend Muriel on the fourth floor received carer's leave when her goat had a prolapse. Charmaine on the ninth floor got two weeks when her hamster contracted scabies and Dolores over in Accounts had nearly a month off when her budgie had encephalitis.'

'Be that as it may, I will await Personnel's advice.'

'Just because I don't have children, I'm discriminated against.'

'It's not my intention to discriminate against you,' said Alan. 'I merely want to be reassured that I would be doing the right thing in granting you leave.'

'Was there anything else that you wished to discuss with me?' Edwina asked.

'No, but I'm very glad Pussils is better.'

Edwina left without any further words. Alan made no attempt to walk with her.

He had barely settled in, back at his desk, when Quentin Quist appeared at his elbow.

'How are you feeling?' Quist enquired.

'I'm feeling fine,' said Alan.

'Isn't that typical of Alan?' Quist said to Morton. 'Not only has he turned up at work after incurring a grievous and potentially disfiguring injury, but he's engaged with the second most senior member of the executive and attended a series of onerous meetings. The rest of you,' he said in a raised voice, 'would be well advised to note the selflessness, resilience and diligence of this exceptional officer.'

Alan smiled weakly.

'Now, off to lunch with you, Alan. You've probably done more this morning than the rest of us combined.'

'I wouldn't say –'

'No, no. On your way.'

'But I've hardly –'

'Off you go,' Quist insisted.

Alan picked up his car keys and, feeling very much like teacher's pet, trudged to the restrooms on his way to the lifts.

28

Alan half expected to see Rasch, in disguise, loitering by the hand basins when he entered the restroom. The director of security was not, however, to be encountered there or at the urinals. Looking into the wall-mounted, waterless, one-at-a-time fixture Alan did, however, see a turd whose delivery would have represented the very pinnacle of the contortionist's art if it had not, in fact, been fashioned out of plaster of Paris by the Trevithick issue – a probability made certain by the way in which it was curled and twisted into a serpentine knot, by the way in which its surface was immune to the erosive pressure Alan applied to it, and by the uncanny resemblance of the object to the copromes which Alan was surprised, on looking around, to see in each of the other niches in the row.

Rasch was not waiting in the car park, either, so Alan had no need to unnecessarily red-line the Morris Minor or take a circuitous route to Bonny Brae with the aim of shaking off an imagined tail.

At the home, Hugo stared impassively at the ceiling. His chart showed nothing abnormal and there were certainly no notes to the effect that he'd spoken since being wheeled out of the recreation room on Saturday.

Alan greeted him in the usual pointlessly optimistic way and poured water from the bedside jug into the plastic tumbler on his trolley table, trying all the while not to look at Clyde Adams in the other bed.

Sitting with his back to Adams, Alan read his way, in a low voice, through most of the To Let advertisements, eliciting – or so he thought – a stronger than usual response: the almost imperceptible hint of a smile at the bottom corners of the old chap's cracked and dribble-sticky mouth.

It wasn't until he was partway through the In Memoriam notices that Alan's self-discipline failed him. He was reading a touching plea to a great grandfather to explain why he had chosen to depart when he did – raising questions about (a) why the dead persisted with newspapers when fewer and fewer of the living were inclined to and (b) why death wasn't thought to be a sufficient explanation for the end of life – when he looked up from the page, straight into the eyes of the True Ginger.

Adams's smile was exultant and Alan could not tear his gaze away.

'Come,' the old man croaked.

Alan prayed that he would not be required to endure physical contact. He took two steps towards the high priest.

'Closer.'

The flame burned more fiercely in the old man's eyes than it had ever done and the obedience he required was as compelling, as complete, as perfect and as uncompromising as that which he'd commanded on the previous Thursday. Alan knew that if obeisance was demanded of him, obeisance would be made.

'Still closer.'

Alan dropped the paper onto the floor – where it formed a low, flaccid pyramid – and took the remaining two steps to Clyde's bedside. Adams looked up at him and Alan prepared himself to again behold the awful embodiment of the life force – that force which had, for so many years, been his nemesis and his antithesis, against whose irrepressibility his whole struggle had been waged.

'Look,' Clyde Adams commanded.

Alan waited for the tray table to be pushed away and the bedclothes to be lifted.

'Look closer,' Clyde Adams commanded, as his right hand – gnarled and spotted and trembling – emerged from underneath the sheets.

Alan peered downwards. The claw of the Master opened and revealed four small white pills.

'Take them,' said Clyde Adams.

'But I'm not unwell,' said Alan, thinking hallucinogenic shamanism unlikely.

'Take them far away,' said Clyde Adams.

'And then?' asked Alan.

'Put them in the bin.'

'In the bin?'

'In the bin, far away.'

Alan extended his hand and the pills fell into it. 'What about our secret?' Alan heard himself enquire.

'It will not be diminished,' Clyde Adams answered.

'Still our secret,' Alan intoned.

'Still our secret,' Clyde responded. 'Now go.'

Alan placed the pills in a tissue and tucked them in his trouser pocket. He returned to Hugo's bedside and was picking up the papers when Matron Frogmore entered the room.

'Ah, there you are,' she said. 'Has our patient been entertaining you with small talk?'

'Unfortunately not,' said Alan, still dazed.

'No gems for my amusement, either,' she said, moving to the spot Alan had just vacated at the side of Clyde Adams's bed. 'And I don't think we'll be hearing anything more out of this one.'

Clyde was lying on his side staring at the wall.

Matron pulled a little bottle out of her dress pocket and shook two smallish white pills from it into her hand.

'The one-hundred-milligram Largactil,' she announced. 'Two of them would stupefy an elephant.'

She pushed the tablets between Clyde's lips and gently closed his mouth shut. The old man remained all the while entranced by the spot on the wall. A note was made on the chart at the end of his bed and Matron turned her attention to Alan.

'And who's been brushing you up?' she said taking in Alan's pasty complexion and the gash over his eye.

'I slipped in the shower and sconed myself,' said Alan, settling into the lie.

Matron sighed. 'Well, I won't deny that I've sought solace in the bottle, myself, at different stages of my life but one eventually learns that it only serves to dull the pain…and, once you're injuring yourself or engaging in fisticuffs, it's time to pull back, don't you think?'

'But I haven't been drinking,' said Alan. 'I was in the shower and –'

'– and denying that you're on it, drinking in secret, pretending that all is well when it clearly isn't – these are signs that things have reached a sorry stage.'

'But –'

'– and the thing is, there's not the slightest need for guilt or self-loathing. We did our best to find out what Hugo wanted to say to us, didn't we?'

'I suppose we did,' said Alan, wondering whether he shouldn't have made a greater effort to locate works for the solo euphonium.

'The sad truth of the matter is that we don't really know what stimulates or agitates the poor things,' she said in a kindly voice. 'We don't know what prompts them to speak or be silent…and we may never understand the whys of it. Our task is only to make them as comfortable as we can until their final moment comes.'

'I suppose so,' said Alan.

'And there is no point in berating ourselves, beating ourselves up or thinking that we've failed our loved ones because they are in retreat from us.'

Alan didn't think of Hugo as a loved one, although he was undeniably family of sorts, and he didn't regard him as 'in retreat' as much as in a state of complete surrender…but the good sense inherent in Matron's statement couldn't be denied, so Alan murmured his agreement.

'The only person who can exert control over your drinking is you,' Matron continued. 'You have to make the effort. However, if you think it would help to have someone to talk to – someone who understands and admires and respects you – who would give her all to save you from the alcoholic abyss and in whose tender breast' – pressed at this point so hard against Alan that he could barely breathe – 'not all hope of romance, passion and intimacy is yet dead, then you should ring me.'

'Yes,' said Alan.

'Lunch won't be long,' she said. And then in a low voice, 'Ring me, soon.'

Alan smiled faintly, feeling anxious, and when Matron left, lowered himself into the bedside chair. It seemed to him that life – even within the safe, close boundaries that he had unwittingly set for himself over time – had recently become too intense to bear. He fingered the edges of the Band-Aid on his forehead to be sure that the plaster was still in place.

A noise – possibly a tumbler tapped against the edge of the tray table – attracted his attention to Clyde Adams's bed.

The old man's tongue protruded between his smiling lips and on it were the pills that had been inserted in Alan's presence minutes before by Matron Frogmore.

Alan heard the rumble of the lunch trolley in the corridor outside.

Clyde Adams spat the pills expertly into his hand, which disappeared under the sheets. 'Our other secret,' said the old man.

'Our other secret,' Alan replied.

29

When Hugo refused his lentils – clenching his teeth to prevent the brown sludge from being spooned into his mouth – Alan had tucked in, shovelling them down before anyone arrived to feed Clyde Adams. Aunty Vi had never abided waste and Alan had hopes of the dish's purgative qualities. So it was that there was no need for any diversion on the way back to the office in search of cascara, psyllium or senna pods.

The doors to the main building were fogged over and, on stepping inside, it was immediately apparent that Burgoyne's labours had, at last, come to fruition. The temperature was easily ten degrees lower than outside. Boris sat at the guard desk with his hands buried in his pockets and the imitation fur collar of his jacket turned up to cover his ears. He waved acknowledgement at Alan but said nothing.

On the seventh floor, Quentin Quist, wearing a jumper and fingerless gloves, spotted Alan returning to his cubicle and beckoned him over. The boxes earlier used to move Quentin's belongings from the palatial executive office sat on the visitor's table, flaps akimbo. Quist was evidently moving out.

'Come in and shut the door,' he said.

Alan pulled the door closed.

'There has been an incident,' Quist announced. 'As a result of which, Carol has decided to, ah, explore other opportunities.'

'An incident?'

'Yes, I'm not able to discuss it. But every cloud has a silver lining. As soon as I've packed up, you can move back in.'

'Thank you,' said Alan.

'Thank me by all means but that's not what I wanted to talk to you about.'

'I see,' said Alan, anticipating news to the effect that Daphne's tenure was also over and that Quist would once again require secretarial support.

'What I'm about to say to you will probably surprise you as much as it, well, shocked me.'

'I see,' said Alan.

Quist dropped into a chair and removed a soggy tissue from his pocket. 'I have been reliably informed that Rasch suspects me of doing ploppies on my own desk.'

'Surely not,' said Alan.

'While my source is not close to Rasch, my source's source is. And it seems there is no doubt. He thinks I'm the poo perpetrator.'

'How can that be?' Alan asked. 'What does Rasch think would possess you to do such a thing?'

'I don't know,' said Quist, twisting the tissue until it frayed and became two. 'I have no idea what he can be thinking.' A tear trickled down his cheek and onto his jumper.

'How unfortunate,' said Alan, conscious of rumblings in his stomach and of a whining crescendo emanating from the same vicinity.

Quist placed the broken pieces of limp tissue on the table, side by side. 'I was hoping,' he continued, 'that you could put a good word in for me – nip this misunderstanding in the bud and so forth – before it gains…' Quist's right hand hurried shallow water.

'Momentum?'

'I was thinking credibility,' said Quist, 'but momentum could do the trick, certainly.'

Alan patted his stomach to silence an especially loud bubbling noise. 'I know Rasch,' he said, 'but don't see him that often and, in any event, I'm not sure he attaches any importance to my views.'

'But anything you could say, of a positive nature, would probably help.'

'Then I'll do my best,' said Alan.

'And if you were to put in a good word for me, I would continue to be your champion here and could employ certain skills – skills most people don't know I have – culinary skills and others in the hospitality area – to assist you in catering for Brian's Christmas drinks…if, of course, no more suitable person could be found.'

Alan might reasonably have reminded Quist at this point of a certain admission earlier in the day re an inability to bake even a bean, but he was, as always, compassionate to a fault and remained silent.

'One doesn't want to be exploited,' said Quist, 'but for a friend who has done me a good turn and demonstrated loyalty in a time of crisis I could…'

'I'll call Rasch, as soon as an opportunity presents,' said Alan.

'And in the meantime some treacherous pig is sitting tight out there' – Quist gestured in the direction of the cubicles – 'laughing at us as our world crumbles.'

'These are certainly not the best of times,' said Alan.

'But if good friends stick together, they will prevail.'

'Yes,' said Alan, wondering how this statement was in any way relevant.

'Let me know how you get on with Rasch,' said Quist, standing. 'I'm counting on you.'

'I'll report back,' said Alan.

Audience concluded, Alan went straight to the lavatories where a long, simooming fart was all that resulted.

At his workstation, he started his computer and halted the air conditioning system. No one responded to the change. An email from Morton, comprised of only a subject line, read, 'Can't talk in the open plan but if you want to know why it hit the fan with Carol, meet me in the toilets.' Alan deleted the message and accepted an invitation, also from Morton, to a section meeting at three p.m. well away from the toilets (for the purpose of reading various pieces of employment-related documentation). Two further emails, both containing official documents to be read at the latter meeting, he forwarded to Trevithick for printing.

He then opened a suspiciously prompt reply to his enquiry about Edwina Troy's carer's leave and Pussils. It stated that 'the term family was not defined in the certified agreement and in related guidelines because of the evolving nature of this social unit', and that he should make his decision, as the approving officer, 'based on community mores, common sense and his understanding of the particular circumstances of the applicant'. This was not, Alan concluded, a useful response. There seemed to him to be nothing commonsensical about community mores or the modern family, except in so far as it was as desirable in the present to share living expenses with familial others as it had been in the past.

'I don't wish to be difficult,' he typed, 'but could you please let me know whether the definition of "family" is thought by the Department to comprehend non-humans?' Satisfied that he was a step closer to resolving the carer's leave problem, he invited Morton to a meeting room.

Secrets were divulged in very short order.

'Carol is in the very hottest water,' said Morton. 'Eris copped a feel from her in the showers after a lunchtime session on the courts…'

'I probably don't need to know any more,' said Alan.

'…and became hysterical.'

'Don't tell me –'

'So the security guards were summoned and they called the police…'

'I probably don't –'

'…with the result that Carol is under arrest.'

'Ghost!' said Alan.

'And Eris is on stress leave.'

'Don't say anything further.'

'That's pretty much all there is.'

Alan thought that he at last understood what the Corporate Foliage Optimisation executive had been alluding to when he prophesied that the graduate would be 'in for a surprise'.

'I hadn't invited you here to find out about any of that.'

'If I'd been dragged down to the cop station every time I'd gone on a foray beyond the bikini line, they'd have allocated me a cell of my own. I actually feel sorry for the woman.'

'I wanted to talk to you about Quentin,' said Alan.

'And there's the graduate, second day on the job – second day at any job – proceeding straight to a lucrative compo holiday. You'll be organising a floral tribute for her before the day is over.'

'Quentin…' said Alan.

'What about him?' Morton asked.

'He just told me that someone, someone with a source close to Rasch…'

'Yes.'

'…has informed him that he was suspected of defiling his own desk.'

'Yes.'

'I've deduced that the informant was you.'

'No denying it.'

'And I wondered what good purpose was served by letting Quist know he was Rasch's principal suspect. I well recall that you don't think much of him, but –'

'To the contrary,' Morton remarked. 'It recently occurred to me that I had misjudged him. He is capable of silliness, of course – aren't we all? – but he has his merits.'

Having heard nothing remotely complimentary about Quist from Morton in the past, Alan was somewhat surprised by this turnaround. 'But if you're suddenly more appreciative of his virtues, why have you been upsetting him by telling him that he's Rasch current suspect?'

'Forewarned is forearmed.'

'But for all we know, Rasch might have moved on.'

'Really?'

'Yes.'

'How moved on?'

'He might, for example, have been dissuaded from his conclusions about Quist by, I don't know, someone able to posit a more credible theory.'

'Is that so?' said Morton, nodding and smiling.

'Yes…by someone able to nominate a more likely suspect or suspects, based perhaps on past animosities.'

Morton paled.

'Christ, Alan, you haven't landed me in it, have you?'

'Of course not – and I'm not admitting anything about discussions I might or might not have had with Rasch – but I can, in fact, tell you that he has moved on.'

'Then I'll let Quentin know, immediately,' said Morton, rising, 'unless there's something else you wanted to discuss with me.'

'No.'

'I don't suppose you'd be prepared to let me know who the latest suspect is?'

'For all I know, Rasch may have reached a different conclusion again since then.'

'But the interim suspects were…?'

'No one of any concern to us.'

'My contact will fill me in, you know.'

'I'm sure she will,' said Alan, still suspecting the voluptuous young woman who took the wonky security pass photos on Tuesday mornings. 'And don't tell Quentin about any part I might have played in events.'

'My lips are sealed.'

Morton left and Alan sat alone in the meeting room. He rubbed the chill out of his hands, thinking about where these developments left him and wondering about the significance of the unprecedented rapprochement between Morton and Quentin Quist.

At his workstation, he restarted his computer, prompting the flow of warm air from the vents above. An email from Quentin Quist informed him that there was now no need to contact Rasch on his behalf, that circumstances had changed and that he wanted to be clear, in case there had been any misunderstanding, that he had offered to assist with the catering for Brian Gulliver's Christmas drinks in only an *advisory* capacity – as executive chef or as menu consultant – but in no role requiring him to 'carry a tray'.

Trevithick had sent Alan breaking news from a media site about a move by supporters of the minister to spill the ministry, and April-May had sent a message to inform him that Edwina Troy had gone home unwell.

Alan pondered the connection between Edwina's absence and their earlier discussion about her carer's leave. He wondered if an application for stress leave would follow. Perhaps a grievance would be lodged with the secretary, a complaint made to the ombudsman or an infraction notified to a rights watchdog. Only time would tell.

Morton carried Quentin Quist's boxes back to the big office vacated by Carol (but still watched over by Daphne) as Alan surveyed, without any real interest, the papers in his In tray. He delegated a meeting to Trevithick, referred a financial reporting task to April-May and approved the participation of various persons in training courses that would, inevitably, be poorly attended, of little use and of even less interest.

At three o'clock the section members minus Robyn (at a health farm), Barbara (unwell), Edwina (sulking) and Eris (assisting the police) gathered in a meeting room to read their way through the documents specified by the secretary and Quentin Quist. Alan, Morton and Trevithick took turns at reading individual clauses, April-May having asked to be excused at the outset. The three men read at high speed, despite the increasing heat. The exercise still had some way to go at the two-hour mark, even though the reading had become, towards the end, too fast to be intelligible. Alan nonetheless called a halt, announcing that they would reconvene to complete the recitation of the Official Secrets Act the next day. All three subordinates – debilitated and disoriented – left the building after the briefest of returns to their workstations.

Alan cleaned the office vacated by Quentin Quist and moved his trappings back in. The reindeer was nowhere to be seen. Although he felt it necessary and appropriate to reinstate his nameplate on the door, he was disinclined to relocate his pot plant, reattach his ticket holder and re-erect the associated signage. It was not clear to him whether this was because the changeable office cimate had sapped his will, because events on the political stage had confirmed to him the transience of position or because he knew that his tenure depended on not having done 'that which he could well have done' during the still missing piece of Christmas Eve. In any event, the rationale hardly mattered.

He left a message on Rasch's answering machine, identifying himself and saying that he was ringing for no particular reason (which was true, except in so far as he wanted to hear the sound of a friendly voice).

Shortly before six forty p.m. – partway through amendments to the section's risk management plan to mitigate the consequences of bio-terrorist incidents – a response to his clarifying email about Edwina Troy's carer's leave pinged into his In box. It read, 'The Department has consulted a prominent zoologist in order to answer your question of this afternoon and is of the view that the term "family" can certainly apply to animals; it can apply in so far as it refers to groups of species and to genetically related social groupings within or constituting communities, especially for the purpose of protection and the raising of young.'

Alan reviewed the question he'd put in the first place and concluded that he'd not been sufficiently specific. He wrote, 'Thank you for this but I wanted to know whether the definition of family for the purpose of carer's leave comprehends animals.' He clicked on Send without a second thought.

On the window ledge, the last few feathers still attached to the delicate bones of the pecking order has-been were ruffled by a sudden gust.

He went home, his In tray untouched, shortly before seven and showered to warm up before retiring. He didn't bother with dinner or the remnants of the news. For what seemed to be many hours, he lay on his back, trying not to place pressure on his distended belly, reviewing the events of the day…and creating follow-on scenarios from the last recalled moment on Christmas Eve when, leaving Brian Gulliver's office, he'd staggered into the lift and descended into his own private hell of unknowing.

30

Alan took things at a snail's pace when he woke. He felt even more tired, more bloated and more doomed than he had on the previous morning. His head was heavy, his nose ran and his eyes watered, presumably as a result of the previous day's plummeting office temperature.

He ignored the lavatory and dragged a patio chair into the shower, where he sat, letting the water pour over him until he heard the front door chime. Then, dressed in a towel, he looked through the security eye hole and spied a swarthy man dressed in Arabic clothing – a red keffiyeh and white thaub – and wearing impenetrable square-lensed sunglasses.

'Who is it?' said Alan.

'It's me.'

'Me who?'

'Me who is the director of security at the department. Let me in.'

'One minute.'

Alan traded the towel for a gown, then unlocked the door.

Rasch of Arabia entered. 'I brought my own coffee,' he said, handing over a small plastic container. 'You look even worse than yesterday.'

'I've got a cold.' This partial explanation seemed less likely to trigger suspicion than an admission of persistent sleeplessness.

'And what's happened to your head?'

'Just a scratch,' said Alan. 'You're looking very…' To his surprise, he did the water-hurrying gesture.

'No one will have any idea I'm me, dressed in this,' said Rasch.

They walked down the corridor to the kitchen, where Alan filled the jug.

'…and it's entirely appropriate apparel, while ever Burgoyne is intent on slow roasting us.'

'I don't think it would suit me.'

'It takes a certain ineffable panache and an unflinching manliness, to carry it off. Not everyone has the necessary qualities.'

'I suppose not.'

'I talked to some of Quist's people yesterday on condition of strictest secrecy. I need to tell you that and I don't have any of them in the frame. None of them had the stomach for it.'

In other circumstances, Alan might have asked what sort of stomach that was, precisely (apart from the obvious answer to the effect that it was, inevitably, a full one). 'That's a pity,' he said, instead. 'Where to from here?'

'I've had the image of the turd enhanced and scrutinised by the best forensic photo-analysts there are,' said Rasch. 'From Virginia,' he added with heavy emphasis, 'using my contacts in the intelligence community.'

This announcement surprised Alan; he thought that Rasch was done with experts after the DNA and criminal profiling specialists had been let go.

'What have they deduced?'

'The object was soft, yet not sitting flat on the blotter. Ergo, it was a short drop, which means squatting, which in turn means Asian-made.'

Alan thought about this. 'Or delivered by a person of retarded stature.' He recalled Alistair McAllister's statement about no one hating Quentin Quist more than the Elk.

'That's a point,' said Rasch.

'Or deposited by someone standing on a chair,' Alan said, 'with their bottom over the desk.'

Rasch sighed and adjusted the tail of his keffiyeh. 'You're not helping, Alan.'

'Probably not. I'm sorry.'

'It seems to me that there hasn't been a single point in this case where things were straight forward. It's always two steps forward and two steps back. Sometimes I wonder if I have unwittingly offended someone important and if this is all some reprehensible, iniquitous hoax to test me: to push me to the limits of my endurance.'

'You think that "it" was aimed at you, so to speak?'

'I know it seems improbable but sometimes, yes.'

'I see,' said Alan, making Rasch's coffee.

'You think I'm unstable, even paranoid, don't you?'

'No, not necessarily.'

'Don't lie to me.'

'Well, your disguise might be taking things a bit far.'

'Why? I had more extreme measures in mind.'

Alan wondered what could be more extreme than the thaub. 'You weren't thinking of crossing the great divide?'

'I was,' admitted Rasch, 'but my legs would have let me down.'

'Their hairiness?'

'Their shape.'

'I'm glad you didn't.'

They took their cups to the lounge and stared at the dead TV screen.

'I can solve it, I know I can,' Rasch muttered.

Alan pretended not to notice.

'How hard can it be?' Rasch asked himself.

Alan sipped quietly on his tea and recalled his overnight imaginings, searching the different versions of Christmas Eve for pointers to the particular version which most resembled the truth.

'Turds don't materialise out of thin air, do they?'

Alan knew that the question wasn't directed at him, so refrained from a lecture on the digestive fundamentals drawing on the too-detailed information imparted by Morton the week before.

From that point on, he and Rasch sat in silence, pondering the events of recent days.

When Rasch was finished, he took his mug to the sink and gave it a rinse. 'I'm not done yet,' he said before leaving. 'I still have one card up my sleeve.'

Alan wondered, watching him drive away, about that card and what it could yet reveal. It could only be, he thought, the security camera footage, about which, bizarrely, nothing had ever been said by Rasch.

On the way into work, Alan decided that a change in scenery might prove efficacious vis-à-vis his bowels and stopped off at the toilet block at the local shopping centre. 'What the World Needs Now' was playing inside the self-servicing cubicle. This did not seem at all appropriate to Alan and nothing, in consequence, resulted.

He bought a newspaper on his way back to the car. The headline read, POO VICTIM GATHERS NUMBERS.

While Alan didn't seriously expect to read of a tilt at high office by Quentin Quist, he nonetheless scanned the article, standing on the footpath, to reassure himself…and was relieved, in a relative sense, to find that it was the minister's claque which was drumming up support for their champion. So much for Quentin Quist's inside information that the minister would be sacked before Monday was over.

Boris engaged Alan in discussion at the security desk. 'We've got aircon again, but I see you're all hunched over, as though you've done a groin. It can easily happen when you're training without experienced supervision. Anselm is lucky to have any groin at all. His was constantly torn in the years before he got a program designed by an expert.'

'It's just a touch of sweat rash,' Alan said, too loudly, hearing his voice echo around the foyer.

'Don't be troubled,' said a woman Alan vaguely knew from another floor. 'We've all got it.'

On his own floor, Alan tried to sneak past Daphne, who was reviewing the contents of Quentin's tray.

'Mr Quist was looking for you, Mr Mewling,' said the EA, without raising her eyes from the document she was examining.

'Thank you, Daphne,' said Alan, trying hard to seem nonchalant.

As he entered his office, he glanced across at the bay occupied by his staff. Trevithick, Morton, April-May and Edwina were present…but dressed in Hawaiian shirts.

Alan pretended he'd seen nothing troubling. The shirts were obviously part of some misguided ironic protest at the temperature in the building. No wonder Quist had wanted to see him; his staff were in revolt.

He put his briefcase on the meeting table and slowed his breathing. He vaguely recalled union-organised protests of less interesting sorts from the early years of his career and there had been, over the decades, individuals who'd done odd or bolshie things, usually in order to expedite redundancy offers. However, he couldn't recall a whole section engaging in an act of civil disobedience short of an industrial campaign. Quist would doubtless blame him and order all of the Hawaiians to be sent home to get changed, with their pay docked for the time away.

If there was something ironic about the situation, it was that the mercury seemed to be in the temperate, unnoticeable range, rather than tropical or polar extremes.

Alan concluded that haste was not warranted and that he could check his In box before making a decision about whether to pre-empt instructions from Quist or feign ignorance of the sartorial disobedience.

Quist entered, dressed in an especially loud Hawaiian shirt and with pink zinc on the parts of his nose that were not covered by the huge black scab that constituted the tip. He didn't bother with greetings. 'What is that awful smell?' he asked, sniffing the air.

Alan's head cold prevented him from smelling anything.

'It smells like number two,' exclaimed Quist.

'I hadn't noticed anything,' said Alan.

'You haven't, y'know…?' Quist made a beak-shaped gesture towards his own bottom and screwed his face up. '…in your pants?'

Alan stood and ran his hands over his buttocks, then checked the soles of his shoes. 'It's not me,' he said.

'And it's certainly not me,' said Quist. 'Have you recently done a smeller? It's always embarrassing when you do one in your office and someone drops by.'

Alan blushed at the thought. 'No.'

'Well, something isn't nice in here, but that's not what I came to talk to you about.' He shut the door and sat down. 'This morning I found a number two in the branch suggestion box.'

'Gosh,' said Alan, in reluctant awe of the flexibility and athleticism of any faecant who could squeeze a bolus through the narrow slit in the receptacle's lid.

'Gosh, indeed,' said Quist.

'A real one?'

'One of Trevithick's.'

'How did you know it was his?'

'It was one of his replicas.' said Quist.

The relief Alan felt was quickly replaced by alarm at the realisation that Quist had been looking inside the branch suggestion box.

'I thought that the suggestion box was only opened by Personnel.'

'I was making a suggestion at the time and noticed something in the box, so took the liberty of prising it open.'

'A likely story,' thought Alan.

'…and found the number two. I was shocked.'

'You would have been.'

'Did you speak to Trevitihick yesterday as I instructed you to?'

'I did and he was very contrite.'

'But not so filled with shame that he felt it necessary to retrieve all of the objects.'

'I understand that his children distributed them on Sunday night. He couldn't know where they'd all been left.'

'Be that as it may, I have had enough. I am taking action under the code of conduct.'

'Is that wise?'

'He had a warning.'

'I'd not act in haste.'

'And while I'm dealing with staffing issues, if you can no longer put in the required hours – if you don't have the ticker for it – let me know and I'll find someone who's still got the drive, someone who can turn up at a reasonable hour.'

'I'm unwell,' said Alan, 'and it's not that late.'

'I call nine o'clock late for members of my branch management team, and this is the second morning running that you've been in after your subordinates. It's as though you've dropped your bundle.'

'It won't happen again,' said Alan.

'See that it doesn't. And why aren't you supporting National Parasitic Nematode Day? Everyone else has made an effort even though it could as easily have been freezing today.'

'I wasn't aware…'

'Even Daphne is wearing a magnolia blossom in her hair. See that you go home at lunchtime and return with an aloha shirt.'

Alan didn't own frivolous apparel of any sort and had no idea what nematodes were. On top of that, he had no recollection that he'd been notified of the day and its special dress code.

Quist left, Alan switched on his computer and the temperature began an upward spiral. He removed his cardigan.

After a short while, Morton knocked at the door. He had opted for white zinc on his nose and forehead. 'Jesus, it's pongy in here. Did Quentin drop one before he left?'

'No, but he gave me a lecture on my timekeeping.'

'Managerial regard never goes to the late starters, no matter what time they finish. You know that. I suppose he told you about censoring the suggestion box?'

'In a roundabout way, yes.'

'Bad times ahead for the old Trevo, I'd say.'

'Does he know?'

'I told him Quentin was not impressed and that it would be wise to recover any of the outstanding copromes.'

'The damage is done, I'm afraid.'

'Recoveries might yet help with the pleas in mitigation.'

'I suppose so,' said Alan.

'I counselled Quentin against precipitate action but he wouldn't listen.'

'I also urged restraint,' said Alan. 'I don't suppose he's given you a look at the incoming minister's brief he's writing?'

'Haven't seen it, but he's almost finished.'

Morton, it seemed to Alan, knew more about key matters of branch business than he did, and not just the matters discussed at the previous day's directors' meeting.

'You look terrible.'

'I've got a cold,' said Alan, 'and a sweat rash and I'm not sleeping. How are things with your…um…down south?'

'I'll live. More interestingly, I saw Rasch dressed up like Osama Bin Laden in the car park *sans* camel.'

'He doesn't seem to be himself,' said Alan, glumly.

'And Trevithick's wearing a skirt.'

'Dear, oh dear.'

'We live in bizarre times but I know what'll cheer you up: twenty-five interesting things I haven't already told you about shit, shitting, toilets et cetera, et cetera.'

'Morton, I don't mean to be unappreciative but I don't have time for the whole twenty-five. I haven't even looked at my emails.'

'There's nothing of any interest on the system, believe me.'

'How about your best ten?'

'What about twenty?'

"I'll take fifteen,' said Alan, 'but only fifteen.'

Morton opened his pocketbook and anxiously studied a list. 'Number one, then: before the introduction of the sauna and the hot box, Australian jockeys could be asked to sit for hours in the stable dung pit, because the generated heat helped with weight reduction.'

Alan's lips pursed. He disapproved of all forms of gambling, even the office lotto syndicate, and had never attended the race track. The thought of already emaciated midgets sitting up to their necks in hot horse excrement disgusted and appalled him.

'Number two: Princess Diana was a colonic irrigation adherent. So, as it happens, is the very lovely Giselle Bundchen.'

Alan hadn't thought much of the princess and he had no idea who Giselle Bundchen was. He would not, though, have been using the term 'adherent' anywhere near a reference to colonic cleansing.

'Number three: there is a West African condiment named "shitto" which is a mix of smoked fish or prawns and chillies, and goes in many specialities of the region.'

Alan wasn't familiar with or interested in African cuisine and didn't think it likely that he'd be remarking on the richness of the shitto in any dish he was likely to be consuming any time soon.

'Number four: if you don't pop the toilet lid down before flushing, a disgusting cocktail of water vapour and bacteria hurtles from the bowl into the bathroom air, where it hovers for a few hours before gently landing on your towel, your toothbrush et cetera.'

Alan always flushed with the seat down, so if this fact had been recounted in order to cause him angst, the strategy had failed.

'Number five: Elvis died on the toilet, probably from the Valsalva Manoeuvre, which halted his heart while he was straining to deliver.'

'One suspects that the papers didn't say he died doing what he loved.'

'You've just made a joke,' said Morton, surprised.

Alan felt terribly pleased with himself.

'After all these years,' Morton added.

Alan smiled. 'Thank you.'

'And Lenny Bruce died in the same place.'

'Lenny Bruce died on the lavatory at Gracelands?' Alan prided himself on knowing very little about popular culture, but he had once been given a snow dome purchased at Elvis's home and had, consequently, read the two Guralnick biographies of the 'King'.

'Ah, no,' said Morton. 'He also died on the toilet, like Evelyn Waugh.'

Alan was dispirited to hear that Waugh had died in such an ungracious way.

'Number six: best shithouse scenes on film include Martin Ferrero getting eaten by a T-Rex while sitting on a toilet in *Jurassic Park*, Joe Pesci trying to put out his flaming head by plunging it into a toilet bowl filled with paint thinner in *Home Alone 2* and Danny Glover almost getting killed by a toilet bomb, triggered when he's rising from the seat in *Lethal Weapon 2*.'

'I'm counting that as two,' said Alan, 'and you're lucky it's not a triple.'

'Then I'm glad I didn't include any Tarantino toilet scenes or the piece in *Unforgiven* where the Kid shoots one of the T-Bar boys in the outhouse.'

'That's definitely now a quadruple.'

'I think that's unfair but there's probably nothing I can do about it.'

'Not a thing.'

'Number nine, then: the most basic invertebrates – your jellyfish and so forth – don't have a continuous digestive system, they regurgitate waste.' Morton looked up. 'It makes you glad to be a mammal, doesn't it?'

'I think that's only one of a number of reasons why you might be pleased,' said Alan.

'Never kiss a basic invertebrate,' said Morton, 'at least not on the lips.'

'I'll try to remember that,' said Alan.

Morton grinned. 'In Japan, well into the twentieth century, there was a toilet god – usually the one – who was known by different names in different locales and was propitiated to avoid occurrences as varied as famine, toothache, ugly children, bladder problems or – probably worst of all – falling in.'

Alan rather liked the Japanese, principally for their orderliness.

'The word borborygmus describes the sound of intestinal gas bubbles working their way free.'

Alan couldn't think of any situation in which he would soon be making use of this addition to his vocabulary.

'God told Ezekiel to bake his bread on a fire of human faeces and when Ezekiel wasn't keen, allowed him to use cattle dung instead.'

'And that was interesting because…?'

'Because,' Morton scratched his chin, 'well, probably because it demonstrates that God isn't only focused on the big picture but is also interested in poo, like we are.'

'I see,' said Alan.

'Everyone is interested in it,' said Morton.

'I'm not.'

'You say you're not.'

Alan sniffed.

'Moving on,' said Morton. 'When conservationists relocate rhino populations they often move dung with them as the crap makes the animals feel less stressed in their new location.'

'There's no place like home,' said Alan.

'Two jokes in the one day,' said Morton, admiringly. 'The Chinese toilet god was known as Zi Gu or Mao Gu or the Third Daughter of the Latrine and was worshipped by women, as well as being used for fortune telling purposes."

Alan looked at his watch.

'Studies show that women tend to be more troubled than men by excreta and bum gas, are more likely to be silent in the lavatory and are more disposed to washing their hands on completion.'

'That must be your fifteen.'

'For the first space shuttle, NASA designed a twenty-three-million-dollar toilet that freeze-dried solid waste so it could be transported back to Earth.'

'Twenty-three million dollars,' Alan exclaimed, thereby encouraging Morton to review the rest of his list for other facts about faeces in space.

Morton knew he had at a least one. 'Ah, yes. Here it is. A two-year trip to Mars involving a crew of six will generate more than six tons of solid organic waste.'

'Gosh,' said Alan. 'We're lucky that's not coming back to earth at some later time.'

'I don't suppose I could give you one more?'

'Only one,' said Alan, 'because I rather think you've already slipped in a few extras.'

'Sigmund Freud theorised that adults' interest in poo is because excreta is the first thing every child is praised for independently producing.'

'And yet the by-product is promptly flushed away.'

'Freud had something to say about that, too.'

'I'm sure he did,' said Alan, 'but that will have to wait for some other time.' Alan turned to his screen. 'And I don't say that in a dismissive way because you certainly seem to know a lot about excreta and, um, related matters.' Alan thought it only fair to acknowledge Morton's fact-gathering efforts.

'I do seem to know a lot of shit about shit,' said Morton.

'I don't suppose you know what National Parasitic Nematode Day is about?'

'Threadworms, hookworms and roundworms are all human parasites from the tropics. Some of their life cycles are too revolting for words. Get the shirt, make the donation, support the research and ask no questions. And make sure that you don't get Quentin started on the life cycle of strongyloides stercorati. Even my stomach churns.'

'Advice accepted,' said Alan, 'and I take it that the Hawaiian shirts are because of the connection with the tropics?'

'What else would you wear? Who's got pith helmets and Bombay bloomers in their wardrobes?'

'Of course.'

'Or a safari suit?'

Alan held his silence.

'Has the stench in here got stronger, or is it just my imagination?'

'I still can't smell a thing,' Alan replied.

'Do you want me to get some air freshener when I'm out to lunch?'

'No thank you, but I'd be grateful if you'd send Trevithick in.'

In the event, April-May came next, wearing a dazzling shirt but no zinc.

'Your office not smell good, Alan.'

'I'm sure it will improve as the day goes on.'

'Smell like da bian. Maybe someone leave brown surprise for you and you keep it hidden to avoid trouble.'

'I've hidden nothing, I can assure you.'

'April-May been thinking a lot about your retirement. Thinking that cleaning keep you fit and busy, and, if you promise tell no one' – her voice dropped to a whisper – 'April-May not only pay you round-eye rate, but give you' – she looked about before continuing – 'cash in hand.'

'Unnecessary but most kind,' said Alan, feeling that he should express gratitude without encouraging the black economy.

'No tax,' said April-May, in case Alan hadn't got the gist earlier.

'Well, I'm not sure that –'

'You hard-working man, too good for commercial job. You clean house April-May.' She gave Alan a cheeky grin. 'Hardly any da bian.'

'That is reassuring,' said Alan. 'Have you enough on here to keep you busy?'

'All good,' said April-May.

'Then we're done,' Alan replied.

April-May moved to the door.

'If you see Trevithick, please send him in.'

'That man in bad shi with Quentin.'

Alan wasn't a hundred per cent sure what 'shi' meant but suspected that it was a term more evocative of da bian than of poor regard or bad standing. 'I rather think he is,' he said.

In Alan's In box was a note from Personnel: 'Your message dated yesterday stated that you wanted to know (past tense) about the definition of "family" for carer's leave. Is it the case that you still want to know?'

Alan replied with a single word in the affirmative. Punctiliousness was, in his book, an admirable trait; pedantry was not.

Trevithick, dressed in a Hawaiian shirt and grass skirt, knocked and entered. One of his eyes was bruised and closed. 'Aloha,' he said.

'Sit down,' said Alan. 'I apologise for the smell.'

'Re the turds,' said Trevithick getting straight to the point, 'I've searched high and low, and even retrieved some from the urinals but I can't guarantee I've got every last one.'

'I don't expect that the threat of disciplinary action will come to anything. However, Quentin is rather cranky.'

'He has no sense of humour.'

'Everyone is on edge. This is not a good time for pranks.'

Trevithick looked uneasy. 'Do you think you need to go to the toilet or get a cup of coffee?' he asked.

Alan didn't drink coffee and toileting hadn't recently been a positive experience. 'I'm fine, in both respects, thank you.'

'Please,' said Trevithick. A tear spilled from his bad eye, down his cheek.

'Why?'

'I just need you to leave for a minute,' he said in a voice choked with emotion.

'But why?'

'I think it's best that you don't know, given the trouble I'm already in.'

'What do you mean?'

'It's another joke. Here in your office.'

'A joke on me?'

'On Quentin.' Trevithick said, sniffling. 'I left something in this office after he moved in. It's the reason for the smell.'

'I see,' said Alan.

"I haven't had a chance to remove it since…'

'Since I moved back in.'

'Yes.'

A shocking thought occurred to Alan. 'It isn't a…?'

'A what?'

'Like the original one?'

'A turd?'

'Yes.'

'No, no. It's a fruit: a durian. I can show you…'

'No. You were right when you said it's best I don't know.'

'If you could duck out for a minute, I could put it in to your waste paper basket, and take it away.'

Alan sighed. Trevithick was a fool and a poor reader of the times but he was not a bad man and he looked to be in enough trouble – domestic and vocational – without further disciplinary action. And what were the alternatives? Searching for the fruit himself? Sitting with the worsening stench, as the day progressed? Moving back into the open plan? None were tenable.

'All right, but don't let Quentin see you…and no parading around the office with it.'

'We might eat it for our lunch,' said Trevithick, brightening up.

'Straight into the bin, double-bagged.' Alan stepped outside and was contemplating a short stroll to the photocopier, so that the stinking fruit could be recovered without his direct knowledge, when Morton gestured him over.

'Have you seen the latest on the minister?'

'I've been tied up. What's happened?'

'See for yourself,' Morton said, pointing to his screen.

Alan could see the heading 'POO MINISTER SPILL' without his spectacles but the text below was an indecipherable blur.

'I don't have my glasses,' he said.

'He's going to move for a spill motion – the vacating of all positions – at this afternoon's party meeting.'

Alan steadied himself by placing a hand on the desk top.

'And the experts are saying it might just get up,' Morton added.

'I'm sure we'll all do our best to serve whoever our next master is.'

'But if he succeeds, it will mean that a turd – probably dropped by one of us – on a desk, mere metres from where we now stand, will have brought down a PM."

'Thanks to our civil institutions, including the public service, the nation will make the necessary transition in an orderly and peaceful manner. I'm sure of it.'

'Alan, we're talking about the first among equals, the captain of the executive and the leader of our people.'

'Yes, it's all most regrettable but we'll pull through.'

Alan's sense of the professional necessitated a display of cautious optimism but, in truth, he thought it likely he would vomit. He had accustomed himself to the possibility of the minister's passing and to the probability that he, Alan Mewling, had – in a drunken, foolish moment – triggered events causing the minister's demise…but to have brought down a prime minister was a sin of an entirely different order.

'Do excuse me,' he said, going straight to the lavatories, where he took the only available cubicle, lifted the seat with his unprotected fingers and dry retched into the bowl.

He thereafter pulled a length of toilet paper from the roll, used a portion to clean his mouth and folded the rest into a single square which, once seated, he used to cushion his head against the cubicle wall.

So upside down had his world been turned that most of the surreal aspects of the day – Rasch's robes, the Hawaiian shirts, the fake turd in the suggestion box and the managerial criticism of his hours – didn't seem in the least odd. Or maybe sleeplessness and the fever associated with his lurgy had distorted his sense of the normal. But to have instigated the fall of a prime minister – that was, he knew, a truly terrible thing.

He whimpered quietly, wondering what else an indifferent universe could throw at him.

31

He was woken by a tug on his right trouser leg. He looked blearily around, realised that he'd nodded off on the toilet, and looked aghast at the hairy hand which had reached under the cubicle wall to pluck at his hem.

'Come on, I'm all out in here,' said the intruder.

No one apart from Quentin Quist had ever spoken to Alan while he was in the lavatory. He was rigid with fear. Would it have been any less horrifying if he'd recognised the voice of his interlocutor? Probably not. He straightened up, pushed his glasses into position and looked at his watch. He couldn't have been asleep for more than five minutes.

'If you can't give me a roll, tear me a good length,' said his neighbour.

Alan picked up the spare roll from the top of the holder and dropped it into the hovering hand.

'Thanks,' came the response as the hand disappeared.

He heard the rattle of the dispenser and then the tumbrel-like noise of a generous strip being pulled free. He placed his index fingers in his ear holes to block out the sounds that inevitably followed.

'That animal, Strasser, was in the cubicle on the other side of yours and tried to engage me in a Mexican stand-off.'

Alan heard sounds of paper being crumpled and dragged across a corrugated surface. He pushed his fingers further into his ear canals.

'You came in at the mid-point and broke his concentration but the man had no chance of outlasting me. I'm made of much stronger stuff.'

Laughter masked the sound of further paper crumpling and dragging.

'People say that we run out of crap paper because of theft,' the voice continued, 'and that, back in the old days, when the stuff was like greaseproof paper, no one nicked it. But let me tell you, even though the shiny stuff didn't have much going for it – remember the zero absorption rating and the problem with slippage – people still nicked it. Why, you ask? Because serviceable crap paper – whether your soft two-ply or your luxurious finger-resistant three-ply – was expensive and if you were bringing up kids, the cost of it could be ruinous. Do you follow?'

Alan didn't answer.

'Alan, are you keeping up?'

Alan was shocked by the mention of his name but, once identified, could hardly pretend that he wasn't himself. 'I follow,' he said.

The dispenser rumbled again.

'Good. So, we've now got nice paper at work – not because management took pity on our arses or got tired of bringing their own soft paper in with them when they needed to go – but because no one makes the shiny product any more. And the persistent theory is that much of the decent stuff is stolen. But let me ask you this: have you ever seen someone leaving the rest rooms with suspicious bulges in their clothing?'

'I tend not to hang around the restrooms,' said Alan. Aunty Vi had always warned him about the types of men who did.

'But when you do?'

Alan had always avoided looking at bulges, suspicious or otherwise. 'I haven't noticed anything.'

'And have you ever seen anybody return to the office at night or make a special visit on the weekend in order to steal toilet paper?'

'No.'

'Right, because toilet paper is, as a proportion of average weekly earnings – even average weekly cleaners' earnings – cheaper than it's ever been. Buy in bulk and it's laughably inexpensive. Agreed?'

'I suppose so.'

'So, if adequate quantities are being distributed, if we're not stealing it and if people's consumption hasn't tripled or quadrupled – an unlikely thing when the product is so effective – why are we always short, Alan? Answer me that. Why are we always short?'

'I don't know,' Alan answered.

'Me neither. Me neither. It's a mystery. That's what it is, Alan: a mystery. Just like the one that surrounds the brown doo doo that appeared on Quentin's desk.'

Alan heard the lid drop and the toilet flush.

'Rasch can investigate until the cows come home, can't he, but there's no video footage of people entering and leaving the building to help him – the cameras haven't functioned since the last lot of cutbacks – and Toni has disposed of the most important evidence. This means that you and I are the only ones who have any idea of what actually happened on Christmas Eve… and neither of us is talking. If we were, we wouldn't be having this discussion.'

Alan knew that this last sentence didn't make sense, but caught its drift, anyway.

The speaker opened the cubicle door and moved to the basins. Alan heard a tap turned on.

'You're not talking, Alan, and neither am I, so we're both *in situ* and the origins of that very thoughtful Christmas gift will stay shrouded in mystery.'

Alan didn't know what to say. He heard the tap turned off and paper towel pulled from the wall dispenser. So much arboreal sacrifice in the cause of human cleanliness.

'How is Quentin coping with the pressure, by the way?'

'Some days better than others,' said Alan, leaning over to peer under the door.

'I really wish I could say I felt sorry for him but I can't. If I feel sorry for anyone, Alan, it's you. You're the faintest shadow of the man you were…and you were hardly substantial at the beginning of the journey.'

Alan could, by ducking down, see his interlocutor's footwear and the bottom of his trouser legs.

'My parting advice to you is, go before you're sapped of any residual *joie de vivre*. I can assure you that even the smallest skerrick of life is worth salvaging.'

The steel-capped boots and green trousers left no doubt as to the identity of their owner.

32

Alan remained in the cubicle thinking about the various things the plant man had said to him. Insubstantial at the outset of which journey? And what had been meant by the description of him as 'the faintest shadow of the man he'd once been'? Alan had actually thought himself to be a more substantial figure with the passing years – one possessed of more gravitas, greater knowledge and enhanced percipience, in addition to accrued wisdom. How was it that someone who had been working in the building for only few months could comment with authority on changes over an apparently longer span of time? What, too, was the reason for his poor opinion of Quentin Quist – a man with whom a Corporate Foliage Optimisation executive could expect, in mostly plant-free times, to have only fleeting, occasional contact?

And what, most importantly of all, was behind the statement to the effect that he and Alan were the only ones who had any idea of what actually happened on Christmas Eve? The implication was clear – that Alan had seen the plant man committing the act or vice versa – but it was also possible that they had, separately or together, chanced upon a third party on top of the executive desk.

Resolution of the turd-specific issue was more than necessary. Alan knew that he would not sleep or recover the *zeitgeist* of his recent years unless he achieved it. Moreover, he feared, illogically, that he would swell and bloat to his doom without it.

The clearest path to resolution was the confrontational one: for him to beard the plant man and, conceding that he could recall nothing about the missing part of Christmas Eve, demand or beg to know what the other clearly knew. Yet he dreaded the outcome and feared that, if he admitted doubt, the truth could still elude him – that is, that the plant man could use his uncertainty to advantage. His welfare was evidently of importance to the man but he could sense that there was disdain – even, perhaps, contempt – also in play. This being so, he could not be certain that he would be given a true account of key events, assuming there could be such a thing.

He rinsed his mouth at the basins, absent-mindedly carried out the hand-washing ritual and left.

As he reached his desk, the fire alarm went off. He noticed, nonetheless, a stomach-churning piquancy to the stench in his office.

The automated warning message instructed occupants of the building to 'evacuate, evacuate'. Normally these instructions, repeated at five-second intervals, could be relied upon to elicit bowel movement jokes from Morton, despite his role as a warden, but he said nothing this time beyond 'Sorry everyone, it's not a drill.'

Alan placed his wallet, diary and workbook in his brief case and took the fire stairs down to ground level. The Committees and Liaison Branch official assembly point was in the fourth bay of the car park across the road. Alan joined his colleagues there.

The zombies stood in line in family name alphabetical order. Otherwise, people were clustered in small groups, the women using the opportunity to chat and the men watching the chief warden flirt shamelessly with the fire truck commander.

Alan observed April-May talking to another Chinese staff member, Trevithick comparing hemlines with Alistair McAllister, and Edwina Troy engaged in earnest discussion with a woman who would, if questioned, probably admit to being the owner of a prolapse-prone goat, a hamster with a history of dermatological adversity or a budgie with extensive cranial scarring.

Everyone, except Alan and a person of Islander appearance, was wearing an aloha shirt. Most of their noses were daubed with pink or white zinc. Trevithick was, however, the only person wearing a grass skirt.

Alan was surprised to see Peaches at the edge of the group one along from Committees and Liaison, talking to some of the other grandmothers. She caught his eye and Alan – uncertain about the protocol for greeting persons with whom one has discovered unanticipated desk-borne excreta – walked over to her, with the intention of making enquiries about her welfare.

'My hero,' she said to Alan, kissing him and then clutching him to her famous décolletage. 'My prince and rescuer,' she announced with even more emotion, before bursting into tears and being ushered away by a colleague.

'She started on a graduated return to work this morning,' explained one of the remaining grandmothers, 'but I don't think she'll ever return full-time.'

'It's heartbreaking,' said another.

'The poor thing can't approach a desk or a table anywhere without fear of encountering a poo.'

Alan mustered a sympathetic look, despite his suspicion that Peaches was exploiting her circumstances to engineer invalidity retirement.

Quentin Quist motioned Alan over. 'Are all of your people present and correct?'

'All present, except Morton and the Graduate.'

'You'd find it easier to tell, if you have them line up.'

'I'll bear that in mind for next time,' said Alan.

Quist motioned Alan close. 'Have you said anything to Trevithick about his apparel?'

'I've spoken to him about the imitation turds.'

'He looks ridiculous,' said Quist, glaring at Trevithick. 'There's always got to be someone taking things that one step too far. I want him out of that skirt asap.'

'I'll see to it as soon as we return,' said Alan.

'And a heads-up: I'm making an announcement this afternoon about stationery. The new school term is only a few weeks off, so all requests for stationery, no matter how small, are to come through me until further notice. I will be considering every request on its merits and I don't want section heads signing any petty cash vouchers for office consumables behind my back. I want our branch to be showing the rest of the division, and the department, the right way to do these things.'

'Understood.'

'One more thing: I've had a complaint from your girl about shilly-shallying vis-à-vis a decision on leave of some sort. Make a decision for god's sake…and report back to me this afternoon. I shouldn't have to be involved in trivia…except in relation to stationery.'

Alan might have offered an explanation of the carer's leave problem had it not been for a commotion at the entrance to their building. A tall person in white robes and a fettiya was pursued from the main doors by Boris and Anselm. That robed personage, clearly unaccustomed to sprinting in sandals, fell and was promptly doused in capsicum spray, to mixed cheers and boos from the massed public servants.

A white van with obscured number plates careered around the nearest intersection. The rear doors were flung open from the inside and half a dozen figures in black rushed over to the figure writhing on the ground. He was mouth-taped, handcuffed and shackled in fast order, and carried like a battering ram across to the back of the vehicle, which was then driven away at high speed.

'It is now safe to return to the building,' the chief warden announced, using her megaphone, at which point all pretence of orderliness was cast aside and people rushed to the entrance, as if dashing to the best bargains at the Christmas sales. Quentin Quist was at the forefront of those surging forward.

Alan waited in the knowledge that it would take as much as fifteen minutes for the foyer to clear. Trevithick was among those who also decided to hold back, so Alan took the opportunity to raise the matter of the grass skirt.

'Quentin has asked me to speak to you.'

'Again?'

'Yes, I'm afraid he wants you – to use his own words – out of that skirt asap.'

'I always knew he coveted my arse.'

Alan blushed.

'Sorry,' said Trevithick. 'What's he got against the skirt?'

'Does it matter? You know how irrational and bloody-minded he can be.' Alan was surprised by his own frankness.

'But this item of clothing is eco-friendly and indigenous,' said Trevithick.

It occurred to Alan that any endorsement of clothing on these grounds was likely to be unwise while ever the penis gourds of New Guinea tribesmen could be justified on the same basis.

'I don't know enough about the relevant production processes or rites or customs to pass judgement on either score…but do you really think Quentin will care?'

'Enough is enough. I'll lodge a grievance.'

'Because?'

'Because…because McAllister doesn't have to wear trousers but I do.'

'I think you'll find that McAllister's wardrobe enjoys a somewhat unique status in the Anglo-Celtic tradition and has been modelled by members of the royal family.'

'And the grass skirt may well enjoy comparable status in the oceanic tradition and have been worn by members of many royal families.'

'Be that as it may, Quentin will doubtless tell you that the kilt is different.'

'Different for him, maybe, but I'll have you know that my cultural heritage entitles me to wear a grass skirt wherever and whenever I see fit.'

'Is that so?' said Alan, unconvinced.

'Yes. A second cousin of one of my great-grandmother's on my stepmother's side came from the Kukae'aina Islands in the Pacific. Quist may well be denying me my heritage and culture by forcing me out of my skirt.'

'I hadn't been aware of this,' said Alan, 'and, now that you have brought your ancestry to my attention, I'd like to acknowledge the customs traditions and culture of your quasi-forebears…but wouldn't it be wiser, bearing in mind the trouble you're already in, to put aside your heritage, pull on some trousers and' – inspiration came to Alan at this point – 'and thereby avoid fines and imprisonment under the Workplace Health and Safety Act.'

'Fines and imprisonment for what?' Trevithick scoffed.

'The fire brigade has just visited our building and you're wearing a grass skirt.'

'Sure, but where do the fines come in?'

'There are fines and prison terms for not mitigating risk, when required by management.'

'Are you sure?'

Alan had no idea what was in the legislation but thought severe punishments very likely. 'If you don't believe me, see for yourself.'

'Hmm. I'm finding it hard enough to pay my child maintenance, without fines or imprisonment.'

Alan murmured sympathy.

'The problem,' Trevithick continued, 'is that I don't have any trousers at the office and I don't imagine Quentin will be happy about me working in my bikini briefs.'

'Why not take an early lunch, duck home and get changed?'

'I could do that, I suppose.'

'Anything we can do to keep you below the radar, would be wise, don't you think?'

'I have recovered most of the imitation turds and your durian is gone, of course.'

'Then let's go,' said Alan, thinking that with the Trevithick situation under control he could now decide how to assist Rasch, how to resolve the situation with Edwina's carer's leave and even how to discover what the plant man knew about Christmas Eve.

'There's just one more thing,' said Trevithick. 'I put a plant in Carol's office – a special plant – and I'll need to get it back, now that Quentin is on the warpath.'

'I hesitate to ask why it needs to be recovered.'

'Its special attribute is that the leaves can smell like shit.'

'Oh, surely not.'

'I can't vouch for it, myself, but the name of the thing, coprosma foetidissima is promising, don't you think?'

'You'll have to come back tonight and remove it.'

'All right, then.'

'Tell me that it's the very last of the practical jokes.'

'Barring an elusive plaster poo or two, it is. Yes.'

'Well, let's hope that Quentin doesn't find any more of those in the next twenty-four hours.'

At the security desk, Alan let Trevithick continue inside, to collect his car keys, while he spoke to the guards about Rasch.

'I think I may know the gentleman in the robes who was involved in the incident outside,' he began. 'I was wondering if I could find out where he's been taken.'

The security guard who'd apprehended Alan at lunchtime the previous Friday looked up from his newspaper and then turned to his partner, the heavy woman with the silver jewellery. 'You know anything about anyone in robes, Devonne?'

'Not unless we talking about the Lord Jesus,' she answered, without looking up from her magazine.

'Well, that makes two of us.' He turned to Alan. 'Can't help you, I'm afraid.'

'He was capsicum sprayed outside the building just ten minutes ago by Boris and Anselm.'

'You know any Boris or Anselm, Devonne?'

'Never heard of them, Curtis.'

'And then a van drove up and men in black took him away.'

'Men in black?' said the male guard.

'Yes.'

'You know anything about any men in black, Devonne?'

'I saw the movie.'

'But hundreds of people saw the incident I've just described,' said Alan

Curtis stopped a passing woman. 'Excuse me, madam, but did you observe anything happening outside a few minutes ago – security guards subduing a man dressed in robes?'

'No,' said the woman.

'Any men in black in a mysterious van?'

'No.'

'Thank you for your assistance.' He turned to Alan. 'There's your answer.'

'I know what I saw,' said Alan.

'Would you say you were an associate of this Arab gentlemen, Alan?'

'We all are,' whispered Alan. 'That man in robes was Security One, in disguise.'

'You don't say?' said Curtis. 'Devonne, Alan here thinks that the Arab person he saw kidnapped outside the building was actually Security One...in disguise.'

Devonne laughed without looking up from the magazine.

'Is there anything else you'd like to bring to our attention, Alan? Sightings of Elvis, messages from outer space unable to be heard by anyone else, that sort of thing?'

'I tell you, it was Security One.'

Curtis picked up the desk phone, punched some numbers into the cradle and said 'Location Six to Security One.' He whistled softly as he waited for something to happen on the other end of the line. 'Yes, I have a Mr Alan Mewling seeking confirmation of your status, over.'

Curtis handed the phone to Alan and moved to the other end of the counter to collect a temporary security pass from a visitor leaving the department.

'Hello,' said Alan.

'This is Security One,' said a voice he didn't recognise. 'How may I assist you?'

'I'd like to speak to the real Security One.'

'This is Security One.'

'You're not Hector Rasch.'

The line went dead.

'Everything sorted out?' Curtis asked.

Alan handed the handpiece back, convinced that no one from Departmental Security was disposed to admitting anything, let alone assisting him. He intuited, too, that if he created further trouble, he could soon experience his own capsicum spray event and the unwanted attentions of the men in black.

'I've got a bad cold,' Alan said. 'And a fever. I'm not myself.'

'We hope you get well soon,' said Curtis. 'Don't we, Devonne?'

'We sure do,' said Devonne, who had at no point made eye contact with either Curtis or Alan.

'Thank you for your time,' Alan said, running his pass over the card reader of the security gate.

In the lift, he wondered what additional efforts it was incumbent on him to make to secure Rasch's release. Taking into account all of the other problems besetting him, Alan reasoned that he'd probably done all that he needed to for the moment.

As he passed Quist's office on the seventh floor, Quist emerged with a communication device in one hand and a bunch of files in the other.

'No, Alan, you have to make an appointment, that's why I have an EA. I can't be at your beck and call.'

'But I wasn't...' said Alan'

'No, don't argue with me. Make an appointment like everyone else.'

'No, you don't understand...'

'Honestly,' Quist said to Daphne, before speeding away.

'What did you wish to speak to Mr Quist about?' asked Daphne.

'Nothing,' said Alan.

'You can't have an appointment to discuss nothing,' said Daphne.

'Then we've got a win-win outcome,' said Alan, walking away.

When he entered his office, he closed the interior blinds and shut the door.

33

There were a hundred and thirty-eight unread emails in Alan's In box. One, marked urgent, required him to justify an underspend of $8.02 for Committee catering in the previous quarter; the response was due by the close of business the day before.

Alan quickly deduced that the problem had arisen because a caterer had given the department a modest discount on the final committee heads' morning tea of the year. Alan instructed Trevithick by email to go back to the caterer and demand invoicing for the full price.

None of the remaining emails interested him, other than a message from Quentin Quist about stationery which, in addition to outlining the requirements Alan already knew of, mandated the provision of a comprehensive risk analysis for each item being requested.

Nothing Alan could conceivably need in the few weeks of employment that remained to him wasn't already in the secret stash he kept in a box marked Personal under his desk. He wouldn't be subsidising the administrative activities of the Commonwealth with purchases from his own pocket or recycling any old stationery submissions, with or without risk assessments, in the weeks ahead.

As he was thinking about the various useful things he'd learned over the years – things like the importance of a secret stationery cache – an answer arrived to the last question he'd asked about Edwina Troy's carer's leave. It read, 'Thank you for your enquiry. Please see our initial response to your queries. You might also find the Q and As helpful.'

Alan found the Q and As and read them. While there was a reference to a dead reptile in one scenario, there was no suggestion that it was either a family member, or that its passing was material to the question being answered: the quantum of first aid officer allowance payable when on war service sick leave at half pay after extended purchased leave ceasing on a working day immediately before a public holiday. And the only other mention of animals was in relation to the reimbursement of relocation expenses for a fish (named Albert) of an unspecified breed.

Alan decided that the only sensible thing to do was to outline the precise circumstances pertaining to Edwina's application – that is, to explain that Pussils was a cat, that he was reputedly of the Burmese persuasion, that he was blue in breed (if not in colour), that he belonged to Ms Troy, that he was the only other member of her household and that discussions about his illnesses, recreational activities and dietary preferences constituted the major part of Edwina's talk (small and larger) not devoted to diets and celebrity amours. He marked the enquiry urgent and included the words 'Response needed this afternoon' in the heading, before pressing Send.

A knock on the door and the entry of the Elk saved him from procrastination about the contents of his physical In tray. Alan looked at his watch. It was twenty to twelve: not long before the dwarf would, according to daily custom, accompany Alastair McAllister out for the afternoon's drinking.

'I need to talk to someone sensible,' said the diminutive Canadian, popping up on to the chair closest to Alan's desk. 'There is a crisis.'

'I'm not sure I'm the best…'

'Of course you are. We are aboard the ship of fools, among flotillas of idiots, all at sea…and who else am I likely to get any common sense from?'

'You know that I've got a cold?'

'McBender says we are not going out drinking.'

'I see,' said Alan, having no doubt as to the identity of the person referred to as 'McBender'.

'He claims he's depressed and going to work through the afternoon. For the first time in fourteen years.'

'What do you intend to do?' said Alan, mindful of the Scotsman's claim that it was in fact the dwarf who was the drunk in need of minding.

'I've got someone watching him, in case he makes a run for it while I'm here talking to you. Otherwise, I intend to keep a close eye on him, to make sure he's not drinking by himself in his office.'

These didn't seem to Alan to be the words of a committed dipso. Perhaps he'd been too hasty, believing what the Scotsman had previously told him.

'Unless you have a better plan,' the Elk continued.

'I can't say I do,' said Alan. 'I am somewhat surprised by this development. Have you recently offended him?'

'We haven't had a civil word to say to each other for more than a decade.'

'Have you recently been nice to him, then?'

'After what my liver has had to endure for that man, hell will freeze over.'

'I see,' said Alan wondering how the two men passed the afternoons, if not in drunken conversation.

'I just don't know what's got into him,' the Elk continued, 'but my feeling is that things around here won't get back to normal until whoever left that poo has been exposed.'

Alan knew in his heart that this last statement was an eminently reasonable one. 'It's had an impact on us all.'

'Between you and me,' said the Elk, 'the Scottish drunk would have been my pick of the suspects, if it hadn't been for the fact that for something to come out, something must go in…and I've never seen solids pass his lips. Do you follow?'

'I believe I do,' said Alan.

'And by late afternoon on most days he can barely stand, let alone mount a desk.'

'Terrible,' said Alan.

'I also know that he laughed until he choked when he heard about the discovery of the stinker.' The little Canadian lowered his voice. 'No one hates Quist more.'

These were words that Alan had heard before but he expressed no surprise. 'There's not a lot to like about the man, but if McAllister wasn't the culprit, who was?'

'I'm thinking it was either one of the senior executive – someone important who came over from the other building to express outrage at the fact that Quentin would temporarily be joining the elite, again…'

Alan wouldn't have thought much of this theory, even before his most recent discussion with the plant man.

'Or there is the most obvious suspect of all, in line with theory that it's mostly the person who discovered the body who committed the crime.'

'Not Peaches.'

'She's at the top of my list,' said the Elk. 'Why should she be ruled out just because she is a woman?'

'Oh, surely not,' said Alan.

"We hear terrible things in Corporate about the state of the ladies toilets."

'Be that as it may…'

'And don't give me that rubbish about her being a vegetarian. Most of the population of India and south-east Asia is vegetarian and they all go to the toilet, every last one of them.'

Strictly speaking, this wasn't true. Hadn't Morton claimed that more than seven hundred million Indians went in the fields every day? Alan, however, wasn't about to quibble.

'And if you blow up the photo of the turd to two hundred per cent,' the dwarf continued, 'you can clearly see corn in it.'

'How is that relevant?' said Alan.

'Her lunch is in the fridge: a rye bread, corn and mayo sandwich.'

Knowing what the plant man had said about only he and Alan being aware of the provenance of 'it', Alan felt obliged to make some additional effort to clear Peaches of blame. 'I'm sure we all like a bit of corn from time to time.'

'I don't,' said the Elk.

'Actually, I don't either,' conceded Alan.

'Now, corn may not be the Perigord truffle of the vegetable world but it is exactly the sort of thing you'd expect to find in vegetarian by-product.'

This statement seemed wrong to Alan in a number of respects but he concluded that it was best to forge ahead. 'Why would Peaches do it?'

'She was going to be Quentin's EA for the next four weeks.'

'That doesn't seem enough motive to me.'

'Then what about invalidity retirement on two-thirds of her current pay?'

'But she's back at work.'

'If she lasts the day, I'd be mightily surprised.'

'We'll see,' said Alan.

'She can pick up invalidity pay while she looks after her grandchildren at home.'

'But aren't some of the grandchildren still in nappies?'

'It's not the prospect of poo per se that she'll claim she's unable to deal with, but unexpected poo – poo in the wrong places.'

This made sense enough to Alan. 'But you know that she was in a state of shock when I went to her aid, in Quentin's office, after the discovery of "it".'

'That woman can weep at the drop of a hat. Feigned shock shouldn't surprise you.'

'I suppose so.'

'So, what do you think of my strategy in relation to the Scotsman?'

'Careful monitoring certainly seems prudent,' said Alan, now inclined to believe that the dwarf was, in fact, the minder…or, to believe, at the very least, that the dwarf and Scotsman had over a period of years convinced each other that each was minding the other.

'I'll keep you up to speed with any developments.'

The Elk departed, leaving Alan to think that his visit had been more to chew the fat about suspects than for any other purpose.

At this point, Alan would like to have shut the door, turned out the light and had a brief snooze under the desk but it was five minutes to twelve and it occurred to him that if he went straight to Bonny Brae, he could check on Hugo and be away before the arrival of the luncheon trolley and any unseemly interactions with Matron Frogmore. He dropped a soggy handkerchief into his garbage bin, selected a fresh one from the pile in his top drawer and headed out.

He took the fire stairs down one floor, to avoid walking past Daphne, and then caught the lift to the ground floor. Curtis and Devonne had been replaced by strangers on the security desk and there was, of course, no sign of Rasch in the vicinity of Alan's vehicle.

At Bonnie Brae, Alan slotted the Morris Minor between two four-wheel drives at the furthest end of the car park. Inside, Hugo Faggoter was lying in his customary position, staring at the ceiling. In the other bed, the True Ginger appeared to be at rest. The TV had been left on low, running advertisements for kitchen gadgets, fitness equipment and underclothing, all able to perform miracles. It appeared odd to Alan that advertisements should have become the program and that they could be considered therapeutic for residents unable to pick up the phone and ring without delay, to take advantage of amazing limited-time offers. There were, though, many aspects of the modern world that were unfathomable to him.

'I'm not staying for long,' he said to Hugo, straightening the newspaper hanging over the bed rail, 'so someone else will have to come and help you with your lunch.'

A woman sobbed, briefly, in another room.

'You're looking rested.'

In fact, Hugo didn't look especially rested or any more rested than he usually did but, as resting was the only thing he seemed to do, an encouraging remark about its efficacy appeared to Alan to be appropriate.

In the other bed, Clyde Adams's eyes appeared to be part open, so Alan approached. 'It's me,' he whispered. 'How is our secret?'

There was no response. He passed his hand across the True Ginger's field of vision. The old man didn't react and Alan feared he might be dead.

Reassured, though, by the slow rise and fall of the pyjamaed chest, he put a different question. 'Our secret – is it safe?'

Again, he received no response.

He went to the doorway and looked up and down the corridor. No one was in sight. Returning to Clyde Adams, he pulled the tray table a few feet towards the foot of the bed and saw all that needed to be seen. The sheets were as smooth as the surface of the grape jelly that always followed luncheon lentils.

With a heavy heart, Alan pushed the tray table back into place. 'Our second secret?' he asked, without any real hope. 'Is there anything for me to take away?'

Silence was all the reply he received.

He pulled a tissue from the box on top of the chest of drawers and gently opened Clyde's left hand which rested, closed, above the covers. Nothing was hidden there.

He dropped the tissue into the bin and passed his own hand one more time in front of Clyde Adams's unseeing eyes.

The old man's ruse had evidently been discovered. The flame would burn no more. Alan was unable to explain the loss he felt and the accompanying feeling of comprehensive defeat.

He took the visitor's chair next to his father-in-law's bed and thought about Clyde, Hugo, life, death and the plant man. He resolved that, if there was a change in the ministry later that afternoon, he would not only seek a meeting with the plant man, to find out what had happened on Christmas Eve, but would take whatever action was then necessary.

No sooner had he concluded that steps of an as-yet-undefined-and-indeterminate nature could and should be taken, than the unthinkable happened.

Hugo spoke. His pronouncement was neither a long nor especially impassioned one, but it was emphatic enough, in its own way, and there could be no disputing its admonitory spirit.

It was the first time in more than four years that Alan had heard his father-in-law say anything, yet the two words which issued from those ancient lips were unmistakably his own and enunciated so clearly as to be beyond any dispute.

'The waste.'

These two words, spoken at precisely twelve twenty in the presence of only Alan – for Clyde Adams could not be said to be there in any functional sense – should have signalled an end to the debate that had taken place in the nursing home since the previous Friday: debate about what Hugo might or might not have said. But no one else was present and, without verification, Alan's claim as to what he'd heard could be given no greater weight than anyone else's.

'The waste?' said Alan, leaning over the old man. Then, leaning even closer, he asked, 'Waste in relation to…?'

Hugo Faggotter's mouth curled into an irritated knot but whether this was because he didn't think his announcement required clarification or because Alan had blocked his view of the TV was not clear.

The waste. Yes, but which waste and why?

Alan followed Hugo's gaze. The advertisements on the TV screen had been replaced by a news bulletin and he saw the switch from reportage outside the departmental building in which he worked to more talk outside Parliament House.

The waste could easily have been a reference to the human waste, the discovery of which, only a few days earlier, had triggered events now playing out on the national stage. But it could as readily have been a reference to the gadgets, gizmos and undergarments endlessly spruiked about in the preceding segment, or to the turnover of ministers later in the day. It could even have been a reference to wasteful public administration, though not in Hugo's own times, as the public service of his day had been a relatively small one, reflecting the more modest aspirations of governments long-past.

Alan reminded himself too that the word 'waste' was a homonym and could also refer to the midriff of one of the girls modelling the miracle performing underwear or even, to the particular waist of one of the kindly, hard-working women who attended to Hugo's daily needs.

'Waste in particular reference to…?' Alan asked, one last time.

In answer, he heard only the distant rumble of the luncheon trolley.

He hurriedly checked Clyde Adams's sight line again – without eliciting an improved response – before hurrying away, having successfully avoided any contretemps with Matron about his failure to call.

He stopped off at the pharmacy on the way back to the office and bought cold and flu tablets, as well as a box of tissues and something to stop his nose. Food was of no interest to him and for the first time in his life he bought bottled water, needing something to help the tablets down.

At the security desk, the same two strangers barely looked at him as he passed. If he had been placed on a blacklist as a result of his earlier questions about Rasch, it was not yet to any effect.

He caught the lift up to the sixth floor and walked up the fire stairs, so as to avoid meeting Quentin Quist and Daphne. April-May, who always brought her own lunch, was minding the phones. Alan waved in her direction, entered his office and locked the door.

The open door policy he'd once been proud of – he genuinely believed that the cause of effective public administration was assisted by unimpeded communication between its proponents – had become a casualty of evil times. He was surprised to find himself in siege mode.

A Hawaiian shirt was draped over one of the visitors' chairs. Alan removed his white nylon, short-sleeved Pelaco and put the brightly coloured replacement on, tucking it in, pulling it out and then deciding to tuck it in again. His tie, he realised after one attempt, was never going to sit properly with a collar that couldn't be buttoned closed. He placed the discarded shirt and neckwear on a coat hanger in readiness for a change back when the day was over, and was positioning the hanger on its hook when he was startled by knocking.

He opened the door and Peaches thrust a large orange envelope into his hand.

'This is for you,' she said, before hugging him, bursting into tears and rushing away in the direction of the ladies' toilets.

April-May, who'd witnessed the incident, made the universal gesture for mystification and Alan responded with a shrug indicating that he too was baffled.

He locked the door and opened the envelope. It contained an A4 sheet headed 'Proposed Structure of Committee(s) Section'. Attached to the sheet was a Post-it note on which was written, 'A certain person left this on the printer and I thought you should see it. Peaches XXXX SWALK.'

The sheet had a box at its top containing the words 'Replacement Director (new and motivated)', a box immediately below it containing the words 'Asst Dir (best of the current three)' and then three further boxes containing the words 'subordinate staff'. A note at the bottom of the same page read, 'Existing director and excess assistant directors to be redeployed/offered redundancies.'

Alan had expected Carol and Quentin to reduce the number of committees and thereby slash the number of committee members but it had never occurred to him that Robyn Rainbird would be sacrificed (presumably because she was absent) and that two of the existing assistant directors would be moved on or cashiered.

Alan's eyes lingered over the 'new director' box and for an instant he thought it possible – forgetting about his great mistake, disregarding the years in which he'd been given low-profile work to do and putting to one side the events of recent days – that he was, at last, to be given his due. It was late in the scheme of things and at a time when it would have little impact on his financial circumstances…but it was his due, nonetheless. His heart soared.

It was an unfortunate outcome for Robyn, who had not been all that bad a manager, but Alan had waited so long and seen so many of the unworthy promoted above him that it would be unthinkable to reject the offer when made. And if he didn't accept the position, someone else (less deserving) assuredly would.

And then doubt – prompted by the recent good relations between Quentin Quist and Morton, fed by Morton's cheerful acquiescence to whatever had been asked of him in recent days and accelerated by the sight of the tennis racquet resting against Morton's drawers – brought Alan

back to ground. The system did not reward the likes of Alan Mewling –
not on the cusp of retirement and not when others even more pliant than
he'd proved himself to be were willing to serve.

He put the sheet back into the envelope and placed the envelope in
his bottom drawer but there was no time for maudlin introspection; three
quick knocks and a knob rattle announced the arrival of another visitor.

Alan rose and unlocked the door.

'What's going on?' Quentin Quist enquired. His pink zinc had faded
and the scab had disappeared from his nose tip to reveal a glistening,
bloody circle the size of a five-cent piece.

'I was getting changed into my Hawaiian shirt,' Alan replied.

'Good,' said Quist. 'You haven't picked anything of mine up from the
printer, have you?'

'No,' said Alan. 'I haven't had to print anything all day.'

'Someone has picked up an attachment to a very confidential
document I sent to the printer by mistake. If you see it, don't look at it
and report straight to me.'

Alan was no longer thrown by the illogical: the requirement to see
without looking. 'Understood,' he said.

Quist looked critically at Alan's shirt. 'It's better worn outside your
trousers, so that you look…' He hurried a small quantity of water.

'Untidy?' said Alan.

Quist's eyes rolled. 'Casual,' he said.

Alan pulled the shirt free and the liberated parts extended from his
hips like a drooping tutu. He tried to smooth them against his body.
Quist observed his efforts for a moment and, thankfully, made no offer
of assistance.

'I'll leave the door open,' said Quist, walking away. 'You can't expect
to foster good communication with a closed door.'

Alan nodded agreement, even though he could think of no good
reason to foster communication with a door of any sort.

He heard Quist making the same enquiries about his lost document
in the next office in the row and made another failed attempt to smooth

the crinkled shirt bottom, so that it hung rather than jutted. After a third try, he conceded defeat and placed his In tray on the visitor's table in preparation for sorting and action.

Trevithick appeared in the doorway. He had swapped his grass skirt for a kilt. 'I see you got the shirt I left you,' he said.

'Thank you, yes,' said Alan, 'and I can see that you've got a kilt.'

Trevithick pirouetted but not so quickly that all was revealed.

'I thought I'd convinced you of the merits of a return to trousers,' said Alan.

'I changed my mind. If the tartan is good enough for McAllister, it's good enough for me.'

'And when Quentin takes you to task?'

'I'll remind him of my right to dress in any way consistent with my heritage.'

'Another great-grandmother?'

'Yes, as a matter of fact.'

'Good luck,' said Alan, wiping his nose and thinking that it was now not a matter of whether there would be a showdown but when.

'And I might also point out to him to the special status of the kilt in Anglo-Celtic culture and remind him of the affectionate regard in which it is held by the Saxe-Coburg-Gothas.'

It occurred to Alan that Trevithick might be making fun of him.

'Never admit defeat,' said Trevithick in a conspiratorial tone, 'except when you are absolutely determined to enjoy your punishment.'

Alan was satisfied, on balance, that he was not being intentionally niggled.

'Perseverance can be a laudable thing,' he conceded. 'Was there something else you needed to see me about?'

Trevithick stepped inside and shut the door. 'Has anybody told you about Daphne?'

'What about her?'

'You saw Quentin's message about stationery?'

'I did.'

'Well, Daphne has claimed that it was a criticism of her – that it implied she was incapable of looking after the stationery cupboard and, furthermore, that she'd not done a good job of it since she came to us.'

'That's unfortunate,' said Alan.

'She told Quentin that she was going to return to her old job, so he grovelled and asked her to think about it over lunch.'

'And how do you know about all of this?'

'Quentin told Morton in case we needed to provide a replacement EA. He authorised Morton to speak to Edwina in your absence.'

Another indicator, Alan thought, that Morton was the chosen one. 'But how do you know what Quentin told Morton?'

'I heard them talking in the men's room, then Edwina complained to me. She is furious.'

If Morton aspired to manage, Alan thought, it was only reasonable that he should experience the sharp end of the task. 'Let's wait and see what Daphne decides to do, before we get ourselves too worked up.'

'She'll go. Mark my word.'

'Thank you for keeping me informed.'

Trevithick rose and left but, before Alan could make any progress with the tray in his lap, Morton appeared, dressed in tennis gear.

'The ancient Greeks used pebbles and bits of broken pottery to wipe,' he announced.

'I'm disappointed to hear that,' said Alan. 'It sounds neither safe nor hygienic.'

'And they emptied their chamber pots straight into channels that ran along the streets.'

'Even more disappointing.'

'Chinese biogas will cheer you up.'

'Perhaps later.'

'Whenever it's convenient. I came to let you know that Quentin asked me, before lunch, to speak to Edwina about filling in for Daphne, should she decide to return to her old position, now things have calmed down here.'

'I see,' said Alan.

'I did as asked and pointed out that you, Trevithick and I had all done EA stints before Daphne arrived.'

'What did she say to that?'

'She's not happy.'

'Well, it may yet be much ado about nothing. Let's wait and see.'

'Nothing is easy, is it?'

'If it was,' said Alan, pointedly, 'we wouldn't need managers.'

'I suppose not,' said Morton, looking away.

'I think another session with the legislation will settle us all down.'

'I'll book us a room.'

'Three o'clock would be good.'

'I'll do it,' said Morton.

'Has Quentin said anything to you about Trevithick's kilt?' Alan enquired.

'I don't think he's seen it.'

'That will be our next crisis.'

Morton nodded agreement.

'You've been having a lunchtime hit,' Alan observed, gesturing at Morton's whites.

'Never too late to improve your serve, is it?' said Morton with an embarrassed look.

'I suppose not,' said Alan.

'I'll organise the meeting room, then.'

Alan slid the In tray onto the table and attended to his dripping nose.

If Daphne decided to return to her normal job, Alan mused, there was every prospect of Pussils suffering a relapse. A resolution to the problem of Edwina's carer's leave was more urgent than he had previously thought, even taking into account Quentin's orders to make a decision before the end of the day. He certainly didn't want Edwina arguing that his failure to promptly reject her application had made her confident about further carer's leave when repeat circumstances emerged.

Alan rang an acquaintance in Personnel and asked if he could speak to someone about a matter of interpretation and the enterprise agreement.

'No one is available, I'm afraid. All of our sophists are in a meeting.'

Alan would have thought this unsurprising on a Friday afternoon… but on a Tuesday!

'A crisis,' said Alan's contact. 'Some troublemaker has been asking complicated questions about animals and carer's leave. It's got everybody in quite a tizz.'

'Really,' said Alan.

'Everyone is terribly worked up.'

'Most unfortunate.'

'There are people in this department who think we've got nothing better to do than sit around all day answering bizarre questions.'

'I'd better let you go, then,' said Alan.

'You might find the Q and As helpful,' said the contact. 'A lot of people do.'

'Thank you. I'll look at them straight away.'

Morton, who was waiting for him to finish on the phone, came in. 'Daphne has gone,' he announced.

'Dear, oh dear,' said Alan.

'And Peaches is only here until three o'clock, because of her graduated return to work.'

Alan looked at his watch. It was two forty-five. 'What are you going to do?'

'Me?'

'I seem to recall that Quentin tasked you with securing Edwina's cooperation.'

'She's not going to wear it.'

Quentin Quist entered without knocking. 'Peaches has just left the building,' he announced, 'in tears.'

'Nothing unusual there,' said Morton.

'I don't think she'll be back. She found one of the fake number twos in the stationery cupboard.'

'Terrible,' said Alan, sneezing before he could locate his hanky.

'According to Personnel, there is some prospect of her suing me, personally, for not providing her with a safe workplace. I'm going to kill bloody Trevithick.'

'I think murdering someone would be a clear breach of your obligations under the same legislation,' said Morton.

'I couldn't give a toss.'

'I suppose Trevithick wasn't able to get into the stationery cupboard to recover anything that was left there,' said Alan.

'I'm not interested in excuses. Is the girl ready to take over?'

Alan looked at Morton. So did Quist.

'I'll go and check,' said the man of the moment.

'I'm very worried about my lost printing,' said Quist, as soon as he and Alan were alone.

'Yes, it's not as if we've got nothing else to worry about.'

Morton returned, looking crestfallen. 'Edwina has also left the building.'

'When?' said Quist. 'I saw her there, moments ago.'

'She told April-May that she has a sick family member.'

'I thought she lived alone,' said Quist.

Alan and Morton exchanged looks.

'Well?' said Quist.

'She has a cat,' said Alan.

'So does every other woman in the department,' said Quist. 'Many own herds of them and if they all went home every time the buggers got sick, where would we be?'

'At the vet?' said Morton, looking pleased with himself.

'This isn't a time for jokes. You know what I mean. The important issue is who's going to be my EA? I'm not going without. Not again.'

'The options in our section are limited,' said Morton. 'There's Alan or me.'

'What does that say about our branch, having staff at your levels answering phones and organising my diary.'

'Or Trevithick,' said Alan.

'I'm not having that man anywhere near me and, anyway, I'm not having people speculating about my sexuality because I've got a male EA.'

It had never occurred to Alan that speculation of that sort could be fuelled by such innocuous things.

'What about a woman to help me out?' said Quist. 'Having a woman looks more…' Furious water-swishing.

'Paternalistic,' said Alan, for the fun of it.

'Conventional?' said Morton.

'Normal,' said Quist.

'Trevithick is wearing a kilt,' said Morton, 'and from a distance, without his beard, could be mistaken for a woman.'

Quist snorted. 'What real women have you got?'

'There's only April-May and she goes home at four o'clock.'

'The only time I've ever spoken to her, I didn't understand a thing. They get other people to do the entry test for them, you know, because we can't tell them apart.'

'I think they say the same thing about us.'

'What about that woman who's never here?'

'Barbara is a director,' said Alan, 'and she works from home.'

'Why can't she come in? Remind me.'

'You've seen her children: the feral ones,' said Morton.

'Oh, this is an impossible…'

'Scenario?' asked Morton.

'Situation?' suggested Alan.

'Business,' said Quist. 'I give up. I just give up. Have someone – anyone except that cross-dresser whose name I never want mentioned in my presence, again – outside my office within five minutes. I'll be following the TV coverage of the party meeting. That couldn't be any more silly than this carry-on.'

'I'll toss you,' said Morton, as soon as Quist was gone. 'Heads or tails?'

'Tails,' said Alan, knowing what the outcome would be, even before the coin was propelled into the air.

Morton flicked a fifty-cent piece upwards, recovered it and slapped it on to the back of his hand. 'Heads it is,' he announced…

But Alan was already on his way out the door with a packet of bacterial wipes in his pocket and with the other things he needed piled onto the top of his In tray.

35

At the EA's desk, Alan wiped the surfaces clean in a perfunctory way and logged on. A message from Trevithick read, 'Depressed. Gone home. Sorry.' An earlier message from Edwina Troy read, 'So you had to send Morton to do your dirty work for you. Pussils has suffered a relapse. I will be in touch when he has fully recovered.' A further message marked 'Secret', without any heading and from an unfamiliar mail address comprised of letters and numbers which made no sense at all, read, 'Cease all questions. Repeat. Cease all questions. Am under ultimate super-deep cover to conclude investigation. All revealed tomorrow. Rasch.'

Alan blinked and this final message self-deleted.

Quist came out of his office with his blackberry, his iPhone, his iPad and a notebook. There was a fresh Band-Aid on his nose.

'All members of the executive have been summoned to an emergency meeting with the secretary.'

'Oh dear.'

'There's no need for catastrophising, Alan. It is our resilience – our ability to deal with the unexpected – that marks us out from the rest of you. I will be back within the hour. Get everybody – the whole branch – together in the recreation room at four o'clock.'

Alan booked the recreation room before any nearby EAs did, and sent out an invitation.

If Quist had been summoned by himself, Alan could have feared the worst for the branch but an all-executive gathering could only have been about ministerial changes. Alan walked over to his own bay to see what Morton knew.

'It was all over in minutes,' said Morton pointing to his screen, on which a rather ordinary man was besieged by journalists somewhere inside the parliament building. 'The spill failed by a vote and our minister is out on his arse.'

Alan felt, as he always did, that big political events took place in another world, far distant from his own, but a lingering sense of causality might have stayed with him on this occasion if his cold had not cocooned him from the world.

'There's no indication yet of who our new minister is going to be,' said Morton, 'but I suppose we'll be working on the emails again as soon as Quentin finds out.'

'He's called a branch meeting for four o'clock.'

'All will be revealed there, to the few who are still around.'

Alan returned to the EA's desk.

An emaciated woman in her fifties, with stringy hair, a neck-encircling tattoo and a pleated miniskirt that would reveal everything if she strayed even slightly from the vertical, was waiting for him, with a trolley. 'Lookin' for Steve Morton.'

On the trolley were eight large plastic tubs. Alan could see that each one was filled with green ministerial folders; each folder would contain a letter from a citizen requiring an answer on behalf of the minister.

'Stephen Morton? Are you sure?'

'That's what it says on the delivery slip.'

'Does he know you're coming?'

'All I got told was "Deliver three trolleys of tubs to Steve Morton, Committees and Stakeholder Liaison Branch."'

'Three trolleys! Goodness me.' That so many citizens could feel compelled to write to a politician about what was really a rather modest pile of excrement was not, Alan felt, a plus for democracy. 'He's down here,' he said, leading the way to Morton's cubicle.

The lucky recipient of the tubs was still watching the coverage of political events.

'Stephen, there's a delivery for you.'

Morton looked at the woman and the trolley, and wasn't surprised.

'Ministerials,' said Alan, 'and there are two more trolley loads still to come.'

'Sure,' said Morton. 'Pop them over there.' He gestured at the graduate's cubicle. 'I don't think we'll be seeing her any time soon.'

The woman pushed the trolley close to the vacant cubicle and began transferring tubs onto the floor. No one offered to assist. Each time she bent over, buttocks separated by the thinnest strip of cloth were on public view. Each time she lifted a tub, she made a strange sucking noise, drawing in air at the ends of her mouth. Everyone looked self-consciously away.

'No one told me that we'd be looking after the follow-up correspondence,' said Alan.

'I had the impression that Quentin was going to discuss it with you,' said Morton.

'He made no mention of it.'

'Seeing as we'd made a start, by getting the early emails sorted, he thought we'd be in the best position to progress the rest of it.'

'On top of our normal work?'

'I believe he may have changes to discuss with you in relation to that in due course.'

'There would seem to be a lot going on that I'm not being made aware of.'

'Like the four million additional biogas digesters in rural China every year.'

'I'm talking about matters in relation to our section,' said Alan, giving Morton his most censorious look.

'Accounting for between one and two per cent of total energy use in rural areas.'

'Records show Chinese peoples have toilet paper before year 600,' said April-May, proudly.

'I'll speak to Quentin when he returns,' said Alan.

'I'll go and get the next trolley load,' said the emaciated courier.

'But the first shit digester was probably built in Bombay in 1859,' said Morton.

Alan walked with the courier as far as the EA's desk, then returned to look at his In box. An email from April-May read, 'Merchant with poor-quality goods should never make display.' Alan knew what she was referring to the emaciated courier but was too despondent to reply with anything jocular. He could rally from most of the other shocks and buffetings which the day had sent his way, but the contempt for protocol evidenced in the allocation of the ministerial correspondence to someone who was, until he was otherwise informed, a member of his staff, without any consultation – or, at worst, instruction – was the last straw.

The departmental executive could do to him whatever – within reason – they wished, but there were still some standards, some fundamental rules, some courtesies that needed, even in the most difficult times, to be adhered to.

Seeking a distraction, he recalled that he'd promised himself further discussion with the plant man about the events of Christmas Eve, if the minister was brought down. Accordingly, he rang the number for Vegetation Optimisation in the department's functional directory and, in his capacity as acting EA for Quentin Quist, temporary custodian of some executive foliage, he left a message for the plant man to get in touch.

'He starts at seven a.m. and finishes at three thirty p.m.,' said the intermediary.

'Then tomorrow morning would be good.'

The intervening hours would give Alan chance to refine his strategy.

The trolley arrived two further times and Alan kept despondency at bay by busying himself.

Quentin Quist returned at three fifty-five and, minutes later, nearly twenty individuals were gathered in the recreation room to be briefed on his meeting with the secretary. Alan had been instructed to walk the floor to round up the gathering averse.

When Quist entered the room and noticed their modest number, he was not pleased. 'Alan, I thought I asked you to get everyone together.'

'This is everyone,' replied Alan. 'It's still school holidays and we have a number of unexpected absences.'

Quentin Quist nodded to himself, as if saying, 'I might have known.'

Alan thought it more than likely that he would have to endure another rendition of the 'Once more unto the breach' speech from *Henry V* (the only piece of Shakespeare Quentin appeared to know by heart) with crucial parts mondegreened, some segments delivered in an unpunctuated rush and others voiced with heavy emphases in all the wrong places.

'That so few could keep such vital processes and important functions afoot…' said Quist, with tears welling in his eyes.

There was no swishing, so the usual culprits left the sentence unfinished.

'I acknowledge the great, proud traditional land of the owners we meet upon.'

Alan adopted his customary look, part contrition and part wonder, with additional remorse, for no other reason than that he'd already been singled out for executive attention.

'I have just been with the secretary,' Quentin Quist said, conveying the impression that he, and he alone, had met with the department head. 'As most of you will know, our minister will be surrendering his commission to the Governor-General this afternoon and a new minister will be appointed soon thereafter. The PM has announced, minutes ago, that our new minister will be –' he named a long-standing supporter of the PM whose principal virtues were a keen appreciation of his own shortcomings and a desire not to be reminded of them by the opposition or the media. 'Our new master,' he continued, 'is close to the leader – which is never a bad thing –' he chuckled to himself – 'and is widely regarded as a safe pair of hands.'

Alan noted that the new minister was not one of Quist's chosen three.

'I will let you know, as soon as we are told, who the chief of staff and advisers will be but, in any event, we are well advanced with our incoming minister's briefing and will do our usual sterling work to make the transition as seamless as it can possibly be.'

Mankiewicz applauded but Quist's glare prevented others from joining in.

'But the news which I called you together to announce is that Denise' – everybody knew he was referring to the secretary – 'has taken the opportunity to step down –' he waited for a gasp that never came '– in order to…' Furious water-swishing.

'Play more tennis?' Mankiewicz suggested.

'Spend time with her family?' said Strasser.

'Become a real professor?' asked Alastair McAllister.

'Deal with some health issues?' said the Sri Lankan, Smith.

'…explore other opportunities,' said Quist. 'She will be a huge loss to the department, and I know you will miss her as much as I will.'

In fact, no one in attendance would miss the secretary in the least. None of them had anything to do with her on a day-to-day basis and Alan, because of the incident in the lift, was the only person present to have ever spoken with her.

'I know you'll want to contribute to a farewell gift, perhaps even join me at a valedictory dinner. Alan will send details in due course. I'd only say at this early juncture, give generously to someone who has given so much for you.'

Alan looked at the expressionless faces of the attendees and deduced that the prospects of any contributions to a farewell gift – for someone whose contract would probably be cashed out and whose annual bonus pay resembled a salary – were not good.

'Brian will be filling in for Denise until a new secretary is appointed.'

Perhaps, thought Alan, Gulliver's race was not yet run, after all.

'Any questions?' Quentin Quist asked.

No one engaged.

'Surely someone must have a question.'

The only enquiries anyone would like to have made were the ones there was no point in making: had the secretary walked or had she been pushed? Had she opted to go because she was blamed for 'it' or because she was seen as someone too close to the outgoing minister? Or was it that someone had to get it in the neck for re-engaging Carol and making it likely that the department would be in the news for new but equally undesirable reasons.

'Someone? Anyone?'

A zombie put a trembling hand up and relieved everyone present of the need to ask something inescapably inane. 'Are you, with your significant experience of organisational change, your emotional intelligence and strategic gifts, going to remain in the branch head's position to steer us through this difficult period?'

In other times, Morton would have simulated vomiting in response to such a sycophantic outpouring but on this occasion there was merely the faintest trace of amusement in his eyes.

'Good question, Nigel. You will go far.' Quist chuckled, alone.

The zombies in the room were all thinking about the punishments which could yet await them for not having put a variant of the same question, earlier. The non-zombies were all thinking how good it was not to be permanently under Quist's control.

'Valerie will return as scheduled at the end of the month but will be able to make use of my advice and experience, such as they are, for as long as she finds it helpful.'

Nigel affected moderate disappointment.

'If there are no further questions, everyone except Alan and Stephen's team can get back to work.'

The reference to his and Morton's team seemed to Alan to be conclusive proof that Morton was on the up in his stead.

Alan, Morton and April-May remained as others drifted away. They gravitated to a table.

'Should I do the acknowledgement of the elders, again?' Quist asked Morton.

'For the four of us?' Morton asked.

'I've always considered four to be the tipping point.'

'I go for a dozen, myself,' said Morton. 'Alan?'

'I've always worked on the assumption that eight was the crucial number but I think that on this occasion, we could regard our meeting as an extension of the larger meeting, just finished, for which there has already been a most excellent acknowledgement.'

'So long as no one feels that I've not done the right thing,' said Quist. 'I'm already worried that we don't have someone to do the stupid signing thing for the deaf at these meetings.'

'But we don't have anybody with a hearing impairment in our branch,' said Morton.

'With respect, Stephen, I don't think that's the point. The deaf are hardly going to be good signers,' said Quist. 'If they can't hear anything, how can they translate?'

'No, I meant that we don't have anybody in the branch who would benefit from signing.'

Quist sighed. 'It's the symbolism that's the thing,' he said. 'It's what the signing says about our preparedness to accommodate the retarded.'

'I don't think you'll find that there is any correlation between deafness and intellectual disability,' said Alan.

'When was the last time you had a decent conversation with a deaf person?' Quist snapped, gesturing with his hands at his shoulders, palms upwards and fingers splayed.

Alan didn't know any hearing-impaired persons, so couldn't recall a particular time.

'That's right,' said Quist in response to the resulting silence, 'and, that being the case, I'll move on. I'll assume that there's no need for a welcome or signing…but never let it be said that I'm not consultative or open to compromise.'

Morton and Alan nodded agreement and April-May followed, presumably because, if the two men thought it appropriate to agree, she should too.

'Very quickly,' Quist said. 'We need to get last week's emails up to the new minister's office asap and I want very substantial inroads made into the trolleys, as well.'

'As you can see, our numbers are somewhat depleted,' said Alan, gesturing towards Morton and April-May.

'This is not a time for defeatism, "poor me" and catastrophising,' said Quist. 'Ask not what your country can do for you.'

'We won't,' said Morton.

'You won't?' said Quist, bristling.

'I mean we will,' said Morton.

'That's the spirit,' said Quist. 'Use the library if you need to. I'll ring at, say, ten to see how far off from finishing you are.'

Morton nodded agreement and Alan, though longing for bed, didn't object. April-May looked worried.

'Do you want me to continue as your EA until the end of the day?' Alan asked, thinking it better to be certain about Quist's secretarial requirements than not.

'You're not indispensable, Alan, and it's not as though I'm helpless without you.'

This about-face was breathtakingly hypocritical and not in the least unexpected.

'Thank you,' Alan said.

'Now that we've got the administrivia sorted,' said Quist, 'I feel compelled to ask the essential question – and you know which one I'm thinking about, don't you?' He took a breath. 'My friends, are we the best public service in the world?'

Alan, anxious to cut short any drawn-out ritual, shot into the air, shouting 'Yes, we are', surprising even himself.

April-May recoiled in shock and Morton was bug-eyed in amazement but Quentin Quist, though dazzled, still had the presence to steady the table and high-five as Alan landed.

'There's life in the old dog yet,' Quist said to the others. 'You watch out June-July, or Alan will be chasing you around the room with intent.'

April-May looked confused, Morton was even more wide-eyed and Alan blushed multiple shades beyond crimson.

'Do you need me to get you organised?' Quist enquired.

'I think we're sufficiently pumped,' said Morton.

'Pumped with what?' Alan wondered.

'Excellent,' said Quist. 'I'll let you make a start.' He left the room.

'You don't need to stay, April-May,' said Alan, in a kindly voice. 'We know you have to go.'

'You give April-May three tubs take home and in morning all done excellent. You see.'

'That's kind of you,' said Alan, 'but I think this is really a job for Morton and me.'

'Then you give me one tub.'

'No, you go,' said Morton. 'Alan and I will look after this.'

April-May left the room.

'Did the ancient Greeks really empty their chamber pots into the streets?' Alan asked.

'No doubt,' said Morton.

'I was afraid you'd say that.'

'Londoners did the same until well into the eighteenth century. What's the problem?'

'I had expected better, that's all,' said Alan.

'Shall we begin?'

'How do you want to proceed?'

'What if I start work on the emails, while you sort the new corro by type, using Friday's system. Then, once you've got the incoming into piles, we can both produce the responses from the existing templates.'

'Sounds good,' said Alan.

They both left the room. Alan took more cold tablets and moved his things back to his office, before moving two visitors' tables together in the open area for the sorting of the folders.

By seven ten, Morton had fixed the weekend email responses and was making notations on the correspondence in the too-hard (multiple issues) piles.

Quentin Quist, the last remaining person on the floor, came by with his trolley and an intention to encourage which never quite became action. 'There are only two of you?'

'But working like a well-oiled machine,' said Morton.

'I hope it isn't going to take you all night,' he replied.

'Us too,' said Morton.

'I'll call at ten,' he said, pulling his file trolley behind him.

'What do you want to do about dinner?' Morton asked some time later.

'I've lost all interest in food,' said Alan. 'You do what you want to do.'

Within minutes, though, Morton's phone rang.

'You've got what?' he asked the caller. 'Fantastic! One of us will come down.' He replaced the handset and looked at Alan. 'April-May has organised dinner but hasn't got after-hours access on her security pass.'

'Do you want me to let her in?' Alan asked.

'That would be good,' said Morton, 'because I'm skint until pay day.'

'Did she say how much we owe?'

'She didn't mention money at all.'

Alan collected his wallet and took the lift to the ground floor. April-May was waiting outside the main doors with two bags of takeaway containers.

'This bag for Morton,' she said. 'Various rubbish dishes popular with round-eyes.' Her lips pursed in distaste. 'But this little one for you: steam pears with honey and sliced almonds, star anise, cinnamon, nutmeg and tangerine peel – for your cold, also your bottom.'

Alan blushed. 'My bottom?'

'You bad colour and look pregnant. You eat steam pears dish and all be good.'

'That really is very kind of you,' he replied, thinking further denial futile. 'How much do we owe you?'

'You no pay. April-May not help with work, so bring food. You look after April-May, April-May look after you.'

'I really don't think...'

'Cold food insult to chef,' April-May warned.

'Yes, of course. Really, very kind.'

Feeling vaguely guilty, as if complicit in unethical practices, Alan swiped his security pass and re-entered the building.

It was when the lift doors opened on the seventh floor that the final piece of the Christmas Eve puzzle came to him in a cyclonic, somersaulting, warp-speed rush that picked him up, threw him backwards, sucked him forward and spun him around, all without the slightest victual spillage.

The doors closed and he was careering out of the lift on the final working day of the previous year, having made his way from the executive suite in his wine-drenched shirt, without his baking trays and with Brian Gulliver's entreaties still ringing in his ears. His imperative was a simple one: to make it back to his desk and, once there, to curl up, out of mind and sight, until such time as the floor no longer teetered unpredictably before him and objects no longer rose up violently to check his progress.

The wall to his left hurtled into him, as did the opposite wall, and he barely remained vertical. Three steps forward, two steps back and three, again, forward – he was making steady progress – and then, out of the corner of his eye, through the gap between the blind and the glass wall, he saw something: a large white shape hovering over the executive desk in Robyn Rainbird's office – before the floor lurched up to block his view, delivering a giddy-making blow to his forehead.

When he looked up, he could again see the pale hovering object: a large blurry mass suspended above the desk top. He rubbed his eyes, squinted, looked again and could see that rather than a phantasm, an alien spacecraft or the strangely refracted rays of the waning sun, he was looking at the bare knees and naked shins of a squatting man.

36

'Christ, Alan.' said the plant man, stuffing a wad of toilet paper into a garbage bag with a latex-gloved hand. 'What do you think you're doing?' Receiving no answer, he pulled more tissue from the roll and wiped again. 'Lucky I'd finished or you might have put me off the job.' He again disposed of used paper.

'What are you up to?' Alan asked, although the words didn't emerge in quite that form.

'You're drunk,' said the plant man, pulling up his trousers. He lowered himself onto the floor and removed his gloves.

Alan stared, unable to make sense of things.

The plant man stuffed the gloves into the garbage bag. 'You're welcome to make your own dark contribution,' he said, 'and I'm happy enough to help you onto the desk, but I can't assist you with the giving bit. You'll have to draw on your own resources for that.'

Alan shook his head and worked hard at sitting up.

'You really are shickered, aren't you?'

Alan nodded, giggled and hiccupped.

'I think we'd better get you out of here. Give me your hand.'

Alan did as he was told and was hauled to his feet. He teetered, however, towards the desk.

'Whoa,' said the plant man. 'You don't want to be falling into that.' He steadied Alan with his free hand and his hip. 'Let's get you back to your own spot. Put an arm around me.'

It seemed to Alan that everyone was taking advantage of his drunkenness to get a hug. Why him?

'If you don't put your arm around me, I'll leave you here…with that.'

The plant man used the hand holding the bag to gesture towards the excreta on the blotter.

Alan swung his left arm over the plant man's shoulder.

It took them three tries to get through the door but after the third attempt, they meandered in short order to the end of the Committees Section bay. Alan's will deserted him at this point. He slid to his knees and remained there, too blithered to get up, yet determined not to slump backwards, all the while surveying the scene through just one eye.

Eventually he offered the plant man his hands and was pulled – then almost carried – to his own seat. From there, a minute later, he wilted onto his keyboard and, soon after, on to the floor.

As Alan's head settled onto the carpet on Christmas Eve, the lift doors opened and closed in early January. He looked about, neither in the past nor the present, hoping that a reality would presently coalesce – that the disparate facts about matters as unimportant as the finish of the metal doors, the darkness of the rubber bumpers that separated them, the spacing of the tiny holes in the ceiling grate, the brilliance of the fluorescent light behind the grate, the rate of his breathing, the weight of the Chinese dinner on his arms and the pressure of his own upright body on his feet – would aggregate to afford him something reminiscent of certainty. And so it was.

He sneezed before he could ground one of the bags and recover his handkerchief, and as the last tiny droplets of spray floated down onto the lino tiles, he realised he was back in the lift on the first Tuesday after New Year, was part way through an evening's work, had custody of two bags of Chinese food and, most importantly of all, was not (and had never been) the source of 'it'.

As the lift travelled back to the ground floor, he wondered how it was that he'd ever doubted himself. How, really, could he have believed himself capable of such unthinking recklessness? How could he have thought himself up to sabotaging all that he'd achieved and all that he yet hoped to accomplish?

The lift doors opened and a middle-aged man got in. He noticed that Alan's hands were full. 'Which floor would you like?'

''Seven,' said Alan, 'thank you.'

Thus was the normal rhythm and trajectory of life resumed.

Alan experienced a profound sense of relief that would, but for his exhaustion, have mutated into bigger emotions requiring embarrassing explanation. In order to eat in solitude, he pretended to have emails requiring his attention. He and Morton resumed work as soon as the meal was done.

When Quentin phoned at ten o'clock, Alan was typing addressee details into a template answer for one category of correspondence and Morton was working on a different category of answers. Alan surmised much from the fact that the acting branch head had called Morton's number, rather than his own, as he'd done the previous Friday night. But not even this could detract from Alan's new lightness of spirit.

At eleven fifteen, precisely, Morton announced that he had done as much as he could do with guaranteed accuracy. 'The rest can surely wait until tomorrow,' he said.

'We've done well,' said Alan.

The draft emails had all been altered and sent to the new minister's office, and more than two-thirds of the letters had been answered. Morton carried the completed tubs of folders into Quentin Quist's office while Alan packed his bag for home and checked his In box. Waiting there was a response to his most recent email to Personnel. It read,

The Assistant Secretary Personnel convened a meeting of experts this afternoon to consider the additional information provided by you in relation to a staff member's request for carer's leave (to look after a cat called Pussils). After consideration of the known facts and the relevant guidelines, you are advised that you should approve or not approve the leave. However, you should do this only after taking into account all of the pertinent facts (including the relationship between the applying officer and the care recipient), bearing in mind any documentation provided in support of the application, weighing up other related information and giving due consideration to local workloads and to the likely impact of any further non-attendance by the applicant on the achievement of work unit output targets, thereby reaching a conclusion which is in the best interests of the Section, the Branch, the Division, the

Department and the wider public service, not giving undue weight to irrelevant or peripheral consideration and evidencing the highest standards of probity, impartiality, transparency and objectivity, while ensuring that all reasonable steps are taken to prevent discrimination, harassment, bullying, favouritism or preferential treatment.

Alan concluded that this answer did not assist him at all and – after two further readings – that it was nonsensical tosh.

In the lavatory he thought about the situation in which his belated knowledge of the true events of Christmas Eve placed him. He concluded, surprisingly, that he was morally obliged to do nothing with the information in his possession and thereby realised that the interests of the department and of public administration were no longer synonymous with his own. What God had once wrought had been, at last, well and truly set asunder.

Stabbing pain had stopped him twice on the way to the lavatory. Irrational imaginings about rampant cancers, cysts the size of apples and growths that obtruded his most vital passages did battle with the more prosaic truth that he was full, fit to burst, of himself.

He occupied the cubicle to the left of the one favoured by Quentin Quist and, in three agonising, convulsive eruptions was delivered of most of his burden. Then, for the first time in his adult life, he looked down between his legs, into the bowl, into the feculent, tenebrous depths. Much had been resolved, but his allotted part in the drama was not yet done.

At home, there was a message from Rasch on his answering machine – 'retribution is nigh' – but he attached less importance to these words than to the weather forecasts for far-off continents. For although his path was not yet clear, he intuited that he had nothing to fear in the future.

He took the adult night dose of cold and flu tablets, went to bed and experienced the deepest uninterrupted sleep.

37

Alan knew, the second his eyes opened, what Hugo's references to the waste – and they were most definitely to 'the waste' rather than 'the waist' – had been about. He knew, too, what the day and the future required of him.

He toileted, showered and shaved, and instead of hurrying to work, ate eggs on toast with parsley fresh from his own neglected garden. He reasoned that Quentin Quist could not expect him to be present early in the day to provide secretarial support, after staying so late the night before. He didn't bother putting on a tie.

At work, there were unknown guards on the security desk and the temperature was in the optimal range for effective public administration.

The Elk was sitting at the executive assistant's desk outside Quentin Quist's office. 'He's off at a meeting about ministerial correspondence. The new advisers don't want their man signing any corro about poo.'

'Why a meeting?' Alan enquired.

'What do you reckon?'

'Don't tell me no one wants their name on it?'

'Then I won't,' said the Elk, 'but don't be surprised if you wind up with the job.'

'It won't be me,' said Alan, in all confidence, 'but can you let me know when he returns? He and I need to talk.'

April-May was the only member of Alan's team in attendance. 'Morton playing tennis. Others call in sick. How your bottom today?'

'In tip-top condition,' said Alan, without any shame. 'I'm grateful.'

'Poached pears fix you up every time.'

Alan nodded and smiled, even though he could think of at least one other reason why his bodily functions were once again in order.

In his office, he didn't hesitate to turn on his computer. While it whirred into action, he checked his phone; there were three missed calls from the plant man. Alan looked at the bird remains on the balcony; only a few of the larger bones were left.

It was nine fourteen and his In box already contained more than twenty new communications. He ignored them all and brought up Edwina Troy's original leave application. Without hesitation, he moved his cursor to the Not Approved button and clicked on it. Then he put a few personal items in to his briefcase: a photograph of the Colonnades at Ephesus, his personal Oxford Concise and his Roget's. He placed everything else he'd moved in with the day before in a carton on his visitor's table.

A new message landed in his In box. It was from the Elk and it read, 'Q is back but Morton and Brian Gulliver are with him. Says he will be free in half an hour. I will call when they are done.'

Alan rang Bonny Brae and informed the clerk who answered that he wouldn't be visiting Hugo again.

'Again as in "never"?' asked the clerk.

'That's right,' said Alan.

'I'm sure he'll miss you.'

'I'm sure he won't but it's nice of you to say so.'

Almost organised, Alan then thought about giving his sansevieria trifisciata to April-May but knew that, as it was neither edible nor conventionally beautiful, it would not be appreciated. He dropped the plant into the bin and, taking his briefcase with him, walked along the corridor, past the protesting Elk and, without knocking, into the meeting taking place in Quentin Quist's office.

Gulliver, Quist and Morton, sitting at one end of the conference table, were all taken aback by his arrival.

'Ah, Alan, there you are,' said Gulliver.

Morton folded up the document the three of them had been poring over and, before Alan could apologise for his rudeness, Quist asked Gulliver whether someone should acknowledge the traditional owners, as Alan's arrival had brought their number to four.

'Let's just move on, shall we?' came the reply.

Gulliver's attention turned to Alan, who said, 'I'm sorry to interrupt but there is something I need to tell you.'

'It's opportune that you've dropped by,' said the acting secretary, 'as I was just telling Quentin and Stephen that the minister has signed off on a new structure for our advisory committees and has ordered full-speed implementation.'

Alan's heart would once have skipped a beat at this point, in the expectation that he was about to be given challenging new responsibilities, a chance to make up for his great mistake and an opportunity to prove himself belatedly worthy of promotion. But he was, at last, a man who knew his hour would never come. Even if he'd been asked to perform an interim role – assisting, perhaps, with arrangements for the new committee while it found its feet – he could no longer accept such a mission.

'In short, we're moving to a single super-committee,' said Gulliver, 'drawing on the best and brightest people from the existing committees, along with some…ah…strategic new appointees, and making use of the consultant's work on priority responsibilities.'

'It's an exciting time for the branch,' said Quist.

'We needed someone with a fresh approach and fresh ideas to be the interim secretariat director,' said Gulliver. 'Robyn has decided that the task isn't for her and is accepting a voluntary redundancy. Quentin has recommended Stephen to replace her, pending permanent filling.'

'I'm sure he'll do an outstanding job,' said Alan, wondering when in the previous week the deal had been done between Morton and Quist.

Morton wouldn't meet Alan's gaze. The archetypal cynical spectator had decided to participate again, after years on the sidelines, and was probably ashamed at the ease with which he'd been enticed back into the game.

'We'll be redeploying excess staff from the Committees Section almost immediately,' said Quist.

'After the necessary and appropriate consultation, of course,' said Gulliver. 'But I – we – we wanted you to know, early in the process, that we've got some special things in mind for you.'

'You're going to be a Centre of Excellence,' blurted Quist.

Alan chuckled.

'That's just one of the options I'll be considering,' said Gulliver.

'Excellence in?' said Alan.

Quentin Quist made the water-hurrying gesture and looked expectantly at Morton.

'Clerkliness, mostly,' said Morton.

'But not special projects,' said Quist.

'Most certainly not,' said Gulliver.

'That's most gratifying,' Alan said, 'but I think that before proceeding you need to know something rather important.'

'Don't tell me you're going to retire,' said Quist.

'I have to inform you that it was me who left the faecal matter on Quentin's desk.'

Gulliver, Quist and Morton all stared at Alan.

Gulliver was the first to speak. 'I'm not sure I heard you correctly, Alan. Can you please repeat that?'

'I admitted, Brian, to opening my bowels on Quentin's desk.'

'Just now?' said Quist, looking over at the desk top, horrified.

'Over the Christmas break.'

'That's a relief," said Quist. 'I thought you were saying you'd done a poo on it recently.'

'You're joking,' said Gulliver.

'He's made a number of jokes, lately,' said Morton. 'Completely out of character.'

'I did it,' said Alan, 'and I'm proud of it.'

'You filthy animal,' said Quist, at last realising what Alan was admitting to.

'He's been acting peculiarly,' said Morton, 'ever since Christmas.'

'After all I did for you,' said Quist.

'I did it,' Alan repeated, 'and I won't be arguing that I was mentally unwell or that it had anything to do with my unhappy childhood. I did it of my own free will, gladly, with a modicum of enthusiasm and with full awareness of the likely consequences.'

In the resulting cacophony of voices, nothing was discernible but heightened emotion.

'Everybody sit…and calm down,' ordered Gulliver.

There was a knock at the door, Gulliver said 'Come in' and Hector Rasch entered, wearing a red, shoulder-length wig and a lime-green twin-set with matching shoes and hand bag. No one seemed surprised.

'I've had a breakthrough…' said the newcomer. 'I had to tell you straight away.'

'Do you think now would be an appropriate time?' Quist asked Gulliver.

'For what?' Gulliver responded.

'The acknowledgement of the traditional owners?'

'Forget the bloody acknowledgement,' the acting secretary said, turning to Rash. 'We've also had something of a breakthrough. Alan has, only seconds ago, confessed to being the phantom shitter.'

'Preposterous,' said Rasch, placing his handbag on the table.

'I have confessed,' said Alan. 'I did it and, given the opportunity, I would most certainly do it again.'

Quentin Quist flinched.

'Don't be silly,' said Rasch. 'I have conclusive evidence implicating…'

'Your evidence doesn't matter a jot. I tell you it was me.'

'When? When did you do it?' Quist challenged.

'It couldn't have been Christmas Eve,' said Brian Gulliver. 'He was drunk with me. Much too drunk to get up onto the desk.'

'It doesn't matter when. Why would I confess if it wasn't me?'

'I have DNA evidence,' said Rasch. 'The experts doubted that it could be done because the sample was so small. Overnight, however, I was provided with details of DNA from the skerrick of crap on the pen that Toni used to poke the turd on the morning it was discovered – the pen she later dropped into the garbage bin. And I have, less than an hour ago, confirmed a match with one of a number of the DNA samples I collected here in the department over the last week.'

He removed a compact from his handbag and applied powder to the places where his beard was breaking through the pancake. 'I only had an analysis done of the pen when all of my other efforts had failed: when I found myself staring disaster in the face.'

'And who do you believe the culprit to be?' asked Gulliver.

'I made a citizen's arrest, disguised as a visiting telephone technician, only' – he looked at the dainty little watch on his right wrist – 'twenty minutes ago.'

'An arrest of whom?' Gulliver enquired.

'The Corporate Foliage Optimisation executive – Dwayne Mencken.'

'Dwayne Mencken!' Alan exclaimed, understanding immediately much that had been unclear in the previous twelve hours.

'Dwayne Mencken,' Morton echoed.

'I know that name, don't I?' said Quist to Morton.

Alan and Morton both nodded agreement.

'No, it can't be. Not *the* Dwayne Mencken?' said Quist.

'The same,' said Alan.

'Someone help me with this,' said Gulliver.

'Dwayne Mencken worked with Alan and me more than twenty years ago,' said Morton.

'He was the first person Quentin ever supervised,' said Alan.

'Harassed, he says, until he suffered a nervous breakdown,' said Rasch.

'That isn't true,' said Quist.

Morton and Alan both knew otherwise.

'And I'll sue anybody who says as much,' said Quist.

'He resigned and booked himself into a psych ward,' said Rasch, 'before anything was decided, but the evidence that he was harshly treated seems clear enough.'

'So, this man was an ex-employee of the department,' said Gulliver, 'and a colleague…but none of you recognised him?'

'He doesn't look, now, like he did back then,' said Alan.

'That's right,' said Morton. 'Back then he was clean-shaven and short haired – very clean-cut.'

'Whereas now,' said Rasch, 'he's your long-haired, bearded, hippy type of person.'

'And he wasn't greying or suntanned like he is now,' said Alan.

'Are you really sure it's Mencken?' said Quist. 'Mind you, he did look vaguely familiar, tending the plants. Alan and I both remarked on it.'

'He didn't have a personal ID,' said Rasch, 'because he was an employee of a contractor, so his name wasn't on his pass and he wasn't listed under his own name in the corporate directory.'

'Has he confessed?' asked Gulliver.

'He claims he's innocent,' said Rasch, 'but we'll see what he's got to say after he's been water boarded, kept awake for a week and forced to listen 24/7 to hip hop, bagpipes and bluegrass.'

'He's claiming he's innocent,' said Alan, 'because he *is* innocent and because he knows your case will never stand up.'

'Rubbish,' said Rasch.

'Tell him why it won't succeed,' said Alan to Morton, who was known by most present to have completed a law degree.

'Well, scientific evidence can always be contested but in this case it lacks integrity for other reasons. We've probably got a broken chain of custody. And then there's the matter of the proposed confession. By being made under duress, it will be inadmissible, whereas an admission like Alan's, made freely and without the prospect of any advantage, would always be given credence when supported by a credible motive.'

'So what is your motive?' said Quist.

Alan believed that any specificity would only enable his story to be tested, 'I have nothing to say about the reasons why I did it.'

'I need to know, too,' said Gulliver, 'because, to my way of thinking, you were everything a public servant should be – everything that everyone in this room isn't.'

'I have nothing to say,' said Alan, 'except that I tender my resignation with immediate effect.' He wrote the words 'I resign, with immediate effect.' on the corner of the chart on the table, adding his signature and the date.

'I don't accept your resignation,' said Gulliver. 'And neither will anyone else, until you tell us what your motive was.'

'Without some explanation,' said Morton, 'it's something of a stretch to believe you, Alan.'

'Tell me,' screamed Quist, lunging across the table to grab Alan by the throat. 'Tell me why you did it.'

Alan recoiled in time to avoid strangulation. Brian Gulliver meanwhile surfed over the top of Quist and grabbed him in a headlock. Morton stood between Alan and his attacker. Rasch pulled a can of pepper spray from his handbag.

'I'm not going to release you,' the acting secretary said to Quist, 'unless you calm down. Will you settle?'

'Yes,' came the muffled reply, 'but he has to tell me why he did it.'

'I agree,' said Gulliver, 'but everyone will resume their seats while we talk this through. Can we all do that?'

There were murmurs of assent on all sides. Gulliver released Quist but Rasch held the spray at the ready.

'Good,' said Gulliver when they were all seated. 'Alan?'

'I did it. Believe me. And don't let matters to do with motive needlessly complicate things.'

'No, Alan,' said Morton. 'Give us a decent explanation. If you expect us to believe you, you can't do anything less.'

Alan sighed. 'I did it because it was there,' he said, recalling his earlier conversation with Quist about the mountaineers' challenge, 'and because I could.'

'No, you'll have to do better than that.' Gulliver said.

'What does it matter?' said Alan.

'We have to know,' said Gulliver.

'All right, then,' Alan said, finally realising that he could not escape a detailed explanation. 'If you want a motive, I'll give you one.'

He pushed himself back from the table. 'Quist made my life hell. A more unprincipled, vain, vicious, stupid, neurotic and…and…perfidious bully I have never encountered.'

Rasch shook the can of pepper spray, in case Quist made another lunge at Alan.

'Perfidious,' said Quist, looking at Gulliver, 'is one step too far. I shouldn't have to put up with it.'

'Of course you shouldn't,' said Gulliver, sensing an opportunity. 'Go with Morton and Rasch up to my office and wait for me there.'

'Perfidious, indeed,' said Quist, glaring at Alan.

'Now, hurry along,' said Gulliver.

Rasch stood between Alan and Quist as Morton escorted the acting branch head to the door. When they were out of the room, the director of security put the pepper spray into his handbag and left, closing the door behind him.

Alan and Gulliver smiled sadly at each other.

'Perfidious,' said the acting secretary. 'Do you think he has any idea what it means?'

'I doubt it,' said Alan.

'Me too.'

Gulliver sighed. 'I know it wasn't you, Alan. Not because you were physically incapable or because you weren't provoked, but because it's not in your nature – even when drunk.'

Alan shrugged.

'Why are you doing this?' Gulliver continued. 'If it's to make amends for not having protected this Mencken fellow all those years ago, what's the point? The past is the past and, no matter what Rasch thinks, there is no official interest in detaining the faecal culprit. Our masters want the whole incident gone and forgotten.'

'It's nothing to do with Mencken.'

'Then who or what is it to do with?'

'I suppose it's to do with me,' said Alan.

Gulliver shook his head. 'Your superannuation will be reduced if you go early and you certainly won't be able to return for temporary employment.'

'It's time to cut the cord,' said Alan.

'I don't understand.'

They sat in silence, listening to snippets of conversation from outside, the hum of the air conditioning and the ticking of the clock on the wall.

Finally, the phone rang. Gulliver picked it up, announced himself and listened intently. 'No, nothing needs to be done. Wait there until I arrive.' He put the handpiece down. 'You're sure this is what you want?' he asked Alan.

'Absolutely,' Alan replied.

'Knowing there can be no going back?'

'Especially knowing that.'

'Then I accept your resignation, effective immediately.'

'Thank you,' said Alan.

'Now, let's get you off the premises, and out of harm's way.'

'Of course,' said Alan, grateful that security guards wouldn't be called to do the task.

'I'll have your things packed up and delivered to your home.'

'No point,' said Alan. 'There's nothing I need. Shall we go?'

'If you're ready.'

Out on the floor, the presence of Brian Gulliver prevented any embarrassing questions.

At the security gates Alan handed the acting secretary his pass. They shook hands.

'What will you do?' Gulliver asked.

Alan might have said, 'I intend to live, to really live', but he couldn't see any point. 'Whatever I choose to,' he said.

'Good luck, then,' said Gulliver.

'You, too,' said Alan, his future filled with all the splendid possibilities a man reborn could wish for.